LOVE'S LABOR'S LOST?

"How old were you when your mother died?" Griffin asked Gates, gently ruffling her curly forelock as she tended to his horse.

"Just twelve," she said. "I learned to expect much less of the world after that."

Something twisted inside Griffin. He too had lowered his expectations from life at that age. The underlying sob in Gates's voice pierced him before he could raise his guard. His hand drifted down to touch her face. Her skin was petal soft and he battled the urge to set his mouth against that creamy surface.

"It will all come right for you. You must believe it will," he whispered in a voice like warm treacle on toast. Gates let her hands drift to his shoulders. No one had ever touched her as though she were something rare and precious.

He pulled back abruptly and stood up, his eyes now distant. "It's time I was back at the house." And then he was moving away from her with determined strides.

Though she had toiled from dusk till dark, she hadn't felt weary or dispirited until Griffin Darrowby had so curtly dismissed her. . . .

The Bartered Heart

Nancy Butler

A SIGNET BOOK

SIGNET
Published by New American Library, a division of
Penguin Putnam Inc., 375 Hudson Street,
New York, New York 10014, U.S.A.
Penguin Books Ltd, 27 Wrights Lane,
London W8 5TZ, England
Penguin Books Australia Ltd, Ringwood,
Victoria, Australia
Penguin Books Canada Ltd, 10 Alcorn Avenue,
Toronto, Ontario, Canada M4V 3B2
Penguin Books (N.Z.) Ltd, 182-190 Wairau Road,
Auckland 10, New Zealand

Penguin Books Ltd, Registered Offices:
Harmondsworth, Middlesex, England

First published by Signet, an imprint of New American Library,
a division of Penguin Putnam Inc.

First Printing, August 1999
10 9 8 7 6 5 4 3 2 1

Copyright © Nancy J. Hajeski, 1999

All rights reserved

 REGISTERED TRADEMARK—MARCA REGISTRADA

Printed in the United States of America

To my grandmothers, Jeanne and Emily,
And to D.E.C., a continuing education

"Such wind as scatters young men through the world
To seek their fortunes farther than at home."

—*The Taming of the Shrew*
William Shakespeare

Prologue

"Get away from that window, damn you," the man facing the fireplace muttered.

Though the man hadn't turned toward the window seat, the child kneeling there winced just the same.

"But, Father," the boy protested, "I still don't understand."

There was no whining in his tone, only a vast incomprehension. He turned his pale, waxen face away from the window with a shuddering sigh. Beyond the leaded panes an elegant traveling coach was speeding down the drive toward the front gates.

"She's gone," the man said brusquely. "And your brothers with her. So there's an end to it. They will be nothing to us from here on. Not even a memory." He pivoted around, his mouth narrowing into a scowl. "Are you attending me, boy?"

The child stood, solemn-faced, before the heavy velvet draperies and nodded once. The morning sun, which filtered in between the parted draperies, danced over his bowed head, turning the paler strands in his honey brown hair into spun gold. As the man moved away from the hearth and approached the window, his hair too was gilded by the bright spill of light. He reached out to tip the child's face up, and the boy flinched involuntarily as the large hand grasped his chin.

"Puling whelp," the man uttered in disgust. "You've no more grit than a simpering schoolgirl. I don't know why I bothered to keep you here with me. If I had any sense, I'd send you after them."

A look of inarticulate hope surfaced on the child's face, but it was dashed away by the man's next words. "But you are the eldest, after all, and a man wants his heir to be in his own keeping, not in the care of a faithless whore."

"Father!"

The man grinned sourly and said in a mocking voice, "Oh, little miss, have I offended your delicate sensibilities?" He gave a grunting laugh. "She's all that, and more. Sold you to me, she did, without even a second's hesitation. You don't like hearing that, do you? Well, it's the truth. I filled her purse and promised to keep her in style if she took herself off to London. It's best that you know her for what she is."

"She's my mother," he said, twisting his head back from the cruel fingers that gripped his chin.

"Aye, and my wife. And so she will remain until one of us departs this wretched planet. But she will be your mother no longer. You will neither write to her nor make any attempt to see her. That was my only stipulation to letting her go—that she sever all ties with you. She will adhere to it or lose her income. And if there's one thing I know about the bitch, it's that she values her own pretty hide more than her children's. Think on that, when you are tempted to mourn her. You are mine now,"—his fingers clamped hard on the narrow shoulder, biting into the tender skin—"and no one will come between us."

The boy felt the nausea twist in his belly as the man's hold tightened. He steeled himself against the pain, as he had done countless times before.

It will pass. It must pass. He repeated the familiar litany and renewed the promise he'd made to himself long ago, that someday, somehow, he would be free of this place and free of this man.

Those who had stood with him, or more aptly, cowered with him, were gone now. His mother, who had been the chief target of his father's rage, had at last gained her freedom. After she'd repeatedly sullied the family name with her indiscreet liaisons, her husband had finally banished her from his home. Although the boy knew her to be a vain, shallow creature, she had occasionally shown him some affection, tossed him a kind word or a fond look. But now even those fleeting tokens, which had made his daily life less wretched, were lost to him. And the two younger brothers who had furnished him with blessed moments of escape, of teasing laughter and companionship, had been swept up in their mother's train as she departed and, under his disbelieving eyes, carried out to the waiting coach.

It was unthinkable that he had been left behind, at the mercy of this man, whom he was forced to call "Father," but whom he privately referred to as the Ogre. His feelings flailed about inside his head like living things, seeking a haven, seeking a sanctuary in the deepest recesses of his mind. Not only from the physical pain, which was his familiar lot, but from the mental anguish of knowing that he had been abandoned by his fellow prisoners. They had made their escape from this house of darkness; he doubted he would be able to survive without the comfort they had offered.

He longed to fling open the window and run screaming down the drive, begging his mother not to leave without him. Then he recalled how she had refused to acknowledge him as he'd stood in shocked silence in one corner of the foyer, while she oversaw the loading of her trunks. She had not even offered him a farewell salute, but had carefully settled the train of her carriage dress over one arm before walking from the house without a backward glance.

As his father moved away to the drinks tray, to begin his daily assault on the various decanters that sat there, the boy felt something stir inside him. Anger and pride welled up in equal measure and overrode his aching sense of loss. He was possessed by a fierce determination to prevail over the mocking, heavy-handed creature who had sired him and the selfish woman who had so blithely departed from his life. Nothing would ever wound him again, not deep inside where his spirit dwelled. He would not wither under adversity; he would use it to make him stronger. One blessed day he would be the one who drove off and never looked back.

Until that time, though, he needed to make a new vow—he would answer his father's cruelty and his endless mockery with utter detachment. And when the pain came, he would endure it in silence. These things he swore with all the passion he could muster in his frightened, twelve-year-old heart.

There were ways of escaping torment, he realized as he slipped quietly from the room, that had nothing to do with boarding a coach for London.

Chapter One

Mr. Pendleton already wished himself a million miles away, and his client had not even come into the room yet. With a nervous motion, he smoothed the wispy strands of black hair that barely covered his round, pink head. He'd tried to engineer the meeting so that it could be held in his own comfortable suite of offices on Shaftsbury Avenue, but after a month of waiting in vain for a response to his urgently worded letters, he'd decided it was time to beard the lion in his den.

Not that the room where he waited was by any means uncomfortable, furnished as it was with deeply cushioned chairs and a handsome mahogany desk. It was just that he preferred to be on his own turf when he had disastrous news to deliver. That way if a client began to behave erratically—which was often the case with gentlemen who had lost their money through intemperate investments—he could call on one of his clerks in the adjoining office to aid him in subduing the man. He had hired several strapping young fellows for just that purpose—longer on brawn than on brains. Recalling the athletic physique and the renowned pugilistic prowess of this morning's client, he wondered if he shouldn't have insisted that one of those young men accompany him.

When the door to the study opened at last and the object of his unhappy mission came sauntering into the room, Mr. Pendleton did not breath a sigh of relief. Rather, his palms began to perspire in a most unprofessional manner, although there was nothing ominous in his client's appearance. Griffin Darrowby, whom he had not seen in two years, did not overpower a room with his size. He was of middle height, though his slim proportions and a goodly length of leg might fool a casual observer into thinking him a taller man. His elegant attire—a superbly cut coat of deep blue melton and inexpressibles of a pale saffron hue—inspired awe, rather than disquiet.

Nonetheless, interviews with Darrowby, in spite of his gentlemanly trappings, always set Pendleton's nerves on edge. On rare occasions the usual expression of watchful assessment in the gentleman's bright blue eyes was supplanted by one of fierce, calculating hunger, which lent his mobile, handsome face a distinct aura of menace, rather like an archangel turned freebooter. The few times Pendleton beheld that look, it had scorched him to his bones.

At present, however, Darrowby was regarding him with a relaxed, open expression of curiosity on his face.

"Pendleton," he said with a slight bow of his head.

"Mr. Darrowby," the businessman responded, quickly rising from his chair. The papers he had been holding in his lap slid to the floor.

Griffin Darrowby knelt swiftly and retrieved them, but did not relinquish them to his visitor. He settled in an armchair and began to read through them.

"I trust you received my letter when you returned from Spain," Mr. Pendleton said with a concerned frown. "And the six others I sent. Of course I understand you might still not be beforehand with your correspondence after being away for two years, but I simply could not let another day pass—"

"Enough," Darrowby interrupted him calmly as he shuffled the sheet he'd been reading to the back of the pile. "You needn't make excuses, sir, for doing your job. It is I who have been remiss; I should have acknowledged your letters." His mouth twisted into a tight smile. "But then I wager no man is in a hurry to hear bad news."

Mr. Pendleton's round face now wore a thin sheen of perspiration, in spite of the cool June breeze that was coming through the open window. "I am not sure how this happened," he began. "When you left for Portugal, your finances were in good order. I myself oversaw all your investments, and, according to your instructions, I chose only the most solid of ventures."

Darrowby shrugged as he handed the papers back to his visitor. "Ships run aground, Pendleton, no matter how well captained. And weevils and blights do attack crops from time to time."

"But the ruby mine in India appeared to be totally sound," the businessman lamented. "Run by a proven corporation, offering a steady income with little risk."

A wistful expression appeared on his client's face. "Ah, but landslides do happen. At least it occurred at night, when there were fewer workers about." He sighed softly. "So tell me, straight out . . . how am I fixed after this series of disasters?"

"I . . . I can't believe you are taking this so well, Mr. Darrowby. Lord Conklin also lost heavily in the mining venture. He suffered an apoplexy and had to be carried from my office on a litter."

Darrowby sucked in one cheek. "Well, until you tell me how my finances stand at present, we don't know if a litter will be necessary, do we?"

Mr. Pendleton now perceived a hard glitter in the younger man's blue eyes, and wondered exactly for which of them the litter might be required. His palms again grew wet.

He coughed slightly to stall for time. During the eight years they'd done business together, he'd learned that Darrowby's reputation for possessing an unflappable temperament that bordered on the cold-blooded was no exaggeration. No man was cooler at the gaming tables, so the gossip went, or more composed over pistols. And if there were also rumors of various indiscretions involving married ladies of the *ton,* those dalliances did not necessarily belie his client's icy nature. Many a rake was hard-hearted, as Mr. Pendleton well knew.

During the past two years he'd heard reports of his client's exploits in Spain—stories of bravery that went beyond the everyday and entered into the realm of fable. Captain Darrowby at the head of his men, leading virtual suicide charges. Darrowby carrying a wounded lieutenant, who outweighed him by two stone, behind the lines in the thick of battle. Darrowby single-handedly taking out a particularly bothersome nest of French artillery.

Lord, if even half the things Pendleton had heard or read were true, the man had ice water in his veins. He'd been thrice decorated in Spain, and had come home this April without so much as a mark on him. At least none that a person could see.

Pendleton prayed his client maintained his legendary sangfroid now, since he had no desire to be tossed out the window on his head.

"There are no liens upon this house," he began. "It is yours free and clear. And of course, there is the estate outside Bath, which is held in entail."

At the mention of his family holding, Darrowby growled softly. "And my liquid assets?"

"Well, there's the difficulty, you see."

Darrowby gave him a relaxed smile that did nothing to wipe out the wary gleam in his eyes. "No, I'm afraid I don't see. Am I rolled up, then? Lord, man, stop trembling in your shoes, and tell me how it stands." He rose to his feet. "I started with nothing, you better than anyone know that. If that is where I find myself now, well then, I shall have to begin again."

Mr. Pendleton also rose, clutching the papers to his chest like a shield. "After the landslide, the local maharajah had his own troops quardon off the mine. They . . . er, refuse to let our corporation reclaim any of their equipment. It's at a stalemate at present, until we can get someone there to negotiate with Sirdir Khan. He holds the corporation responsible for the loss of the workers and is apparently in no mood to be cooperative. Not only that, he wants reparations made and is asking for a great sum of money. Though I doubt his people will see a penny of it; he is a greedy old fellow from what I hear."

Darrowby frowned. "In my recollection, landslides are acts of God. How then are the investors responsible?"

"It is all nonsense, of course," Pendleton concurred. "The bigwigs at Whitehall and in the diplomatic corps are working on the problem. They don't want to create an incident. But until they have sorted things out, your funds are tied up." He added softly, "What there is left of them."

Darrowby crossed his arms and raised a fisted hand to his mouth. He ran his teeth across his knuckles thoughtfully for several seconds. "Mortgage this house," he said at last, in a clipped voice. "I shall need money to live on until Sirdir Khan is made to see reason."

Mr. Pendleton looked hesitant. "That seems a drastic measure. Your mother is well off, is she not? Your father left her a handsome jointure . . . perhaps you might—"

Darrowby's face darkened. "Mr. Pendleton," he said with strained patience, "when I came to you eight years ago, willing to place my future in your hands, what was the sole stipulation to our doing business together? Don't tell me you have forgotten."

Pendleton looked sheepish. "No, sir, I have not. It was that I was never to bring up either of your parents. But, please, Mr. Darrowby, I am only thinking of—"

"You have ceased thinking," he interjected softly, "if you have so run out of ideas, that throwing myself on the mercy of that harpy is the only solution you can come up with."

"But she's your *mother*."

Darrowby gave a harsh laugh that set the hairs on the nape of Pendleton's neck on end. "Ah, my tender dam. Pendleton, there are sea cucumbers who foster their offspring with more care than my mother ever bestowed on her children." He waved a dismissive hand. "Now, see to the mortgage, and I will see about reversing my fortunes in my own way."

Mr. Pendleton was halfway to the door, his relief at escaping virtually unscathed washing over him in waves, when his curiosity brought him up short. "How will you do that, sir?" he ventured.

Darrowby turned from the window where he'd gone to gaze out at the garden.

"Why, how do you think a clever fellow like myself would go about regaining his wealth?"

"You're not thinking of taking to the high toby?" he asked. He doubted there was little his client would not risk to restore his fortune, including his neck.

To his surprise, Darrowby gave a loud chuckle. "Pendleton, you amaze me. And flatter me, as well. But even I have some scruples about illegal gains. And, no, don't remind me of that nasty little smuggling venture I backed some years ago. That's in my sordid past. A good thing too, considering my current goal."

Pendleton's brows were knotted in bewilderment.

Darrowby crossed his arm over his chest. "I shall pursue a more legal, though no less dangerous course. Taking my cue from Petruchio, I shall endeavor to 'wive it wealthily.'" He then offered his man of business a dazzling smile.

Mr. Pendleton thought, as he made his way out the front door, that if Darrowby could bring a fellow male practically to his knees with such a smile, he would have no trouble winning a veritable Croesus of a bride.

Griffin waited until he heard the front door close before he allowed the mask of relaxed goodwill to fade from his face. It was replaced by the stricken expression of a man who has suffered a terrible blow. He moved away from the door of his study and slouched into his desk chair, crossing his booted legs before him on the carpet.

"Rolled up," he muttered. "Eight years struggling to get my life in order, and now it's all wiped out by a bloody landslide and a greedy maharajah." He smiled in sour amusement.

No wonder old Lord Conklin had suffered an apoplexy; Griff felt like he was very close to one himself, though not a soul would have been able to detect it by his appearance. But he felt the blood drumming in his head, an endless pulsing that echoed *doom, doom, doom,* as the ever-present fear of being reduced to dependency once again clenched at his heart.

He'd sworn in his youth that he would never marry, and never,

ever, sire a child. Yet he'd also sworn that he'd never again be at the mercy of anyone named Darrowby. It was a pretty contretemps, and it occurred to him now that he'd made far too many vows as a child. It positively constricted a man. Well, one of those vows would have to go, and he knew that marriage was a far more bearable fate than having his mother witness his downfall.

It had been a foolhardy notion, haring off to Spain two years ago. It was one time in his life he'd given in to Darrowby caprice, the wayward, self-indulgent behavior that had ruled—and ultimately ruined—his family for generations. His unholy father was dead by then, which meant there was no one left in England for him to battle, so he'd decided he might just as well apply his restless energies against the French. It had never occurred to him that he'd return to England to find his finances in shambles.

He had built up a tidy fortune in the years after he'd left Darrowby, using as his stake a small inheritance from his maternal grandmother. He'd gambled, both at the tables and on the 'Change, until he'd seen a few hundred pounds increase to thousands. Which was a good thing since, upon his father's demise, he discovered he'd inherited only the entailed estate, a sprawling Elizabethan pile, but none of its furnishings and not a groat of currency.

As Pendleton pointed out, his mother had received a large jointure, but that was through no benevolence on his father's part. Rather it was due to her marriage settlement, which had been agreed upon before those two grossly mismatched people set up housekeeping together. What his father had done with the rest of his money, Griff never bothered to question. For all he knew the demented old sot had burned it.

The sad fact was, he should have stayed in England and looked after his own affairs, rather than seeking a vague absolution in the service of his country. But lamentations were for the weak-natured; if what Pendleton told him was true, then he needed to rectify things with all haste. Marriage seemed the only practical solution to his financial woes.

Furthermore, the task of finding a mate might possibly dispel the ennui he'd been suffering since he sold his commission. Lord, he'd welcome almost any distraction. He'd been home for nearly six weeks and had yet to recapture the allure of his sporting life in London. The nights out with his friends, the drinking, gambling, and frequent wenching, left him feeling stale and strangely unsated. Even the mistress he'd set up on his return, a buxom opera dancer who was more skilled between the sheets than she was on the boards, had lost her sparkle.

He blamed this uncharacteristic restlessness on the war. He'd learned that when you faced annihilation on a regular basis, when artillery shot rained about you like hailstones and death stalked relentlessly up and down the entrenchments, life became your only precious possession. Griffin doubted he'd been allowed to survive the deadly skirmishes and heated battles of the Peninsular war, merely so he could win a monkey at faro or dance a waltz with a come-out miss. He'd never before examined his place in the scheme of things—he was Darrowby of Darrowby, the scion of a notorious family, and that had been more than enough to tax a man's brain. It rankled him now that he should question his existence with such increasing frequency.

Several of his friends had gotten leg-shackled while he was in Spain. *Idiots,* he'd muttered, when he'd learned of their defection from the ranks of bachelorhood. As he slouched even lower in his chair, he wondered if they too had begun to find life in the *ton* constricting and pointless. Was it possible for a man to regain his appetite for life by giving up his freedom?

It was a plaguey notion. He had fought too long for his freedom to relinquish it on the puny chance of achieving some peace of mind. But he knew he *could* barter his independence for material gain with relative ease, as long as he kept his inner self intact. A woman of substance could win his handsome face and his agile body . . . but there was not a female in the galaxy who possessed enough money to purchase his soul. This was no Faustian arrangement he intended to seek out, but rather a mere commercial exchange—his gilded Darrowby looks and his centuries-old family name in return for good English gold.

He'd have to act quickly, before the rumors of his ruination spread through the *ton.* And he would need to maintain an aura of wealth until he found a likely candidate. He'd best go out and order up a half-dozen new coats, just to allay suspicion.

He reached for the decanter of brandy that sat on the edge of the desk and poured a healthy tot into the tumbler beside it. After downing it in one swallow, he immediately refilled the glass. Though he rarely got drunk, he knew there were times when it was the only sane thing to do.

Chapter Two

Taking the shortcut through the woods had been a very bad idea. Griffin reined in his horse and narrowed his eyes, looking for some semblance of a trail. If there was one, the tangled ground cover of bushes and vines obscured it. It was too long since he'd been in Cheshire, he realized, too long since he'd visited the estate of Bellaire and shot grouse in these woods with its late owner. He hated to admit it, but he was hopelessly lost. Which was a galling indignity—when he'd been fighting in Spain, his men had trusted his ability to lead them back to camp, no matter how far afield they'd roamed in search of provisions. But Spain had been open country, where a canny man could follow the stars or the movement of the sun overhead. It boasted no dense woodlands like this one, where the sky above was nearly obscured by the webbed canopy of beech, oak, and towering elm.

In his impatience to reach Bellaire, he had forgotten one of his abiding adult precepts, one that had served him in good stead in the army—assess the terrain before you advance. However, a man at the mercy of his appetites did not always heed his wiser voices, and this case was no exception.

Lady Minerva Stargrove was the cause of Griffin's uncharacteristic haste. Four days earlier the delightful Lady Min had sent him a note—the paper awash with her heady jasmine scent—to invite him to a house party at her country estate. It was by way, he prayed, of cementing the relationship that had been building between them since July.

Shortly after his distressing interview with Pendleton, he'd embarked upon his mission of discovery—to determine if there was a well-dowered woman in England who could tempt him from his solitary state. He'd spent the remainder of the Season assessing the merits of the young ladies who displayed themselves at the parties and balls of the haute *ton*. He had even occasionally strayed into Almack's, that most dreary bastion of all that was proper and prim in society.

Despite his efforts, he'd begun to despair of finding a respectable female he could tolerate for more than five minutes at a time. He balked at the notion of marrying a schoolroom miss, heiress or not; he could muster no interest in wide-eyed virgins. So Griff gave up on the Marriage Mart and cast around for a more mature woman, a widow perhaps, of some means, and dashed if Lady Minerva Stargrove didn't hove into his sights like an elegant, streamlined schooner.

Tall and classically featured, with raven ringlets and cornflower eyes, she had been the prize of the Season some five years earlier. Old Lucas Stargrove had snatched her up before any of the younger men had had a chance to court her, and then he'd had the good sportsmanship to pop off four years later, leaving his wife still possessed of her glorious looks and his fortune to boot.

Griffin and Stargrove had been casual friends before the older man's marriage. Griff had twice spent a month at the sprawling estate of Bellaire, shooting game birds and playing at billiards. But after his marriage, Stargrove and his new wife had retired permanently to Cheshire and invitations to the estate were no longer forthcoming.

Recently of mourning, Lady Min had come to London in July to spend the quiet summer Season with an aunt. During her first week there she had attended a musical evening where she and Griffin had been introduced. He'd been instantly enchanted, as much by her serene manner as by her beauty. Here was a woman whose studied poise and queenly bearing was a promising counterpoint to the infamous Darrowby temperament. For her part, Lady Min did not seem to be put off by Griff's past dalliances or his unfortunate parentage.

She quickly became the object of his single-minded pursuit. He accompanied her to picnics and champagne breakfasts, rode with her in the park and escorted her to the opera. They became a familiar sight in London, the dark head and the gold, bent over a theater program, or tipped intimately toward each other at a dinner party. When she left London in the middle of August, she promised Griffin they would not be apart for long.

After receiving Minerva's note, Griffin had promptly posted his acceptance and set off for Bellaire in a most pleasant state of expectation. He decided to forego his usual transportation—a curricle and pair—and instead chose to travel in state. His valet, Wilby, accompanied him inside the gleaming black coach, while his liveried coachmen sat on the box. Farrow, his gray-haired groom, rode behind on a blood-bay stallion. The impression was one of wealth and taste, exactly the aura Griffin intended to foster.

They made good time on their journey; Farrow saw to it that only the swiftest teams were hitched to his master's coach at each posting house. Griffin was impatient to reach the lady, though he would be the first to admit that romantic love was not what spurred him. Darrowby men were quite incapable of that tender emotion. Griffin had never troubled to make the subtle distinction between *could* not love and *would* not love, he only knew that Darrowbys *did* not love: their parents, their children, their maiden aunts, or even their dogs. And most shocking of all, it was rumored that they had little fondness for their horses. At least Griff was innocent of that lapse—his Turkish stallion, Gaspar, meant more to him than most of his acquaintances in London.

But if Griffin was not following the beckoning lure of romance, he was heeding other voices that were as insistent. Love may have been in short supply among the men of his clan, but physical desire was a perpetual appetite. There were also the obvious financial considerations that prompted him to haste. Lady Min was by way of offering him, in one celestial creature, the solution to his two most pressing needs.

Greed and lust, he'd thought wryly as they set out. Of the seven deadly sins, those were the two to which Darrowbys were most prone. At least it was lust on his part. He wasn't sure how the widow felt about him in that respect. Though she'd flirted with him over the summer, she had allowed him no intimacies, not even the occasional chaste kiss. He began to fear that her cool poise reflected an equally passionless nature. This was of some concern to Griff, since he'd given the opera dancer her congé shortly after meeting Minerva, and his long spell of celibacy was testing his nerves to the breaking point. But once a man was properly wedded there was no law, save a few bothersome Biblical ones, to prevent him from seeking his pleasure outside the home. That was one Darrowby trait he saw no reason to jib at.

Still, he hoped Minerva's invitation to her remote country estate meant she had at last decided to fulfill the promise that had glittered in her eyes for the past two months. And if the lady continued to behave coyly, he imagined he was not beyond a bit of seductive coercion. He did, after all, have marriage in mind. Especially since the Indian contretemps looked as if it would drag on through the autumn. His funds were at a dangerously low ebb, in spite of the money he'd borrowed against the town house.

With any luck, he'd bring his courtship to its inevitable conclusion in the wilds of Cheshire. Minerva was proud, beautiful, and rich; a man could not ask for more in a wife. And if a tiny voice in the vast emptiness of his heart cried out for something more substantial, an emotional completion, perhaps, he disregarded it, as one would the caterwauling of a fractious child.

By the afternoon of the third day—as the entourage drew to within a few hours of Bellaire—Griff had wearied of sitting idle inside the coach. He traded places with Farrow and mounted the stallion. Gaspar had no patience with the rambling pace set by the coach and showed his distemper by dancing fretfully along the road. Griff was equally eager for a show of speed, so he had given the horse his head.

Once he'd passed beyond the tiny village of Paultons and entered Bellaire Wood proper, Griff recalled a shortcut to the main house, which was not far along the road. He held the stallion to a slow canter until they came to the stile that marked the path.

It soon became evident, though, that the path he'd diverted onto was not the shortcut of his memory. The rough track had quickly become a meandering deer trail, which had then petered out after only a quarter mile or so. Griff had doggedly ridden on, keeping the setting sun always before him. But he knew that once it grew dark he would never find his way to the estate.

He now leaned back in the saddle and took stock of his surroundings. The dark woodland that enclosed him was a maze of towering trees, the spaces between their trunks overgrown with vines and spreading thickets of laurel. In the flat light of dusk, it was an eerie setting. The air about him seemed to hum with hidden voices, and he wouldn't have been surprised to come face-to-face with a withered Merlin, or a throng of pixies bent on mischief. He shook off a shiver of disquiet.

The stallion snorted as if he too felt the charge in the air. He champed at his bit and rolled his eyes.

Griffin wondered if he would be best served by retracing his steps, and then realized with a rueful grin that he had no chance in hell of finding his way back to the road. From the streaks of red that marked the western sky, he knew he was still headed toward Bellaire, however haphazardly, so he set his heels against the horse's side and moved on. He let Gaspar choose his own course, hoping that the beast would instinctively head toward some sort of habitation.

The stallion made his way cautiously through the trees. When an animal rustled in the bushes beyond him, the horse gave an abrupt, stiff-legged buck. If Griffin hadn't been riding from the time he was breeched, he would have come out of the saddle. As it was, he had to find his stirrups and regather his reins. His mellow, expectant mood was darkening as rapidly as the sky overhead.

He was cursing his rashness for the hundredth time, when he came to a wide, shallow stream. It was strewn with jagged rocks that rose up from the water like a miniature mountain range. In the cooling air, tendrils of mist rose ghostlike from the stream's surface, and the rangy bushes that overhung the water thrust out their branches like eldritch, bony fingers.

Gaspar snorted again and danced back, loath to step off the bank.

"Idiot," Griff muttered, though he might have been referring to himself. The horse responded to the pressure of his master's thighs by rearing up. Some creature splashed in the water nearby—probably only a hungry trout—but the horse was having none of it. He tossed his head and circled repeatedly in the small muddy clearing. The idea of dismounting to lead the stubborn beast across the stream—and ruining his best pair of riding boots in the process—was not something Griff even remotely considered. He gave the horse a light flick with his riding crop and Gaspar at last moved forward into the water.

Griff was guiding him around a group of rocks near the center of the stream, when something leaped from the bushes and came splashing toward them through the water. He heard an unearthly cry, and had only an instant to observe a dark, shambling creature, before Gaspar screamed in fright. The horse twisted violently up and away from the approaching specter, flinging Griffin sideways from the saddle. As he landed on his back in the water, his head glanced against a jagged rock. Just before his eyes clenched shut from the searing pain, a thin, white face loomed over him in the misty light.

Water sprite, he thought, illogically. *Done in by a damned water sprite.*

* * *

Gates threw herself down beside the fallen man and struggled to lift his shoulders from the water, but he was a sodden, inert weight. If she couldn't remove him from the stream, he was likely to take an inflammation of the lungs and die. Which would be a pity, because, by her reckoning, he was exceedingly fair. Not that all souls, comely or not, didn't deserve an equal effort for their salvation, but this particular soul had thick brown hair streaked with spun gold and a perfect cleft in his strong chin.

She had been gathering berries along the stream, singing softly to herself, when the horseman had come out of the trees. She'd stopped to watch him from behind a screen of berry bushes as he tried to calm his nervous mount. There was patient strength in the hands that held the reins and supple grace in the arch of his back as he moved in cadence with the stallion's fretful dance. Her admiration turned to alarm when she realized he was planning to cross the stream at that exact spot. Her fear for him had sent her splashing into the water; she'd never intended to frighten his horse, she'd only wanted to warn him before he reached the opposite bank.

She slapped gently at his fine-boned cheeks, feeling the faintest trace of bristle beneath her hands. Even if she hadn't deduced from his clothing that he was a gentleman, she would know it from the noble brow and wide, sculpted mouth. Surely only members of the gentry bore such refined features. Furthermore, only very wealthy men rode such handsome horses. Her gaze swept to the stallion, who luckily had not crossed the stream. He now stood on the near bank, idly lipping at some leaves, the picture of amiable docility.

Mindless of the cold water, she crouched down and wedged one shoulder behind the man's upper body, lifting him away from the rock. He muttered incoherently as she shifted him, which she took as a good sign. But then—when he opened his eyes and snarled, "Sweet, bloody hell, stop fidgeting with me!"—she was not so sure.

His eyes were pale in the gloaming light, blue or green, and they glared at her.

"Can you rise, sir?" she asked, tugging at the lapels of his coat. "You'd be better of out of the water."

"I'd be better off if I were still on my horse and riding up the drive to Bellaire," he rasped crossly. He tried to stand, and then fell back against the rock with a groan. Gates tried to aid him, wrapping her arms around his chest, but he pushed her away with another oath and tottered again to his feet. Small rivulets of water ran down from his coat and breeches into his top boots.

He staggered back to the bank—never even looking behind him to where Gates stood, calf-deep in the stream—and leaned down to catch the trailing reins of the horse. The beast shied away from him, dancing back, deeper into the trees.

"Shall I help you catch him?" Gates asked, not moving from where she stood.

"Oh?" The man turned to her. "I didn't think water sprites were allowed to leave their streams."

She almost grinned, but then realized there had been no humor in his voice. He reached again for the horse and cursed softly, as the animal moved even farther away.

"Damn!" He was leaning against the trunk of an alder, clutching it for support. "Yes," he gasped after a few moments. "Yes, I do need your help." The words were uttered without the least measure of cordiality. "Get beyond him if you can. Send him back toward me." He motioned to her with a peremptory swipe of his arm. "Well, get on with it. Or are you going to stand there in the blasted water until winter comes?"

Gates shook herself. It was obvious he was used to giving orders and having them obeyed instantly. She had a thought to wander off downstream and leave him to his own devices. But that would not have been a very charitable thing to do, even if he was a rude, ungrateful bully. She sighed that such a shimmering, gilded facade should have been given to a man of poor character.

"Don't go near him," he warned as Gates slogged through the water and stepped ashore just beyond where the horse was browsing.

"I'm not afraid," she sail. "Animals like me."

"He'll have your arm off if you try to touch him. He's the devil's spawn around strangers."

As Gates approached the horse, he raised his head and assessed this bedraggled upstart who was making soothing noises deep in her throat. Once he'd decided she was harmless, he allowed her to get within a foot of his reins.

"No! Get back!" the man cried. "Are you daft, girl!"

The horse's head shot up in alarm, then he turned and pelted off into the woods.

"I almost had him," Gates called out across the space that separated them. "You frightened him away."

"*I* frightened him? I raised that beast from a foal, you damned, impertinent chit."

She bit back her angry protest and clenched her hands. She'd always thought her two brothers had cornered the market on obnoxious behavior. It now occurred to her that perhaps this was a universal male tendency, and not one restricted to her own family.

She fought her way through the prickly bushes, back to where the man stood. He was weaving slightly, but his face was stern and fixed. "Now what?" he asked. "Now that you've sent my mount fleeing off to God knows where? I suppose it's too much to hope there's a horse somewhere that I could hire."

Gates shook her head. "We've no horses at our farm. Only goats and chickens. Nattie West has a farm cart, but he's off to market in Chester and won't be back for several days."

The man eyed the sky through the dark silhouettes of tree branches. The little that could be seen of the horizon in the west was now deep indigo stranded with fiery red.

"How far is it to Bellaire? Could I walk there before full dark?"

"I don't think, sir, after your fall—"

"Are you a physician?" he asked with a pronounced sneer.

"No," she muttered. "Of course I am not, but—"

"Then I suggest you keep your medical opinions to yourself. Now, how far?"

"Two miles," she said begrudgingly.

He turned from her and stepped into the stream.

"No!" she cried, reaching out to him. "You mustn't."

He spun around, crossed the bank, and stalked her until she was backed up against an oak trunk. "I have had quite enough of your interference. If you hadn't leapt up under my horse's nose and frightened him into a fit, I should no doubt be halfway to Bellaire by now. And if you hadn't chased him off into the woods, I would be riding there instead of being forced to walk in these damned, wet boots." He leaned down menacingly, his pale eyes narrowed. "Now, do I make myself clear?"

Let him go, a mean-spirited voice urged. *Let him discover for himself what lies beyond the stream.*

The man was apparently waiting for some response from her. His body was still holding her trapped, and he'd planted one long finger against her damp tucker.

She threw her head back. "I didn't save you from drowning to watch you get sucked into a bog."

His eyes narrowed even further. "You're lying."

She shrugged. "Cross then. I won't stop you." She sidled away from his touch, purposely setting the trunk of the tree between them. The sensation of his finger pressing upon her chest had made her a little breathless. Besides, it was past time she was home; her brothers would be coming in soon, looking for their supper.

The man cocked his head, opened his mouth to say something, but Gates had already drifted back into the thicket. When she could no longer see him, standing in a posture of barely contained anger on the bank of the stream, she turned and raced for home.

"Faded into the woods like a damned faerie," Griff muttered as he strode along the edge of the water, pushing brambles out of his path as he went. What a strange, unlovely creature she was, more like the offspring of a hedgehog and a gnome than a human child. Twigs and heather sprigs had sprouted from her wild brown curls, not merely lacing the surface as though she had laid her head upon a pillow of bracken, but rather they had been woven deep into that bizarre coiffure. It had only increased the unearthly, elfin look of her pinched face, with its slanted, peat-colored eyes.

He recalled her clothing with a shudder, not sure how he would describe the motley collection of rags she had worn. The largest and most prominent layer, which had been swathed about her waist with a vile orange sash, looked to have once been a brocaded, velvet drapery. Beneath its frayed hem, a tattered lace petticoat had dangled limply. In spite of the cool September weather, her feet had been bare. Bare, but surprisingly clean. No, not surprising at all, considering how she had splashed through the stream before she spooked his horse out from under him. No wonder Gaspar had bolted; the girl was surely the queerest creature Griffin had ever seen.

Stargrove must have been a lax landlord to allow such ragged tenants on his land. Gad, tinkers and Gypsies dressed better than that chit. But ragged or not, the girl seemed to think there was danger on the far side of the stream, and the way his luck was running, Griff thought it prudent to find another crossing.

"Gaspar!" he called out as he walked along, hoping the animal had recovered his wits enough to heed his master's voice. Once he reached Bellaire, Griff would send Farrow out to search for him. The groom was the only person, besides Griffin himself, whom

Gaspar tolerated. But he knew it might be hours yet before he found his way to the estate and he prayed the beast did not end up mired in a bog or lamed by his dangling reins before they found him. At least Griffin would be making his undignified, sodden arrival under cover of darkness. There was some small solace in that.

There was no solace, however, in the knowledge that Lord Pettibone had doubtless beaten him to Bellaire. The night before he left London, Griffin had learned from a crony that Lady Min had also invited the baron—who was the closest thing Griff had to a rival for the lady's affections—to attend her house party. Pettibone was a spindle-shanked fop on the shady side of fifty, who happened to own half of Surrey. If the Divinity was seeking a connection of wealth and title, then Pettibone was her man. However, Griff suspected she'd had enough of bloodless, matchstick fellows in her marriage to Stargrove. He fancied she might require someone more vigorous in her next marital arrangement.

Griff's coach had passed Pettibone's vehicle that morning outside of Taunton, but the victory had been short-lived. Now that he was hopelessly mired in this tangle of forest, Griff feared the baron might very well carry the day. Or the night, to be more precise.

He slowed his steps when he came to a small clearing. The bank across from him looked solid—a wide shelf of pebbles laced with moss. He was weighing the notion of crossing, when he heard a rustling behind him.

That dratted girl, he thought as he turned to send her on her way.

A tall, narrow-shouldered young man stood before him, holding an ancient fowling piece in the crook of one arm.

"Look here, Demp. A fine gent out for an evening stroll." He was speaking to the young man at his shoulder, who grinned ferociously. Both appeared to be nearing twenty and wore loose-fitting canvas coats that were soiled and threadbare. They were not an inspiring sight.

"I am one of her ladyship's guests at Bellaire," Griff said in a tight voice.

"Lost, are we?" The one with the gun smirked. " 'T'isn't safe to be roamin' these woods with night falling. You'd best come along with us."

"I'm certainly not lost," Griff insisted coolly, "I've just wandered away from my friends."

"There's no one else about in these woods," the second young

man pronounced. "Or we'd have come across them. You just hark
to my brother, Sank, here, and come along with us."

Sank raised the barrel of the gun meaningfully. "We'll make
sure you're quite comfortable."

This is preposterous, Griffin fumed as he strode along in front
of the two young men. He had been waylaid by these yokels a
mere two miles from Bellaire . . . at gunpoint, no less. Pray God he
never again ran into the ragged girl who had unseated him from his
horse or there would be such a reckoning.

As Griff walked along, occasionally prodded in the back by the
one called Sank, he was repeatedly assailed by the highly unsatis-
factory image of Lady Min melting into the embrace of Lord Pettibone. To the victor go the spoils—although Minerva could hardly
be called spoils. The thought of being cut out by that popinjay was
enough to make him turn on his two captors and wrap the muzzle
of the ancient gun around their scrawny necks.

But he was still a bit dazed from the blow to his head and knew
he wasn't yet in fighting trim. And he was damned if he was going
to let his desire for Minerva make him do another foolhardy thing.

"Oh, no! You haven't . . . not again! Sank, no! Oh, Demp, how
could you let him?"

Through the door of the woodshed, or wherever the hell it was
they had imprisoned him, Griff could hear only a muffled version
of the altercation that was taking place in the farmyard. A woman
was berating the two men who had abducted him.

"Sank had the gun," the one called Demp replied. "So what
could I do? And this fellow looks flush. Even flusher than the last
one. That's a diamond in his neckcloth or I'm Jack Sprat. And such
boots as I've never seen. He'll have a fine, fat purse—"

"—and a family who will be happy to pay his ransom," the tall
brother piped in. "He smells of money. Papa will be so proud."

"No!" the woman cried. "This isn't Papa's way at all."

There was a joint guffaw from the brothers. "You know the
Book says that God helps those who help themselves. And that a
rich man is an abomination in the eyes of the Lord. It's all there in
Papa's Scriptures."

"What about charity?" she asked. "That's in the Book as well."

"We could use some charity about now," the younger man said

with a chuckle. "This place isn't fit for the crows. Not since Papa went off on his last ministry right in the middle of sowing season."

"Don't you blame Papa," she railed. "You two could have finished the sowing, even without his help. But no . . . you sold the plow horses and sat about all spring, until the money ran out. And then you went off and abducted a cloth merchant and expected his poor wife to pay for his release."

"Hey, Demp, you think this one's got a wife? He's a pretty-enough fellow. A woman'd pay up real quick to get that one back in her bed."

"I won't stand here and listen to this!" the woman exclaimed. "You set him free this instant or I will go and fetch the magistrate."

"What you will do, missy," Sank said, his voice low and threatening, "is remember your place. A woman heeds the word of her menfolk, and we say he stays. Now fetch him out something to eat, while Demp and I have our supper. We don't want him to starve, being Christian men and all." The two brothers went away, sniggering softly.

Griff slid down onto the rough plank floor and rubbed the tender, swollen spot on his skull. This was infuriating. In the two years he'd spent fighting Napoleon, he hadn't once seen the inside of a prison. It was ludicrous that here, in the serene and secure reaches of England, he now found himself incarcerated by two larcenous farmers. He wondered fretfully what the brothers had done with the cloth merchant after his wife had paid his ransom. It occurred to him that there were plenty of places to hide a body in the dark recesses of Bellaire Wood. The bog beside the stream came immediately to mind.

Some minutes later, a plate slid under the crooked door of the woodshed, followed by a shallow bowl.

"Please," Griff said in a low voice. "Listen to me. I'll make it worth your while to aid me."

He waited for a long moment but there was no response.

"If you help me escape," he called more loudly through the planks, "I'll see that you are held blameless."

There was only the sound of someone hurrying away across the graveled yard.

After he'd eaten the pitiful stew and downed the watery cider from the bowl, Griff tried to pry away some of the rotting wood from the walls of his prison. At first several planks gave way easily, but beyond them were more planks, newer, sounder. It appeared the brothers had merely hammered good, stout boards over the rotting ones, rather than repair the outbuilding properly. His distaste for the two men was increasing by the minute. Not only were they lazy layabouts, if the woman's complaints were to be believed, he suspected they were also incredibly stupid.

He recalled how they had led him for some time through the woods, and then, when they reached a clearing, had covered his eyes with a ragged, dirty handkerchief, as though to prevent him from identifying his surroundings. Yet they continued to call each other by name. Once he was released, Griff would have no trouble identifying them for the authorities. How many yokels named Sank and Demp could possibly live on the outskirts of Bellaire? Perhaps they were planning to kill him after the ransom was paid, in which case they had no need to be discreet. Then why bother with the blindfold? He cursed in impotent fury.

And who was the woman? She was clearly an ally of sorts, for all that she'd refused to speak to him when she brought his meal. He'd have to work on her tomorrow. That was one area where he was on sound footing—cozening women had been his specialty since his days at Oxford.

He spent the night tossing restlessly on the dirt floor, tugging the collar of his coat up to his ears to ward off the cold, damp air and vowing with every chilled breath that he would see them all rotting in Newgate for keeping him from Minerva's side.

Chapter Three

*I*t has to be the same man, Gates reflected bitterly the next morning as she prepared the prisoner's lunch. It had to be the gilded stranger she had unhorsed at the stream. What was the likelihood that two gentlemen would be roaming Bellaire Wood in the same afternoon? Unfortunately, she hadn't gotten a glimpse of him last night; Sank had him locked in the woodshed by the time she emerged from the house to discover why her brothers were whooping so gleefully in the yard.

Now Sank and Demp had left for London, where they would attempt to extort money from the gentleman's family. They had gone into the shed first thing that morning and relieved him of his valuables. Sank had found a calling card in the man's waistcoat, and seemed to think he could ask a tidy sum for the safe return of one Griffin Darrowby of Mayfair. They had also taken his purse and his watch, his onyx signet ring, and the diamond stickpin. Unfortunately the man's fine boots had proven too narrow for either of the brothers, and they had thrown them angrily across the yard before they replaced the stout padlock on the door.

"Stay away from him while we're gone," Sank had warned her. "Except to give him his meals. If you bring the law down on us, you know it will break Papa's heart. We're doing his work here, in our own poor way, saving souls from perdition by removing their earthly possessions."

"But—"

"Don't argue," Demp had said harshly. He often defended her from Sank's bullying, but now his eyes were lit up with greed, just like his brother's. "We stand together as a family, you know that. Against anyone who doesn't share our belief in Papa's version of the Book. You believe in his Book, don't you?"

"Yes," she had answered softly as they went striding off.

But it was a lie. She often disagreed with her father's bizarre interpretations of the Bible, though she had to acknowledge he possessed a genuine calling to preach. However, even more vexing than his traveling ministries, which kept him from home for months at a time, was his constant refusal to see the true nature of his two stepsons.

Four years after the death of her mother, when the evangelical spirit had first come over him, her father had married a farm woman whom he'd met at one of his prayer meetings. The Widow Marsden had children of her own, two sly, conniving boys, both slightly younger than Gates. Now, after four years in their company, Gates knew that neither of her stepbrothers would follow in her father's footsteps, as he'd hoped. It was more likely that they would follow in their own father's footsteps. She had learned from her stepmother, on her deathbed a year earlier, that the woman's husband had died in prison after a bungled robbery attempt. When Gates had broached her father on the brothers' unfortunate patrimony, he had chided her for her uncharitable thoughts and reminded her that the sins of the father, by his Book, were not visited upon the sons.

However, it seemed that the sins of her father had been most truly visited upon her.

She had tried to keep the farm running after her father left in April, but there was little she could do alone. Especially since her stepbrothers had sold the two plow horses to a neighbor barely a week after their stepfather's departure.

A month ago they had also sold the one remaining horse, an elderly mare, to a passing tinker. Without the mare, Gates felt stranded on the farm. Taking long rides across the countryside had been one of her few pleasures, which she'd indulged in only when her father was away, since he frowned on using animals for anything but work. Unnatural, he pronounced it, to make one of God's creatures toil for a human's pleasure. But it made no sense to her, especially since the mare seemed to enjoy it when they went racing up the grassy hill behind the farmhouse.

Gates suspected the money her brothers received for the horses had gone directly to the publican at the Badger Burrow in Paultons—heaven knew she never saw a penny of it. At least her father sent home the occasional pound note, which kept them in cornmeal and molasses.

By late summer, in spite of Gates's efforts, the once-tidy farm had become an eyesore. When a corner of the farmhouse roof was staved in by a tree limb during a storm, Sank had merely shrugged and called it the Lord's work. She had climbed a ladder and forked straw into the hole, in an attempt to keep out the elements, and had

nearly broken her leg when the rickety ladder had collapsed under
her. Sank had laughed at that, but Demp had helped her into the
house and offered to cook their supper that night.

He had also warned her the same night that Sank had started
noticing things about her. "What sort of things?" she had asked.
Demp had given her an exasperated look, but he'd never mentioned it again.

Then Gates began to see it for herself, how Sank's eyes followed
her when she did her chores, his mouth hanging open, like a hungry hound's, when she washed up at the outdoor trough. Her stepbrothers had been gangling boys when she first came to live on the
farm, and she had quickly fallen into the role of older sister. But
during the past year both Sank and Demp had matured—at least in
body—into young men. Gates was not callow enough to believe
Sank would respect their sibling relationship—he was barely a
year her junior and no blood kin at all.

To ward off this unnerving threat, she began purposely to disguise her appearance. She ratted her hair into a tangled mass each
morning and swathed herself in billowing lengths of cloth that she
found in the attic. She also began to spend more time in the woods,
keeping her contact with Sank to a minimum. As long as they got
their breakfast and dinner on time, her stepbrothers didn't give a
fig for how she spent her days. So she was free from morning till
early evening to roam across the fields and dream away the hours
in the dappled glades of Bellaire Wood.

After they'd abducted the cloth merchant, she had stayed away
from the farm entirely, subsisting on berries and wild fruit. She'd
wanted no part of her stepbrothers' wicked schemes. It was bad
enough they'd begun pilfering goods from the stores in Paultons
and stealing chickens from the neighboring farms. She knew the
infrequent rabbits they brought home had been poached from Bellaire Wood. But when they turned up on that July afternoon with
the stout little shopkeeper from Nottingham in tow, blindfolded
and trussed up like a spring hen, she realized they had moved far
beyond petty crimes.

A few nights later, while her brothers were off delivering their
ransom note, she had slipped back to the farm and freed the man,
prying open the locked door with the handle of an ax. She had tied
his hands and blindfolded him again, and then led him for miles
before she left him sitting on a tombstone in a churchyard. She
knew she should have taken him to the local magistrate, but it

shamed her to think of that gentleman, whom in the past she had counted as a friend, discovering how low her brothers had sunk.

Sank and Demp had been furious when they returned home and heard that the merchant had escaped. Not only had his wife refused to pay them a penny, they now feared the man would bring the law down upon them. Even though Gates knew they were safe from prosecution, she said nothing to ease their fears. It was her only way of ensuring that they would curb their larcenous tendencies until her father returned.

She now laughed sourly at her own naiveté as she ladled soup into the shallow bowl. Barely a month had passed, and there was a new prisoner in the shed and a stout new lock on the door.

How had she gotten into this dreadful situation, and more to the point, was there any way out of it? This summer she had begun to dream of getting away from the farm, but responsibility to family had been drummed into her during her father's endless nightly sermons—it was one of his favorite themes. A pity his stepsons had taken it so little to heart.

It was impossible for her to credit that the cheerful, intelligent man who'd been devoted to his wife and young daughter, had somehow been transformed into a bleak prophet, whose only goal in life was the spreading of his own personal gospel.

She recalled how frightened she'd been when he first began to experience his strange episodes, or enlightenments, as he called them. Voices and visions overwhelmed him, urging him to share his evangelical insights with the masses. He had left his home in Chester then, and gone on the road, carting Gates along with him like a sack of beans. As little as she'd liked traipsing over the country with her father, sleeping in hedgerows and living like a Gypsy, at least she'd learned to look out for them both. They had survived those rough days only due to her well-developed sense of economy. She could stretch a shilling into next week if she had to. Then her father had married the Widow Marsden. Gates suspected he'd done it—allied himself with a woman far below him—so he would have a place to leave her while he was away on his ministries. But even with her knack for economy, Gates couldn't make the farm prosper, not without men willing to work it.

Now, the seductive whisperings of freedom assaulted her. Sank and Demp were not there to stop her from leaving. She had no idea how long they would be gone or if they would even come back. It was the perfect time for her to get away. There was no longer any

money for food—her father had sent nothing in over a month—
and she doubted her brothers would have even a ha'penny left between them when they returned. She had been awaiting some sign,
something that would portend a change in her life. If she looked
about her, she realized, she would see those signs in every rotting
board of the farm.

If it weren't for the man in the shed, she could have fled the
farm. Yet she dared not set him free, as much as her conscience
prodded her. He wouldn't allow her to bind up his hands and blindfold him, as the merchant had, or follow her docilely to a distant
churchyard. He was much more likely to tear her limb from limb—
she'd seen yesterday what a wicked temper he had.

It was pointless to weigh the repercussions of releasing the prisoner, she thought as she crossed the yard with his lunch, since
Sank had taken the key for the padlock with him. Gates doubted
she had the strength to force the heavy lock.

"Talk to me," the man entreated her hoarsely, as she slid his
plate under the door. "You must let me out of here. I promise you
will come to no harm if you do."

"No key," she said tersely.

"Then break down the door." His voice was louder now.

"No ax," she replied. Sank had sold it to a peddler only a week
before.

"Then how the devil do you chop firewood?" he fumed. "It's a
blasted farm, isn't it? There must be an ax or a pry bar."

"I can't say," she answered truthfully. She had no idea what remained of their farm tools. She'd begun avoiding the barn after
Demp had warned her about his brother—it was too easy to get
cornered in such a place.

Gates saw his boots, dusty now and a bit mauled by the goats,
lying beside the fence. She rose and fetched them back to the
woodshed. "Here," she said as she maneuvered them through the
space beneath the crooked door.

"Thank you," he said softly. Then his hand slid out through the
narrow opening, palm up, a sign of entreaty that was hard to mistake. She had a fair idea of what such a gesture would cost an imperious man. Without thinking, she laid her calloused hand over
his smooth palm.

"Please . . ." he crooned from the other side of the planked barrier. His fingers tightened slowly on hers, a warm clasp that sent
her heart rocketing to her throat. "Help me."

"I'm sorry," she whispered raggedly, pulling back from that stirring contact. "I must go now."

"No!" His strident voice echoed behind her as she ran from the yard in the direction of the woods. "Sweet Jesus, you must let me out!"

Gates found the man's horse in a thicket near her favorite climbing tree. The stallion's reins had become hopelessly snarled in the branches, and he had worked himself into a lather in his attempts to break free. He reared up as she came toward him. Gates gentled him with her voice as she drew closer. Once his ears were cocked toward her in an inquisitive manner, she reached forward to stroke his nose. He whickered softly, and then stood calmly while she untangled the reins from the branches.

She led the horse through the woods to the farm. A fearful cacophony was coming from inside the woodshed as they went past it, which made the horse set his ears back. The prisoner seemed to have found a tool of some sort, and was banging it energetically against the planks. Gates was unalarmed; her brothers had reinforced the shed's walls during the cloth merchant's sojourn there.

Inside the doorway of the dilapidated barn a clutch of scrawny chickens roosted on an overturned thresher; beneath it one of the goats was napping on a torn burlap sack. Gates removed the horse's saddle and bridle, and then shut him in one of the stalls, tying the broken latch shut with a bit of twine. She knew there was no fodder for the beast—the animals that lived on the farm were used to foraging for themselves. The horse lipped at the dry, dusty straw that littered the floor of his stall, and then looked up at her with reproach. This was clearly not the sort of reception he was accustomed to.

After prodding the goat off the sack, Gates carried it out to the base of the hill that lay behind the house, where wild grass grew in profusion. She filled the sack with handfuls of the sweet-smelling stuff and carried it back to the barn. As she swung it over the stall door, and scattered the grass at the horse's feet, she noticed there was a battered pitchfork leaning against the back of the adjoining stall. She might be able to pry the padlock off the woodshed door with the handle. And the tined end might serve to keep the man at bay until she could escape to the woods. She went into the empty stall and lifted the tool away from the wall, hefting it in both hands. It seemed sturdy enough.

A violent cracking noise erupted out in the yard. Gates spun around in alarm just as the man came tumbling out through a splintered hole in the shed.

He threw down the large, rusty hinge he had been clutching—obviously his tool of escape—and looked wildly about him. Before she could duck down behind the stall door, he caught sight of her and came racing toward the barn with black rage written across his lovely face. Skirting the stall door, she fled across the floor and went flying up the rickety ladder to the hayloft, still clutching the pitchfork. The man was only a few steps behind her; when she turned to draw up the ladder, he was already clambering up after her.

"I should have known it was you," he seethed as he cleared the edge of the loft. She scrambled back from him, tucking herself beneath the low eaves. "I should have expected that those two larcenous wretches were related to you."

"They're n-not related to me," she stammered.

"Then you must be married to one of them, God help you. God help all of you, for you'll most likely hang for this business. Kidnapping, robbery—" The stallion in the stall below them gave a nicker of welcome at the sound of the familiar voice. "Horse thieving," he added.

"I had nothing to do with it," she insisted. "I didn't steal your horse. I rescued him from the woods."

"Not bloody likely," he growled. "You're nothing but a thieving little liar. You and those two knaves you live with." He was very close to her now. The sunlight that filtered in through the holes in the barn roof was making a blazing halo of his gold-streaked hair. "So where are they? Hiding somewhere to save their miserable skins? Letting you take the brunt of my anger?"

"They've gone to London," she managed to rasp out. "To get your ransom."

He gave a brittle laugh. "Good. My butler will have them thrashed and thrown into Newgate."

He slid forward on his hands and knees till he was directly in front of her. He lowered his head a notch so that his eyes were on a level with hers. They gleamed like pale blue ice.

Gates poked at him with the tined end of her weapon. "Stay back!"

An expression of wry amusement shifted across his face. "So it has a bit of spirit after all."

She set the sharp metal points against his chest. "You won't sound so smug when you've got four holes in your belly." She realized then that the pitchfork was missing one of its tines. "Er, three holes," she amended.

He laughed outright. "And it can count. How refreshing."

"Stop saying that," she said crossly. "I'm not an *it,* I'm a girl."

"Yes," he purred. "I'm just beginning to notice that." His eyes darkened ominously and she swore she felt the heat rise off his lean body and jolt into her.

"Tell me, little jade," he said in a dangerously soft voice, "do they share you, those two brothers?"

She gasped and increased the pressure of the pitchfork. "That's a horrid thing to say! This is a godly house!" The protest sounded feeble, even to her ears. "My father is a preacher! A man of the Lord!"

"Last time I looked, the Lord didn't sanction kidnapping and thieving."

"They are headstrong!" She was quoting her father now. "And inclined to sloth. But they are not wicked, sir. They are not!"

"Maybe not," he said softly. "But I can be. Wicked, that is. Especially when I've been deprived of my sleep and my dignity, and forced to eat slop that's not fit for swine." She felt the pressure of his knees, where they straddled her legs. "Yes . . . I think I can be quite wicked."

Before she had time to react, he thrust the pitchfork away from his shirtfront and swiftly wrestled the handle from her grasp. He tossed it from him into a pile of hay and turned back to her. Gates quickly slid back as far under the eaves as she could, until the nail tips that protruded from the roof spiked into her back.

"Whichever of those louts you belong to, it's no matter to me. I'll take my revenge on you all eventually. But you'll be first." He set his hands around her waist and tugged her roughly forward, out from her sanctuary. When he lowered himself onto her again, his thighs were straddling her hips.

He flicked open the tucker that had been loosely tied over her bodice. The feel of his fingertips on her chest was like a brand of fire. With his other hand, he reached down and began drawing up her skirts. She felt like a young deer who had strayed into the sights of a wolf; blind, panting fear was mixed with a bemused, fatalistic curiosity.

"Jesus," he muttered under his breath. "How many petticoats are you wearing? This had better be worth all the effort."

"No," she said, surprised at how calmly the word came out. "You don't want to do this."

"Don't I?" he said with a sneer. "I don't think you have any idea of what I want."

She slapped at him, and then, when he continued his exploration undaunted, she hardened her hands into fists and began raining blows on his arms and shoulders. He quickly caught both her wrists with one hand and held them tight against his chest.

He had overpowered her as easily as an adult curbs a small child. But more frightening than his effortless mastery of her flailing arms was the fearful set of his face. The angelic beauty she'd seen at the stream had darkened into a demonic intensity. His eyes sparked with blue fire and his lips were drawn up into a harsh mockery of a smile.

"If you fight me," he observed almost gently, "it will go the worse for you."

"I will fight you," she cried out raggedly. "Because you are too cowardly to fight yourself."

Gates began to struggle with renewed energy, writhing beneath him in a mindless frenzy. Her short, panicked sobs echoed down from the rafters. She was unaware that the man was no longer trying to subdue her, but was instead attempting to soothe her. When she felt his warm fingers upon her shoulders, she gave a long, strangled cry. Then her vision swirled sickeningly and the world went black.

Griffin threw himself back from the swooning girl and pressed his knotted fists to his brow.

Lord, he was half out of his mind with icy rage. And hunger. The empty hollowness throbbing in his gut was now joined by the tearing pangs of guilt. He *never* let his temper get the better of him, even when anger popped and sizzled inside him. Though the blood beast often surged against the cage of Griff's making, the mindless brutality never got past his guard. But twice now this ragged chit had riled him into anger and this last time to something quite near violence.

He waited in the shadowed loft until his breathing grew more regular. All he'd really wanted to do was frighten her, he told himself, to get a bit of his own back after the indignities he'd suffered from her kin. There was no way in heaven he would have actually lain with the chit. He did have some standards, after all.

The girl in the straw sighed, and Griffin's gaze shifted to her face. The pinpoints of sunlight that danced over his hair were also dappling her cheek and brow. He leaned closer to check her breathing and was surprised to discover that she was not so ill-looking as he'd first thought.

In the shadows beside the stream he'd seen only her tattered clothing and the pinched, elfin face with its dark eyes. Now in the filtered light of the loft, her features appeared softer. Her cheekbones were high and widely set, and her eyes tilted provocatively up at the ends. Her mouth was a deep rose color, an enticing contrast to the pale olive of her complexion.

Though her limbs were thin—her arms and long legs barely made an impression beneath the rumpled layers of her clothing—they were shapely and there was a ripeness to her form that stirred him.

"Steady on," he cautioned himself, drawing back from her forcibly. It was madness to even contemplate it. Not when he had the Divinity awaiting him at Bellaire. But as the girl shifted slightly in the straw, and Griff glimpsed the rise of her breasts beneath the disarranged tucker, his whole body tensed in anticipation. No opera dancer, no lady of easy virtue, not even Minerva Stargrove, had ever drawn such an instantaneous response from him. Though his brain had registered only white-hot anger as he'd tussled with the chit, his body had clearly acknowledged the ripe, supple female beneath it. Griff sighed. He really had to learn to curb himself.

"It's only hunger," he murmured reassuringly, merely his body mistaking one appetite for another.

Once he had mastered his unaccountable lust, he moved forward and lifted the girl into his arms. The wise course would have been to saddle his horse and ride away from this place. However, some uncharacteristic chivalry prompted him to wait until she had revived from her swoon.

She was limp and lifeless against his chest as he swung his legs over the side of the loft and settled his feet on the ladder. He chuckled softly; he'd never before had any of his conquests faint under him. At least not before the act of coupling. A few ladies had paid him the ultimate compliment of swooning away afterward, though he suspected there was an element of playacting to their response. But this fey creature was dead to the world. No amount of playacting could have accounted for that.

Once he felt the ladder take his weight, he hoisted the girl over his shoulder and carried her down to the barn floor. Gaspar gave an angry stamp as his master went past with his inert burden.

As he crossed to the house, Griff had a chance to observe the farm. Beyond the weathered fences that bordered the yard lay lush green meadows, rolling in green swards to the very edge of Bellaire Wood. No animals grazed there, which was a pity; he recognized fine horse pasturage when he saw it.

The yard itself was in an appalling state. No corner was free of debris—broken farm equipment, mildewed harness traces, and tattered grain sacks littered the gravelly expanse. Scrawny chickens pecked among the healthy crop of weeds, and a herd of bony goats was milling about on the sagging front porch. The stone farmhouse appeared a decent enough dwelling, until one noticed the gaping hole in the corner of the roof. Griff dreaded going inside the house, but short of leaving his charge on the rickety wooden porch chair, and at the mercy of the foraging goats, he could think of no other course.

He went up the steps, thrusting several of the nosy beasts aside with his knee as he unlatched the front door. The interior was less distressing. The main room boasted a large fireplace and a plank floor, and was furnished with a pine table, a narrow-seated settle, and several straight-backed chairs. He scanned the room, looking for a place to set his burden down and frowned at the unwelcoming austerity of the place. To his left a set of worn stairs clung to one wall; he shifted the girl onto his right shoulder and trooped up to the first floor.

After ducking his head into an attic bedroom, whose floor was awash with gin bottles and stray clothing, he came to a charming chamber, as unlike that other room as a lily was unlike a nettle. The plank floor had been scrubbed to a soft patina. A faded rug lay before a narrow bed, which was draped with a dimity spread. Frayed lace curtains were pinned over the dormer window; the sunlight filtered through them in a rich golden haze, highlighting the watercolor drawings of plants and animals that hung upon the whitewashed walls. These were amateurish, he noted, but done with a good eye to detail.

Griff laid the girl gently upon the spread. A little color had returned to her cheeks, but, as he placed his fingers against the side of her throat, he could feel her pulse still fluttering. Poor mite, he thought, to live in such a grim homestead. No wonder she sought refuge in the forest.

He stood for a moment, battling the stern voice that insisted he leave her. Ignoring that voice, he drew the bench from the vanity up beside the bed and straddled it. Both vanity and bench were French and of very fine workmanship. His mother had a similar set at Darrowby, and he wondered where a farm girl had acquired something so valuable. *Probably stole it,* he muttered to himself.

He watched her for several minutes, following the slow rise and fall of her breasts. Today she was dressed like the lead character in a provincial play—*The Shepherdess of the Hills,* or something like—in an old-fashioned black bodice that laced over a flowing white blouse. He wagered her voluminous blue calico skirt had at least a dozen petticoats beneath it.

That image recalled to him the feel of her skin under his hand as he'd stroked it along her calf. Smooth as china silk, she'd been, and so warm. No ice maiden, like his intended. Fiery and fierce, she'd defended herself with every ounce of energy she could muster.

Ah, but that's always the way with virgins, he observed silently, hoping that the warning would cool the heat that was again licking through him. Was it his fault that the clean, graceful lines of her coltish limbs were so enticing, or the pagan curves of her body? She was a young Diana, he thought, a budding goddess of the forest.

He was distracting himself by examining one of the watercolors when he heard her stirring on the bed. Her eyes remained closed, though. He turned back to her and set his elbows on his knees. "There's no point in pretending any longer," he said, leaning forward. "I can see that you've recovered."

She opened one eye. "I am waiting to see what you will do," she said.

He could have sworn he heard a note of amusement in her tone. Quite a surprise, since he expected an exhibition of mortified, maidenly weeping. "What would you like me to do?"

"An apology might be in order," she said as she tried to sit up.

"No, stay," he cautioned, coaxing her back to her pillow with one hand. "You've had a bit of a shock."

She turned her head and met his eyes. "How could you have used me so? After I saved you from the bog."

"I have not used you at all," he said simply. "I did nothing more than frighten you out of your wits. Then you swooned."

"From fright?" she asked with resentment. "More likely from lack of air, with a great lummox like you sitting on my chest."

Griffin nearly laughed out loud. No woman in memory had ever called him a lummox. It had a novel charm. "Well, whatever the reason, I can't recall a single female ever reacting to me that way."

"And how many females have you forced yourself upon?"

"Not more than a dozen or so," he said. "Usually it's the other way around."

"Oh, I see. You no doubt have to beat them off with a stick."

"I am never that rash. A look of boredom usually suffices."

She looked at him through her lashes. "So I am still as you found me? Truly?"

He gave a little cough. "You don't have to take my word for it. I believe you would know it, if there had been any, um, well you know, between us."

"Congress?" she said.

"Yes, for lack of a better word." He knew plenty of better words—nice, effective Anglo-Saxon words—for that particular act. He was also quite sure she knew none of them.

"Why did you stop then? I'd have thought my fainting would have made your task a lot easier."

"I find myself rather indifferent to women who are unconscious. It's a little quirk in my nature." He lowered his head a fraction of an inch. "In truth, it was you who stopped me—you brought me to my senses when you said I was too craven to fight myself."

"I said that?" Her eyes widened in disbelief. "And that alone made you stop?"

He cleared his throat. "It *was* cowardly of me to have ... um ..."

"Attacked?" she interjected.

"Yes, if you insist, to have attacked you like that. And whatever the Darrowbys may have been accused of over the centuries, they've let few men call them craven."

"What about women?" she asked artlessly.

"Women, on the other hand, have been calling us far worse than that since the time of Eleanor of Aquitaine.

"She was a queen of England," he added quickly, when it dawned on him that a farm girl would know nothing of medieval royalty.

And of France, she murmured under her breath.

But Griff didn't hear her. "I can only say, in my defense, that being abducted at gunpoint and locked in a woodshed is likely to make any man peevish."

"P-peevish?" she echoed.

"Well, furious, then. But you must admit I had every right to feel that way. Then you refused to help me, you wouldn't even speak to me . . ." His voice deepened. "I am not used to being ignored, you see. It plays havoc with my self-esteem."

He offered her a slow, canted grin. Numberless ladies had been made breathless and acquiescent by that grin, and Griffin knew it. The girl on the bed merely frowned, her expression anything but forgiving.

"You, sir," she said briskly, "are a cozening man. My father has warned me of such. I've often wondered if I should ever meet one."

"You are not disappointed, I trust?" he said slyly. "And if you like, I could furnish further demonstrations—" He set both hands on the edge of her comforter and leaned forward.

"I think I've had enough cozening for the present. It appears a little goes a long way."

As he was drawing breath to respond to that subtle knife thrust, she suddenly cried out and took his two hands between her own. "Oh, Jehosephat! Look what you've done to yourself."

"Wh-what . . . ?" He could have sworn he was stammering. He looked down at his hands, wondering what had come over the girl. In his urgency to free himself from the shed, he'd scraped and torn his fingertips and knuckles. The rusty hinge that had at last levered him out of the place, had left behind several raw blisters. He'd suffered worse after a bout of fisticuffs at Jackson's, but he wasn't about to tell her that.

"Stay here," she said as she slid from the bed. An instant later she was back with a soft flannel cloth, which she had doused in her washstand basin.

He watched in amazement as she carefully pressed the cloth to one hand and then the other. As a rule, he did not enjoy being

touched. Especially not by strangers. Even the act of coupling, for
all its pleasures, required him to overcome his particular dislike.
Not that he didn't enjoy being the one to do the touching when he
sported with a woman. But all his conquests sensed, or quickly
learned, that it was he alone who initiated and engineered their
play.

Griffin found he was suffering the girl's ministrations in a tolerably good spirit. In fact, there was a soothing delicacy to her touch.

"Sit still," she chided him when he squirmed slightly as she
dabbed at an open blister. "Hmm, I need to put some ointment on
this."

His cheeks drew in wickedly. "Perhaps you could kiss it better."

"Cozening man," she muttered as she again left the bed and
went to rummage in her dresser.

"I was under the impression," he said, twisting on his bench to
watch her, "that you were the one who required nursing."

"Ah!" she cried triumphantly, unearthing a small tin from beneath a billowing mound of fabric. She turned back to him. "What
was that?"

"I am only amazed that you have recovered your . . . self-
possession so rapidly."

She shrugged, and then came to kneel at his feet. "I'm fairly
stouthearted," she proclaimed. "I've no sensibility to speak of. I
don't need looking after, which is a good thing, as there is no one
here to do it." She gave him an easy smile and proceeded to smear
an evil-looking green ointment over his palms.

Griffin recognized the lie behind the words she had uttered in
such a matter-of-fact manner. It was the same lie he'd been telling
himself for the past sixteen years—that he needed no one. Griffin
had lived that lie, and made it work for him. He'd grown accustomed to fending for himself, of taking charge of his own destiny.
He had learned to dominate his environment, and never let it overpower him. It was a quality that had served him in good stead in
his financial endeavors. But it had also exacted a toll—he was as
solitary now, in his adult life, as when he'd lived in total isolation
at Darrowby, with only the Ogre and the servants for company.

He wondered as he gazed down at the tangled mass of curls that
was lowered over his hands, if this young woman was as self-
sufficient as she claimed. It was clear she had no idea of how to
dominate so much as a goat. But then, females were ever more tol-

erant than males. Doubtless she did not simmer and smolder at her
wretched lot in life, as he had done.

He thought she was finished with him once she'd closed up her
tin and settled herself on the side of the bed. But she merely took
his head between her hands and tipped it forward. For a brief,
breathless instant, he thought she was going to kiss him, but she
merely said, "I need to see where you hit it yesterday. I worried all
night that you might have got concussed."

"I was not very pleasant to you at the stream," he said between
his teeth as her fingers prodded the right side of his head beneath
the spill of hair. "I wonder that you should have spared a thought
for me."

"It seems the lost lamb always receives the most attention," she
responded.

Griff nearly laughed. First lummox, and now lost lamb. What
unlikely names she leveled at him.

He flinched when her forefinger touched the jagged scrape
above his ear. When she leaned over for a closer inspection, he had
to shut his eyes to avoid coming face-to-face with her rounded
bosom. Her whispery touch was already sending tendrils of flame
licking into his belly; he'd have her beneath him in an instant, if he
gave in to his urge to look past the gaping material above the
quilted bodice.

"Not so bad," she pronounced, as she sat up. Her fingers were
still resting below his ears. No, not resting, stroking slightly. Making his spine feel like molten metal. "Nothing like the time Sank
hit Demp with a horseshoe. I had to stitch up his head with a needle and thread."

Griffin stifled his disappointment when her hands fell back to
her lap. "Well that's a fate I'm grateful to have avoided."

"I have a very neat stitch," she said primly. "It barely left a
scar." She smiled at him then, a wide, Gypsy smile that lit up her
eyes.

They were a vivid amber color, he saw now, awash with swirls
of gold and copper, like veins of precious ore in a sandstone cavern. With her eyes shut she'd been appealing, but now that they
were wide open and vibrant with life, she was much more than
that. Some spirit of the woodland had been miraculously captured
in those eyes, lending her whole face a pagan beauty.

Griff pushed the bench back, scraping it along the floor away
from the bed, again trying to fight off the heady onslaught of de-

sire. She wasn't a wood nymph after all, he thought as he tried to calm his racing pulse, but Circe, the fatal enchantress. Though she was looking at him with a playful expression, there was an ancient wisdom in those amber eyes. He had an uncanny feeling that she'd known exactly how her touch had affected him.

"Why don't you pretend to be the patient now," he said in what he hoped was a relaxed voice, as he motioned her to lie back on the bed. "And I will fetch you something from the kitchen." He rose and moved toward the door. "Tea or cocoa, perhaps."

"The problem is we have no tea or cocoa in this house." She brushed her tangled hair back from her face. "Or molasses or flour. Only turnips."

He made a nasty face. "Now I know why that stew you fed me tasted so foul. I hate turnips."

"They're the only things that grew in the fields this summer."

"What of the goats and chickens? Surely that's something for the pot."

She shook her head and looked solemn. "I cannot bring myself to eat a one of them. I've rather made them into pets, you see."

"Strange pets," he muttered.

She shrugged and sighed. "They've been better company than my stepbrothers."

Griff grunted. "The less said about those two, the better." He scratched at his chin, which was now covered with fine bristles. "Er, whatever happened to the cloth merchant they kidnapped?"

"He escaped before they returned from collecting his ransom."

"Were you a party to his abduction?"

A martial spark leapt into her eyes. "I should say not! During the time he was here, I stayed in the woods. Praying for his deliverance, if you must know."

"A note to the local magistrate would have been a bit more effective, don't you think?"

She gnawed her lip. He watched her fine white teeth trace over the soft pink surface, and felt the slow simmer begin again. He could see she had no answer for him, and so continued, "Why didn't you hie yourself off to the woods when they brought me here?"

"I suspected you were the man I had met by the stream . . . and I felt responsible for you, I suppose. Also, I didn't dare anger my brothers again . . . they were very cross when I wouldn't help them look after the cloth merchant."

He took a step nearer the bed. "Beat you, did they?" he said under his breath.

Her head snapped up. "Oh, no. Papa would never allow them to strike me. They merely sold my little mare to a passing tinker." Her face had grown so forlorn as she spoke that Griff felt a new anger rise up in him toward her brothers.

"Another pet?" he asked softly as he returned to the side of her bed.

"Mmm," she said. "She wasn't young or very pretty, but she had such nice eyes. I like to think the tinker is taking good care of her, because he told Demp that she had a rare, bright look about her."

When she raised her eyes to his face, Griff's lust fizzled instantly and was replaced by the fierce urge to wrap his arms about her and comfort her. He drew back from the bed and went to lean against the door. It was safer here, away from that waiflike aura. "Is there no one nearby you can go to now? I mean, I don't think it's safe for you to be here alone."

He quickly heard the absurdity of that statement—the two louts she'd been living with were probably the most dangerous men in the district.

She regarded him thoughtfully. "My father would be very angry if I left the farm."

"It seems he hardly warrants such loyalty," he observed.

"It is my duty to remain here." Her voice grew wistful. "But I do feel such a temptation to get away."

"Perhaps you should follow your father's example. Maybe your destiny also lies beyond this farmstead, and you have been denying it by staying here."

Griff wondered for an instant if the blow to his head had scrambled his wits. He couldn't recall speaking to anyone about such things in his entire life. His voice became brisk. "Did your stepbrother happen to take his gun with him to London?"

"No. It should be hanging over the mantel in the parlor. But why would you—"

"Stay here and rest. I'm going to do something about the lamentable state of your larder."

He opened the door, and then turned, "I am sorry for frightening you in the barn. As for those hooligans you call kin . . . well, I will keep my own counsel on the matter. However, you must promise me that the next time they . . . er, stray from the path of righteousness, you will alert someone in authority."

"I will," she said with a little smile.

He let his gaze wander over her one last time. The lambent light from the windows had blanketed her in pale gold where she reclined against her headboard. He shrugged off the nagging desire to recross the room and lay down beside her.

"I'd best be off," he said gruffly.

The sooner he was away from this place, the better. His life had slipped from his grasp somewhere about the time he'd plummeted off Gaspar's back, and he wanted desperately to get things back to normal. No more larcenous yokels, no more goats and chickens, and definitely no more amber-eyed farm girls with enticing smiles. Minerva Stargrove awaited him, and he was sure that once he was in her presence, this ragged, strangely sultry waif would vanish from his thoughts like a morning haze.

Chapter Four

"A cozening man," Gates murmured to herself after he'd gone striding from her room. Since her father had first warned her of the idle, vain, rascally sort of man who preyed on innocent women, she'd wondered if she would ever meet one. Griffin Darrowby had far exceeded her expectations. She doubted if there was a farm girl in Cheshire, or in the whole of England, for that matter, who'd ever been cozened by such a wickedly beautiful man.

She had regained consciousness halfway up the staircase, to find herself slung over his shoulder. Unsure of what he intended to do with her and still a bit woozy, she had decided that it was best to continue her swoon. But the tender way he'd laid her on the bed, and the apparent concern on his face, which she had seen as she'd peeped at him through her tangled forelock, had allayed her fears. And though she still felt shaky and weak, she knew instinctively that he had not violated her in the barn.

Gates now heard him moving around in the room below, and then the sound of a door slamming. At least he hadn't fetched the gun back upstairs and taken a shot at her, she thought with a grin. Ah, but he had frightened her in the barn, dreadfully, if truth be told. She had seen the devils that turned his eyes from pools of shimmering blue to dark cauldrons of rage. She could not know that very few people had seen him in such a state, or that those who had, had never been able to shake off the sight.

It was a wonder she had been able to sit there on her bed and banter with him so calmly afterward. But when he wasn't in a horrid fit of temper, he was extremely easy to talk to. Intelligent, especially for a wastrel member of the *ton*, charming, and amusing.

There was also that stirring masculine beauty that made looking at him a joy. In the daylight he was even more impressive than he'd been beside the twilit stream. The hands that she had so tenderly bathed were refined and long-fingered. Well kept, but with a steely strength beneath their pampered surface. The hair she had parted with her fingers had been like thick strands of silk, and a thousand shades of honey and gold.

He was possibly the most glorious being Gates had ever encountered. Compared with her two brothers—Sank, with his bulbous eyes and bony physique, and Demp, with his tangle of red hair and haphazard teeth—Griffin Darrowby was a demigod, molded by a celestial sculptor. Angels surely did not possess such beauty in their faces or such grace in their forms. She instantly regretted such irreverent thoughts, but then grew mutinous. He was one of God's creatures and could be admired the same way one admired a hawk in flight or a stag on the run. There could be no disrespect in acknowledging that the Lord had done outstanding work on the day Griffin Darrowby was born.

Sighing with a vague discontent, she climbed from the bed and went to her dressing table. It had been her mother's, part of her dowry. Gates had managed to have it sent from Chester after her father's marriage to the widow. The gleaming fruitwood was dulled now and the mirror had partially lost its silvering, but Gates valued it for all the memories it held. So many nights she had sat at her mama's knee, watching as she combed out her long hair and braided it into a thick plait.

She leaned down and peered at herself in the glass. No wonder Griffin Darrowby hadn't wanted to deflower her—she looked like a troll. Just then hoofbeats sounded in the yard. She shifted to the window in time to watch him ride off, the gun crooked in one arm. Maybe he really was going to find her something to eat. Maybe he really would return. Gates wasn't taking any chances. If he returned, he wasn't going to be met by this unkempt creature. She hurried down the stairs and into the kitchen.

The water from the pump was ice cold, but she grit her teeth and thrust her head under the forceful stream of water until her tangle of hair was soaked. She lathered it with her own lavender soap and then rinsed it twice, washing out all the twigs and flowers that had adorned it. Sank was on the road to London; she no longer needed her disguise. Next she stripped off her clothing and washed herself all over. Shivering and dripping wet, she raced back up the stairs and dried herself with a sheet. Only one decent dress remained in her narrow wardrobe, a beige muslin sprigged with green leaves. It still fit her, although it was a bit snug in the bodice. She took a fresh tucker from the wardrobe and draped it over her shoulders. The image that now appeared in her mirror was in all ways satisfactory. She pinched some color into her pale cheeks and lay down again on the bed to await the stranger's return.

She must have slept for several hours, for when she awoke the late-afternoon sun was slanting in through her window. She sighed as she lay there, saddened by the realization that the man had not come back after all. He was probably signing a complaint with the authorities this very minute. If she was wise, she would make speed for the woods, and hide there until she was sure it was safe. But, no, he'd promised he would not make trouble for her, and she knew gentlemen rarely went back on their word.

Hunger was gnawing at her belly as she went out onto the porch to watch the sunset, and the thought of more turnips only made it grumble the louder.

A dead pheasant hung from the porch rafters. The fowling piece was propped against the porch railing; one of the goats was lipping at it with a blissful expression on its face. Gates shooed the animal away and carried the gun back into the house. As she was hanging the weapon above the fireplace, she noticed five gold buttons sitting on the mantel shelf. They had, until recently, adorned the embroidered waistcoat of Mr. Griffin Darrowby of Mayfair. She picked one up and buffed it against her skirt. Not real gold, she thought, but surely worth enough to trade for some tea and flour at the store in Paultons.

She tried not to feel forlorn as she sat on the porch step and plucked the feathers from the game bird. Why should she be sad . . . she was going to dine like royalty tonight. Only she had been lonely for so long, and for a part of the afternoon, while she had spoken with him, her loneliness had faded away. It was a pity he hadn't gotten a chance to see her in a proper dress, with her hair combed into soft curls.

He had left her the bird, it was true, but she'd rather have eaten turnip soup in his company, than dined on roast pheasant all by herself.

Griffin rode south along a cowpath until he came to a rutted lane. A farm wagon pulled by a pair of oxen was toiling along the track. Several young farmworkers lounged in the back on a pile of straw, laughing and joking. He called out to the driver for directions to Bellaire and the man pulled up his team.

"I'n't more than two mile," he remarked with a gap-toothed grin. "You just follow along with us now and I'll point out the turning."

Griff drew Gaspar into a walk and settled beside the wagon. He sighed at the slowness of the oxen, but then he recalled what had happened the last time he let his impatience goad him. The farm lads in the back of the wagon were eyeing him with good-humored assessment and so he called out to them. "Is there a farm near here, where two men called Sank and Demp live?"

One of the youths shook his head slowly. "I'd stay away from them, Cap'n. Nothing but trouble, those Underhills. My uncle runs the dry-goods store in Paultons, and whenever they come around, things go missing. If you take my drift."

Another fellow nodded. "Pity they're such a shiftless pair. The sister used to come to our farm to sell eggs—my ma always bought some because she felt sorry for her, even though we've chickens to spare."

The first one added, "But she's as daft as the rest of the family. Runs wild in these woods, like a madwoman. My da says she's a witch and to keep away from her."

"But I understood the father was a parson of some sort."

They all hooted. "Parson of Addlepates," a third fellow crowed. "That's what he is. We all follow the Methody hereabouts, but that Underhill has his own religion. He stands outside our chapel and rants at us, threatening our folks with hellfire. Been before the magistrate for it, he has. More than once."

Griff sighed. It was far worse than he expected. There was clearly to be no relief for the girl, even if her father came home any time soon. At least he'd done something for her, left the pheasant he'd shot. When he returned with the bird, he'd peeked into her room and found her asleep. He knew it would be best for his peace of mind to leave her to her slumbers. By way of apology for his brutish behavior in the barn, he'd also left her the buttons from his waistcoat, which her greedy brothers had overlooked when they'd searched him that morning. Real gold they were, and would fetch more than enough money to keep her into the cold weather. And there was an end to it.

He forced himself to think of Minerva, to rekindle the anticipation that had marked the first days of his journey. He frowned, though, when all he could summon up was a pair of haunting amber eyes.

The main house of Bellaire was constructed of red brick, with a sweeping facade that fronted a flagged courtyard. Ancient cedars lined the pebbled drive and surrounded the house. It was a dark house, Griff recalled, because the encroaching woodland let in little light. But it was also an extremely beautiful house, famous for the double staircase in its entry hall and its high, ornate chimneys.

He knew his appearance at the moment left a lot to be desired, so rather than ride up to the front door he made for the rear of the house and left Gaspar with a goggling yard boy.

"Sir?" the cook said as he came through the kitchen entrance. "Can I be of assistance?"

"Wilby," he said. "My valet? Is he about?"

"Mr. Darrowby?" The cook's eyes brightened. "Oh, my stars, we have all been so worried. Your people arrived yesterday afternoon, but when you didn't appear by suppertime, her ladyship was ready to send for the Bow Street Runners. As it is, she's had her grooms searching the woods for you." She turned and spoke to a young boy who was peeling potatoes. "Perkin, show Mr. Darrowby to his room."

Wilby practically had tears in his eyes when Griffin came striding into the bedchamber. He forgot himself enough to grasp his master's sleeve. "Sir, oh, sir . . . I have been that upset. You should never have gone riding off on that wicked beast. 'It's been the death of him,' I said to Farrow. 'That creature has thrown him off in the wilderness.' But he assured me you haven't been unseated since you were seven."

"I just lost my way in the dark," Griff replied, wondering what Farrow would have thought to see his prize pupil sitting in sopping disarray in the middle of a stream.

Once he had regained his composure, Wilby took stock of his master's attire. "Sir, never tell me you have slept in your clothing," he observed fretfully. "I fear there are some wrinkles I will never be able to remove from that coat." He eyed the denuded waistcoat, which hung open over Griff's grimy shirt, with alarm. "And whatever have you done with your buttons?"

"Never mind that," he said brusquely, wondering when his stiff-necked valet had turned into a fussing nursemaid. "You can burn these clothes. Just peel me out of them—I am badly in need of a bath."

Griff appeared in the drawing room before dinner looking as though his incarceration at Underhill Farm had never taken place.

His golden brown hair was artfully disarrayed, his Hessians gleamed, and the brandy-colored coat he wore fit seamlessly over his biscuit-hued inexpressibles.

Only after a prolonged bath had Griff allowed Wilby to shave the bristles from his chin, and to minister to him with a soothing facial tonic of sandalwood and balsam. He was now feeling refreshed, restored, and wholly fit. And damned hungry.

He spotted Lady Min shortly after entering the spacious drawing room; she stood beside a partially opened French window, speaking with several of her guests. Lord Pettibone was engaged, Griffin was happy to observe, on the opposite side of the room.

The Divinity had chosen her colors well—the deep violet gown, with its startling décolletage, was complemented by a tiered necklace of sapphires and opals. Sprays of sapphire flowers were scattered in her ebony curls. She turned to him as he crossed the room and held out one hand, where an enormous diamond glittered. As he approached her, he was unaccountably reminded of the Underhill waif. Lady Min's ring alone would have fed and clothed the chit for a decade. He quickly stifled the wayward thought, as he raised her hand to his lips.

"Lady Minerva," he said in a deep voice.

"Griffin," she said with a delicate smile. "I was so relieved when I learned you had arrived at last. It is wretchedly easy to lose one's way in those woods; I've done so myself, a dozen times."

"I am returned to your side without so much as a scratch, my lady," he responded, purposely omitting any mention of the bump on his head, and hiding his bruised hands behind his back.

"I believe I gave you leave to use my name in London," she chided him playfully. "Surely we don't need to stand on ceremony, especially here in the country."

"Minerva, then," he said, offering her a winning smile. He tucked her hand under his arm in a proprietary manner and led her back to her guests. She introduced him to a portly squire, his equally stout wife, an aging viscountess, and Sir Thomas de Burgh, the local magistrate. Griffin recalled that de Burgh, who was a tall, courtly gentleman of forty-odd years, had been a close friend of Lucas Stargrove's.

"Sir Thomas," Griff bowed.

De Burgh nodded in greeting. "Darrowby . . . a pleasure to see you again. I believe we shot woodcock together here at Bellaire, what was it, five or six years ago? I remember being in awe of your skill with a shotgun. Minerva tells me you've recently returned from the Peninsula—so I imagine our French friends were equally impressed."

Griffin chuckled softly. "At least woodcock don't shoot back; not to mention the French were a damned sight harder to flush."

The corners of the magistrate's mouth edged upward into a half smile. "Indeed. Ah, but I understand you were waylaid on your journey here. I hope you did not meet up with any of our local ruffians."

In light of his promise to the Underhill girl, Griffin quickly stated, "Not waylaid. Lost my way, is more like it. I had to overnight at a farm."

"There are several farm families east of Bellaire Wood. Was it perhaps the Wests or the Benchleys you stayed with?"

Griff squirmed. "Truth to tell, I never learned their name while I was there. I . . . er, took shelter in one of the outbuildings. Didn't want to cause a stir."

"The Underhill place is nearest this estate," Sir Thomas remarked. "But you'd have known it, if you'd strayed onto *their* land."

"How so?" Griff asked idly.

"It's the home of those ruffians I mentioned. I've been magistrate here for less than a year—I took over for Stargrove, you know—but in that short time the father has been before me on six different occasions for disturbing the peace. And the two sons will be bound for Australia, if the local shopkeepers ever get up the nerve to lay charges against them."

"Why haven't you taken any action against the sons?" Griff asked. "If you believe them to be thieves."

Sir Thomas sighed. "I know something of the father's past. He was a lawyer in Chester . . . and a gentleman."

Griffin's brows knit. "A gentleman, you say?"

"Yes, but after his wife died, he began suffering from evangelical visions. Just like poor William Blake. He now roams the countryside, our own John the Baptist, if you will, preaching to anyone who will listen."

"How did he come to be settled here?"

"Married a local woman, some years after his wife's death. She had a small farm and two worthless sons. Underhill himself had a daughter. Actually, she is the reason I cannot see my way to jailing her brothers or her father. I became acquainted with her after she rescued one of my dairymen. He'd been unwise enough to wander into the same pasture with a rather nasty-tempered bull; she managed to distract the beast, until the man got away—"

Probably made friends with it, Griffin muttered under his breath.

"She's a lively sprite," Sir Thomas continued, as his gray eyes narrowed into fine lines.

Griff hid a polite yawn. "And does she have a name, this offspring of the mad preacher?"

Sir Thomas grinned. It enlivened his long, rather dour face. "When she lived among normal folk, her name was Katherine. But when her father got the calling from God, he changed it to Gates of Heaven."

Griff tried to restrain a snigger. "You're not serious?"

"Unfortunately, I am. Poor child. And her stepbrothers Gerald and Raymond were rechristened Sanctification and Redemption."

Griff thought those two louts were the least likely candidates on the planet for such righteous-sounding names. "A most unusual family," he said softly.

Lady Min was thinking that Sir Thomas had usurped enough of Griffin's time. She wasn't fooled, either, by the expression of boredom on Griffin's face as he'd listened to her old friend—his body was tensed into a posture that conveyed extreme interest. A pity she was too well-bred to eavesdrop; she'd give her best earbobs to hear what Thomas was saying to make him react that way.

She sailed up beside him and touched his sleeve. "Griff, Lord Pettibone will be taking me in to supper, but I fancy a game of whist afterward. Will you partner me?"

"I am completely at your disposal, my lady."

As she turned to greet another guest, Lord Pettibone, resplendent in ochre and pale blue silk, came sidling up beside Griffin. "Ah, Darrowby. We had quite given you up for lost." His reptilian eyes drifted over Griff in a manner that combined insolence with enormous self-consequence.

Griffin merely drawled, "Sorry to disappoint you, old man. I trust you looked after her ladyship for me during my absence." Just then Lady Min glanced over her shoulder and gave him a very warm smile. "And, do you know, I find that being the lost lamb is not without its benefits."

Pettibone growled imperceptibly as he moved away.

*   *   *

Griffin had dutifully partnered his hostess at whist, and then applauded enthusiastically after she'd entertained her guests with several piano pieces. But he found himself avoiding her afterward, giving in to a yen to smoke a solitary cigar on her ladyship's wide terrace. The Underhill chit's problems seemed to have supplanted his own monetary concerns, and he chewed over the girl's dismal prospects as he took in the night air.

Sir Thomas found Lady Min standing at one of the drawing-room windows, watching with barely concealed irritation as her errant guest paced along the balustrade.

"He won't dance to your tune, Lady Minerva," he said quietly. "The boy's never been broken to a bridle. The more demands you place on him, the more he will resist."

She spun on him. "Little you know of the matter, Thomas. He made his interest in me quite clear in London. And if he asks me, I intend to wed him."

"And what of Lord Pettibone, who looks at me so menacingly now that I have your ear?"

She shrugged her white shoulders, and then tossed a brief smile at his lordship, who sat across the room. "I believe a man needs a bit of competition, it adds spice to the game. And Darrowby is never more attentive than when I am encouraging the baron."

"This is not a game, my dear child." Sir Thomas overlooked her pettish frown at being called a child. "A man of Darrowby's cut will only be teased for so long. I am just warning you . . . your widowhood protects you less than you think."

Minerva looked at him from under her long lashes. "Thomas, are you suggesting Mr. Darrowby would . . . force himself on me?"

De Burgh sighed. "I am merely advising you, as a long-time friend to both you and your late husband, that you'd best be sure he has matrimony in mind before you offer him any . . . inducements."

The lady scowled. "It is clear you think little of my morals, Sir Thomas. And it is not his marital intentions that worry me . . . it is his lack of ardor."

"That's not something any Darrowby man lacks, if the tattle from London is true."

"Oh," she said crossly, "I am not speaking of his amatory intentions; I can surely recognize desire when I see it in a man's eyes—"

"Can you, my dear?" he said almost to himself.

"It is his lack of . . . of emotion that troubles me. I sometimes sense he is going through the motions of courtship without any of the deeper feelings."

"Yet you have said you will wed him. It is most curious."

"Just look at him, Thomas," she whispered fiercely. "What woman would not desire such a man?"

The magistrate's gaze wandered to the shadowed figure on the terrace. The waxing three-quarter moon had set a blaze of silver gilt around Darrowby's head, and the lights from the drawing room danced over his spare, muscular form. De Burgh nodded in understanding.

"But he has to love me, Thomas, before I will wed with him. He *must* love me."

"You ask a lot from a fellow," he said brusquely. "Especially one as cold-hearted as that whelp is rumored to be."

She put up her chin. "Is it wrong to expect a man to love me? My late husband did, quite to distraction, as you very well know. And I will not settle for less in my next marriage. But Darrowby is going to come round—he will be perishing for love in no time at all. My dresser has a touch of the Sight, if you must know, and she promises me it is so."

"The Sight," Sir Thomas repeated with gentle mockery. "Lord, Minerva, you sound like a schoolgirl when you speak of love in such a way. Stargrove should have taken you to London more often, so you could have gained a bit of polish."

"You think me rough and unschooled?" she asked challengingly. "Then I wonder why you waste your time counseling me."

She smoothed the frown from her brow and went sweeping across the room to speak with Lord Ashcroft, another of her admirers. Sir Thomas watched her go with a troubled expression in his gray eyes. "No, Minerva," he said quietly, "I believe you are quite without flaw."

The following morning Griffin sent a message to his butler in London. Any persons attempting to extort money from the household, he wrote, were to be threatened with the constable. He assured Bucket that he was in fine health and in no one's clutches—except Lady Min's, he added to himself. He hoped that the nefarious Sank and Demp would then slither off back to their farm, empty-handed, but with a wealth of experience, especially when it came to coercing a Darrowby.

He passed the next few days in idle contentment. It was clear that Lady Min was playing him against her other suitors, but he found it amused him more than it vexed him. He refused to be baited by her behavior; his occasional remoteness brought her to his side more often than if he'd acted the lovesick swain.

Lord Pettibone, with his world-weary air, and thin, dissipated face, was still in the running, as was Lord Ashcroft, a new contender. Even though the man sported a dashing cap of jet black curls, and possessed a physique that did his tailor proud, Ashcroft was hardly a matrimonial prize. For years the man had kept a mistress in Hempstead and had sired no less than five by-blows. Minerva might have been sequestered in the country for the past five years, but during her stay in London she had surely learned of Ashcroft's infamous brood.

Sir Thomas also continued on at the house party, though his own estate was but five miles away. Griff found him to be an amiable, if somewhat acerbic, companion and a worthy opponent at billiards. He wondered why the magistrate had never married, in light of his courtly address and his impeccable breeding. Though not precisely handsome, Sir Thomas possessed the trim, muscular physique of a horseman; his waving brown hair was still thick and barely laced with silver. Griff could have easily accounted him another suitor for Minerva's hand, except that de Burgh and his hostess seemed to be constantly sparring.

It was late afternoon on his fourth day at Bellaire when Griff came in from riding to find Lady Min being entertained by Ashcroft. He was rowing his hostess across the ornamental lake that lay beyond the stables. Minerva was laughing at something he'd said, her head thrown back with happy abandon. Griff inadvertently tightened his hold on the reins until Gaspar snorted in protest.

"She needs a bit of reining in," Sir Thomas remarked to Griffin as he came strolling up from the terraced gardens. He walked with a gold-headed stick, but Griff doubted he required it. The man was nothing if not fit.

"Gaspar is a stallion, sir," Griffin pointed out.

"I wasn't referring to your horse, Darrowby," de Burgh said dryly. "Lady Minerva is a trifle headstrong. Her husband spoiled her, I'm afraid."

Griff gazed across the lake. "A woman like that deserves to be spoiled. She would expect it."

"Ah," said the magistrate, "but she also expects to be loved."

"That is no difficult task."

Sir Thomas paused a moment before speaking. "I knew Stargrove well in the days before his marriage. He was not like other men of the *ton*. He was . . . a thoughtful man, a philosopher, if you will."

Griff had always thought Stargrove a bit of a prosy old fool but he kept this opinion to himself.

"When he met Minerva," the magistrate continued, "it was as though something inside him flowered. She became the center of his world, and he of hers."

"He was her senior by nearly thirty years," Griff reminded him.

Sir Thomas gave a graceful wave of his hand. "I doubt it mattered to her. She was willing to give up society for him, to play the dutiful country wife. But now that she has tasted freedom, she will not relinquish it to a man who does not stir her heart as her husband did."

Griff shrugged. "It is not difficult for a man to convince a woman that he loves her."

"There speaks the voice of experience." Sir Thomas shook his head. "My dear Darrowby, do you honestly think a woman who has known real love will fall prey to a few pretty speeches? That she will mistake flattery and cajolery for abiding affection?"

Griff slid from the saddle and leaned one shoulder against his horse's side as he crossed his arms. "I mislike your implications, Sir Thomas."

The magistrate smiled patiently. "Steady, lad. I am merely making an observation . . . She needs someone who will cherish her. It is what she was accustomed to with Stargrove."

"Cherish her?" Griff echoed. "Do you think me incapable of such a thing?"

"I believe you covet her. Like a prize or a token of merit."

"I am beginning to think I have a rival in you, sir," Griffin muttered. "That you are so worried about her future."

The older man shrugged. "You mistake the case. She is the widow of my dearest friend. I am only interested in seeing her made happy."

"I think it is for the lady to decide what will make her happy."

"Quite true. But you are, Darrowby, for all your recent heroics and your standing in the *ton,* the offspring of a notoriously faith-less family. Your grandfather carried out his infidelities in public, and your own parents were equally open in their . . . adventuring."

"That is none of your concern," Griff bit out. Sir Thomas was treading on very shaky ground.

"Indeed it is," de Burgh responded, tapping the tip of his stick idly upon the ground. "Seeing Minerva wed to a man who loves her faithfully, one who even remotely understands that concept, is my concern."

It took all of Griff's considerable control not to snatch the walking stick away from the fellow and break it over his head. "If you have nothing but contempt for my suit, Sir Thomas, I wonder that you shared with me the key to Minerva's expectations. Has it not occurred to you that I will now do everything in my power to convince her of the earnestness of my feelings?"

The magistrate raised one brow. "I never expected to keep you from the course; I only wanted to warn you that some of the hur-dles may be beyond your ability to negotiate. Food for thought, my young friend. Good day."

Chapter Five

Gates feasted on roast pheasant for two days. Then she boiled up the bones and made a savory soup. But on the fourth day after Griffin Darrowby's departure, she was again faced with an empty larder. She wished one of the chickens would keel over from old age, so she wouldn't have to wring its neck. However, for all their scrawniness, they continued to be in surprisingly good health.

Every morning as she passed the five gold buttons that lay on the mantel, she touched each of them briefly. It was only a matter of time before she would be forced to take them to Paultons to trade for food, which was, she was sure, why he had left them behind. A man might lose a button from his waistcoat, even two, if he were really untidy. But it was unlikely he'd lose five or that they would all end up on a mantel shelf that was five feet off the floor. She knew in her heart why she hadn't yet redeemed them—they were her only tangible link with him. It was true he had been irritable and angry with her in turn. Yet in the end he had been kind. Kinder than anyone on the farm had been in a very long time.

By the afternoon of the fourth day, Gates came to a decision. Rather than wait for her brothers' return and risk their anger when they discovered another pigeon had flown, she was going to leave the farm. Since she doubted the few skills she possessed were of any value, it was her intention to go into domestic service. By her reckoning, servants—even the lowliest ones—were fed regularly.

Some of the blame for this unfilial decision fell on the stranger's shoulders; he had pointed out that her father had been repeatedly abandoning *her* for years. Their brief encounter had furnished her with the sign of change she'd been awaiting. There was now a thrumming restlessness inside her, some recently awakened voice that urged her out into the world. She knew she would never meet anyone to match him, but surely there was a man somewhere who might value her, in spite of all her faults. If she was extremely lucky, there might even be a man who could love her. That was the legacy Griffin Darrowby had left behind—besides the bird and the buttons—for the first time in her life Gates was experiencing the stirrings of desire and the longing to be loved.

She wrote a brief, unapologetic note to her father, and then packed up her few belongings—her mother's silver hairbrush, her watercolor paints, and her volume of Homer, which she had assiduously kept hidden from her father, who would have been shocked to discover such pagan literature in his home. She then folded her one good gown and placed it atop her bundle. The five buttons she placed in the pocket of her purple overskirt, being careful to pull the wide orange sash down over the opening.

She went outside to fuss over the goats one final time, threw the last of her supply of cornmeal to the chickens, and then walked out to the lane beyond the rickety fence. Her first stop was Nattie West's farm.

Mrs. West tut-tutted when Gates told her of her intention to find work. But she made no attempt to stop her, neither did she offer her a place on her prosperous farm, which Gates had hoped she might do. She did, however, give her a fresh-baked loaf of bread and a small apple tart. When Gates took one of the buttons from her pocket to ask her what she thought it would fetch in the village, Mrs. West insisted that it was made of gold. Gates remained dubious until the woman scratched at the back of it with a pin, proving that the rich color went past the surface.

This information threw a wrench into the works for sure, Gates grumbled to herself. She had planned to head east, toward Chester, but now she would have to travel in the opposite direction. It was one thing to accept a gift worth a few pounds from a stranger, it was another thing altogether to be carrying around a small fortune in her skirt pocket. Gates knew her father had very strict views on accepting charity, regardless of her stepbrothers' loose interpretation. They were ones she shared.

"Tell your husband he can have the goats and chickens, Mrs. West," she called as she went out through the farm gate. "If he can catch them, that is."

Unlike Griffin Darrowby, Gates knew the proper shortcut through the woods to Bellaire. She expected to get there before dark, but hadn't realized that traveling on foot took the stuffing out of you if you had been living on turnips for weeks. So it took her longer than she'd anticipated, and it was nearly dusk before she crossed the boundary fence that marked the beginning of the estate proper.

She had never been afraid to be alone in the woods after dark. There were times when her own bedchamber was a much more ominous place. She tramped on, her bundle tucked under one arm, nimbly skipping over the roots and brambles that blocked her path. The feeling of complete freedom was thrilling, being on her own, not bound to the farm or to the sullen brothers who made her life a chore. Her father would no doubt consider her an ungrateful child for abandoning the farm, but that was surely preferable to being a dutiful daughter who starved devoutly to death. She sighed that she hadn't the makings of a martyr.

When she came to a little clearing, she sat down and ate some of her bread and every last crumb of the apple tart. It was so peaceful and quiet, she knew she could have spent the night there, watched over by the denizens of the forest. As it was, she dozed off for a few hours, curled up on the grass, and awoke feeling refreshed and eager to push on. She had a mission, now, and the object of that mission was at present staying at Bellaire. So she climbed to her feet, plucked up her bundle, and continued on her way.

Griff was not sure how much credence he should give to Sir Thomas's warning. Even if what he felt for Minerva was nothing more than physical desire and, of course, the nagging need to replenish the Darrowby coffers, he certainly wasn't going to balk at a few murmured endearments to achieve his ends. He wondered if the lady was, as the magistrate had insisted, acute enough to detect his subterfuge. In Griff's recollection, he'd never said those particular words to a single living soul. Still, they were only words . . . three syllables that must surely be easily spoken when one was in the arms of a goddess.

There was dancing that night after supper. When the squire's wife offered to play the piano, couples quickly formed into the lines of a reel. Griff sought out Minerva and remained her partner for the next two dances. He relinquished her at last to Ashcroft, but when the squire's wife began to play a waltz, he neatly separated Lady Min from both Ashcroft and Pettibone and led her to the floor.

It was exciting to hold her in his arms and watch her eyes beam up at him. What a wife she would make, he thought, beautiful, accomplished—regal, even. A woman whose exquisite face still had the power to make men stop and stare in wonder.

As the last note of the dance faded, Griff guided her through the open French windows and onto the terrace, where the night air offered a refreshing change from the closeness of the drawing room. Lady Min sighed and moved away from him, into the shadows of an overhanging cherry tree.

"Minerva?" he said haltingly as he followed in her wake.

She turned to him and smiled. "See this tree? My husband planted it as a young boy. He swore he would endure as long as the tree did."

"He was sadly off in his calculations," Griff observed softly.

"Oh, no," she said. "Last year the tree was struck to the very core by lightning, and though it bloomed this year, it is only a matter of time before it dies. So you see, he was not far off at all."

Griff took up her hand and held it against his chest. "But it did blossom, Minerva, regardless of the damage that was done to it. As you will blossom again, in spite of the loss you suffered."

"I know that is true."

"And you will love again. You are a woman made for such things . . ." He raised her hand and set his lips at the base of her wrist where the skin peeked through the white satin glove. He watched in satisfaction as her eyes closed.

"I have no doubt I will love again. But the question remains as to whether I will *be* loved."

Damn, he thought. De Burgh hadn't been spinning him a Banbury tale after all. What was more, it was clear from Minerva's tone when she spoke of her late husband that she had loved him very much. Living rivals were one thing, but Griff suspected it was extremely difficult to compete with a ghost.

"That is a foolish question, my dear. Every man you encounter is laid low at your feet."

She drew her hand away. "That is hardly love. You speak of adulation, and I of lasting affection."

"Do you doubt my affection for you?" he said, trying not to let irritation sully his mood. She was starting to sound confoundedly like Sir Thomas.

She stepped back farther into the shadow of the cherry tree.

"Ah, Minerva"—he reached out and took hold of her shoulders—"you are everything a man could desire. Since we met in London, I have been beset by thoughts of you. I . . . I . . ."

"What?" she whispered, stepping closer.

I wish I had never been born, Gates thought wretchedly as she gazed down through the branches of the cherry tree at the couple below her.

She had only wanted to watch the dancing, to see how the members of society passed an evening in the country. She had also wanted to get a glimpse of Griffin Darrowby before she made her way to the servants' entrance to ask for work. It had never been her intention to spy on him, or to eavesdrop on his wooing of Mr. Stargrove's beautiful widow.

It was the most humiliating moment in her short, uneventful life. She clutched her bundle and laid her head upon the branch, trying to hold back tears of mortification.

"What I am trying to say," Griff uttered hoarsely, "is that I am . . . that I . . ."

With a sharp crack the branch Gates was perched on broke partially away from the trunk, and she was jolted forward against the silvery bark. Her bundle slipped, and without thinking she reached for it with both hands. The next instant she was plummeting down through the leaves, her fall broken only when she grasped frantically at another branch.

A loud, wavering scream echoed out beneath Gates. Not far beneath her, she realized; the lower half of her body was now dangling below the foliage.

"Come down here!" Griffin ordered in a voice of ice.

"I'm afraid to let go," she cried back.

Hands closed firmly around her bare ankles and tugged hard. She tumbled out of the tree and into Griffin Darrowby's arms.

"Miss Underhill," he said in a low voice as he set her on her feet. "Why am I not surprised?"

"I—I—" she stuttered.

Lady Minerva was wilting back against the stone balustrade, holding one hand to her mouth. All the guests and several of the servants had rushed out to the terrace. One of the footmen, a tall fellow with a mouth full of large teeth, pulled Gates abruptly away from Griff and clouted her sharply on the side of the head.

In twenty-one years, no one had ever struck Gates. As she fell awkwardly onto the flags of the terrace, she realized that being hit hurt your pride as much as your hide.

Griff snarled and leaped toward the footman, his hands outstretched in anger. Sir Thomas quickly whisked the intemperate servant behind him.

"It's that Underhill chit, the parson's brat," the footman cried out in his own defense. "A thieving lot, they are! All crazy or wicked. Everyone hereabouts knows that." He tugged at the magistrate's sleeve. Sir Thomas was regarding Gates with a sober expression in his gray eyes. "Tell him, sir. Haven't you seen her father in court a dozen times this past year.?"

Sir Thomas moved forward and aided Gates to her feet. "There, child, no one will harm you now."

"Thank you," she said as she bent to retrieve her bundle from the flagstones.

Once Griffin saw the girl was no longer at risk from the footman, he turned back to his hostess and took up her hand. "Are you all right, Minerva?"

"You know that creature?" she whispered, pulling her hand away.

He squared his shoulders and nodded. "It was on her farm that I stayed the other night. I slept in one of the outbuildings, as I said."

"Whatever is she doing here now?"

Griff turned his head toward the girl, saw the numb confusion that had widened her eyes. He knew if she was charged with trespass, she could end up in jail. However, if he lied to protect her, she would likely be the only one to find fault with him. In the *ton,* lies were most folks' stock in trade. In truth, he felt some responsibility for her being here—he was the one who had encouraged her to leave the farm.

"I told her," he began, "that if she ever needed work, she should apply to you."

"You told that . . . that Gypsy . . . to come to my home?"

There was a muffled guffaw from Lord Pettibone, who now advanced to capitalize on Griff's apparent fall from grace. "There, there, Minerva," he said, taking up one of her hands. "Mr. Darrowby surely had the best of intentions. He couldn't know that you hire only respectable people to serve you." He turned to Gates. "Be off with you, baggage, before we have you whipped for frightening this lady."

"There will be no whipping—" Griff started to say, when Sir Thomas interrupted him.

"Minerva," he said in his most reasonable voice. "Look at this girl." He prodded Gates forward a bit. "She is well known to me—"

"Not as well known as her crazy father," the footman interjected.

"And," the magistrate continued, "I will vouch for her character. She will serve this house honestly. I can promise you that."

Lady Minerva leaned forward and peered at Gates. Gates gave her a hopeful smile, all the while thinking that this beautiful woman was wearing a deal too much scent, and wondering too why there was so much sadness lurking in her eyes.

"She looks clean enough," the lady pronounced at last. "But she's very . . . unkempt."

"I will see that she is properly outfitted," Sir Thomas intoned. "Out of my own pocket."

Lady Minerva turned away from Gates, muttering, "As if I can't afford to clothe my own servants . . ."

She motioned to her butler, who had been hovering nervously in the background. "Stubbin, take this girl away. See that she is fed . . . and then find something useful for her to do in the kitchen."

The look Minerva flashed at Sir Thomas was politely victorious. He bowed as she swept past him, calling behind her, "Lord Pettibone, I believe you have the next dance."

Griff remained beside the balustrade as Minerva and her guests reentered the drawing room. He watched without a word as a subdued Miss Underhill was led off by the butler and a troop of footmen. Like a prisoner of war, he thought.

Sir Thomas came to stand beside him and leaned back on his elbows. "So you *did* pass the night at the Underhill farm."

Griffin shrugged. "It seemed best not to dwell on it, once I was away from the place. I'm sorry if I gave you the wrong impression."

"It explains the curiosity you had about Miss Underhill's family. It doesn't explain why you nearly throttled the footman who struck her."

Griffin turned and looked out over the night-shadowed garden that gave way to the encroaching cedars. "No man enjoys seeing a woman struck. I merely reacted as any gentleman would."

Sir Thomas pondered this in silence. When he spoke again, his voice was whisper soft. "There was a lady in London, whom I befriended years ago. At times she didn't leave her town house for days, and when she did she was often heavily veiled. The tattle was that her husband was a bit hasty with his fists when he was in his cups. Unfortunately, I knew this to be true. As I recall she had several children." His voice lowered another notch. "It would mark a child to see such things, don't you think?"

"Children are more resilient than you might give them credit for," Griff replied in an offhand manner. "And they are rarely affected by the actions of others. Not deeply, not forever."

"Do you honestly believe that, Darrowby?"

Griffin pushed away from the wall. "It doesn't matter what I believe. I am speaking rhetorically." He bowed curtly to the magistrate. "And now it's time I pried my lady from the hands of that popinjay. Min has done her good deed for the evening by aiding Miss Underhill, and I want to commend her for it."

"I wish you joy of her," Sir Thomas said.

"Who? Minerva?" Griff had turned halfway to the French door. De Burgh cocked his head. "Whom else would I mean?"

Griff made no comment. He entered the drawing room and was lost among the guests. Sir Thomas stayed behind, pondering what he had seen in Griffin Darrowby's eyes when he'd flown at the footman.

Everyone in the *ton* knew that Darrowbys were godless, to a man. Neither vicar nor prelate, scholar nor diplomat, marred their ranks. And Griffin was a true Darrowby, you had only to look at him to know it. The shimmering hair, the startlingly blue eyes, and the graceful form that each generation generously bequeathed the next, had all been allotted to him. Just that evening, Sir Thomas had overheard Viscountess Upworth remark to her companion, as they observed Griffin dancing with their hostess. "Darrowby men may be unholy," she'd said with a wink, "but they are never, ever unhandsome."

But, as Sir Thomas's mother had always been quick to point out, handsome is as handsome does. Still, he had seen the expression of fierce, protective anger that twisted Darrowby's face the instant the girl had been struck. It would take a lot to shake such a primal response from a man who was famous for his cold-blooded detachment. He also recalled the look of gratitude in Gates Underhill's eyes when she'd gazed at her defender. Gratitude and something a bit warmer. Sir Thomas wondered exactly what had transpired between the two of them the night Darrowby stayed at her farm.

Considering the fellow's rumored tendencies toward the fair sex, Sir Thomas determined to ask his valet to keep an eye on the girl. And maybe he'd better enlist his groom as well.

The following day there was an excursion to visit a Roman ruin. The more sedate guests chose to travel in her ladyship's brougham, but Minerva herself preferred the more robust recreation of riding. Griff had to admit she looked splendid mounted on her gray mare, wearing a royal blue habit and a rakish, feathered shako. As he was complimenting her on her appearance, he simultaneously wondered if someone had found a suitable garment for Gates Underhill to wear, something to replace the rags she had arrived in. He himself would volunteer to burn that wretched orange sash.

"Er, what was that?" He dragged himself back to the present.

"I asked you why you were growling at me, Griffin," Lady Minerva said with a laugh.

"It's nothing," he said, returning her smile. "I'm merely anxious to be off."

Once they reached the ruins, Pettibone and Ashcroft positioned themselves on either side of Lady Min and she seemed delighted by their company. For the first time, Griff began to have doubts about his suit. It was not uncommon for widows who were comfortably situated to maintain their single status for years. Was the lady merely toying with her beaux? Was Griff destined to be held at arm's length, Season after Season? That was unthinkable in light of his dire financial situation.

He growled in earnest. He vowed to give the lady one more week, and if she did not single him out from the pack, then he would hie himself back to London . . . or maybe travel to Brighton to see what Prinny was up to. There were other rich woman in the *ton,* by God.

But then, as they took their luncheon on a blanket beneath a wide-spreading elm, Lady Min contrived to seat herself beside him. She sparkled with such gaiety, laughed so prettily at his jests, that Griff forgave her for her defection and renewed his intention to marry her.

A storm blew up as the returning party approached Bellaire. The riders kicked their mounts into a gallop and made it back to the house just as the first drops began to fall. They handed their horses to the waiting grooms and then all ran, laughing and hooting, into the central hall, sounding more like unruly children than well-bred ladies and gentlemen. Only Sir Thomas maintained his unhurried pace and entered Bellaire a minute or two behind the others. He called Griff aside.

"Your horse," the magistrate said. Griff's ears immediately pricked up. "He seems to have nicked himself on the foreleg. Your groom is looking at it now, but I thought you'd want to know."

Griff went immediately to the large fieldstone stable. Farrow stood up as his master entered the stall. "It's not bad, sir. Forged with his hind leg, it looks like. There's a bit of swelling in the tendon."

Griff knelt and ran his hand knowledgeably down the horse's pastern. A shallow, six-inch gash marred the sleek skin. "A wet compress, I think," he said as he rose. "We'll see how he fares in the morning before we call in a farrier."

He strode back to the house through the pelting rain, wondering at the irony—after a day spent running loose in Bellaire Wood, Gaspar had suffered no harm, yet now had managed to injure himself during a trifling excursion. Griffin was not a superstitious man, but he had an edgy premonition that this visit to Bellaire was ill-starred. He'd not merely gotten lost in the woods, he'd been thrown, drenched, and knocked on the head. Then he'd been abducted, imprisoned, and unceremoniously frisked. And now his favorite mount had been injured.

He shrugged off his feelings of unease as he went in through the front door. The only ill-starred thing about this visit was the irksome presence of Pettibone and Ashcroft.

Lady Min's guests were weary after their outing, and so the party broke up early. Several gentlemen asked Griff to join them in the billiard room, but he politely declined. He made his way through the continuing drizzle to the stable—he wouldn't rest easy until he had checked on Gaspar.

There was a lantern lit near the center of the stable row—he walked beyond it to Gaspar's stall. The horse nickered softly and set his chin on the edge of the stall door. It was difficult to credit that this creature who showed such affection for his master, was a veritable terror with any strange handlers. Griff tugged at the horse's forelock and whispered a soft hello.

"Stand still, will you!" The irate words floated up from the depths of the stall.

Griff's eyes widened at the sound of that voice. He craned his head over the wooden door. She was kneeling in the straw bedding beside Gaspar, within range of his fatal hooves.

"I do believe you have a death wish, Miss Underhill. I suggest you come out of there. Now."

"He's fine as long as you don't startle him with shouting," Gates said as she laid a soothing hand on the horse's shoulder. "As you did beside the stream."

Griffin's jaw tightened. "You're not going to start that again, I hope. And you might not know this, but my orders are that no one is to look after him but my groom, Farrow. Only Farrow."

Gates didn't even look up, but continued to wrap wet gauze around the horse's injured leg. "When your groom came in to supper, he mentioned your horse had been hurt. I made up this poultice while the others were eating and left it to thicken a bit. I think it's just what he requires."

She climbed to her feet and laid a soft kiss against the horse's neck. Griff watched in amazement as the irascible creature turned his head and nuzzled her arm.

With a smug smile she turned to him. "See, I told you. Animals like me."

He wanted to grind his teeth in irritation. Instead he reached over the side, hauled her off her feet, and set her on the edge of the stall door.

She perched there, shifting a little to gain her balance. "People," she continued, "now that's another story."

"I am not at all surprised to hear that."

She grinned. "I am not very . . . at ease with most people. My tongue ties into knots and my brain seems to freeze. Well, you saw how it was last night. All those people milling about . . . I couldn't think of a word to say. I suppose I should thank you for speaking up for me."

"I saw how frightened you were," he said.

Her eyes narrowed. "Frightened? You thought I was frightened?" She grinned. "Tongue-tied is not at all the same thing as frightened, Mr. Darrowby."

He sniffed. "You looked scared half out of your wits, if you want the truth."

She looked down at her pinafore and plucked at the fabric. "It wasn't fear," she repeated.

They'd furnished her with a uniform, he saw. It was of gray

serge and about six sizes too large for her slim frame. The pinafore she wore over it had been laundered to a yellowish gray color, and had been mended so often it looked like a patchwork. It was possibly the ugliest ensemble Griff had ever seen, and he felt himself unaccountably mourning the loss of the purple drapery skirt and the vile orange sash.

"They've clothed you, I see," he said gruffly.

"It itches," she said. "My things were not so rough on the skin."

"And what duties have they set you to perform?"

She took a piece of scone from her pocket and fed it to Gaspar as she answered. "I work in the scullery washing dishes, pots, trays, and cutlery. Oh, and I wash glassware. 'You 'ave to be very careful with milady's glassware,'" she said, aping someone else's voice. He grinned in spite of himself. "That's Mr. Stubbin, the butler. I broke three glasses tonight." She frowned slightly. "He said their price will be deducted from my wages and that in three months' time they will be paid off." She cocked her head. "That can't be right, can it, Mr. Darrowby? Three months' wages to pay off three wineglasses?"

Griff felt something twist inside him. Her waiflike aura had him in its spell again. "I expect scullions don't receive much of a wage," he said gently. "And Lady Minerva's crystal is no doubt from Ireland."

"Oh, Ireland," she said, nodding sagely, as if that explained their exorbitant cost.

He realized with a shock that her hair had been cut; it looked to have been sheared off above her ears. All that was left was a forelock of dark waves that curled over her brow. It made him want to throttle someone again, the thought of that lush mass of curls going under the scissors.

"It's a pity about your hair," he said, reaching out to touch the side of her head.

"My hair?" she echoed. "Oh." She put one hand behind her and tugged a badly braided plait over one shoulder. "He made me bind it up. Stubbin did. He said I looked like Hecate." Her brow wrinkled.

"She's a witch . . . from the play Macbeth," he explained.

"Yes, I know that," she said indignantly.

Griff smiled again. He shouldn't bait her over her lack of education. He wondered if she could even read or write. She spoke well enough, almost like a lady of quality, and he recalled the skillfully rendered paintings in her bedchamber. There were paradoxes here he was sure he had no desire to grapple with.

"They are feeding you, I expect," he said.

"I had some soup last night. This morning I slept through break-fast—in spite of having to sleep in the scullery."

"You slept in the scullery? Does Lady Minerva not supply beds to her servants?"

Gates hitched one shoulder. "There are no beds available in the house right now. All these guests, I expect, with too many servants. Perhaps I will have a bed once the house party is over."

Griff was frowning. "So you slept on a stone floor?"

"They keep the fires banked in the hearth overnight. That's why I slept so long—it was lovely to be so warm. But I did miss my breakfast, then I missed lunch—I was in the dairy, helping with the cows."

"Is that one of your duties, as well?"

"No, I just wanted to see how a proper dairy was run."

"Miss Underhill, you lived on a farm . . . How could you not know about dairies?"

"There was one cow when I came to live under the hill, but—"

"Let me guess . . . one of your brothers sold it to a tinker?"

Her low, musical laughter pealed out, mingling with the dust motes in the air. "No," she said with a shake of her head. "She died. She was quite old, you see, and we never replaced her. The Benchleys sold us milk for a time. But after my brothers set fire to their privy, they would have no truck with our family."

Griff propped his elbow on the edge of the stall, laid his brow upon his hand, and slowly shook his head. "How is it that no one has garroted those brothers of yours?" he asked without looking up.

"Stepbrothers," she reminded him. "Though I do think some-times that the Lord watches over them, in spite of their wicked ways." Her stomach growled audibly in the quiet space.

Griff raised his head. "So when exactly did you eat today?"

Gates bit her lip. "After I was done washing the dishes, all the food had been put away. I did manage to find this scone."

"Which you have just fed the better part of to my horse."

"He liked it," she said simply.

Griff wondered why he even cared. If she was so dim-witted, so guileless, that she couldn't even manage to forage a meal in this extravagant household, why should he be concerned? Yet the strange thing was, he did care. He lifted her down from the stall door and took her by the hand.

"You may not have the wherewithal to feed yourself, Miss Under-the-hill, but I surely do."

He dragged her along the wet path and into the kitchen. A spit boy was sleeping beside the hearth, and Griff spared a moment to wonder how many other houses he'd stayed in where the servants were forced to sleep on a stone floor. He drew the girl past the sleeping boy. "Where is the larder?"

Gates pointed to a stout wooden door. "But it's kept locked," she hissed.

Griff gazed around, looking for the proper tool and his eyes lit up when they came to rest on a large carving knife. He lifted it from its wooden block and pried the padlock off the larder door.

"This, Miss Under-the-hill," he said, tugging it open, "is what you should have done for me, when I was locked in your wood-shed. But see, I don't bear any grudges." He stepped back and allowed her to enter. "And if His Highness Stubbin complains, tell him Darrowby of Darrowby was his midnight bandit."

She plucked up a cooked cutlet and a slice of cheese from a tray and laid them on a small plate. He noticed the way her eyes brightened at the sight of a plum cake. "Take it," he said under his breath. "Otherwise the squire's wife will have it for breakfast, and Lord knows she doesn't need it."

Gates snatched at it, and he grinned as it disappeared into her pocket.

"That's for you," he said as he ushered her out of the larder. "Not for my blasted horse. Understand?" She nodded. "There's a good girl," he said as he reached out to tug on her braid.

Then he headed for the doorway, back to the abovestairs world of fine ladies and elegant gentlemen.

"Gor," said the spitboy as he sat up, rubbing sleepily at the side of his face. "Who the devil was that? Bleedin' King Midas?"

"No," Gates pronounced primly as she headed toward the scullery with her plate, "*that* was Darrowby of Darrowby."

Chapter Six

The rain continued unabated the next day. Tempers frayed as Lady Min's house guests grew bored with billiards and card games. What was the point of staying in the country, they complained to each other, if you couldn't be out-of-doors?" Griff found a collection of Swift in the library, and so holed up there, immersed in his favorite author. Gentlemen and ladies occasionally wandered in, looking for something entertaining to read. Some attempted to pass the time with him, but he was not inclined toward conversation, and they all eventually drifted away.

It was late afternoon when Griff at last laid the opened book upon his chest, and sprawled back in his armchair. The light in the room was fading, but he hadn't the energy to rise and light a candle. He couldn't remember the last time he'd spent so many hours with a book, or the last time he'd been so content to do nothing but read. His days in London were full of social obligations, but here in the country there was a tranquillity that was foreign to his life in town. He now understood how the Underhill girl had been able to spend her days alone in the woods, without company or any source of distraction. There was a serenity in solitude, and he found himself relishing it.

Lady Minerva disturbed his reverie some minutes later.

"They told me you were in here reading." She looked pointedly at the open book, which was still resting on his chest. Griff slid the book closed, clasped it between his hands, and made as if to rise.

"No," she said, impatiently waving him back into his chair. "No formality between us, remember."

"Very well." He watched as she prowled restlessly around the perimeter of the library, her fingers brushing lightly against spine after spine. This was a different Minerva than he had ever seen before. Her stately composure was missing, but in its place was a barely controlled energy that was even more intriguing to him.

"This was my husband's favorite room," she said from over her shoulder. "I used to tease him that Moroccan leather and bound paper meant more to him than flesh and blood."

"I daresay a man can go too far in either of those directions."

Her expression grew wistful before she turned back to the stacks. "Lucas was not a man of extremes. Oh, but he did love his books."

There it was, Griff thought a bit irritably, that word again.

"He spent hours cataloging this collection," she continued as she turned to face him. "His life's work, he called it. But there were too many books . . . he'd left it too late, you see."

Griff was often impatient with reminiscences of others, but he schooled his features into a polite semblance of interest. Perhaps if he knew more of her history with Stargrove, he might have a better idea of how to woo her himself.

"He could have hired someone to assist him," he said. "I believe that's what my grandfather did at Darrowby when he wanted to set his library in order."

"*I* was his assistant," Lady Minerva responded with more than a touch of pride.

It was difficult for Griffin to equate Minerva, the graceful and beautiful adornment to society, with a dutiful helpmeet who helped her elderly husband sort through his books.

"This must be a place of sadness for you, Minerva," he said with sudden insight.

"Yes, it has been. I've hardly set foot in this room since Lucas died. I only came here today because I . . . I thought you might be better company than my other guests."

He rose then and crossed over to where she stood before the long window. "Then I am flattered beyond words."

She looked up at him and smiled. "I believe you might be the only person in this whole house who is not spoiling for a fight. The rain has made everyone as cross as crabs . . . I have a mind to send them all packing." She crossed her arms over her chest and shot him a mutinous look.

He laughed aloud in response. "You'd get no argument from me, my lady, as long as I was allowed to remain behind with you." He reached out and boldly took hold of one of her hands, running his fingers over the palm. A tiny tremor rippled through her and he rejoiced at that subtle vibration. She was not immune to his touch after all. He took advantage of her acquiescence and moved closer, sliding one arm around her waist. His mouth danced against the soft skin of her throat "Min," he crooned, "let me ease you."

She stood unmoving as his mouth traced a path along the underside of her jaw. When he tipped her face toward him and sought her mouth, she gave a tiny cry of protest.

"It's too soon," she said fretfully, looking away from him to the window where the gray rain obscured the view of the gardens.

He knit his brows, unsure of her meaning. "Min?"

"Too soon for this," she said, withdrawing her hand from his warm clasp. "For all of this. For entertaining, for being among people. It's too soon for me to have taken up this mask of gaiety. I don't wear it well, Griffin. Not at all well."

"It's never too soon for life, Minerva," he said, barely masking his irritation. He was beginning to wonder if he was losing his touch with women.

She drew a long breath. "If you knew how difficult this has been for me. Society dictates a year of mourning, and then expects one to resume their life without a hitch. As though it were bad *ton* to still care for someone after that prescribed time had passed. I can't make my heart adhere to that schedule."

He'd let his gaze wander to the window, where the relentless downpour had stippled the glass. He saw a slim figure come flying down the path from the stables, heading toward the back of the house. He had no trouble recognizing Gates Underhill, in spite of the rain. Her thick braid trailed behind her, and her skirts were hiked up in woeful disregard for the proprieties.

Lady Min was looking at him expectantly.

"What?" he said, trying to regain his expression of concern.

She smiled ruefully. "I said, I cannot make my heart adhere to that schedule. And so I must ask you to have patience with me when I hold you at arm's length."

"You must certainly go at your own pace," he said with great forbearance. "But perhaps you ought to send us away. I mean it, Minerva. If solitude is what you seek then it is your right to have it. No one will say a word against you."

"At least not to my face," she replied with a small chuckle. "Ah, but think of the tattle back in London. No, I will muddle on here and play my role of hostess. I feared this might happen, after I'd sent out the invitations but by then it was too late. And see now, some good's come of it. I have learned that you are a man of great understanding."

And great frustration, he added silently.

*   *   *

Gates was just unwrapping the gauze from Gaspar's leg when Griff opened the stall door. Unlike the night before, he now seemed unperturbed to find her with his horse. She stifled the elation she was feeling as he knelt down beside her and murmured, "Let me have a look."

He was dressed for a dinner party. His coat was a velvety midnight blue, and in the subdued light it was a stark contrast to his white shirt collar and ruffled cuffs.

He traced his fingers along the healing gash. "Hmm . . . not much swelling."

"No," she said. "The poultice has seen to that. But I've made up another one, just as a precaution." She indicated the earthenware bowl in the straw beside her.

He raised it under his nose and sniffed. "Witch hazel," he said, "And something sweet."

"Honey," she said. "It has healing properties. And a bit of willow bark for the pain." She took the bowl from him and began to slather the thick mess onto Gaspar's leg.

"Tell me," he asked, shifting back against the stall door and drawing his knees up. "How is it that you know so much about horse doctoring? From caring for your little white mare?"

There was a pleased, secretive smile on her face as she said, "I am surprised you remembered that. But we did have other horses at our farm in the beginning. And my stepmother had been a country woman all her life—she taught me about poultices, and remedies for colic, and such."

Griff said, "Perhaps you could recite her recipes to Farrow and he could write them down."

Gates was about to reply that she would be happy to write them down herself, when Gaspar shifted and stepped on the bowl. It cracked beneath his weight.

Gates slapped at his shoulder to shift him away from the broken shards. "Move over, you great lummox," she chided him playfully. The horse snaked his head down and blew a soft breath into her hair as she quickly gathered up the bits of broken crockery. Griff continued to regard these equine displays of affection with disbelief; Gaspar was clearly smitten. It was a pity Gates Underhill was a female. He'd have snatched her away to work in his own stable if she'd been a lad. Anyone who could handle blooded horses with such calm assurance was worth her weight in gold.

She was rewrapping the bandage over the poultice, when he

leaned forward to assist her. "No," she said, pushing his arm away with her elbow. "You'll soil those elegant shirt cuffs. Hold his head, if you want to help."

"Yes, ma'am," he said as he climbed to his feet and twined his fingers through the horse's headstall. "So tell me, have we managed to eat anything today?"

"We," she said with a chuckle, "have eaten so much we are fit to burst. His Highness Stubbin was most displeased that someone broke into the larder last night, but the spitboy told him it was a tall, golden-haired nob who'd done the deed, and that he shouldn't get his garters in a twist over it."

Griffin laughed. "So you didn't suffer for our pillaging then? Good."

"Not a bit," she said as she rose to her feet and began to brush the wheatstraw from her skirt.

"But what's this?" He caught her chin in his hand and tipped her face up so that the diffused lantern light fell more directly upon it. He traced the angry purple bruise that lay beside her right ear.

"Oh that," she muttered darkly, pulling back from his touch and tugging down some stray wisps of hair to cover the spot. "The footman, if you recall."

"Damn it, that's not where he struck you the other night. He cuffed you on the left cheek, as I very well recall. This looks to be more of a backhand blow."

"It's nothing," she said as she ducked down to pick up an imaginary shard of earthenware from the stall's floor.

He tugged her upright, a hand on each shoulder and marched her out of the stall toward where the lantern hung. "Now stop squirming and let me see."

She closed her eyes and suffered the indignity of having him examine her face close up.

"I wonder a blow this hard didn't knock you into next year."

"I'm tougher than I look," she said between her teeth. "I didn't even fall down. Not like the first time, when he hit me on the terrace."

Griff's breath whistled as he drew it in. "So it was that blasted footman again."

"I—I—"

"Don't pretend to be tongue-tied, Miss Under-the-hill. Just tell me what happened like a nice sensible girl."

Gates twisted away from his hold, unable to meet his eyes as she said, "He kept . . . trying to touch me . . . in a familiar way . . . every time he came into the kitchen. The housemaids think he is handsome—I've heard them giggling over him—but he has far too many teeth for my taste."

"What happened?" Griff repeated.

"I was serving the upper staff at table, carrying the soup tureen. He pinched me and . . . I poured the soup into his lap."

Griff didn't know whether to laugh or groan. It was a delightfully painful image.

"He leaped up and started shrieking . . . and then he caught me by the hair and struck me on the side of the head." She added as an afterthought. "I expect I ruined his fine breeches."

He couldn't hold back his grin. "I suspect you did a bit more damage than that, my little savage."

Gates blushed. He'd made the word savage sound almost like an endearment.

"He'll stay away from me now," she pronounced. "I'm not accustomed to being hit. My father held very firm views on the striking of children."

Griffin thought that was possibly the first thing he'd heard in Parson Underhill's favor.

"You're wrong there, I'm afraid," he said as he drew her to a nearby bench and sat her down beside him. "I mean about the footman leaving you alone. Your toothy friend will find a way to pay you back. I fear you've made a nasty enemy, Miss Underhill."

She pondered this with troubled eyes. "Perhaps I should leave this place. There are other estates, other houses that might hire me."

"Where you wouldn't know a soul? I don't think much of that solution." He leaned back against the wall and sighed. "Have you no relatives who could aid you? What of your mother's family?"

She drew her braid over one shoulder and began to toy with it. "When she died from the scarlet fever, Papa was distraught, so it fell to me to send a message to her family in Trouro. But they never responded. I believe there was some discord between them and my parents before I was born . . . so I wasn't really surprised."

"Did her family have money? That is often at the root of discord."

"They were not poor," she said. "My mother was the Honorable Maria Bembroke before she wed."

Griff shook his head. "My dear girl—" He reached across the

space that separated them and gently ruffled her curly forelock. "That would mean she was the daughter of a baron, at the very least. You must have misunderstood."

"Oh," Gates said, paying no heed to his words as his long fingers stroked over her brow.

Griffin dropped his hand and began to fidget with his cuffs. "How old were you when she died?" he asked without looking up.

"Just twelve," she said. "And then afterward my father . . . well, he turned away from me and from the life we'd shared when he found his calling to preach."

"So you lost both of them, in effect."

She nodded. "It was difficult to go on . . . I learned to expect much less from the world after that."

Something twisted uncomfortably inside Griffin. He too had lowered his expectations from life at the tender age of twelve. But at the same time he'd vowed never to bend to adversity, but to fight back with everything he had. This young woman was hardly a fighter, and yet he sensed she possessed a serene acceptance that he'd never been able to discover in himself. It made no sense at all.

He shifted slightly on the bench. "You might try to contact your mother's family again. People change over time, their feelings change." Griff nearly choked getting the words out—they ran so contrary to his own experience. But she needed to hear some words of comfort.

Instead of appearing grateful, her eyes flashed in irritation. "They do not want me. Which is a perfect arrangement, because I do not want them. They did not even acknowledge my mother's death. I am sorry I am even related to such people."

He heard the underlying sob in her voice, and felt it pierce him before he could raise his guard. *No, don't,* he cautioned himself, even as his hand rose to touch her face. His palm moved slowly up and down her bruised cheek. Her skin was petal soft and he battled the urge to set his mouth against that creamy surface. He had no doubt she would taste like heaven.

Gates leaned into his hand, her first instinct to pull back immediately overridden by the warm comfort of his tender caress. No one had ever touched her like this. As if she were something rare and precious. She heard his soft sigh as his hand slid to the back of her neck.

"It will all come right for you," he whispered as his fingers found and then stroked the smooth skin beneath the rough collar of her gown. "You must believe it will."

He lowered his head, till their noses were nearly touching. His eyes held her, so intensely blue that it was like gazing into a mountain lake. Gates felt the outside world recede. She and the gilded man beside her seemed to be floating in their own oasis of light, surrounded and protected by the soft, somnolent darkness of the stable.

"Gates?" he murmured in a voice she'd never heard him use before. Like warm treacle on toast.

Without conscious intent she let her hands drift to his shoulders. They were supple steel beneath her fingers. Touching him, feeling the strength in him, made her heart swell and her body tremble.

He pulled back from her abruptly and stood up. His eyes had clouded over, they were now opaque and distant. "It's time I was back at the house." His gaze was directed to the planking above her head as he spoke. "You're doing very well with my horse, Miss Underhill."

Her *thank-you* died unspoken on her lips. He was already halfway down the stable row, moving away from her with determined strides. She shifted back on the bench, letting the wall of the stall behind her take the weight of her shoulders. Though she had toiled from dusk till dark, though she had been struck on the cheek hard enough that she'd seen a constellation of stars, she hadn't felt weary or dispirited until Griffin Darrowby had so curtly dismissed her.

It would be best if she avoided the stable in the hours after dark. There was no profit that could come of meeting him again. He had already woven his way deep into the fabric of her life, this man whom she'd not even known existed until eight days ago. The more time she spent with him, the harder it would be to watch him ride off to London. And if, as she suspected was the case from the downstairs gossip, Lady Minerva had determined him as her future husband, she couldn't remain at Bellaire unless she forced herself to remember the wide gulf that separated them.

It was the only way. She must keep her distance, battle her stubborn heart into submission, and restrict the wild flights of fancy that whispered that a man of beauty and grace could learn to care for a preacher's daughter, even one who currently masqueraded as the lowliest servant in a fine lady's home. She made a low, bitter noise of disgust. There were no flights of fancy wild enough to convince her of anything so improbable.

Harris was exceedingly pleased with himself. He twitched his elegant footman's coat into unwrinkled perfection before he took the luncheon roast from the sideboard and carried it to his mistress. The meal would be over soon, and then he would have some time to himself before dinner. He had learned where she disappeared to each afternoon, that untamed chit with the blazing amber eyes. She had affronted his dignity yesterday, as well as scalding the general environs of his most prized anatomical possession, and so needed to be reprimanded.

Carrying out his punishment wouldn't be difficult—there was an empty stretch of woodland between the main house and the dairy barn, where a strong man might accost a thin, raggedy girl as she returned from the cow byre. He smiled at the thought of holding her down in the grass, while he erased the saucy expression from her face with a few expert kisses. And if she struggled, well then, who would blame him if he had to get a bit rough with her? In his ken, women expected that sort of treatment.

"Harris!" the butler hissed from his station at the door.

Harris looked up. One of the gentlemen at the table was motioning to him. He immediately went to stand behind the man's chair. "Sir?" he asked, bending low.

"Ach," the gentleman said in dismay, "I seem to have spilled my claret." He fretfully fingered his shirtfront, which bore a dappled red stain. "Will you attend me? I need to change my linen and I've given my valet the afternoon off."

Harris bowed gracefully and pulled back the gentleman's chair.

Griffin rose and excused himself to the small company gathered in the dining room. The sun had come out that morning and a number of the guests had gone off to Paultons, seeking any entertainment, however humble, to relieve their boredom. The tall footman followed in Griff's wake as he made his way up the sweeping staircase. When Griff got to his room, he waited until the footman opened the door, before he preceded him inside.

Harris, who had aspirations of one day rising to the position of valet, immediately went to the walnut-veneered armoire and took out a folded cambric shirt.

Griff had peeled himself out of his coat and waistcoat by the time the footman set the shirt on the end of the bed. Griff looked across at him as he began to undo his cravat. "Take off your coat and shirt," he ordered. Harris stood rigid, an expression of confusion fixed in his eyes. "I said, take off your jacket and your shirt."

The footman blanched. "Sir?"

This gentleman, Harris knew, was Griffin Darrowby, who was reputed to be very much in the petticoat line. Harris wondered if the rumor mongers were wrong for once.

Harris took a step back. "Sir, if I may say . . . I am not inclined that way . . ."

Griffin laughed softly as he drew the wine-stained shirt over his head, but there was no mirth in his ice blue eyes. "I find myself quite uninterested in how you are inclined. Now you will remove your coat and shirt or I will do it for you."

The footman, who was easily half a head taller than Griff, eyed him speculatively. There were sloping muscles all along the blond man's arms and upper chest. And Harris knew that the gentlemen of the *ton* practiced at fisticuffs with professional prizefighters. He shrugged with manufactured indifference and began to work the buttons of his bullion-trimmed coat.

After Harris had drawn the loose-fitting cambric shirt over his head, he stood, hands clasped before him and waited. As Griffin walked slowly around him, his eyes narrowed. Once he was done with his perusal, he said, "Sit down," and motioned to the bench at the foot of the wide bed. The footman sank onto it, trying to hide his uncertainty. Griff crossed the room to where a tray of decanters sat on a side table. He poured out two glasses of brandy and then returned to the footman.

"Drink up," he said, proffering glass. "I'll see that you're not reprimanded for it."

Harris downed the fiery liquid in one swallow.

"Now," Griff said as he toyed with his own glass, "tell me how often he hit you."

The footman made a noise that sounded like he'd swallowed his tongue.

"Tell me how often you watched him strike your mother."

When there was still no answer forthcoming, Griff took a step back and turned to one side. "See this," he said, running his index finger along a narrow, red welt that curved along his rib cage. "This was from a red-hot fireplace poker. I was nine." He held out his left hand. The two smallest fingers were slightly misshapen.

"This was from the one time I held him back from hitting my mother. He closed my hand in a door as punishment."

The footman was trembling visibly.

"Now you tell me, young Mr. Harris," Griff continued implacably, "who taught you to hit? At whose knee did you learn that it was proper to lay punishing hands on a woman?"

Harris leapt up from the bench and rapidly crossed to the bottle of brandy. He splashed a measure into his glass and threw it down his throat. It was several long seconds before he spoke.

"It wasn't my da," he said in a low voice as he turned around. "It was *his* da, my grandfather. He looked after me while my parents were at the mill. He beat me when I didn't listen. And he beat my sister Laura, when she was slow with his pipe or his dinner. She lost the hearin' in one ear, because of him."

Griffin looked grim. "And what of your parents? Did you tell them how he treated you . . . how he treated Laura?"

Harris shrugged. "'Twas no different for them, growing up. They got beat as well, I expect."

Griff mulled this over. "Yes, but they didn't ever hit you, did they?"

"Well, no," he admitted. "Except for a cuff now and again. But never like my grandfather."

"But you believe it is a fine thing to take your fists to a woman. To use your strength against someone who has no defenses, no means of retaliation . . ."

"I had no defenses!" Harris cried. "I was a babby when he began. Broke my arm, he did."

"Yes," Griff said, "I can see where it was badly mended. And he used a horsewhip, if those scars on your back are any indication."

The footman shut his eyes. "I know what this is about . . . that preacher's brat . . . you know that I . . . I struck her yesterday."

Griff shrugged. "My servants talk among themselves. I overhear things sometimes."

"She dumped a bloody pot of soup on my privates!"

"You were under the misapprehension that she desired your advances, Mr. Harris. Now, perhaps, since you know otherwise, you will not trouble her again."

The footman nodded twice. "No, I'll not trouble her. I only thought she was a pretty little thing under all that hair and miles of serge."

"Yes," said Griff as he slipped the clean shirt over his head.

"She is a very pretty little thing. And, just as your sister Laura did, she needs someone downstairs to watch over her."

Taking his cue from the blond man, Harris tugged on his own shirt. "I doubt she needs me, sir," he grumbled as he took up his coat and went to the door. "Not when she has the likes of you on her side."

"She needs any ally she can find right about now. And yes, Harris, you may go. I didn't really need you—I got in the habit of dressing myself on the Peninsula."

The footman touched his brow with one hand. "As you like, sir."

"And, Harris—" the man stopped halfway through the door— "the things he did to you . . . they might not ever go away. But if you are wise, you can learn something from them."

Griff was surprised at the intent look the toothy young man leveled at him. "I've never spoken of it to another soul."

He was out in the hall, beyond the closed door, when Griffin whispered back, "Neither have I."

As Griffin fussed with his cravat in the bedroom mirror, he pointedly avoided looking at the reflection of his face. It was uncomfortably like the face of another—the man who had whelped him. Griffin knew it was pleasing to women and so he didn't despise it as much as he might have. But it was a trial to him all the same. Not a week went by that he didn't pass a shop window and stop in shock when he saw a startling facsimile of the Ogre gazing back at him.

Once his cravat was arranged to his satisfaction, he smoothed his hair back with one hand and unwittingly caught sight of his face in the glass. It was almost as though a stranger were staring back at him. A stranger who, except for the vivid coloring, bore little resemblance to his father.

There was a soft mobility to his mouth and a lazy crease of humor around his eyes. The nearly stern set of his brow was now eased and the tight line of his jaw had relaxed. Though his features had certainly not rearranged themselves, they were not quite the ones he was used to.

He was musing over this remarkable metamorphosis when Wilby came into the room.

"I thought you'd taken the afternoon off," Griff said over his shoulder.

"I am weary of the country air, sir," the valet said with a slight moue. "I yearn for the congestion of London." He picked up Griff's discarded shirt from the floor. "What happened here?" He held the shirt up under his master's nose. "First the missing buttons on your French waistcoat, and now red wine on one of your new shirts? You are a trial to me, sir."

With a wink Griff sailed past him toward the door. "It was for a good cause, Wilby. A very good cause."

Sir Thomas found Minerva on her knees in the library, surrounded by piles of books.

"Carrying on Lucas's work?" he asked as he propelled himself toward her, leaning slightly upon his stick.

"Mmm, I've been avoiding it for a long time, Thomas."

"You've been avoiding a great many things," he said gently.

"Have I? It seems I can always count on you to be my conscience. Lucas used to say that you were an old sobersides, in spite of being so many years his junior."

Sir Thomas merely smiled. "That comes from my time in the diplomatic corps, I suspect. My youthful enthusiasm quickly tarnished among that jaded lot. So you think me something of a martinet?"

She closed the book in her lap and looked up. "Do you want my honest opinion?"

"Always," he said as he settled on the chair nearest her.

"I think you are an observer of life. You watch the rest of us scurrying about, trying to find our way, but you never join in. And yet you presume to judge those of us who are trying to make something meaningful of our lives."

"That is plain speaking," he said with a slight wince. "And perhaps a trifle unfair. I am not so remote from life as you think; I take my duties as magistrate quite seriously."

"Ah, more judgments," she uttered. "I think even Lucas feared to be found wanting in your eyes. And I shudder when you have caught me out at some foolishness."

De Burgh blinked. "I make you shudder, Minerva? After the five years we have known each other, you tell me you fear me?"

"Oh," she said, lowering her head over her book, "I am not afraid of you. Only of your acerbic pronouncements."

"You are still angry, then, that I cautioned you about encouraging Darrowby?"

"Perhaps a bit miffed . . . you made me feel like a callow girl chasing after a dancing master. I wonder . . . am I foolish in wanting to marry again so soon?"

"I never cautioned you against marriage. I wanted you to understand that if you sought to replicate the happiness you had with Stargrove, you'd do better to choose a man like your late husband."

"There is no man on the planet who is like Lucas." She sighed. "You and I both know that."

Sir Thomas steepled his fingers in his lap. "Then choose a man who has some of his qualities at least. Not the offspring of a wicked, profligate family."

She sat up on her knees. "Why do you dislike Griffin so much? You believe I want him merely because he is handsome and attentive. But there is much more to his character . . . I had evidence of it only yesterday." She moved closer to his chair. "Remember what Lucas was like when we were first wed, how remote from life . . . lost in his books and studies for weeks at a time? And do you recall how eagerly he came to embrace life within the first year of our marriage? My love for him worked that magic, Thomas. And his love for me. He danced with me in Paultons on our first wedding anniversary, this man who had not been to a village fete in his entire life. He danced and drank very bad wine. And he laughed all the way home."

Sir Thomas rose abruptly and took a turn about the room. "And what has this to do with Darrowby, pray? He surely has embraced life, if the tales they tell of him are true. He doesn't need your guiding hand to lead him into revels, my dear. What magic is it then that you seek to work on him?"

She tipped her head back. "He is as remote from his softer feelings as Lucas ever was. How could he not be, coming from a family that is a byword for infidelity and marital misconduct? You and I, Thomas, we had parents who nurtured us. We can only imagine how a child would be affected as he watched his parents try to destroy each other in public."

"It sounds to me," he pronounced darkly, "that you have more pity to offer the man than love. That is not a good foundation for a marriage."

With a sigh she set down her book and climbed to her feet. "I

will tell you one thing, the thought of marriage has not distracted
me from my pain. My grief recedes for weeks at a time, and then
it washes over me until I am drowning in it. I . . . I thought that if
I allowed myself to love again, the grieving would cease. But it has
not."

The magistrate crossed to where she stood and put his hands on
her shoulders. "Perhaps you are not so in love as you think."

She blinked up at him. He was quite tall, even taller than Lucas
had been. "Do you think so?" she said quietly. "No, I know my
own heart now. Which means this house party has served its purpose and I can send everyone on their way."

His hands dropped and he moved away from her. "When will
you tell Darrowby of your decision?" he asked over his shoulder.
"I expect you will want to be married with all haste, now that he
has told you he loves you."

He didn't miss the stricken look that crossed her face. "I . . . that
is, he has not. Not in so many words." She sank into the chair he
had vacated. "I need to give him time, Thomas. I am at an im-
passe—if I marry him now, I cannot be sure his feelings for me
will ever change to love. And I couldn't bear that. But if he goes
back to London without a commitment from me, I fear he will return to his old habits, and, well, take up with ladybirds and such. I
don't think I could bear that either."

Sir Thomas looked thoughtful for a moment. "Then send him
away for a short while, say, two months, and charge him to prove
his loyalty to you by giving up his former pastimes. I fancy only
love could make a man of Darrowby's inclinations toe the line,
Minerva."

She mulled this over. "And how shall I know if he is behaving
in town?"

The magistrate shrugged. "I have many correspondents in London, among them Lady Jersey. Little goes on in the *ton* that she is
not privy to. And there is your aunt in Hyde Park."

"It might just work," she said as she rose. "I fear Griffin will not
like it, but it suits my purposes."

And mine, Sir Thomas thought as a tiny dagger of guilt twisted
inside him. *But all's fair in the pursuit of love,* he reminded himself. And who knew, Darrowby might surprise everyone and behave like a paragon.

"And while we wait to see how he conducts himself, I will con-

tinue to be at your disposal"—he coughed softly and did not try to
hide the wry gleam in his eye—"as your nonjudgmental friend."

"Thank you, Thomas." She rose on tiptoes and placed a chaste
kiss on his cheek. "But, nonjudgmental?" she said playfully. "I will
believe that when I see it."

He set her away from him and took her arm. "And now I think
you require a stroll in the garden. To chase away the cobwebs."

"The ones in my mind, do you mean?" she asked as he led her
through the doorway.

"No," he said as he fondly brushed the gossamer strands from
her dark hair. "I mean the real cobwebs you have acquired from
poking about in your husband's dusty library."

Chapter Seven

She isn't here, Griff thought dismally. It was foolish to think she would come. He'd seen that afternoon that Gaspar's leg was nearly healed. There was no further need of her doctoring.

He went up the stable aisle, past his horse's stall, until he reached the door to the tack room, peering over each stall door, thinking that perhaps she had found a new patient. But he was alone in the stable except for the lads who slept in the high loft beyond the raftered ceiling. It was for the best that she'd stayed away. Something had shifted between them last night, had charged the air when he'd touched her. He'd seen the sudden melting expression in her eyes and felt the equally sudden quickening of his own body when his fingers traced over her smooth, warm skin.

He'd never taken a serving woman to his bed. Why would he, when there were any number of well-bred ladies to do the honors? Even his first time, while he still dwelled in the unhallowed halls of Darrowby with his father, had been with a charming lady who was cousin to his father's latest paramour. She had seduced him over a game of chess, and then had the wisdom to pretend it was his overtures she'd responded to. A most encouraging initiation into the world of eros, which left him with his dignity intact even if his virginity was forfeit. He had been all of fifteen.

He had not looked back after that first week with Helene. He'd discovered there was one thing in the world he could do well. Something his father's black looks and ready fists could not diminish. Something his sire's cutting disdain could not destroy. Griff's ultimate victory had been when, while still a student at Oxford, he had managed to steal the current leading lady from Covent Garden out from under his father's nose. That it had scandalized the *ton* for a short while meant nothing to Griff. All that mattered was that his father had retreated to Darrowby with the sound of his cronies' mocking laughter still ringing in his ears. Payback, Griff reckoned, was as sweet as a ten-guinea whore's kisses.

But Gates Underhill was not an opera dancer or an actress. She was certainly not a well-bred lady with dalliance on her mind. That placed her beyond Griff's sphere of seduction as surely as if she were guarded by a hundred stepbrothers. Not that those brothers of hers were likely to guard her virtue. A disturbing thought crossed his mind that perhaps they had even threatened it, and his fingers itched again to throttle each of them in turn.

He heard a slight noise from inside the tack room. No light showed from beneath the door, but he quietly thumbed the latch and pushed it open. She was sprawled atop a large trunk, backlit by the moonlight that streamed in through the leaded window. As he came through the door, she turned and held out one hand.

"Come and watch," she whispered excitedly as he crossed the room. As he settled behind her on a corner of the trunk, he saw what it was that held her so enthralled.

A large garden spider was in the process of spinning a web across the entire span of the window. The exquisitely fine tendrils of silk shimmered in the pale light. The spider labored on, casting out a line, tethering it and then swinging back to form another part of the web, oblivious to his human audience.

Griff laid a hand on her shoulder. "This is pretty magic," he said as he moved closer to her, swinging one knee up onto the trunk. Somehow his body had forgotten his recent edict to leave her untouched.

She canted her head to one side. "It's a daily miracle," she whispered into the waves of hair that feathered over his ear. His body's response to that unwitting caress was instantaneous and unremitting.

He groaned softly. And then said in an attempt to distract himself, "A daily what?"

She leaned back even further, so that he was able to smell the clover scent that clung to her hair, and the sharper tang of lye soap from her hands. There was also an undertone of cinnamon, rich and spicy, wafting up from her pinafore.

"First," he said, "show me what you have in your pocket."

She drew the sticky bun out and carefully peeled away its paper wrapping.

"Gaspar gets all the treats," he grumbled.

"Gaspar has been ailing," she said. "Here, then." She broke off a piece and popped it into Griffin's mouth.

He nearly choked in surprise. He could see her eyes laughing at him, even in the moonlit darkness. She was toying with him, he realized, like the most seasoned belle at Almack's. Well, two could play at that game. Nothing in his rule book said he couldn't *flirt* with servants.

He lifted her fingers, where she'd held the morsel, and slowly licked off the remains of the sticky honey. She closed her eyes and smiled. A tiny dimple cleft her cheek, below the fading bruise the footman had given her. He had concurred with that fellow, Harris, that Gates Underhill was a pretty little thing. What an understatement that was. Even though in his experience scullery maids were rarely even presentable, this particular scullion was undeniably exquisite. The moonlight worshipped her, making an exotic mystery of her angular face, deepening the slope of her almond eyes, and heightening the span of her high cheekbones. She might be a princess of the Levant, playing truant in this paltry English house.

"Gates," he said softly, unwilling to break the spell that had been woven about him, as surely as the spider in the window spun his fatal web. "Let me undo your hair."

He had already found the piece of twine that held the braid in place. With sure fingers he unworked the plait, feeling the soft waves spring free under his palms. The scent of clover seemed to be all around him now. She shook her head slightly so that the unconfined mass fell into a cloud of dark curls that billowed over her shoulders.

"There," he said as he forced himself to lean back from her. "That is much better. Now tell me about the daily miracle."

Gates didn't know if she was able to speak. The touch of his hands, so gentle on her hair, had fogged her brain. But no more than the feeling of his mouth against her skin had, when he'd licked the stickiness from her fingers. She had no idea of what was happening between them; her only thought was a sort of surprise that there was so much pleasure inside her. And that this man, this gilded, achingly beautiful man, was drawing it from her, summoning it from beyond the protective walls she had erected so many years ago.

"The daily miracle," she began in a husky voice, which was all she could muster just then, "is something I invented. My father doesn't believe in miracles, not the ones in the Bible, at any rate. In Papa's version of the Book, our Lord Jesus was goodness incarnate, and so did not have to perform miracles to prove his worth."

Gates stopped to assess his response to this particular aspect of her father's heretical views. Griffin was nodding as he spoke.

"Radical," he said, "but hardly novel. I have heard that Mr. Thomas Jefferson wrote a version of the Bible which also omitted the miracles. Though, if for the same reasons as your papa, I cannot say."

She stared at him openmouthed.

"Mr. Jefferson was the third president of the United States . . . of America."

"I know that," she responded, again wondering why he persisted in thinking her so ignorant of everyday things. "I am only astonished that Mr. Jefferson and my papa could have had the same vision."

Griff tweaked her chin. "Perhaps Mr. Jefferson did it without the vision. But you still haven't told me . . . about the miracle."

"Oh, I forgot," she said chidingly. "I fear you distract me, sir."

There it was again, he thought, that coy, baiting grin, which any budding debutante knew could bring a strong man to his knees. He felt his own self-control starting to slip. It had been a mistake to tamper with her hair. Now more than ever she looked like the sultan's favorite houri, with that dark, untamed spill of silk framing her face and spreading over her shoulders. He instantly imagined her hair fanned out behind her on a satin pillow, while her slim body arched beneath his, not in distress, as it had once done, but in shared delight.

"I'm sorry to distract you," he rasped out. He slipped off the trunk and went to lean against the door.

She swung around to him and tucked her knees up under her skirt. "Very well. I *will* get this out before the night is through. Since my papa's Book doesn't allow for grand miracles, I look for less grand ones, which might be more acceptable."

"And what are these daily miracles you have discovered in this little corner of Cheshire?" he asked as he crossed his arms over his chest. "Besides your industrious spider."

Gates sat looking thoughtful for a moment.

"Can't think of another?" he teased her amiably.

"Oh, no," she replied. "There are so many, I don't know where to start. I find one or two every day. There are the honeycombs in Nattie West's apiary—perfect tiny hexagons, made without a measure or a rule. And the feather of a sparrowhawk, held up to the sun. Delicate and light, but it will not break in the strongest wind." Her voice took on a haunting quality. "And the spray of color over a waterfall, as though a thousand hummingbirds danced there."

"Go on." Griffin breathed out the words. He was leaning away from the door now, needing to see the play of emotions on her en-raptured face. He doubted he'd ever made a woman look that way, doubted he ever could.

She too was leaning forward, as if her words would eradicate the space he had intentionally set between them. "Dragonfly wings, river snail shells, the nest of the weaver bird high in the cedar boughs. Beech leaves in the full of autumn, aspen leaves in the spring, the bright swirls on a turtle's shell, the dappled coat of a newborn fawn."

As her voice drifted to a halt, he crossed to her and took up her hands. "Ah, Gates, I was wrong. You have seen a great deal in your corner of Cheshire. There are soaring cathedrals and mighty cas-tles I have visited that might possibly compare in beauty to a drag-onfly's wing. But I suspect you do not find your daily miracle in things made by man."

There was a wistfulness in her face as she said, "I have seen lit-tle of the world. Chester, where I lived as a child, is only a hazy memory to me. The buildings there did not speak to me, though, not as the wild things do."

His hand was upon her hair again, against his will and much against his better judgment. "You are full of fancy, Miss Under-the-hill. But I understand now how you could have survived on that farm. It was never really your home. It was as I surmised that day by the stream—you are a spirit creature and not bound by mor-tal ties."

She turned her face and laughed softly against his wrist. "What nonsense you talk, Darrowby of Darrowby."

His fingers tightened in her hair; he drew her forward until her head rested beneath his chin. She was frail beneath the arm that en-closed her shoulders, still gaunt from her turnip-eating days at the farm. But she was strong as well. He felt the strength of muscles honed by running and climbing. By God, she was a little savage—as wild and exotic and sweetly supple as a desert cat.

"There was something made by man that I once added to my list," she said, her voice muffled in the folds of his cravat.

He tipped her head back and watched the moonlight dance over her long, white throat. "What was that?"

"There was a horseman who came upon me one day, while I was in the woods—" Griff felt an instantaneous rush of jealousy for this unknown man. "He was having a bit of trouble with his stallion, and as I watched the flex of his fingers on the reins and the arch of his back in the saddle, I said to myself, 'Gates, here is your daily miracle.'"

"It was me?" Griff asked with a relieved smile. "I was your miracle?"

She nodded, her head again tucked beneath his jaw. "I had never seen anyone like you . . . fair and graceful and gilded by the sun."

"The sun was setting, as I recall."

"Then you had your own aura, which made it all the more special."

"I was a rather wet miracle, as I also recall."

She laughed aloud and pushed back from him. "You are a wretched man to make light of my admiration."

"No," he said in the softest of whispers, "Your admiration is a miracle in itself. A grand one, Gates, not a daily one. Right up there with the loaves and the fishes."

"Which Papa disbelieves, as I've told you."

The mention of her parson father quickly brought him back to his senses. He'd nearly let her beguile him, with her foolish talk of miracles and auras.

"I will never look at the world in quite the same way, Miss Under-the-hill." He regretfully drew back from the warmth of her body and the cool serenity of her moonlit face.

The spider in the window behind them had finished its work— the new web vibrated slightly on its wooden frame—but its architect was nowhere in sight. He'd be waiting off in the shadows, Griff knew, waiting for some unsuspecting fly or beetle to enmesh itself in the web.

Just as there was a dark side to the spider's lovely miracle, there was a dark side to the feelings that had coursed through him when he'd held the girl against his heart. This was no chaste affection he was experiencing, no matter how much he tried to convince himself otherwise. The ripe curves he'd first seen in the barn loft at her farm were not obscured by the loose gown and pinafore she now wore. His fingers twitched to touch those curves and to trace the length of those long, sleek legs.

Herein lies madness. The warning refrain started slowly and then grew to a fever pitch. He backed through the door and fled without a farewell.

Gates was becoming accustomed to his abrupt departures. They gave her an odd sense of power. She pulled a horse blanket off a nearby rack and wrapped it around her before she shifted onto her back on the wooden trunk. It felt softer under her backbone than the stone floor of the scullery. And who would notice if she spent the night here? The horses would wake her in the morning, as they stamped and snorted for their grain, and she would be at her post in the scullery right on time.

This is a heavenly place, she murmured as she drifted into the early stages of sleep. *Griffin Darrowby held me in this very room, and then told me my admiration was his own daily miracle.*

She doubted there would be another moment in her life when the yearning in her heart would march so closely with the reality of her existence. Gates might not have traveled the world or seen the great cathedrals, but she was wise enough to know content-ment when it slipped out of the shadows and settled over her.

Sir Thomas gazed down at the girl who was cocooned in the canvas horse blanket. Only her nose and chin protruded, like a red Indian papoose in its cradleboard.

His groom had come to him at daybreak to report that the young miss was asleep in the stable. Sir Thomas hastened there at once; it was the perfect opportunity to speak with her away from the house. But now, seeing how comfortable she looked, he hesitated to disturb her slumber. With as little noise as possible he gathered up bridle and saddle, thinking he would have an early ride. But as he was sidling through the door, Gates opened her eyes and mur-mured, "Good day, Mr. Grump."

He gave her a proper bow in spite of his encumbrances. "Good day to you, Miss Gumption."

She sat up and swiped her loose hair back from her face with her forearm. "So you still remember our foolish game, Sir Thomas."

He dropped his tack in a heap on the floor and crossed back to her. "It was only two months ago that you stopped coming for lessons. I may be ancient, but my memory is not yet that faulty."

"You're not an ancient, Mr. Grump," she said, stifling a yawn. Her eyes peeped at him over her hand. "Only you do insist on walking about with that ridiculous stick, and wearing a coat that must be a dozen years old."

"And what do you know of men's fashions, Miss Gumption?"

"Oh," she said idly, "I've been studying them with some inter-est of late."

Yes, that's what I am afraid of, he said under his breath.

He crouched before her, his gray eyes dark with earnest intensity. "How are you faring here, Gates? I've been afraid to approach you—you didn't acknowledge me that first night, when you dropped out of Lucas's cherry tree. I thought . . . I feared that you were angry with me for some reason. You'd stopped coming to the house . . . And when I rode by your farm to ask after you, your brothers sent me away with a flea in my ear. I didn't tell them that you'd been coming to me for lessons . . . but I wondered why you'd stopped."

"My brothers sold our mare to a tinker," she said. "So I no longer had a way to get to Burgh Hall. I know I should have gone to see you one more time to explain, but I was ashamed."

"Ashamed of what?"

She frowned and said crossly, "You are always so full of questions, Sir Thomas. But, never mind. Sank and Demp have gone off to London now. And I am come here."

"There are other houses, Gates. Other people who would take you in. I worry about you in this sort of place."

"I thought Lady Minerva was your friend. How can you say this is not a good place?"

The magistrate sighed and stood up. "Minerva attracts a rather fast set of people. Do you know what that means?"

"You mean rakes and loose screws." She grinned. "I learned those words from Demp. They are men who take advantage of women." Her eyes widened in disbelief. "You don't think one of those fast men would try to take advantage of me, do you?" She crawled out from under the horse blanket and stood up, holding her arms out at her sides. "Perhaps you need spectacles, Mr. Grump. Look at this dress they have given me . . . look at this tatty pinafore I must wear." She held up her raw, reddened hands. "See what the lye soap has done to my poor fingers." She sighed deeply. "The only thing fast about the men who come near me, sir, is the speed with which they then depart." She sat down with a thud on the trunk and folded her arms. Her expression dared him to refute her.

"Dear me," he said weakly. "You still have no idea . . . Listen to me, Gates. I will be going home to Burgh Hall in a week's time. Return with me then. I will see that you have a pleasant room of your own . . . you can help me with my accounts and my ledgers. You still have a better head for numbers than I do, in spite of my years at Cambridge." She was looking less martial now. "And we can continue your lessons . . . the Punic Wars, I believe is where we left off in ancient history."

"And Cromwell and the Roundheads," she recited, "in English history."

"So you will come and assist me at Burgh Hall?"

The decision was out of her hands, she realized. She only wanted to be where *he* was, and she was fairly certain *he* was not going to Burgh Hall.

"You are the kindest man I know, Sir Thomas," she said with true regret. "But I have been under someone else's thumb my whole life. I need to do this now, to be on my own."

"Even with the tatty pinafore and the lye soap?"

"Even so," she said stoutly. She raised one hand before her and observed it. "I wasn't very fond of my fingernails anyway."

He touched her arm once before he turned to retrieve his gear. "I will seek you out again before I return home just to see how you are getting on. And remember, if anything or anyone troubles you while you are here, you must come to me."

"I promise, Mr. Grump," she said in a dutiful singsong voice.

"You are a rascal and a rogue, Miss Gumption," he said irritably, but he was smiling as he made his way down the aisle toward his gelding. He doubted there was a man in the *ton*, fast or otherwise, who could break her spirit. Even the lye soap hadn't done that.

Minerva checked and rechecked her appearance in the mirror over the mantel in her sitting room. She knew the sky blue morning dress was a perfect foil to her dark coloring. Lucas had commissioned a portrait of her wearing a gown of that exact shade, but he had died before it was completed. Minerva hadn't the heart to continue the sitting, not when her beloved would never set eyes upon the end result.

She coaxed a few tendrils down from her elaborate coiffure and bit her lips to enhance the carmine tint she had applied there only minutes ago. There was a soft knock on the door, and then Griffin Darrowby opened it and stepped into the room. He too wore blue; his coat was a deep indigo. She took that as a positive omen.

"Minerva, you wanted to see me?"

She nodded, praying her voice did not waver. "Please sit with me, Griffin." She perched nervously at the edge of a long couch and he placed himself squarely at its center. "After we talked the other afternoon, I began to see the wisdom of disbanding my house party. My nerves are not yet settled enough to entertain guests day after day."

"You seemed fit enough in London," he interjected. "Perhaps you need to return there. This house . . . is a house of mourning still."

The compassion in his tone disabused her of the notion that he wanted her in London for his own ends. And the house may have held sorrowful memories for her, but for this man, she sensed, it had somehow become a place of renewal. Griffin Darrowby was no longer the wry, guarded, man-about-town who had danced attendance on her in London. Something in his nature had begun to mellow, here in her home. She flattered herself that she was the cause of it, but whatever the reason, it heightened his attractiveness a hundredfold.

"If you recall," she said softly, "I limited myself to a few public entertainments while I was there. And this house, in spite of my own particular specters, is my true home. So I will remain here and bid my guests to seek other diversions. But I didn't want to send you away, Griffin, not without a special farewell."

He swung toward her and took up her hand. "That is some consolation, my dear. I believe you know my intentions toward you, though I have not said the words outright. Shall I—"

She quickly laid a hand upon his mouth. "No, oh, please no. Not yet, not now."

"Then tell me when, Minerva," he said between his teeth. "When will you know your heart?"

"When you know yours, my dearest Griffin." She stopped his angry words from erupting with the pleading expression in her eyes. "You do not love me. And, no, don't make protestations that you do. I believe you are fond of me, and I think that you desire me. But I would know it, as sure as the moon follows the sun, if you truly loved me."

With a muttered oath he bolted up from the couch and went striding off to the mantel, hooking both hands over the high marble ledge. "This is de Burgh's work, isn't it?" he charged her from over one shoulder. "He's been nattering on to you about my wicked, profligate forebears and the rotten odds of my making a good husband."

Her bosom rose noticeably as she cried out, "Sir Thomas has

nothing to say in this. But even if he did, he has always given me good counsel. Lucas used to say there wasn't a finer man in—"

"Then why don't you marry Sir Thomas, my lady?" he bit out. "He spends enough time trotting about after you on that damned walking stick."

"Mr. Darrowby!" she cried, her hands fisting in her lap. "This is not why I asked you to see me, not to brangle with you."

He turned and gave her a dark, searching look. "What else has the estimable Sir Thomas told you about me, Min?"

She appeared flustered. "What else is there?" Then the worried expression faded from her eyes. "Oh, do you mean your finances? Lord, Griffin, I heard the rumors while I was in London—that the Darrowbys were rolled up. But I rarely pay heed to idle gossip."

Griff took a deep breath. He had the unaccountable urge to gamble his future on one turn of the cards. "And what if those rumors were true?" he asked in a ragged whisper.

Minerva canted her head back and looked at him for several heartbeats before she spoke. "I've already told you what I require from you, sir. And I don't recall that adding to my already substantial fortune was on that list."

His sigh of relief was nearly audible. "You wouldn't refuse a man who came to you with empty pockets?"

"Not if his heart was full. Not if he pledged his love to me."

He moved back to the couch and cast himself at her feet. "This is what you want, isn't it, Min? A man on his knees? I'll kneel for you, but I swear I won't crawl. Not for anyone."

She laid her hand upon his tawny hair. "You won't even have to kneel, Griffin."

He shifted to the cushion beside her. "What then?" His eyes beseeched her. "Tell me what dragons I must slay, then, before I can return and ask for your hand."

"No dragons," she pronounced, refusing to be distracted by his boyish earnestness. "But since you aspire to play knight errant, I will set you a task." She drew a steadying breath. "For the next two months I want you to prove to me that your heart is engaged. No carousing on the town, no carriage races . . . no, um, ladybirds. In the middle of November you may return to Bellaire and I will give you my answer."

At her words, a look of simmering defiance had clouded his face. This was marching very close to an ultimatum and Griff was prepared to balk. Lady Min saw that look and whispered her fingers over his cheek. "It's not meant to be a punishment, my dear. But you need to examine your feelings for me, and discover if they are strong enough to keep you from your former, er, rather unsavory path."

"I make no excuses for my life, madam," he said stiffly. "I am no worse than any gentleman in the *ton.*"

Christ, he thought, this is what you got when you courted the widow of a prosy old stick. Prim lectures about bad behavior. He had a sinking notion where this lecture was heading, and he was not wrong.

"And then there is the unfortunate matter of your parents," she said with an intent gleam in her cornflower eyes. "They were both notorious for their flagrant infidelities. Sir Thomas did not need to point this out to me—it has been a source of scandal in the *ton* for decades. When I wed, it will be to a man who has armed himself against temptation. I will not permit myself to love someone unless he can promise to be completely faithful. And I place my trust in your sense of honor, Griffin, that you will not make me such a promise, unless you believe you are capable of keeping it."

A puzzled frown chased the budding anger from Griff's brow. "You will forgive me if I am confused, my lady, but is being in love an involuntary state or does it involve choice? You speak of love on one hand, as though it were a powerful force that one cannot fight. But then you say you will not 'permit' yourself to love. How can this be?"

"In the early stages," she pronounced, "I believe one can choose to allow it to blossom or not. But later, once it has flowered, oh no, there is no choice whatsoever. You love and there's an end to it."

Griff stood up and tugged at his waistcoat. "I wish you would be a rational woman for once, Minerva, and understand that attraction and affection are both sound reasons to wed. Especially for people in our station of life. Does it count for nothing that what I feel for you is as near to love as any Darrowby man has ever come?"

She rose up beside him and took hold of his shoulders. "Mock turtle soup, my dear sir, is still not the genuine article, no matter how earnest the turtle. Now, I trust I will see you in November."

She offered him her hand, then sailed from the room. As the door shut behind her, Griff swept up the nearest bibelot—a hideous statuette of cherubs swathed in starched lace—and raised his arm to heave it at the door. But he stopped himself in midthrow and set it gingerly back on the table.

There was still too much of his father lurking inside him for his own peace of mind. Anger, temper, even black rage at times. Drinking did not distill it, neither did any type of physical activity. Well, there was one activity that always cooled his temper even as it heated his blood, but that outlet was now to be denied him. Minerva's edict was clear. He had to "arm himself against temptation" and prove himself an exemplary character for two months, before she would consider his suit. A mere sixty days of celibacy, sobriety, rigid abstinence . . . it sounded interminable. But then he recalled how effortlessly she had absorbed the news of his failing finances and so regained some of his charity with her.

A man was supposed to walk through fire for the woman he intended to wed. Hell, what was a paltry two months of good behavior compared to that?

The cow byre was Gates's favorite place on the estate—her secret haven. It was deserted in the midafternoon, the cows turned out in their pasture, the dairy men away—probably chasing the dairy maids, she thought with a wicked chuckle.

At the far end of the byre there was a high stack of hay bales where she could while away the few hours of respite she had between scrubbing endless pots. Though the woods beckoned to her, she knew once she was amidst the trees again, she would forget the time and suffer the wrath of the butler. No, it was better to stay here, close to the house, and yet a thousand miles away. The sweet scent of timothy and alfalfa mingled with the pungent odors of cows and manure. It was earthy and intoxicating.

She stretched back lazily along the topmost row, which rose a dozen feet above the stone floor. The bales in front of her cascaded down in haphazard steps. If she slid to the back wall, she was sure no one could see her at all in the shadows beneath the arched roof.

Sleep traced its insistent fingers over her brow and her eyes fell slowly closed. It was so pleasant to dream. There were no larcenous stepbrothers in her dreams, no wandering parson fathers. Hunger disappeared as did the chill of winter and the fierce heat of summer. It was always spring or autumn in her dreams, the seasons of change. . . .

The man came upon her quietly. She didn't need to open her eyes, his scent was as familiar to her as her own, the crisp brace of balsam and the soft amber-hued scent of sandalwood. He nuzzled her neck with his chin and she felt herself smile. He murmured something low against her throat, words that had no meaning other than that they were for her ears alone. When his mouth traced over her cheek, she purred out a tiny sigh. He echoed it with a hitching moan that made her stomach swoop like a swallow over a lake.

His hands were gentle as they lifted her head and released her hair from the confining braid. She felt him carry the tresses to his mouth, heard those murmured endearments again. She wanted to murmur back, to share with him all that was in her soul. But before she could find the words or form the syllables, he had slipped one arm behind her back and raised her up from the straw. His mouth took hers, opened slightly and full of heat. He was drawing on her lips . . . coaxing . . . coaxing, all the while holding her hard against his chest.

Gates responded by opening her own mouth, feeling the lovely slide of his tongue as it dipped and darted with heartstopping abandon against her own tongue. There was nothing to do but arch up in his arms, nothing to prevent her from crying out when his hand slid beneath the bodice of her pinafore and pressed against the roundness of one breast.

She heard the whispered curse, the word whose meaning she shouldn't know, but did. And then he was kissing her less urgently, the tension in his arms not quite so steely, his breath on her cheek not so halting or uneven. When he drew back from her, her arms reached out to bind him.

"Sleep, my love." The whispered command was a ragged sigh. "And dream of me."

Gates did as her specter bid and drifted off unresisting. Which was odd, she mused groggily, since she was already asleep.

Chapter Eight

Gates lurched awake and her eyes flew open in sudden panic. Someone had been here, beside her on the stack of bales. She could still feel his presence, strong and tangible. She peered over the edge of her shelf. The byre was empty. Not even a mouse nosed about in the scattering of hay on the floor.

Foolish girl, she muttered to herself, *starting at shadows like a baby.*

She brushed the loose straw off the front of her pinafore, preparing to climb down and return to her post at the scullery sink. Something clinked together in her patched pocket as her hand slid over it. She emptied the contents out into her lap and then sat staring for several moments.

Beside her sorry-looking handkerchief lay five jet buttons, each containing at its center a dazzling white stone. Gates had seen those buttons on Griff's waistcoat last night; the diamonds, if they were diamonds, had sparkled in the moonlight-drenched tack room. She rubbed her eyes and looked again, thinking these must be her gold buttons. But those, she knew, were hidden with her other belongings on a deep shelf in the scullery. Somehow five new buttons had found their way into her pocket.

A sudden frantic fear shot through her. Her mind was screaming in denial as she boosted herself off the top bale and scrambled down to the stone floor. She ran from the byre and raced down the path that led back to the main house. She saw the dairy men walking toward her—several doffed their caps as she flew past. The stable lay ahead on her left. Oh Lord, it was such a large stable! Stall after stall in endless sequence. She counted them breathlessly as she raced along the aisle. There . . . there was the lantern that hung at the center of the row. Now two more . . . oh, no, that stall was empty. Gaspar's must be the third stall after the lantern . . . or the fourth.

But they were all empty. Nearly every stall that had housed the cattle of Lady Min's guests was empty.

A riding expedition, she told herself. They've gone off again to look at ruins, or to harass the shopkeepers in Paultons. She was being a ninny. He hadn't gone, hadn't left her without a word.

Someone blocked out the sunlight near the entrance to the stable. It was a man; she could tell by his height. Taller than Griffin, she saw, nearly as tall as that heavy-handed—

Oh, God! It was him. She'd managed to avoid Harris ever since the soup incident, but now he had her trapped in the barn. She tried to muster up a dollop of fear, but it was difficult since her heart was breaking.

"He's gone," the footman said as he approached her. "He asked me where he could find you, and I told him about the cow byre. But he must have missed you. I'm sorry, I know he . . . looked after you a bit." Harris motioned to the empty stalls. "They've mostly all gone now. Lady Min came down with a head cold and has taken to her bed. Sir Thomas announced to her guests that she needs a long, quiet rest. They all took the hint except for Pettibone and Ashcroft. But your Mr. Darrowby rode off not ten minutes ago. Bound for London, I do hear."

"Why are you being kind to me?" Gates raged as her voice broke. "I wish you would hit me again . . . then I would have an excuse to punch something." She crumpled into a small heap on the floor as the depth of her anguish overwhelmed her. "Oh . . ." she sobbed against her hands. "I . . . I just want to strike at something. Anything to make this pain go away . . ."

Harris knelt down beside her. "Hit me then. You owe me that twice over."

"Stop being nice!" She'd cried the words in such a shrill, theatrical voice that she nearly laughed through her tears.

"There, that's better. I swear I saw you grin just now."

"I am dying," she declared peevishly.

"Then you'd better do it inside, over the scullery sink, or Stubbin will grind your bones." He hefted her to her feet and guided her along the stable aisle.

"Why do you care what happens to me?" she asked as he stopped to slide the stable door shut. "I thought you hated the sight of me."

He shrugged as he took her arm. "You remind me of someone. Someone I'd forgotten until Mr. Darrowby recalled her to me. Now come along, and if his nibs rails at you for having a swollen, blotchy face, you tell me, and I'll sprinkle a bit of coal dust in his stew."

Gates decided that if she was not going to die of a broken heart, then having Harris, the toothy footman, as an ally was no bad thing.

Sir Thomas had just finished consoling a weepy Minerva—who was now convinced that she had done an unforgivable thing in sending Mr. Darrowby away, not to mention canceling her house party, which might mean being ostracized by some high sticklers in the *ton*—when there was another soft knock on his bedroom door. He retied the sash of his dressing gown, set down the book he'd been reading, and went to discover the identity of his second nighttime visitor.

Gates looked up at him in mute, glassy-eyed appeal. He didn't even hesitate, but drew her into the room, put his arms around her and held her. She didn't shed one tear, but he could see from the state of her face, she'd shed plenty earlier in the evening.

"They're not beating you down there in the kitchen, are they?"

"No," she said, breaking free of his hold. "Though they should. I broke four more glasses tonight and Stubbin says I will have to work for six months to pay them off . . . and . . . I must get to London."

He made a noise of frustration deep in his throat, but then calmly suggested that she sit, as he lowered himself into his own chair.

"London is quite far from here, Gates. And a dangerous city for one so inexperienced. Has your papa sent for you, perhaps? Or your brothers?"

"I'm not going to lie to you, Mr. Grump. I am not able to give you a reason, except to say that I have a debt to repay. I missed my chance to repay it here at Bellaire. I dawdled, you see, thinking I had plenty of time to get down to business. And now I am even more in this person's debt."

His gray eyes narrowed. "You haven't been dealing with moneylenders, have you?"

"Good heavens, no. Why would anyone lend me money?"

Sir Thomas thought it best not to pursue this line of conversation. The less an innocent like Gates Underhill knew about moneylenders the better.

"You'd best direct me, Gates, for I still cannot follow your lead. What is it you want of me?"

"There are at present still two men from London in this house. Lady Minerva's other suitors."

"Her other suitors?" His face had gone a bit pale.

"I meant besides Griffin Darrowby," she said. "Whom did you think I meant?"

"It's not important. Go on."

"Just this morning you said that I could call on you for a favor. And this one should be fairly simple. What I need is to secure a position with either Ashcroft or Pettibone. Then they will take me with them to London, and once I am there, I will be able to repay my debt."

"I could do a great deal more for you, Gates, if you'd let me. I'd gladly give you coach fare."

"No," she said adamantly. "I will earn my own way. All I ask is that you pay for the wineglasses I broke, so that I am not bound here for another six months. A loan, mind you."

"It seems I have no choice but to aid you, since I am a man of my word. I will speak to Pettibone in the morning—Ashcroft is less suitable, I fear."

She held out her hand to him. "Done then?"

He took it with a weary sigh and shook it dutifully. "Done."

She went to the door, but then turned back to him and said in a halting voice, "Is it wrong, do you think, to covet something that belongs to another?"

His head darted up. Her brisk manner had evaporated and she now clung to the door frame with white-knuckled hands. Guilt and hope warred in her eyes. He knew those feelings only too well, and so it took him several seconds to compose himself before he answered. "That's the general belief. But the wrongness of it doesn't stop the wanting, Gates."

"Yet sometimes there is joy to be had, in spite of everything?"

"Sometimes," he concurred softly.

She nodded, as if to herself, and then slipped into the hall. Sir Thomas picked up his book and tried to read, but his brain wouldn't cooperate. The girl was following Darrowby to London; if he were a betting man, he'd lay money on it. His own groom had passed along the tattle that the blond gentleman and Miss Underhill had met in the stable for several nights running. The fact that he himself had found Gates sleeping in the tack room was circumstantial at best, but it lent credence to his groom's story. And if his suspicions were correct, it meant he was allowing his sometime student, a girl for whom he had real affection, to place herself at risk. He weighed his options. He could stand back while Gates went off to London, where he fancied she would furnish a very potent distraction to Griffin Darrowby. Perhaps enough of a distraction to blind him to Minerva's charms. Or he could insist that Gates stay in Cheshire. And then, in the course of time, Darrowby would return to claim Minerva's hand. There was a third possibility, one he did not even like to voice in his own head—that Darrowby would take the girl as his mistress while he continued his pursuit of Lady Minerva.

Still, Sir Thomas doubted Gates would be so easily led astray. Her father had fairly bludgeoned her with his Old Testament beliefs. And he knew further, that she would not be turned from her mission to repay her mysterious debt. It was pointless to try to dissuade her from going.

The next afternoon Gates found herself tucked into Lord Pettibone's baggage coach. She shared the cramped space with his perfumed French valet, and his less-fragrant groom. She couldn't decide which of them was giving her the worst looks. The Frenchman sneered and the groom squinted, and neither expression boded well for their enforced confinement during the three-day journey to London.

Lord Pettibone himself had interviewed her briefly in the back parlor of Bellaire. He'd walked around her several times, inquired after her health, and had asked to look at her teeth. She had grimaced for him dutifully. There were no indignities she would not suffer to achieve her ends.

"You'll do," he'd said after his perusal. "My tweeny's had to leave my house in London . . . the chit got herself into an . . . interesting condition. Gather your things, then, and wait in the stableyard."

While she'd waited for the baggage coach to be brought out, she'd pondered what sort of interesting condition the tweeny had gotten into. She thought it boded well for her future. Life could never be too interesting.

But now that she was sitting across from his lordship's two sour-faced servants, she wasn't sure of anything. Sir Thomas had made his farewells to her in the kitchen. After admonishing her to write to him of her progress, he had pressed three gold coins into her hand, insisting he would feel better about things if she took them. "Godspeed, my dear," he'd said before he left the kitchen. "And don't forget my offer still stands." She wished he hadn't looked so grim.

She slept through most of the trip—sitting up in the baggage coach by day, and in the crowded attics of posting houses by night. She almost longed for her solitary spot under the scullery table.

The worst part of the interminable journey was that it afforded her too much time to think. She had blocked out all thoughts of her hazy dream in the cow byre from the moment she realized that Griffin Darrowby had gone away. But as the slow miles passed, and her taciturn companions continued to ignore her, she had no will left to hold those thoughts at bay.

She still referred to it in her mind as a dream, but she knew that what had taken place on that high ledge had been no phantasm. That same night, after the tearful swelling of her face had gone down, her lips had remained swollen and sore. There had also been a tender spot on her cheek where the golden bristles on his chin had left a slight burn. It was inconceivable that the elegant Griffin Darrowby had climbed into a hayloft and kissed her delirious. But the evidence—the telltale signs on her body, and the five jet and diamond buttons in her pocket—could not be ignored.

And by far the worst part was that she had slept through the entire thing. Well, not slept precisely. It was as though she had been drugged by the languorous, heady atmosphere in the byre and then further drugged by Griffin's deep, sweet kisses. He couldn't know she had not been fully conscious during his tender assault. She recalled moaning into his mouth and tugging at his hair with urgent fingers. No, he had surely thought her a willing accomplice.

Yet however intently she tried to relive the moment, it remained fuzzy and indistinct. It was depressing to think that the most thrilling encounter she was ever likely to experience would forever be a blur.

Gates was not completely unhappy in her new home, but she felt constricted. Lord Pettibone's large town house faced a pleasant square, which was enclosed behind iron railings. Since only the upper servants were allowed to walk in the gardens beyond those railings, Gates, as a humble tweeny, was denied access to her beloved greenery.

Her only glimpse of London had been on the night the baggage coach arrived. Some narrow houses and high-steepled churches were all she'd been able to see through the half-open canvas shade. The city air had smelled fetid and rank, especially while they'd driven beside the Thames, and Gates had wondered why the wealthiest people in the land would choose to dwell in such a noisome place.

Now her scenery was limited to the endless walnut spindles of his lordship's three staircases. Every morning she polished them with a solution of turpentine and beeswax and then buffed them with a square of lambswool. She had to admit the polish had done wonders for her lye-damaged hands. But the endless crouching and stooping was playing havoc with her back.

When Gates arrived, his lordship's housekeeper had taken one look at her ill-fitting gown and dingy pinafore and summarily ordered them burned. Gates barely had time to retrieve her buttons from her pocket before she was stripped down to her ragged chemise. The woman gave her a castoff gown to wear, which had belonged, Gates inferred from the housekeeper's muttered comments, to the tweeny with the interesting condition.

Gates was taller and somewhat more rounded than her predecessor, and so found the dress uncomfortably tight in the bodice and definitely wanting at the hem. The first time Lord Pettibone came upon her in her new gown, while she was buffing spindles on the upper landing, he made her stand up and turn around. She grimaced at him, thinking he'd also want to reinspect her teeth, but he merely gave her a tightlipped smile and went on his way.

At least she had a proper bed in this household; she shared an attic chamber with the other housemaids. However, there was no privacy at all in that narrow space and she feared to leave her possessions in the open. So she stitched together a cloth pocket for her buttons and the coins from Sir Thomas and pinned it to her chemise.

On her first afternoon off, three weeks after her arrival in London, Gates prevailed upon one of the other housemaids to walk through Mayfair with her. As they strolled along, she casually mentioned the name Darrowby to her companion.

The girl squealed as though someone had jabbed her with a pin. "Griffin Darrowby?" she cried.

"Yes," Gates said. "He was staying at the house where I used to work . . . I just wondered where in Mayfair he lived."

"O'course I know where he lives. There's not a nanny, house-maid, or tweeny in London who don't know where that handsome rascal lives."

"Why?" Gates asked. "Does he employ so many female servants?"

Her companion giggled. "Lord, no. He don't employ a one. Only men go to work for Mr. Darrowby. We ladies jus' likes to pass by his house, in case we can catch a glimpse of him. I saw him one time—he was dressed all elegant, for a dinner party or such. I says to Margie, my cousin, as we passed by, 'Have you ever seen the likes of that hair?' Pure gold it looked to be, under his fine hat. And she says back, 'Aggie, lookit them legs o' his. No paddin' in those calves, not like your Lord Pettibone.'"

Gates did not ask Aggie why a man would want to pad his calves, or any other part of his anatomy, for that matter. But she was relieved to discover that Griff's impressive stone town house was only a five-minute walk from her employer's home. She memorized the street names on the return trip.

Her revelation about Griffin had given her some cachet with Aggie and the other female servants. They crowded around her bed that night, prodding her to tell them what he looked like up close. Gates lied and said she'd never gotten within twenty feet of him. It was disconcerting to discover that the man who had stolen her dreams was also the object of adulation to so many other women. It began to occur to her that her mission was a very foolish one, and that she'd have been better off helping Sir Thomas in Cheshire than hankering after an unattainable man in London.

She spent the night tossing and turning. She dreamt of her father for the first time in months. He stood upon a high precipice, launching bolts of fire and brimstone at her from his fingertips. A man with gilded hair threw himself in her path and transformed the bolts into gold and jet buttons that rained down on her like the softest wheatstraw. But then one of the flaming streamers struck the man and set him ablaze. He reached his hand out to her through the licking flames. "Help me!" he cried. "Please. . . ." But when she grasped his hand, she saw it had turned to stone. And then he was gone, and she stood alone in a bleak, moonlit landscape.

She awoke with an aching inside her, a deep, fathomless longing that would not be stilled. There were tears on her flattened pillow and her body was trembling with distress. The darkness of the attic frightened her, in spite of the slumbering maids on either side of her. She needed the light.

Slipping from her bed, she crossed the narrow room and went down the stairs to the lit portion of the lower hall. She sat on the fourth step and laid her chin upon her fisted hands trying to puzzle out the meaning of the troubling dream. She was jolted out of her musings when she heard someone coming along the corridor. She'd forgotten that she was no longer in the servants' attic, but on the floor where Lord Pettibone slept. And it was none other than his lordship himself who was making his way toward her, the skirts of his belted banion swaying with each step he took.

Gates sighed as he came to a halt before her. "Stand up," he said with a flick of his fingers.

She did so and again performed her pirouette. "This is getting tiresome," she muttered between her teeth.

His lizard eyes lit from within. "You'll do, girl," he said softly. "You'll do very well."

Gates ran barefoot through the fog-shrouded streets of Mayfair, her feet beating an erratic tattoo on the damp cobblestones. She heard the ragged cadence of her own breathing and felt the panicked pulsing of her heart beneath the torn bodice of her chemise. As she ran, she clutched the woven shawl tighter around her. She had snatched it off his lordship's bedside chair to cover herself before she pelted down the stairs and out the front door of his house.

The street names she had memorized that afternoon became a blur. *Tillbury or Millbank?* She screamed the question silently as she came to a corner and skidded to a halt. A loitering jarvey gave her an assessing look and took a step toward her.

"Darrowby?" she cried pleadingly.

He cocked a thumb over his left shoulder. "Two blocks down and the second square in, love. And may I wish Mr. Darrowby a fine evening."

But Gates had already raced on, her hair, now mostly out of its braid, streaming down her back.

Yes, she thought as she turned a corner. *Oh yes.* This was the right street at last. She recognized the spearheads that topped the fence in the square and the red brick church at the corner. It gave her the will to struggle on in spite of the piercing stitch in her side.

Suddenly his town house loomed before her. She pushed

through the gate and stumbled up the steps to the porch. As she hammered with all her might upon the door, someone came along the pavement behind her. She quickly crouched down and huddled in the shadows. But whomever it was kept on walking, after casting an unsurprised glance at the half-naked woman on Griffin Darrowby's porch.

Gates resumed her hammering, praying that someone was home. There were lights showing in several of the windows, but perhaps Londoners did not answer their doors so long after dark. Her heart lurched at the possibility.

She had nearly exhausted all her strength, when the door swung open a crack and an irate voice growled, "Go away!"

"Oh, please . . ." She threw herself against the wooden panel, obviously surprising the person behind it, who wasn't expecting such a blatant frontal assault. The door gave way under her weight and she staggered into the hallway. A portly, middle-aged man in honey brown livery stood staring at her.

"Darrowby of Darrowby?" she gasped. "I know this is his home."

Still the man gaped at her.

A youth with golden brown hair came wandering out of one of the side rooms, carrying an open book. "Who was making that hellish noise, Bucket?"

"Darrowby of Darrowby?" Gates repeated her litany.

The young man's eyes widened. He shut his book and came forward. "I am Darrowby of Darrowby."

"No." She wasn't sure the word had passed her lips. What cruel joke was this, that there were two golden-haired Darrowbys living in Mayfair?

"And *I* am Darrowby of Darrowby," proclaimed yet another golden-haired young man as he came rapidly down the staircase. He reached the foyer and came shoulder to shoulder with the first young man.

Gates was trembling in disbelief and shock as her gaze shifted from one to the other. It occurred to her that she might still be dreaming, and she prayed intently that this was truly a dream.

Then she heard another set of footfalls on the stairs and a clipped voice that stopped her heart. "What in blue blazes is going on down here? Cort? Wescott?"

She looked up and met his eyes. He stumbled and missed the

next two steps. By the time he'd righted himself, she had rounded the newel post and was on her knees before him.

"Sweet Jesus!" he cried as he leaned down and took her shoulders between his strong hands. His head snapped up. "Bucket, bring me the brandy. And, Cort, if you could stop goggling long enough to use your brain, you'd see that she needs a blanket."

"What can I do?" the first young man inquired as he leaned over the banister for a better look at the exotic creature who was clinging to his brother's ankles.

"Put your damned tongue back in your mouth," Griffin snarled. The young man looked chastened but did not move away from his vantage point.

By the time the two men returned, Griff had wrapped Gates in his coat and was sitting on the stairs with his legs angled down on either side of her. As yet he'd been unable to get her to move and he didn't want to force her in case she'd been injured somehow. Bucket handed him a goblet filled to the brim.

Griff tipped her head back. "Drink it now, there's the girl."

He stroked her throat, making sure she'd swallowed, before he offered her another sip. Cort had joined his brother at the banister, and they both watched Griff's tender ministrations toward the girl with puzzled disbelief.

Finally Gates sputtered and sat up, coughing as the last of the brandy seared its way down her throat.

"I'm sorry," she said hoarsely, looking up at him. "This isn't at all how I'd planned it."

Heedless of his siblings' stares, he stroked his hand over her hair. "Life seldom turns out as we plan, my dear. Are you feeling stronger now?"

She nodded. Cort slung the blanket he'd fetched from the library over the banister and Griff drew it around her shoulders. "I think you might be in shock," he said, leaning down. "If the color of your complexion is any indication."

The taller of the two brothers leaned over for a closer look. "Pale as an albino's—"

"Cortland!"

Cort bit his lip. "Sorry, Griff. Wasn't thinking."

"What happened to you, miss?" Wescott asked as he shifted to the foot of the stairs.

Gates smiled at him sadly. "It was my own fault. Because I am foolish and ignorant and—"

Griff set his hand against her mouth. "We can catalog your shortcomings later. Just tell me what has happened to you. How is it you are in London?"

"I left Bellaire . . . Lord Pettibone offered me a job as tweeny. It sounded better than being a scullion. And his last tweeny found herself in an interesting condition, so I thought that was a good sign . . ."

Both the brothers commenced to chuckling until a flash of Griff's eyes silenced them.

"I've been in his house for three weeks . . . and I haven't broken even one glass."

. "Commendable," Griff remarked softly.

"But tonight . . . I had an upsetting dream. So I went to the landing . . . and Lord Pettibone came along and asked me to come into his bedroom. I . . . I thought he might have spilled something and need it cleaned up. I had no idea he would . . . because he is so old, you see, and not at all like the fast men Sir Thomas warned me about."

Griff shook her slightly. "What happened, Gates? What did he do to you?"

"H-he t-told me to take off my chemise." She clutched the blanket tighter around her. "And when I wouldn't, he lunged at me and ripped it. And then he opened his banion. He . . . wasn't wearing anything beneath it."

"Lord!" said Cort. "*That* must have put a good fright into you."

"No," Gates responded. "It was really quite . . . insignificant."

She had the unwitting privilege of seeing all three Darrowby men blush.

"But what is worse," she added in a reedy voice, "I fear I made that observation out loud. He came after me with a fire iron then, swearing he would have me jailed if he didn't murder me first."

"And so you fled and came here to me."

"Yes. Just this afternoon I'd asked one of the housemaids to show me where you lived. I'm so sorry I disturbed you this way. But I am willing stay here and work for you . . . without pay, if you like. I polished the spindles in Lord Pettibone's house, three floors' worth." She hiccuped out a sob. "I would much rather polish your spindles, my dearest Mr. Darrowby."

The brothers all blushed again.

"I think we've heard enough," Griff said abruptly, as he stood up and lifted Gates into his arms.

"She's foxed, ain't she?" Cort chortled.

"So would you be," Wescott said, flying to the girl's defense. "If you'd drunk that much brandy."

"And who says I haven't?" Cort responded belligerently.

"Boys!" Griff called down from the head of the stairs. "Could we hold off on the fisticuffs until tomorrow. Try to remember that we've a lady in the house now."

"She ain't a lady," Cort complained. "You heard her say it, she's a tweeny."

Griff's searing look could have sliced granite. Cort lowered his head and muttered under his breath to his brother, "She did say it, you heard her."

Wescott rolled his eyes. "I believe Griff was speaking of her sex, not her station. But Lord, she was pretty, don't you think?"

Cort wrinkled his nose. "Too pretty. I don't like the way he was looking at her. Never saw him look at anything but a nag with that much interest."

Since it was out of the question to sequester her in the attic with his footman and his valet, Griffin carried the girl to one of his guest rooms and laid her on the bed. She murmured something as he drew the soft coverlet to her chin.

"What?" he whispered, as he stroked a damp tendril away from her cheek.

"You got me drunk and I made a fool of myself."

"That's only halfway true, Miss Underhill. I did get you drunk. But as for making a fool of yourself . . . I'd wager that after your somewhat unorthodox arrival here tonight, my two worthless siblings will be your devoted slaves."

"That's nice," she said dreamily.

"Let's see what you think in the morning. I can have them flogged if they annoy you."

"Mmm," she sighed. "That would be nice too."

He watched with grave misgivings as she snuggled deeper into the bedcovers. This was precisely the person he didn't want in his home. Not when he was supposed to be leading a life free of scandal or intrigue. If Lady Min got wind of the barely dressed damsel who'd been pounding on his door, he was sure he could kiss his chances with her good-bye.

The thought of kissing recalled immediately to his mind the day he'd left Bellaire. The day he'd found Gates Underhill drowsing in the hayloft. He was always discovering her in stables and barns it seemed—which explained why her hair always bore the damned, erotic scent of clover.

He still wasn't sure why he'd kissed her. Her cheeks had been flushed with sleep, her tempting mouth half open and so lush. He'd meant to offer her a brief good-bye, but instead he'd raised her in his arms and kissed her. Kissed her until his head spun with longing and delight, and his body ached to lose itself in her dark, silken depths. And he'd done it not an hour after Minerva's strict pronouncement that he behave himself.

For weeks now he'd relived that fevered moment, when he'd torn himself away from Gates Underhill, wanting her with a need so keen that climbing down from that blasted pile of hay and walking away had been pure torture. And now here she was, tucked up in bed in this bachelor household, with not one soul to look out for her.

He should put her on a coach and send her back to Cheshire, back to the tumbledown farm and the goats and the chickens. But something had stirred inside him there on the stairs, when she'd looked up and said, "my dearest Mr. Darrowby." He had thrown away so much in his lifetime, but he'd never before turned his back on such untarnished adulation. And he wasn't sure he had the wherewithal to do it now.

"I think we're both fools," he said softly to the sleeping girl, "my dearest Miss Under-the-hill."

Chapter Nine

Griffin spent the night in fitful slumber. Both his body and mind were intent on betraying Minerva in the arms of an amber-eyed, long-legged farm girl. Though he remembered little of his disturbing dreams when he awoke, muzzy-headed and cross, they'd left him with a stern resolve to see the girl gone from his home and, furthermore, to do it quickly. Lord knew how many of her London acquaintances Minerva had instructed to keep a watchful eye on him.

He nudged away the irksome notion that *anyone* was monitoring his actions, and turned his mind to determining the fate of Gates Underhill. A position was the obvious answer. With a nice sedate family. No lascivious lords or lusty bachelors. Unfortunately Griff's social circle was exclusively made up of such men. As he mentally cataloged the least objectionable of his acquaintances, one of his hazy dreams from the night before shifted into focus. Vividly into focus.

Her sweet, hot mouth was on his, open and urgent, while her hands swept along his body in a shivering, silken caress. He cupped her face with one hand, feeding again and again from her parted lips, while with his other hand he possessed the fullness of a warm, rounded breast. Their entwined bodies moved in a slowly increasing cadence . . . Griff nearly cried out at the phantom sensation of her slim body arching beneath his own, and the utter bliss that rippled through him when he at last—

"*Christ!*"

Throwing back the covers, he leaped from the bed. He crossed rapidly to his washstand and thrust his head into the basin of cool water. When he returned to sit on the edge of the bed, shaking water droplets from his hair, he had dispelled the vision from his brain. But the desire still sizzled inside him.

A voice, one he'd not heard for some time, whispered silkily, "You've already got a position picked out for her, haven't you?"

Griffin collapsed back on the bed with a groan. It was insane to even imagine it—not with the vigilant specter of Minerva Stargrove hovering over him. Jesus, it galled him to be scrutinized in such a way. For the past two weeks he'd not even set foot in any of his clubs, for fear that Minerva would think sharing a glass of claret and a harmless game of cards with friends was too rackety a pastime. And he'd certainly not dared to visit a brothel.

Which no doubt accounted for his prolonged, erotic dreams last night; he was just not accustomed to celibacy. He'd endured it well enough in the war—but then he hadn't had a tangle-haired wood sprite sharing his bivouac in Spain and making him crazy with lust.

When Wilby came in to help him dress, Griffin was still uncertain of how to proceed. Sending the girl back to that bleak farm in Cheshire would be cruel. Finding her work with strangers might be equally cruel. He pondered, as he slipped his arms into the riding coat Wilby held out, whether making Gates his mistress was not the safest and kindest solution.

He was not so blind to his own motives that he didn't see the rationalization lingering behind his logic. But he wanted the girl and would grasp at any argument that justified that goal. Griffin rarely lied to himself, but he was not above an occasional self-deception.

Of course he would have to wait until he'd settled things with Lady Min, before he set the girl up as his mistress, but in the meantime he could keep her under his wing, so to speak. He had no intention of employing Gates as a servant—he wanted her to gain a bit of polish, but not the sort one acquired from buffing furniture. And since he was now forced to bow to propriety, he would need to bring another female into the house to lend countenance to his arrangement, someone of whom the starchy Minerva would approve. Griffin smiled as he twitched his cravat into place. He knew the ideal person for the job.

He finished dressing and went out into the hall. Cortland and Wescott were lingering on the landing, sprawled on the window seat beside Miss Underhill's room, obviously hoping to catch a glimpse of her when she emerged. Cort, who was tossing dice onto the velvet cushion, looked up as he approached.

"After all that brandy," he said, "she's going to have the deuce of a headache. I know of a tonic that will chase away the blue-devils—if you like I could bring it in to her." He eyed his brother expectantly.

"And I have chosen several books from the library, which I thought she might enjoy," Wescott added, pointing to the volumes that were piled at his feet. "Though I wouldn't presume to enter her room without your permission, Griffin." He shot an arch look at Cort.

"You'd be in there fast enough," Cort hissed, "if Griff wasn't here to draw your cork if you tried it."

Griff tried not to scowl. It appeared his brothers were now firmly launched in the petticoat line, all in the space of a few hours. Another vexing development he could lay at Miss Underhill's door. If he had any doubts about the necessity for a chaperon, his brothers' fatuous expressions quickly dispelled them.

"You can return these to the library, Scotty." He nudged a volume of Milton with his boot. "I doubt she's up to such ponderous reading. She is a farm girl, after all." Wescott opened his mouth to protest, and had the words knocked out of his head when Griff added, "And since I will be inviting Aunt Delphinia to come here, your concern for Miss Underhill is unnecessary."

Wescott's face crumpled as he uttered bleakly, "You're bringing Aunt Delphie here? To this house?"

Cort jumped to his feet. "Lord, Griff, the woman would as soon box your ears as look at you. I think that's a bloody awful idea."

The edges of Griff's mouth curved down ominously. "I don't have to justify my actions to you, Cortland. You are in this house on sufferance if you will recall, having lost your entire quarterly allowance in a . . . what was it? Ah, yes—a duck race."

Cort's face darkened. "Well, if that don't beat the Dutch! You, of all people, cutting up stiff over a little matter of a bet. They still talk about the time you wagered your curricle and four on the amount of time it would take a fly to crawl up a windowpane."

"Yes," Griff replied smoothly. "But I won. And that's all the difference in the world."

Miss Delphinia Darrowby was a byword in the *ton* for her various eccentricities, among them her radical bluestocking leanings and a consuming interest in canary breeding. But her most notable quirk was an aversion to members of the male sex. That prejudice, fortunately, did not extend to the eldest of her three Darrowby nephews—Griff knew she'd always had a soft spot for him. Furthermore, she was the only respectable woman he could think of to look after his guest on such short notice.

She had lived for years in Greenwich, in a suite of rooms above a bake shop on the High Street. He toyed with the idea of sending her a note, but then reasoned he could be more persuasive in person.

His aunt did not hide her surprise at finding him at her door. He'd called on her briefly after his return from Spain, but usually years passed between his visits. She ushered him into her sunny parlor, which, with its abundance of aspidistra plants and trilling canaries, evoked the atmosphere of a tropical jungle.

Delphinia had been a handsome woman in her youth, tall and stately, with the fair Darrowby coloring. Now nearing her fiftieth year, she still carried herself like royalty, but her long face had taken on an almost masculine aspect. She settled in a chair and motioned him to be seated.

"So what brings you here on this fine morning? Is White's not open yet?"

Griffin shook his head and grinned as he sat back in his chair. "I have a favor to ask of you, Delphie. There's a young woman I need you to look after. Someone I met in Cheshire—"

"You've been off courting Minerva Stargrove," she interjected. "If the gossip is correct."

He nodded. "It is. But this girl was not part of the house party." He briefly told her of meeting Gates Underhill after he'd lost himself in Bellaire Wood, omitting any mention of his abduction. "I spent the night on her rundown farm," he said. "Shortly afterward, she came to Bellaire to work in the kitchen. And then three weeks ago she arrived in London to work as a tweeny for Lord Pettibone."

"Almost sounds as if the chit's been following you about," she remarked with a frown.

Griffin's head jerked up. *Damn, he'd forgotten how astute she was.*

He cleared his throat. "Yes, well, I'm sure it's a coincidence. I don't know why she even needed to work; I left her something for her troubles before I departed the farm, enough to keep her into the winter. And then I left behind another gift as I was leaving Bellaire."

"So she's come here to look for more pickings, eh?"

"No, of course not," he said crossly. Somehow his story was not coming out right. "But I feel responsible for her, even though I did nothing to encourage her to come here."

"Except looking like a maiden's dream of paradise," she noted softly. "And giving her presents."

Griffin got up from his chair and ran one hand through his hair. "For God's sake, Delphie, she was a scullion at Bellaire. You know I have never trafficked with servants."

"Do I?" she asked, wide-eyed, as he squirmed visibly. "Oh, very well, I will leave off baiting you. Tell me what happened next."

"Last night she arrived at my house, barely dressed and in a state of shock. Lord Pettibone . . . attacked her, and she was forced to flee into the street."

"How ironic," she said with a twinkle, "that *you* were the one to offer her sanctuary from the wicked lord. Still, I never liked that man. He's an oily rogue for all his rank . . . and it's my belief he dyes his hair."

"Well that certainly places him beyond the pale," Griff remarked dryly.

"The girl's clearly a fool to have been taken in by him."

"She's not a fool," he said. "Just incredibly naive. She speaks well; you wouldn't know her for a farm girl to hear her talk. Her manners are genteel, if you discount her tendency to show up at the most unexpected times. Her father is an itinerant preacher, but I have it on good authority that he was a gentleman, once upon a time. So you see, she's something of an enigma."

His aunt cocked her head and frowned. "Why was she working as a tweeny in Pettibone's home. Surely a girl with some refinements could do better for herself."

"I doubt she's had much education." He leaned back against the high chimney breast and rubbed thoughtfully at his chin. "Though she does possess a sort of rustic wisdom, which is surprising since she's virtually untouched—Oh, don't roll your eyes at me, Aunt. What I mean is, she's like a creature from some distant galaxy. Knows nothing of how to go on in the world or how to look after herself . . ."

"Sounds simpleminded to me," the lady said with a sniff.

"There is nothing simple about Gates Underhill." He sighed. "When I met her she was running wild in Bellaire Wood, dressed in an old velvet drapery, with twigs and flowers in her hair."

She cocked her head to one side. "So you discovered your own Titania there in Cheshire. I wonder that you want me to stand guard over the girl, since you sound quite enamored of her."

Griff's eyes flashed and he swallowed his guilt as he spoke the lie boldly. "I assure you she means nothing to me. I merely want to keep her safe. And I would like your assistance."

"I'm afraid it's out of the question. I have no room here for guests." She chuckled then. "Barely have room for my birds. Two of my hens bred this spring, and I've only been able to give away five of the chicks. I don't suppose you'd be interested in a nice pair of songbirds?"

He shook his head. "Thank you, but no. And you misunderstand me, Delphie. I want you to come to London, to stay at my house. I doubt it will be for more than a month. If I can't find someone to employ the girl in that time, then I will send her back to Cheshire."

"Why not send her back now?"

Griffin had prepared himself for that line of argument. "She is overwrought at present. And I doubt her father or brothers will be back home any time soon. No, she needs looking after—" He eyed his aunt meaningfully as he added, "And she deserves the chance to make something better of herself."

Delphie took the bait like a bream rising to a mayfly.

"As every woman does," she said intently. "We can find a suitable occupation for her, if she is clever and honest. Several of my friends in the *ton* have grandchildren—perhaps we can place her as a nursemaid or nanny. And there is your third cousin, Beatrice, who married that squire off in Cornwall. A farm girl might be just the ticket to help them with their holding."

"Beatrice used to pull the wings from flies," he remarked sourly.

His aunt shrugged. "It was just a suggestion."

"But you will help me? It will get me out of the devil of a fix."

"Afraid of the gossip mills for once? That's not like you, my boy."

"It's not *town* gossip I fear. Minerva Stargrove has some misgivings about my rakish reputation."

"No, really?" Delphinia interjected dryly.

Griff ignored her sly remark. "She might not like it that I've got an unchaperoned young woman living with me. Not to mention, Cort and Scotty are staying at the house and I'm hoping your presence will keep them in line around the girl. You should have seen them when she arrived last night. I hadn't thought they'd discovered females yet, but apparently I was wrong."

"They are nineteen and twenty-two, as I recall. Well past the age for Darrowby men to have discovered . . . er, fleshly delights. I'm surprised they waited so long, after the example you have set."

He partially stifled his ire; he couldn't risk antagonizing her. "I forget you're a harsh critic of my sex."

"You wonder that I have no love for men, after a youth spent with your father and your grandfather?"

He bowed stiffly. "I don't wonder. But I fancy your unfortunate childhood was no worse than mine."

"That's probably true." Her eyes softened as she regarded him. "Your father was a brutish man, Griffin. I don't know what your mother was thinking to allow him to keep you after they'd separated."

"My mother," he said with barely disguised bitterness, "was thinking that he'd cut off her allowance if she didn't leave me behind. She bartered me so she could live in style in London."

Delphinia rose and laid a hand on his sleeve. "Don't stir it all up, my boy. It wasn't the worst scandal in the *ton,* but it was surely the saddest."

He moved away from her touch. "You may dislike me for being male, Aunt, but don't blame me for being his whelp. I have spent every day of my adult life battling his influence."

Her mouth drew up into a smile. "To paraphrase that old saying about the Scots—much might be made of a Darrowby, if you catch him young enough. Perhaps you fled from him in time to salvage some of your character." She led him toward the door. "Now give me a chance to get sorted out and packed up. You may send your coach here in the morning—you will have to keep your brothers at bay until then."

"Thank you, Delphie." He bowed over her hand. "I knew I could count on you."

She watched him go with a small secretive smile on her wide mouth. He had been with her for over half an hour, and in that time he had only fleetingly mentioned Lady Minerva. On the other hand he had spoken at length about Miss Underhill and when he did his eyes had gleamed with a rich light.

He'd certainly piqued her curiosity—she couldn't wait to meet the young woman who had shaken her blasé nephew from his usual reserve. *Darrowby of Darrowby, enamored of a scullion.* She chuckled at the thought. And then grew solemn when she realized that no good could come of it, only a deal of trouble. But then stirring up trouble was what Darrowby men did best.

Griffin was feeling distinctly relieved as he rode away from his aunt's house. Though the woman did have a knack for putting his back up, even when he'd determined not to let her draw him out. And the worst of it was, she had every right to preach at him. She knew better than anyone how little he'd made of his life, always counting on the Darrowby charm and the Darrowby looks to see him through.

She had gained strength from her wretched childhood, the strength to stand up to her father and brother and leave Darrowby, even if it was for a life of genteel poverty in Greenwich. He'd gained nothing from his years with his father, when the two of them dwelled together in the great stone house, except for the desire to see the man in his grave. He'd never taken up a cause as his aunt had, never battled for anything of meaning. Even in Spain, he'd fought for the adventure of it, not for Country or for King.

It wasn't until Gates Underhill appeared in his life that he'd felt a need to slay dragons. It was odd that he'd used that phrase to persuade Lady Minerva of his affection; she least of all required a knight to do battle for her. It was her lowly scullion who'd needed him—to protect her and defend her.

And here he was, scheming his way toward her eventual seduction. Which didn't mean he'd lost the desire to look after her. Once Gates belonged to him, he vowed he'd be the most benevolent of caretakers.

It was just past noon when Griffin reached London. His next order of business was to find the girl something to wear. He couldn't have her wandering about the house in nothing but a ripped chemise. It was bad enough his brothers had seen her in such a state, with an indecent amount of her lovely bosom on display. He forced himself to block out the stirring sight of Gates Underhill on her knees before him on the stairs. Time enough for such visions when he could make them a reality.

Griffin was no stranger to the various modistes who catered to London's elite. He'd often sat and sipped a glass of sherry while his current ladybird modeled a new ball gown or a walking dress for his approval. But those frivolous and outrageously expensive confections were not what he had in mind for Gates. At least not yet. She required a serviceable gown, preferably one that had been made up already.

Fortunately Madame LaSalle of Oxford Street had several dresses from which to choose. The first two were in dark, matronly colors, and had been cut for a much broader figure than Gates possessed. When the modiste held up a delicate muslin gown in a shade of pale apricot, Griffin forgot his edict.

"This one will do" he said. "It looks to be her size. She will also require a chemise and stockings."

"And slippers?" she asked, trying to hide her disappointment that the usually extravagant Mr. Darrowby was placing such a paltry order. She then recalled the rumors she'd heard recently of financial reverses in his family.

"Of course slippers." Griffin had another momentary vision of Gates crouched on the stairs, her bare feet peeping out from beneath the ragged hem of her chemise.

He strolled about the shop while Madame LaSalle packed up his purchases. A display in the window caught his eye—several bonnets, embellished with egret feathers and velvet ribbons sat jauntily upon their stands. He leaned over and plucked one from the display. The ribbons were a rich amber hue, as close to the color of Gates's eyes as anything he'd ever seen. "I'll take this, as well."

I'll give it to Minerva, he promised himself.

Madame looked up from her wrapping. "Those bonnets came in just this morning . . . I sell them on commission. The milliner's prices are quite dear, I'm afraid."

"I said I would take it," Griff replied through gritted teeth, wondering when had he gained the reputation of a nipfarthing. "And I want you to send someone to my house to measure the young lady for several more gowns."

He went from the shop in no good humor.

When Gates awoke it was just two o'clock. She knew the exact time because there was an ormolu clock chiming the hour on the mantel across from her bed. At first she thought she must still be dreaming, as her gaze roamed across the spacious room. Silk draperies hung at the two windows, a soft violet-blue that matched the hangings at the head of her wide bed. A cream-colored carpet, sprinkled with a riot of woven flowers, covered the parquet floor.

Even though Griffin himself had carried her to this lovely chamber, she knew it must have been a mistake. Perhaps his servant quarters were full and he'd placed her here only temporarily. But it didn't matter where she ended up—she'd sleep out in the garden, if it meant she could stay on in this house.

She sat up and examined the tear in her chemise. It was not quite beyond repair. The shawl she had taken from Pettibone's room was tumbled at the end of her bed; she crawled out from under the covers and wrapped it around her shoulders, tying the fringed ends behind her back. She was peeking out the bedroom door, wondering if she dared go in search of sewing supplies, when Griffin appeared on the landing, carrying a bandbox in the crook of one arm.

"Oh, no you don't," he called out as he came swiftly toward her, breathing a brief prayer of thanks that his brothers were no longer on the landing. Christ, the skirt of her chemise was nearly transparent.

"But I just—"

"Inside," he said briskly, holding the door wide. He followed her into the room as she returned to the bed and perched on the edge.

"I only wanted a needle and thread . . . so I could repair my chemise." She laid a hand on her breast by way of reminding him of the damage that had been done there.

As if I needed a reminder, he muttered to himself. He purposely turned away, setting the bandbox on a chair. "Never mind that; I've brought you something to wear."

"Oh." Her eyes brightened. "That was very thoughtful of you."

"Not thoughtful," he said turning back to face her. "Merely practical." Her head lowered slightly. "I gather, since you are up and about, that you are feeling better."

She nodded. "Much better. It seems as though last night was a horrid dream."

He took a half step toward her. "You're safe now, Gates. No harm will come to you in this house."

She had an uncanny notion that this was not quite the truth. In her desperation to flee from Lord Pettibone, she had run unthinking to Griffin's home. But she was not so callow that she did not recognize the dangerous emotion that simmered in his eyes as he watched her. She'd seen that look several times at Bellaire—the one that twisted her insides into giddy knots.

"I've sent for my aunt to look after you," he continued. "She is a peppery old thing, but I think you will like her. She's the only woman I know who is as heedless of authority as you are, Miss Under-the-hill. I expect you two will get on famously."

A furrow appeared on her brow. "Why would she want to come here to look after me?"

"Because I asked her to. Delphie will like nothing better than to take you in charge. She is a tireless reformer, and you, my little savage, will be prime grist for her mill."

Gates looked skeptical, but Griffin merely chuckled. "Unless you manage to convert her to your wild ways, and then all of London will be shaking in their shoes."

Clasping her hands in her lap, she said, "I promise to be on my very best behavior."

It was Griff's turn to look dubious. "Yes, I suppose you will try. Though opinions vary as to whether that is even a possibility." He moved off toward the door. "Now that you're awake, I'll send the footman up with some food. That way you needn't come down tonight"—Gates heard the command inherent in his words—"and by tomorrow, when my aunt arrives, you should be feeling totally fit."

Once he had gone, she slid from the bed and went to investigate the bandbox. After prying off the cover, she smoothed away the folds of tissue and drew out the apricot gown with a reverent sigh. Beneath it she saw a neatly folded chemise, a pair of silk stockings and two dainty slippers.

Bless him, she thought as she held the gown up against her torn chemise. For his generosity and for his ability to see into her heart. It was wrong to covet material things. But she'd always dreamed of owning such a pretty dress. And such delicate slippers. It was as though she had wandered into a fairy story, where all her desires were fulfilled. Well, some of them, at any rate. Her greatest desire, she knew, was beyond even the magic of jinnis or sorcerers.

After she bathed herself at the washstand, she drew the lacy chemise over her head, vowing that she would work for years, if necessary, to pay him back. And then she wondered what monetary value she would place on the happiness he had given her. There were some things that were far beyond price.

"It's not good news," Farrow said to his master.

It was nearing ten o'clock, and the two men stood in the dark mews lane that ran behind the town house. "As you requested, I tracked his lordship's groom to his favorite pub after supper. Pettibone called in the watch last night and swore out a warrant for the girl's arrest. Claims she assaulted him and then stole several valuable items from his home."

"The devil he did," Griff muttered. "The man should be horsewhipped."

Farrow shrugged and kept his opinions to himself. "The groom told me that his lordship's housemaids were arguing over who was to get the girl's belongings."

Griffin's face darkened. "A lot of harpies," he said, "fighting over her miserable bits of clothing."

"I believe there was also mention of a silver hairbrush," Farrow said dryly.

Griffin recalled seeing that hairbrush in her bedroom at the farm, as finely wrought as the vanity it had lain upon. In spite of her dire situation, she had not pawned it. He had an uncanny notion that she had likewise not pawned his gold buttons in Paultons. She was a beknighted little fool, but he was beginning to think himself equally beknighted, because his only thought at that moment was to reclaim her things and to clear her name with the constables.

Lord Pettibone, that loathsome midnight predator, would discover that Gates Underhill was not without a champion.

Rippon's was a recent addition to the myriad gaming clubs in London. Situated in a private house in Belgravia, it had become, Griffin knew, one of Lord Pettibone's favorite haunts. He entered the elegant foyer, greeted a few acquaintances who were lounging in the front rooms, and then wandered through the place until he found his lordship playing faro in a small back parlor. The men with whom Pettibone sat were well-heeled members of the nobility who thought nothing of risking great sums of money on the turn of a card. Griff had often played against them in the past and he was almost tempted to join them now—Dame Fortune had always favored him at the tables. But he was enough of a gambler to sense when his luck had run dry. And his instincts were telling him things were fairly parched in that area. So he merely leaned against one of the faux marble pillars that flanked the entrance and watched Pettibone at play.

The pile of coins and markers stacked before his lordship grew steadily in the next hour. Occasionally men relinquished their seats to those who had been waiting to play. At one point, as a vacancy occurred, Pettibone himself looked directly at Griffin and motioned to the table with a languid hand. Griff shook his head, offering him a tight smile. Pettibone shrugged and returned to his game.

Another hour passed before his lordship left the table. He scraped his winnings into his purse, bantered with the men, who insisted he stay and give them a chance to recoup their losses, and then headed in the direction of the small dining parlor.

Griffin followed in his wake. "You've lost something," he remarked pleasantly.

Pettibone stopped and swung back to the card room, fearing he'd left a coin behind unnoticed.

"Not there, my friend," Griff said, coaxing him forward. "It was last night that you mislaid it. Fortunately it came to light in a safe place."

Griffin chuckled at the perplexed expression on the older man's face; Pettibone was not an ideal foil. "She's not quite the friendless creature you assumed her to be."

Pettibone stopped walking again and his face twisted into a sneer. "If you are referring to my runaway tweeny, it might interest you to know I have lodged a complaint against her. She stole a valuable cashmere shawl from my home and will see Newgate if she is caught. And since the shawl in question is easily worth fifteen pounds, she might even hang."

Griffin laughed softly. "You must be sadly lacking in diversions, old chap, to waste your time swearing out complaints against housemaids."

"And London must be sadly lacking in ladybirds, if you have to turn your attention to tweenies."

Griff's jaw tightened. "Perhaps I am only following your example, Pettibone. Except that when I get a woman into my bedroom, she doesn't end up fleeing in distress."

Pettibone's pale complexion darkened to a mottled crimson. "What the devil do you want?"

"Your hide, if the truth be told. But I'll settle for having the girl's belongings returned and the charges against her dropped."

His lordship sputtered an oath. "You can go hang. She's a thief *and* a harlot . . . she came along to my room as eagerly as any fancy piece. But that's why you want her, isn't it? It's bad enough you're determined to win Minerva away from me . . . now you want that little fox-faced baggage, as well? I think that's a tad greedy of you, my friend, even for a man with the Darrowby appetite for vice."

There was an unperturbed smile on Griff's face as he took Pettibone by the arm and maneuvered him into an empty room. His lordship found himself seated in a chair gazing up at Griffin.

"You will do as I ask, return the girl's things to my house, or I will see that you are made a laughingstock in the *ton*."

His lordship colored up again.

Griff nearly chuckled out loud, remembering Gates's vivid description of the man's anatomical shortcomings. "No," he said softly, "I'm not so remote from charity that I would pass along Miss Underhill's . . . ah, insights with regard to your person." Pettibone growled softly. "Rather, I will reveal to a few influential friends that I saw you cheating at cards tonight. Which would be most unfortunate since, unlike the Darrowbys, you Pettibones have a rather pristine reputation. Funny isn't it, how little truth there often is to public opinion?"

Pettibone leapt to his feet and scowled down at Griffin. "I should call you out for such a slander."

"Ah, but you won't. Because you've seen me shooting at Manton's. And I've had a deal more practice in the last two years with targets of French design. But I wouldn't let it come to that. Not only to keep Minerva out of the gossip mills, but also because, as much as I'd enjoy putting an end to you, it would be irksome to have a fribble's death on my conscience."

His lordship was visibly trembling with rage. "I . . . I can't believe you would make an enemy of me over that worthless chit. I could ruin you, Darrowby, and you have the gall to threaten me?"

Griffin shrugged negligently, and then glanced out into the hall as several men strolled past. "Oh, look, there's the Earl of Stowe. He lost heavily to you last week, as I recall. I imagine he'll be quite interested in what I observed tonight."

He started after the men, but Pettibone held him back. "Damn your wretched interference," he snarled. His voice lowered, "Very well, I will see that the chit's things are sent to your home."

"And the charges against her?"

His lordship coughed slightly as his eyes shifted away. "I will have my butler speak to the constable."

Griffin smiled serenely. "Then our business here is concluded."

As Pettibone pushed past him, Griff took hold of his arm. "One other thing. I want fifty pounds—"

"What!"

"To be sent to the tweeny you cast off. And, no, don't tell me that she was a trollop who was asking for it. I wager she was just another country girl you preyed upon."

Pettibone opened his mouth to protest but Griffin gave him such a challenging look, that he merely shut it again with an audible snap. "You go too far, Darrowby," he said under his breath.

"It's a family trait. I'll expect your footman in the morning with Miss Underhill's things."

He sketched a bow to his lordship and went into the hall feeling well pleased with his victory, and wondering at the same time why the hell he had brought up the disgraced tweeny. Worrying over the fate of total strangers was definitely not a family trait.

The next morning at first light, Gates dressed in her new gown, struggling gallantly with the row of tiny buttons down her back. She paraded several times in front of the long mirror on the wardrobe, turning this way and that, watching as the frilled hem swirled above the delicate slippers. None of the maids in Lord Pettibone's home, even the exalted parlor maid, owned such a fine gown. Then she recalled Aggie's pronouncement—that Griffin Darrowby employed no females. He probably didn't know the proper attire for serving girls. And she was certainly not going to tell him.

She made her way down to the kitchen, stopping off to peek into several rooms on the main floor. If the front parlor was impressive, with its brocaded sofas, silk wall hangings, and white marble firebreast, the library was breathtaking. The tall mahogany stacks, which rose above a dazzling Persian carpet, were filled to overflowing with books and portfolios.

The entire house was well kept, every stick of furniture was polished to a glossy sheen, and not a speck of dust was evident. She had a sinking feeling that Griffin might not require another servant, not if the ones he employed were so efficient.

The kitchen was warmed by the fire blazing in the hearth and enlivened by the dozen or so copper pans that hung against the whitewashed walls. Mr. Bucket was sitting at a long pine table, reading a racing form. Beside him a young man, also in honey brown livery, was making short work of a plate of eggs and kippers. Gates steeled herself in the doorway, preparing to be her most genial, obsequious, and obliging self. Both men rose as she approached the table.

"I have come to receive my work assignment," she said with a tiny curtsy.

Mr. Bucket looked confused. "Miss?"

"I can wash dishes," she added brightly. "And polish and buff. Oh, and I can cook."

The chef turned his sallow, narrow-boned face toward her and muttered something darkly in French.

She moved closer to the pot he was furiously stirring and sniffed the air. "*Mmm,* that smells like the fishhead soup I used to make for my brothers."

Mr. Bucket whisked her at once from the kitchen and into the hallway.

"I believe if my master wanted you to work," he said, "he'd have instructed me to that effect."

Gates was bewildered. "But you must surely have some duties for me to perform."

He shook his head. "Robert and I manage very well without outside help," he proclaimed.

"Oh, yes, I can see that. This place is much better looked after than Lord Pettibone's house."

There was a distinct softening of Bucket's expression. "Perhaps you might like to walk in the garden, miss, until my master comes downstairs."

Gates nodded. She went out through the kitchen entrance and up the shallow steps that led to the garden. Plenty of work for her here, she noted. The house may have been shipshape, but it was apparent Mr. Bucket's domestic talents did not extend beyond its four walls. The bricked paths of the garden were overhung with broken blossoms and rife with weeds, and several rose trellises were coming down from the brick walls. She made her way down the winding path, past a charming gazebo—which badly needed a coat of paint—to an arched gateway at the rear of the garden. Beyond the gate was a cobbled lane where a small stone stable lay, its double doors opened to the morning sun.

Farrow was moving about inside, forking hay into one of the stalls. Back at Bellaire he'd always had a kind word for her, and he now offered her a welcoming smile.

"Morning, miss," he called out. "You're up and about early."

"Hello, Mr. Farrow," she said. Six sleepy-eyed horses watched her approach from over the tops of their stalls. Gaspar, who stood nearest the door, let out a whicker. She reached out to scratch his ears.

"He recalls you, I see."

"He thinks I've brought him a treat," she said. "I've nothing for you, greedy fellow."

"Here," Farrow said, stepping up beside the horse's head. "He likes this even more than a treat."

He showed her how to rub the indentations above Gaspar's eyes with the ball of her thumb. She watched the horse's eyes close in pure equine bliss and then smiled at the groom over Gaspar's long nose. When Farrow offered her a grin in return, Gates was instantly struck by its similarity to another, much-beloved grin—Griffin's. The fleeting but distinct resemblance was uncanny.

She wondered if Farrow might have been a by-blow of Griffin's grandfather. He was built along the same spare, muscular lines as Griffin and was of a similar height. Though his graying hair had once been blond, it was impossible to tell if it had matched the golden honey shade of the Darrowby brothers.

But when he cocked his head at her, curious over her lengthy silence, she saw that his eyes were a bright, grassy green. Gates knew that all the Darrowby men had blue eyes.

"Sorry, Mr. Farrow," she said, dropping her hands from the horse's warm face. "I was just woolgathering. I suppose you have worked for Mr. Darrowby a long time."

"Since he was born," he said. "I worked for his father, actually, until young Mr. Griffin left home."

Gaspar shifted restlessly, annoyed by this sudden neglect, and a shaft of sunlight struck his gleaming red coat. Gates leaned over the stall door, peering at the numerous whirls of white hair that laced his sides. She'd not noticed them when she'd unsaddled him at the farm or in the shadowed stall at Bellaire.

"When did that happen?" she asked, pointing to the strange markings.

Farrow moved away from her, his genial manner suddenly gone. "Best ask my master," he said gruffly. "Not my place to speak of it."

Gates watched him move off toward the back of the stable. She knew the marks on Gaspar's side were scars, long healed and grown over with gray hair. They had been inflicted by someone who cared very little for another creature's suffering. She wondered how Griff had allowed such a thing, and it was a testament to her faith in him that she never allowed he might be the one responsible.

Griffin was fighting off a headache as he sat, now blessedly, alone in the dining room. It had been impossible to keep the peace between Cort and Scotty at breakfast—they brangled with each other incessantly. In the past, the three Darrowby brothers had rarely sat down to a meal all together. Before his disastrous wager, Cort had kept a suite of rooms in Kensington. He had moved into Griff's town house unannounced while Griff was in Cheshire. Westcott had arrived only days after Griff's return. His term at Oxford had been interrupted by a severe outbreak of measles and he'd implored his brother to take him in, insisting he'd rather stay in London than return to their mother at Darrowby.

Though he could well understand that sentiment, Griff's first instinct had been to refuse. He had stopped hankering after either brother's company years before and, in spite of occasional encounters with Cort in London and infrequent visits from Scotty when he was in town with his mother, Griff had little fraternal feeling for them. But they were family, after all, and he reckoned it was time he started taking an interest in their lives.

He had also known that housing his brothers would serve to scotch any rumors of his financial ruin—a man on the verge of penury did not invite his relatives to sponge off him. So he had overridden his misgivings and agreed to Scotty's request.

Now after three weeks in their company, Griffin was regretting his decision. His once-tranquil home had become a battleground. The two argued on every topic and seemed to come to blows over mere trifles. That this was a normal state between siblings and had no bearing on their affection for each other never occurred to Griffin. He was unable to detect the strong bond behind their discord, in spite of the fact that Cort was forever dragging his younger brother off to cockfights and gaming hells.

The butler entered the room and coughed to gain his master's attention.

"Yes, Bucket, what is it? You needn't creep about like that."

"The young lady has come downstairs, sir, and has asked me to apprise her of her duties." Bucket squirmed slightly. "I was not sure what you intended for her, sir. That is, what you planned . . ."

"I take your meaning," Griff interrupted him with a scowl. "I will speak with her."

"She is in the garden at present. I sent her from the kitchen . . . she was making Marchand nervous."

That's all it requires, Griff though irritably as he went in search of his charge. His French chef was temperamental at best, and downright sullen at worst. And if Miss Underhill had put him out of twig, everyone in the household would suffer the culinary consequences.

He spied Gates at the far end of the garden, deadheading chrysanthemums. He stopped beside the gazebo to assess the effect of her new clothing from a proper distance. The gown was a bit large, having been fashioned for a woman who'd been eating regular meals. It was also insipid, with its flounced hem and high, lace-trimmed bodice. Not at all the sort of dress Griffin preferred on a woman.

He'd had some vague hope when he purchased the damned thing that it would lend the girl a modicum of demureness. He needed her demure if he was to spend a month with her and not succumb to his incipient lust. The dress was all he expected, but Gates still looked like an enticing wood sprite.

Regardless of how she was dressed—in rags or serge or bland muslin—she sent his body into a humming state of physical awareness. She was not beautiful, not in the classical style of a Minerva Stargrove, but she had something, perhaps the rich olive tones of her skin or the oblique slant of her Levantine eyes, that was equally potent. Though she'd trapped her hair neatly behind her ears, it insisted on being curly and waving with less-than-ladylike abandon, as if it had been tousled by the hand of a lover.

Griffin growled softly in frustration. Gates looked up from her pruning and gave him a wide smile.

"Miss Underhill, I want to speak with you." His voice sounded, even to his own ears, icy and remote.

Her smile faltered at his tone. "Yes, of course. I've started on your garden, but you need to tell me what my other duties will be."

"There are several things we need to discuss. Will you come inside?"

She dutifully followed him into his small study, which lay beyond the library. It was clearly a man's room, she saw, redolent with the scent of tobacco and the faintest hint of horses. She imagined him coming here straight from riding, to do his accounts or to write letters. There was a spectacular inkwell at the corner of the desk, shaped like a writhing dragon. Its bronze scales glistened in the soft light, and Gates fancied it was captivating enough to be in contention for her daily miracle.

Griffin motioned her to one of the two armchairs, and then sat down at the desk. He lifted a wrapped parcel from its surface and passed it to her. "These are the things you left behind at Lord Pettibone's house. His footman brought them around this morning."

"Oh," she said, with some surprise as she placed the parcel on her lap. "Thank you. He was so angry at me, I'm surprised he didn't burn them." Her eyes darkened. "But how did he know to send them here?"

"I sought him out last night at his club and warned him not to make trouble for you."

"W-was he going to?" She had blanched slightly.

"He'd sworn out a warrant for your arrest." He added quickly, "But you are in no danger, Gates. I made him promise to drop the charges. All it took was a bit of . . . friendly blackmail."

"I'm sorry you had to resort to such a thing."

"The ends justify the means," he replied. "His behavior toward you that night went beyond what is acceptable. I was not going to allow him to compound it with trumped-up threats."

This is not about me, Gates murmured to herself, the realization tearing at her heart. What a fool she was to have thought it, even for a moment. Griffin Darrowby was retaliating against Lord Pettibone because the man was his rival for Lady Minerva. The game they had been playing at Bellaire, jockeying with each other for favor with that lady, had now merely moved to London.

She knotted her fingers above the parcel. "Again, I must thank you for your concern. And now you must tell me what my duties will be while I am here. And where I will be sleeping."

Griff cocked one eye at her. "The room you are in displeases you?"

"Of course not, how could it? But I am aware you only put me there because you thought I was ill. Even I know that servants do not sleep in guest rooms."

He blew out his breath in exasperation. "Will you stop this nonsense, Gates. You put poor Bucket off his feed this morning, tagging after him in the kitchen and asking for work. Why the devil do you persist in thinking yourself a servant in this house?"

Gates felt her throat close up. "It is what I am," she said

hoarsely, avoiding his gaze by focusing her eyes on the splendidly barbaric inkwell. "What else would I be?"

Griffin dug his left hand into the folds of his neckcloth and tugged until the pristine fabric was creased beyond repair. "What you are," he said gruffly, "is a damnable inconvenience, a lone chick among the foxes. But you are not—and I will say this only once—a servant in this house. For one thing, I do not employ females . . . I have something of a reputation in the *ton,* and most women would prefer to work for less . . . notorious employers."

"Like Lord Pettibone, you mean," she said with a pronounced sneer.

"Yes, well, it seems I have flaunted my . . . um, indiscretions, while he—"

"Creeps about like a slithering reptile," Gates finished for him with a great deal of heat.

Griffin chuckled. "Indeed. And he frightens my friends, which I find intolerable."

Her head shot up. "He frightened someone else you know?"

It was no use; he couldn't prevent himself from laying the back of his hand gently against her cheek. He'd manufactured a nice testy head of steam to keep her at arm's length, but all it took was one plaintive look from those beguiling elfin eyes, and his resolve was dust.

"I was speaking about you, my little turnip."

"Oh." Her eyes went from clouded and doubting to brightly jubilant in an instant. He didn't want to see that stunning transformation, he certainly didn't want to be the cause of it. He wasn't interested in her damned admiration.

"And that answers your earlier question," he said as he drew his hand away. "About your status in this house. You are my friend and, therefore, my guest. If you can contrive to amuse my aunt and distract my brothers from fratricide, I will consider my hospitality well repaid."

Gates mulled this over and then drew a steadying breath. "I cannot stay here, not if you won't let me work for you. It isn't fitting." Her eyes flashed briefly. "But I am not without resources; I'm sure I can find other work in the city. So thank you for your kind offer, but since I arrived here uninvited I am unable to accept your . . . hospitality. It's just that I needed a place to go that night, and I thought . . ." Her voice grew husky. "I thought you wouldn't mind so much if I came to you."

He was minding less with every passing minute. "That's not an issue, Gates. You found yourself in a bad way and were wise to seek me out. And now I must decide what is best for you."

She bristled noticeably at his presumption. "And what have *you* decided?"

"Don't say it in such a way. You must admit I have a slightly wider experience of the world. You are no match for the depravities of London—your encounter with Lord Pettibone is proof of that. You can't know this, but callow country girls are the usual fodder for the bawdy houses in this town." He winced slightly, recalling that he had often sampled such women—newly deflowered and eager to please for the price of a few coins. It was unthinkable that Gates might find herself in such a situation.

"You are not being fair," she said with a frown. "I may have been foolishly trusting of Lord Pettibone, but you can be sure I won't ever make that mistake again. I will not assume a man to be honorable merely because he is a gentleman. Well, not unless he has proven himself to me, as you have done."

Griffin wondered if the heat he felt creeping up from his throat could possibly be a blush. He pivoted around to toy with his letter opener. "If you trust me, Gates, then you must let me guide you. I have a position in mind, one which will offer you security and financial reward."

"I don't understand; if I'm to go to work for someone else, why can't I stay here and work for you?"

"It's not open for discussion" he said stiffly. "But it will take some time to work out the details of my plan. In the meantime, this is your home."

"My home is in Cheshire!" she cried, rising to her feet and clasping the parcel to her breast. "And if you won't employ me, then I shall return there."

"The devil you will!" He was on his feet now. "I am trying to help you, you ungrateful girl."

"I d-don't require your help," she stuttered miserably. She needed to end this interview now, before the lurking tears overwhelmed her. He had not spoken to her so harshly since that day on the farm.

"Please turn around," she said. A puzzled furrow appeared on his brow. "Please," she repeated, motioning with one hand. "Just turn away for a moment."

After he did as she asked, she quickly hiked up the hem of her gown until her fingers found the small pocket she had pinned to her new chemise. She drew out the gold and jet buttons and laid them on the desk. When he turned back to her, she pointed to them and watched as his eyes narrowed in confusion.

"I came to London . . . to return these," she said haltingly. "Because the Underhills do not take charity, and because I still owe you for the money and jewelry my brothers stole from you. I went to Bellaire to return the gold ones, but I got distracted." She smiled at him wanly. "And then you . . . you left these other five, which more than doubled my obligation to you. You should know that I . . . I do not require anything from you, Mr. Darrowby. Except perhaps your good opinion."

She fled then, scurrying out of his study without another word. He wanted to call after her, tell her that they had been a gift, not blasted charity. But she was gone and the shadows in the room seemed to deepen with her departure.

He flicked at the buttons with his finger and felt something unfamiliar shift inside him.

All his life people had taken from him. His mother had taken his two young brothers, whisked them out of his life. His father had taken his confidence and, sometimes Griffin feared, his soul. The army had taken his idealism. And Helene had taken his innocence, though he had gratefully offered that gift at the time. There was not one person in the *ton,* he reckoned, who did not want something from him—friends required his advice on investments, ladybirds desired his caresses and the contents of his purse, and marriageable young misses sought after the status of his ancient name. One of Minerva Stargrove's greatest charms had been that she seemed to want nothing from him. Now he knew she required the ultimate offering—his undying love.

Yet this half-tamed girl, this plain-speaking parson's brat, who had so little expectation from life that she thought nothing of sleeping on a stone floor, had returned to him a small fortune in jeweled buttons. Because all she wanted from him was his good opinion.

"Ah, Gates," he whispered as he scooped up the baubles and dropped them into his desk drawer. She was not going to make this easy for him—he wondered if he had the stamina required to seduce a saint.

*   *   *

Gates threw herself across the bed, fighting back her tears. She refused to be overset by her interview with Griffin. Even if he'd frowned at her in the garden as though she were a hat he had just purchased and was having second thoughts about. Or called her an inconvenience and implied she was a hapless bumpkin. These were not reasons to turn into a watering pot. So what if he wouldn't consider letting her work in his home? He had every right to that decision. She had no desire to behave like the butcher's boy in Paultons, who threw himself at every turn in the path of the mayor's pretty daughter. The lad's lovestruck antics had been a source of great amusement to the villagers.

With a sinking heart, Gates realized that must be exactly how she appeared to Griffin. A pitiful, moonstruck girl who had aspirations far above her station. She had no refinements, no graces. Her only claim to gentility was a severed connection to a Cornish family whom she had actively detested since the death of her mother. She doubted that tenuous connection would raise her up in Griffin's eyes. In her experience, people judged you by your present circumstances, not by your distant relations.

She'd do better to stop mourning the loss of Griffin's kindness and begin making plans to return to Cheshire. Sir Thomas's coins were still in her hidden pocket; he'd assured her there was enough for coach fare to his home. Once she was at Burgh Hall she would immerse herself in her studies and help Sir Thomas with his accounts. Then, surely, the memory of Griffin Darrowby, the man who'd held her in his arms in a musty tack room and made her feel like the light of his world, would completely fade away.

Chapter Ten

After indulging in a short fit of weeping, Gates forced herself to get up. Though she had no intention of staying on in this house, she distracted herself by sorting out the contents of the parcel—which took all of two minutes. She hung her muslin dress in the wardrobe and placed her silver hairbrush on the wide dresser, beside the tortoise-shell one that a kind soul had left there for her use. She tucked her paint box under the night table, and then settled down in the chair nearest the window to read her volume of Homer. Maybe the mythic problems of Odysseus would put her own petty concerns into perspective.

Very soon thereafter she heard a thudding and banging out in the hallway, accompanied by the sound of muffled cursing. Ten minutes passed and the noises repeated themselves. Unable to contain her curiosity, she set down her book and went to peek out the door.

Griff's brothers and Robert, the footman, were trooping past, laden down with luggage, birdcages, and at least three large potted plants. A tall woman in a vivid green traveling costume followed in their wake, calling out orders in a brisk, flinty voice.

"Be careful, Wescott. If you drop my birds, I'll boil you in oil. Cortland, those aspidistras need to be kept upright. *Tcht,* you've spilled the dirt all over the carpet. Set the trunk down here, Robert. Good fellow. You seem to be the only one in this house with any brains."

"Thought this required brawn," Gates heard Cort grumble as they vanished into the room next door.

So this was the peppery Miss Darrowby who was going to take her in charge.

Gates thought it fortunate that she was leaving for Cheshire in the morning. She would not have to worry about pleasing this formidable woman, whose gunnery sergeant's voice could be heard barking orders through the common wall. Gates suffered a momentary pang of guilt—the lady had clearly turned her own household upside down to come here on a pointless mission.

Gates sighed. She was herself now well acquainted with pointless missions.

*   *   *

"We've got to tell Griffin," Westcott said, tugging at his brother's sleeve.

The two were in the gazebo hiding from their aunt—in case she needed more heavy lifting done. Cort turned away from the railing. "It ain't the right time, Scotty. Lord, I wish I hadn't read the letter Mother sent him while he was off in Cheshire."

Westcott rolled his eyes. "Don't gammon me, Cort. You've been prying open other people's mail since you were breeched. You were probably hoping there was some money in it."

Cort snorted softly. "Money? From the Gorgon? Don't be an idiot."

"Well, if she was a nipfarthing before, just think what she'll be like now that she's lost her entire jointure to bad investments."

"What she'll be," Cort intoned, "is planted on Griff's doorstep, cajoling him into supporting her."

"You'd know about that," he quipped, and then ducked when Cort reached out to cuff his head.

"Which is why you are going to write a letter to her, in Griff's hand, fobbing her off for a few months. Tell her she can sell some of her jewels, if she needs to. But I don't want her coming here—once she shows her face in London and starts hobnobbing with her friends, half the *ton* will know she's rolled up. And that could jeopardize Griff's chances with Lady Minerva."

"But he's flush, Cort. He's made a pile of money on his own in spite of getting nothing from Father's estate. So what if the Gorgon's lost her income? Griff could probably pay her debts and keep her in pin money with what he loses at faro in one night."

Cort's good-natured face turned somber. "I wasn't going to tell you this—I found several other letters in his desk. Very distressing letters. While he was in Spain, he instructed Pendleton to purchase shares in a mining company in India. There was a landslide in the spring—half the mountain came down upon the mine works and now the entire operation's been abandoned. There were other losses, as well, from shipping and farming. I'm afraid Griff's rolled up too, Scotty."

Shocked disbelief shone in his brother's eyes. "He isn't behaving as though he'd lost his blunt."

"He wouldn't now, would he. Got to keep up appearances at all costs. Especially since he won't want Lady Minerva to think him a fortune hunter. Which is why he mustn't learn about our mother's disaster—we can't let anything distract him from the rich widow, not before he returns to her in November. She's going to be the saving of the Darrowbys."

Wescott wrinkled his nose. "It sounds rather cold-blooded. I fancy Lady Minerva won't be happy when she discovers she's married into a family of paupers. Well, I mean, you and I will get our trust funds when we turn twenty-five, but that paltry sum isn't enough to bring Griffin to rights."

"If our trust funds are even intact," Cort said darkly. "For all we know, the Gorgon's been helping herself to our blunt."

"Jiminy," Scotty whispered, reduced to a childhood expletive at the thought of losing his much-anticipated inheritance.

"Exactly," Cort said. "Now you'd best write to her instanter. She wrote again this week—I, er, intercepted her letter before Griff saw it. But she's spitting nails that he didn't answer her first one."

"I'll do it, but only under protest. And I promise I won't say a word to Griffin. Still, you'd best burn Mother's letters—he'll have our heads if he ever discovers we knew about this and didn't tell him."

"He'll be wed to the fair Minerva by then," Cort said with a sly wink, "and much too busy entertaining his lady wife to waste any time on his brothers."

Half an hour after the disruption in the hall, Gates was roused from her Homer by a soft knocking; Robert called out, "Miss Darrowby would like to speak to you, miss." He offered her a sheepish smile when she opened the door. "In a bit of a mood, she is."

She grinned back. "So I heard."

"Chin up," he said before he moved off, tugging the lady's trunk behind him. It echoed hollowly as it thudded along in his wake.

She took a deep breath and tiptoed down the hall. The door to Miss Darrowby's room was ajar, and Gates went inside cautiously. The lady was ensconced in a wide armchair, surrounded by her birdcages and a veritable forest of leafy plants.

"My lady," Gates said as she performed a wobbling curtsy.

"I am not your lady, gel," the woman responded tartly. "I am nobody's lady, thank goodness. I am Delphinia Darrowby of Greenwich. Now come closer and let me have a look at you." She spent several long seconds observing Gates and then grunted softly to herself. "I'm not surprised. Not surprised at all."

"Ma'am?" Gates was still feeling shaky from her interview with Griffin and wondered if it would be proper to sit down. "Shall I fetch you a footstool?"

Before she could reply, Gates had tucked a petit-point stool beneath her feet. Then she crouched there on the rug, watching as Miss Darrowby lifted a tangle of skeined wool and knitting needles from her lap and began knitting furiously.

"I never like to waste a minute of my time," she pronounced as she held up the partially completed scarf. "This is for one of my girls."

Gates was puzzled; she was sure Griffin's aunt was a maiden lady. "How many girls do you have?" she asked politely.

"A dozen at least in the home where I do my charity work."

"Oh, charity work," Gates said under her breath.

"Poor things they are, fresh from the country most of them. Caught in the coils of wicked men and then left alone when they find themselves in . . . an interesting condition. And when the babies come, there is no one to look after the poor mites, for the mothers as often as not return to the streets."

Gates nodded sagely. She now knew that getting into an interesting condition was the same as being with child—she'd had that insight the night she fled from Lord Pettibone. Her poor, banished predecessor had likely been another of his lordship's late-night victims.

She cocked her head. "Why would they want to be on the streets? Wouldn't they be better off staying inside?"

Delphinia lowered her knitting and gave Gates a narrow-eyed stare. "Griffin said you were a naif, but I fear he understated the case."

With a little chirp of discontent, Gates wrapped her arms around her knees. "I am all that and more."

"It's nothing that can't be cured," Miss Darrowby said encouragingly. "Now stop lolling about on the floor, child, and sit in a chair like a civilized person." Gates did as she was ordered, settling herself on a spindle-backed side chair. "And stop fretting with your cuffs . . . and put your feet together, for heaven's sake. You're sprawled there like a lad."

Gates pulled herself upright, slid her toes together, and clasped her hands in her lap.

"I see that you're a biddable creature," Delphinia observed.

"Not inside my head I'm not," Gates muttered.

The woman gave a startled chuckle. "Well, well. Now that's a sentiment I can share. Sometimes it's better to keep mum, eh? Best not to rile those around us. But you simmer, don't you, young miss?"

Gates looked at her blankly for an instant and then offered her a guilty smile. "Yes. Sometimes."

"That means you've got a bit of spine. Can't abide females without spine. Can't abide a lot of things. Idleness, for instance." She locked her gaze onto Gates and pronounced, "You can't stay on here—"

"I know that," Gates interjected. "I am planning to return to Cheshire in the morning."

Miss Darrowby snorted. "Are you indeed? I fancy that's news to my nephew. He said you'd be here at least a month. Until he could find you—"

"I will find my own situations," Gates said crossly, interrupting her again. "I was reared by a man who thought he knew what was best for me, and all it ever got me was a bed in a hedgerow." Miss Darrowby's brows rose alarmingly. "I will never again let a man direct my course. Not father, or brother, or interfering Darrowby of Darrowby."

The lady grinned at her. "Well said, Miss Underhill! I see we have a great deal in common. But since I have uprooted myself and my birds to come here and look after you, I think you should reconsider your plans. What is a mere month in the scheme of things? Perhaps in that time I can find something that appeals to you in the way of occupation."

Gates was now totally bewildered. "But you just said I cannot stay here."

"You never let me finish, Miss Impetuous. I was saying that you cannot stay here unless you make yourself useful."

Gates's head shot up.

"That's what you're accustomed to, isn't it? Griffin tells me you are a parson's daughter—serving others should come naturally. I could use someone like you in my charity work." She fastened her blue eyes on Gates. "Now tell me about yourself, Miss Underhill, and especially how you came to be running tame in my wicked nephew's house. And don't be afraid to shock me . . . I got over being missish when I turned fifteen. I am particularly interested in hearing about the hedgerows."

Gates related her personal history with very little embellishment. She kept her voice steady and prayed there was no hint of her true feelings for Griffin in her tone. At one point, early in her narrative, the older woman's eyes widened in shocked surprise. Gates stopped speaking then and looked at her expectantly, but the lady said nothing, just motioned her to continue.

When Gates was finished, the woman's long face bore a thoughtful expression." I suspect there are things you've told me here that you've not told my nephew."

Gates shrugged. "I've told him, Miss Darrowby. But he doesn't always attend me."

"Then I would not edify him. Men do best with the least amount of information. Otherwise it taxes their pitiful brains. Now, what have you decided? Will you stay and help me with my girls?"

"Yes, Miss Darrowby," Gates said intently, holding back her jubilation at this reprieve. She truly had no desire to return to the farm, and even if she and Griffin had lost their easy camaraderie, at least she would be sharing this house with him. "I would be pleased to assist you. It will give me a chance to repay your kindness in coming here."

"And," the lady added, "it would also offer you a distraction."

"From what?" Gates asked cautiously.

Miss Darrowby smiled gently. "Why, from whatever it is that has made you cry, my dear."

"Oh." Gates lowered her head and rubbed at her nose. "I expect I am just a bit blue-deviled."

"And no wonder, living among these savages. But never fear, I will make sure you are looked after. My first order of business is to see that you get something to eat. You are as thin as a coatrack. Luncheon should be laid out by now." She set aside her knitting, then stood up and held out her hand to Gates. "We'd best go downstairs, before those rascally boys have taken all the best tidbits."

She leapt to her feet. "You want me to d-dine with you? With Mr. Darrowby and his brothers?"

The lady huffed. "Of course I do. It's only fitting if you are to be my companion."

"I could eat in my room," Gates suggested hopefully.

"Nonsense. Where's your spine, Miss Underhill?"

Gates gave her a rueful grin. "I believe I left it back in Cheshire."

*   *   *

Griffin entered the dining room, took up a plate, and began to fill it from the chafing dishes at the sideboard. Unless he was entertaining he dined informally at breakfast and luncheon, to save wear and tear on his small staff. Since he did not consider his brothers guests, he hadn't changed the protocol after their arrival. And Delphie was certainly not one to stand on ceremony.

His brothers came in as he was seating himself at the long mahogany table.

"Wilby tells me you went to Rippon's last night," Cort remarked, as he lifted the lid off a compote of oysters. "I've never been there—a bit above my touch these days."

"I should think so," Griffin said dryly. "But I didn't go there to play." His brothers turned to him. "I went there to speak to Pettibone. He was going to press charges against Miss Underhill for the theft of his shawl."

Cort was sniggering when Griffin's eyes speared him. "It is not in the least amusing, Cortland," he uttered in a voice of ice. "Thieves are still hung in this country, or have you forgotten? Often for any item costing more than five pounds. Pettibone reckoned that cashmere shawl was worth at least fifteen."

"You paid him, I expect?" Scotty ventured.

He shook his head slowly. "No, I told him if he dared to bring charges against her, I would drop the hint in all my clubs that I had caught him cheating at cards. He eventually backed down."

"Had you caught him cheating?" Cort asked.

Griff's eyes narrowed. "Not exactly. That's the best part, because he obviously has been."

"Well, I'll never sit down to cards with him again," Cort declared stoutly. "Not that I ever liked the fellow. I believe he dyes his hair."

Griffin chuckled unexpectedly, and then reapplied himself to his meal.

Delphie came in a short while later, followed by Miss Underhill. Griffin had not expected to see the girl so soon after the unpleasantness in his study and he felt himself tense. It never occurred to him that his aunt would ask her to dine with them. But then he himself had told Gates she would not be treated as a servant. He just hadn't counted on having to sit across from her at his own table.

He schooled his face into a polite smile. "Ladies," he said as he rose from his seat.

"Sorry we're late," Delphie said. "Miss Underhill required some convincing. Didn't think it proper."

From the look on the girl's face, she might have been facing a court of inquisition.

"What would be proper, Miss Underhill," he said lightly, "would be for you to sit down and have some of this delightful salmon my overpriced chef has prepared. I expect you recall my brothers—Cortland is the one wearing that atrocious neckcloth, and Westcott is the one hiding a book under the table."

Griffin coughed meaningfully, and both young men quickly rose to their feet and nodded in her direction. Gates saw the puzzled expressions in their eyes. They knew, even if their brother didn't, that farm girls were not invited to sit at the table with gentlemen.

As she slid stiffly onto the chair he'd pulled out for her, Griff leaned down and said close against her ear, "And, Miss Under-the-hill . . . please try not to break any of my wineglasses. I'm rather fond of them."

She turned her face up to him. "They'll be safe, I promise—I never drink wine."

Once Cort and Wescott heard that, they spent half the meal teasing her to try a sip, until she finally relented. When she realized that the sweet liquid relieved a great deal of her nervousness, she allowed them to refill her glass two more times.

They also showed her how to remove the bones from her salmon, and how to negotiate her way around a standing rack of lamb. When, at the end of the meal, Cort demonstrated how to peel an orange skin in one long, continuous strip, she laughed like a delighted child.

Observing this display, Griff had an inkling his two indolent brothers might have the makings of decent men after all. The girl apparently brought out something benevolent in their natures, the way a playful kitten charmed the crustiest of fellows.

During the meal she had only spoke when she was directly addressed and had not attempted to enter the general conversation that circulated around the table. But it was clear she took in every word. *She's like a little sponge,* he thought, *absorbing new experiences, and with such open appetite.*

Even Delphinia seemed taken with the girl. She coughed discreetly into her napkin when Gates took up the wrong fork for her lamb, and then nodded briefly when she chose the proper one. A minor exchange, but one that surprised Griffin. Delphie may have fled from her Darrowby roots but she was as self-centered in her own way as any Darrowby born.

Griffin now watched Gates as she attempted to duplicate Cort's feat with her own orange. After she'd succeeded in peeling a snakelike whirligig of skin from the fruit, she held it up for his approval. Her wide, victorious smile made her eyes dance. It also made the blood race from his head to his belly and back again, in a rapid, dizzying swoop. And the result of that tumultuous jolt was a stirring in his lower body that he could do little to prevent.

This is not going to work, he thought irritably. Not if he had to sit across from her three times a day, and constantly fight off the insistent clutch of desire. Mealtime would soon become a torture. He wondered where his famous self-control had disappeared to. He'd be a gibbering idiot by the end of a month if he didn't think of a solution. Perhaps an icy bath prior to his meals would do the trick.

He'd be the cleanest gibbering idiot in the kingdom.

After lunch, Delphinia settled in the parlor for a short nap. Griffin and the boys had gone out and her new charge had offered to go upstairs and look in on her canaries.

She had to admit the girl had conducted herself well during the meal in spite of her apparent unease. However, her fledgling table manners were the least of her problems—Miss Underhill had far weightier issues to grapple with.

Really, Delphie grumbled to herself, Griffin must think her a blind old fool if he believed she would swallow his tale—that he was looking after the girl merely because she needed a haven. Darrowby men were not renowned for their charity. And Griffin was a Darrowby to the bone.

No, there was something afoot here between her wayward nephew and this misplaced girl. She had not missed the simmering hunger that flashed in Griffin's eyes every time he let his gaze stray to Miss Underhill. A starving wolf showed less appetite as he circled a spring lamb. But if Delphie had any say in the matter, this particular lamb would not be forfeit.

Not that Miss Underhill would understand the danger she was in. Delphie had to agree with Griffin's assessment—the girl was completely unworldly. And more than likely had no idea of her own allure.

Delphie had expected her to be pretty but she was not. At least not in the spun sugar way that most gentlemen seemed to prefer. Still, Delphie had been struck by the girl's appearance and she knew, furthermore, that there was something beyond a pert nose and china blue eyes that drew a man to a woman. Whatever that ineffable quality was, Gates Underhill possessed it in abundance.

Delphie again wondered why Griffin had asked her here; he knew that she, of all people, would not take her responsibilities as chaperon lightly. Why had he purposely placed an impediment in his own path? Few men of Griffin's cut would balk at seducing an innocent girl, and none would intentionally invite outside interference. Perhaps she misjudged him—she had never known her nephew to be overtly cruel, just casually heartless.

After some consideration, she chalked up Griffin's behavior to the influence of Minerva Stargrove. If he was intent on marrying such a paragon of virtue, he'd need to learn to keep his appetites in check. Even, Delphinia suspected sadly, with his intended.

Delphie was of the opinion that Stargrove's ice-princess widow was not the sort of wife her equally cold-blooded nephew required. Griffin's mother had been such a woman; she had eventually elicited from her husband such icy rage that they had nearly frozen each other to death before the need for warmth sent them both into the arms of lovers.

No, Griffin needed a different consort. Someone who could pierce the armor of remoteness he'd fashioned about himself since childhood. Delphie pondered whether such a creature even existed, and then remembered the smoldering expression in Griffin's eyes when he'd watched Miss Underhill. The heat of desire had flickered there, surely, but she'd also seen another, more tender heat.

It would be a wonderful vindication, she mused, if the lamb turned the tables on the wolf. And she would gladly do her part to help such a reckoning come to pass.

She heaved a sigh that erupted into a tiny belch. It had been foolish to indulge in that second slice of rum torte, she thought sleepily as her chin nodded against her chest.

That night Griffin dined with his brothers at White's. It was a neat way of avoiding both the females in his household. He was still vexed with Delphie for bringing the girl down to lunch and out of charity with Miss Underhill for reasons too numerous to count.

Over their dinner of braised veal, he dropped a few subtle hints to Cort and Scotty regarding the girl. Nothing too heavy-handed, just a nudge to remind them that they were gentlemen first and Darrowbys second. The last thing he wanted was either of his siblings forming an inappropriate attachment to the girl. That was his province.

"What're you getting at, Griff?" Cort asked with irritating thick-headedness as he buttered a roll. "You mean we ain't to dally with the chit? Well, there's no need to warn us off—she's hardly a pocket Venus. More of a harum-scarum miss." Griffin did not observe Cort's sly wink to Westcott.

"That's not quite true," Griffin said, stung into defending the girl. "She has a rough sort of charm."

"I'm certainly not in the petticoat line," Scotty proclaimed. "Thought you knew that, Griff. Though now that you mention it, she does have a dashed pretty pair of—"

"Westcott!" Griff's voice erupted in the quiet dining room.

"Eyes," Scotty finished blandly, trying desperately not to chuckle at Griff's outraged expression.

As the two brothers strolled back to the house—having left Griffin behind with some cronies at White's—they congratulated themselves on drawing him out.

"He's turned prosy as an old maid," Cort said with a frown. "And it's all Miss Underhill's doing."

"I don't mind," Scotty responded. "He's never bothered to lecture us before. It was rather refreshing. Makes me think he might give a tuppence for the two of us after all."

"No," Cort said dolefully. "Makes me think it's Miss Underhill he gives a tuppence for. And that don't march with our plans for Griffin marrying Minerva Stargrove."

Scotty mulled this over. "Did you see how he smiled at lunch when she hid her Brussels sprouts under her napkin? He'd have rapped our knuckles for doing that. Maybe she's good for him, Cort. He never smiles like that over anything we do." His voice softened. "And I wish he would, you know. It only makes me think how wretched his life must have been living with Father for all those years."

Cort grunted. "No worse than our years with the Gorgon. I'd take a brute over a nipfarthing any day."

Scotty kept his own counsel on the matter; he hadn't forgotten his tenure at Darrowby and the fear that had been his daily companion. He was only surprised that Cort had been able to dismiss those phantoms. "Well," he said, "what's to be done with her? At least she's presentable now that Griffin's tricked her out in a decent gown."

"But why is he spending so much blunt on her, if she's to be sent off to serve in some lord's household eventually?"

The young man put his head back. "I think I know the reason, but you're not going to like it."

Cort's brows converged. "You ain't suggesting he's going to marry the chit, are you? That's preposterous. She hasn't a feather to fly with, for one thing."

"True enough. But remember what I just said—he barely took his eyes off her at lunch."

Cort mulled this over as they walked. "It's possible he has other, er, plans for her. But, no, if he had dalliance in mind, he'd not have brought Delphie here. Lord, we'd best make sure to keep her out of his way, just in case he is forming a *tendre* for her."

"We could fill up her days with the sights of London," Scotty said. "You know, take her to Astley's and show her the Tower Menagerie."

Cort still looked doubtful. "I can see," he moaned, "that this is going to be a deuced lot of work."

To Griff's dismay, his aunt was waiting for him in the front parlor. It was nearly one o'clock, but she looked bright-eyed and chipper. He couldn't know that her frequent daytime naps made her a veritable night owl. He slouched onto the couch opposite her and prepared to be browbeaten.

She merely smiled softly and said, "Leaving us to dine alone tonight was a bit cowardly, don't you think? Miss Underhill is now convinced you don't want her at your table."

"I don't," he stated flatly. "I assumed she would continue to dine in her room. But I shall bear up under the stress. At least I am relieved to see that you have properly taken her in hand."

"And a good thing too. She was planning to return to Cheshire tomorrow morning, though by what means, I cannot guess."

He rolled his eyes and heaved a weary sigh. "Knowing Miss Underhill, she would likely cadge a ride from a loose screw and end up on her back in a hedge tavern." It took him several seconds to banish the unpleasant and highly inflammatory image of Gates being tumbled by a stranger. "So, what has made her change her mind?" he asked at last.

"She is going to help me with my charity work; I expect she will prove herself quite useful."

"Fine," he said as he shifted to his feet. "Anything that keeps her out from underfoot."

Delphie tipped her head back. "I've written to several of my friends, mentioning I had a young female connection who required genteel employment. Just to get things rolling, you know."

Griffin's jaw tightened. "I will see to her future, Delphie. You needn't concern yourself with it."

She opened her mouth to protest, but he had already headed for the door.

The following morning, Gates repaired to the garden after breakfast, bearing a rusted pair of shears and wearing a tattered pair of canvas gloves, which she'd unearthed from one of the kitchen cupboards. Griffin had specifically told her she was not to toil inside the house, but she didn't think he would object if she set his garden in order. Furthermore, she had several times seen Lady Minerva snipping blossoms among the late roses at Bellaire, so gardening was surely an unobjectionable occupation for a lady. Gates was nothing if not observant.

She was wrestling with a wayward trellis at the rear of the garden when she heard the sound of raised voices coming from the gazebo—Cort and Scotty, arguing over something. The words "marriage" and "money" drifted over the heads of the plants. Gates continued her clipping and pruning, listening with one ear to the brothers' halfhearted brangling. She could see that Westcott had carried his schoolbooks into the gazebo and was attempting to study. Cort, meanwhile, was stacking the books into towers on the planked floor and then knocking them down.

"Stop that!" Scotty finally snapped. "How can I concentrate on Latin declensions when you are crawling around my boots like a toddler?"

"Latin?" Gates asked, coming up the shallow steps.

"It's a language," Scotty explained.

"A dead language," Cort added sourly as he got to his feet. "And rightly so."

"I always enjoyed Latin," Gates said as she peered over Scotty's shoulder. She pointed to a sentence that he had scrawled on his pad. "But I believe you have used the wrong word there in that paragraph about Plato tutoring Alexander the Great. His name should be *Alexandrum,* not *Alexanderum.*"

Both brothers were goggling at her.

"What?" she said, once she'd noticed their incredulous expressions. "Oh, I am sorry. I shouldn't be bothering you?" She stepped back abruptly, but Cort caught her by the arm.

"How the devil do you know Latin, Miss Underhill? However Griffin sees fit to treat you in this house, you were a tweeny in Pettibone's home. Never heard of a tweeny that could read Latin."

Scotty set down his pad and stood up. "Griff said you're not much of a scholar. Show's what he knows. Have you been at school, Miss Underhill?"

"No," she said. "My father taught me at home. English and a bit of Latin. Before he received the calling to preach he was a lawyer. And my mother taught me my sums and how to play the pianoforte." She then recalled Miss Darrowby's suggestion that she not speak of her background. "But you must not tell your brother. Please. He might not like it."

"*You* are a very silly girl," Cort stated.

"Yes, but one who knows Latin better than I do," Wescott interjected, with a smile for Gates.

Cort spun on him. "What I meant, dash it all, is that she is foolish to think Griffin would mind."

"My father minded," she said with a sigh. "I had to go behind his back to continue my lessons."

"Griff thinks your father's dicked in the nob, to have gone off and left you," Cort remarked.

Gates drew herself up. "I know exactly what Mr. Darrowby thinks of my family. And especially his views on my father."

"They're no worse than what he thinks of his own father," Scotty said soothingly. "But Parson Underhill does sound a bit daft. If you were my daughter I'd take better care of you. Er, well . . . that is, if you take my meaning."

"Thank you, Scotty," she said. "I do take your meaning and it was very nicely said. You have all been so kind. I only wish there was more for me to do here, to repay you in some way. But what does your brother do? He buys me pretty dresses and sits me down at the table with his family."

"We ain't that bad company," Cort muttered.

"She is not complaining," Scotty said as an aside. "She means she didn't expect to be treated so well, and it's confusing her. Just think how you would feel in such a situation. Going from tweeny to young lady in the space of one day."

"Never been either thing," his brother replied. "Wouldn't want to be, especially not a tweeny."

Scotty sighed and offered Gates a facsimile of Griff's rueful grin. "See? See what I have to put up with, Miss Underhill?"

She grinned back at him, unable to help it—he looked so much like his elder brother at that moment.

"I think you make a rather nice young lady," Scotty added. "And if your father was a lawyer, then you are a gentleman's daughter. Perhaps you should reflect on that. I wager your mother was from a similar background, as well."

Gates sighed. "No, Mama was from a very different station in life than my father."

Both brothers looked sympathetic and Cort said briskly, "Well, it ain't the first time a man married out of his class, I daresay."

Before she could think of a response, Delphie came marching into the garden and announced to Gates that the modiste had arrived to take her measurements. Gates looked back at her blankly.

"You require several more dresses," Delphinia explained. "And a wrap."

Gates turned to the brothers. "Will you come with me . . . I am not sure I know what to do."

Before they could respond, Delphie had taken her by the hand and was hauling her toward the house. "Honestly," she huffed. "More hair than brains, this one."

Cort glanced at his brother, who was watching Miss Underhill's departure with amused regret. "Astley's it is," he murmured sourly as if accepting the verdict of his own beheading. " 'Cause if Griff's buying her gowns, there's no telling what he has planned for her."

Gates suffered her fitting with fair patience; overlooking the occasional pinpricks and the modiste's tickling fingers. Miss Darrowby hovered in the background like a general on a ridge and barked out orders to the harried seamstress. She had quickly scotched the woman's suggestion of insipid whites and pinks, and had instead chosen a sea green muslin sprigged with violets and a deep lavender sarcenet with a pale yellow stripe. She had also ordered a biscuit-colored pelisse, a pair of jean half boots and four pairs of kidskin gloves.

"Autumn weather's coming on," she said to halt Gates's protest. "You need something warm."

"But I have Lord Pettibone's shawl," Gates pointed out.

Delphie saw the modiste's ears prick up, and merely offered Gates a severe, quelling frown.

After luncheon, where Griffin was again conspicuous by his absence, Delphinia whisked Gates off to Whitechapel in a hackney cab. To the Ladies Benevolent Society Home for Fallen Women, to be precise. Gates watched out the window as the elegant streets of Mayfair and the City gave way to the littered, crowded thoroughfares of the East End.

The cramped brick building that housed the charity home was dirty, with small clouded windows and little ventilation. Gates was not surprised that the women who stayed there seemed less than grateful for the attention they received. She imagined many of them had once been prosperous in their chosen profession, and now resented the fact that they were dependent on charity. She knew well enough how that felt.

The gray-uniformed children, who scuttled along the sooty walls, were pale shadows of the robust country children she had known in Cheshire. It wrenched her heart to see them, and she was awkward at first, uncertain of how to win them over. But when one little girl came forward and asked for help with her rag doll, whose cloth leg had come off, Gates quickly appropriated a needle and thread from the dour-faced matron and performed the necessary surgery. By the time she was finished, a whole circle of raggedy children had gathered around her. "More," they said, handing her corners of their skirts or jackets to stitch. She asked each of them their names and then proceeded to embroider their initials on the garments. She suspected not a one of them could read, but they were nonetheless impressed by the brightly stitched emblems. When the matron called the children into the kitchen for their suppers, Gates was sorry to see them go.

"Well," Delphie asked as they walked along Fenchurch Street to look for a cab, "what do you think?"

"I think," Gates said slowly, "that I have been wasting my life in Cheshire."

"You are not repelled then, by the dirt and the poverty?"

"No, I was only wondering when we could come again. I

promised little Jane I would stitch her up a doll like Betsy's. And that rascal James told me he would hold his breath until I returned." Her eyes misted. "How can you bear it, Delphie?" she said, forgetting her manners. "They have so little."

Delphinia patted her hand. "They have people like you and me to help them, my dear. And the ones with a bit of pluck and luck will succeed in life. Not much different from most children, really. You need to bear that in mind for yourself, as well."

"What do you mean?"

"You've got the pluck, Miss Underhill. With a bit of luck thrown in, I fancy you could succeed at anything."

Gates eyed her suspiciously, sensing the lady was referring to something more profound than a choice of occupations. "I am content with my life," Gates countered. "I have no aspirations."

Delphie looked down her long nose at her. "Then it's time you started acquiring some. At any rate, I am delighted the children took to you. I suspected you would have a way with the young ones."

"How could you? I have rarely been around children."

The lady smiled broadly. "I knew anyone who could handle Cort and Scotty would have no trouble managing real children."

Griffin was still not home at dinnertime. Gates wondered if this was his usual habit or if he was staying away on her account. The brothers amused her during the meal and even offered to teach her whist in the parlor afterward, providing Delphie would make up the fourth player.

When Gates retired to her room, her mind was still replaying the images from the charity home. Though she had said nothing to Delphie, those waifs had reminded her painfully of another lost child—herself. The Gates Underhill who had been wrenched from her home by a frighteningly distant father and made to tramp half across Cheshire and back. Since her father had given up his law practice—and given away most of their possessions in a fit of religious zeal—he and Gates had had no source of income, save the few pence she was able to collect at her father's evangelical meetings. When you preached to the poor, she learned, your tithes were virtually nonexistent.

She rarely thought back to those times. Her love for her father had been sorely tested and she knew she had not always looked upon him in a forgiving light. Now, seeing those disloyal feelings through the eyes of an adult, Gates knew they had sprung from fear. Fear of going hungry, fear of sleeping in the open, fear of angry strangers who hounded them from their villages.

Somewhere on the road to Paultons, where her father was soon to meet his second wife, Gates had conquered her fear. She had been fifteen at the time and had counted it a sort of epiphany. Some rude boys had been throwing rocks at them from the far side of a stone bridge. Her father pulled his ragged collar up and started in the opposite direction, but Gates had had enough. She kept walking toward the boys. One of them threw a stone that landed at her feet. She picked it up and carried it to him.

"Here," she said. "I make a better target close up."

The boy's eyes had narrowed in bewilderment. He did not know how to deal with a victim who looked him straight in the eye. His friends all ran off then, but he had stayed and walked with Gates and her father until they reached the village. That night her father met the Widow Marsden at his meeting behind the dry-goods store. Gates saw it as another sign—she had faced her fears and now her father would settle down and become a farmer. Not that it had worked out exactly as she'd hoped. Papa had farmed for less than a year before he was called again to preach.

She curled up on her bed and wondered where he was. His last note had been sent from Yorkshire. It consoled her that she would be performing good works with Griffin's aunt, work that her papa would approve of. On the other hand, she doubted he would approve of her stylish new clothes or her recently acquired taste for wine. But then, the absent cat was hardly in a position to criticize the errant mouse.

Chapter Eleven

During the next week Gates found every minute of her day occupied. In the mornings, Cort and Scotty squired her around London with Delphie in tow for propriety's sake. They shared with her all the amusing spots of the city, and purposely kept her from the less savory reaches that they traversed at night. She goggled appropriately at sites of historic import and grew duly reverent inside the various churches and cathedrals she insisted on visiting—much to Cort's chagrin.

On most afternoons she and Miss Darrowby visited the charity home, often choosing to walk to Whitechapel when the October weather was clement. Gates made dolls for the girls and painted picture books for the boys. She helped Delphie teach the adult women to spin and weave, so that they would have a trade to take out into the world. And when Delphie was otherwise engaged, Gates quietly questioned the women who lived there about their lives. Some were reticent, but many were frank, and in the space of a few days, Gates learned as much about the ways of men as any married lady in the city.

Not that her new accumulation of knowledge aided her with Griffin. She rarely saw him at the house, and when she did, he merely nodded and gave her a distant smile. He appeared, to her discerning eyes, distracted and careworn. Her new gowns had arrived two days after the modiste's visit, but even the sight of her in such elegant finery did not provoke him into commentary.

Delphie, however, did not withhold her approval. When Gates donned her new pelisse, she'd proclaimed, "We shall now have every coxcomb in the *ton* following us about."

Gates had merely laughed at the overblown compliment.

But they *were* followed one day as they left the charity home—by two ragged young men. One was tall with protuberant eyes and the other was red-haired, with higgledy-piggledly teeth.

Sank and Demp had been loitering near the entrance of a grog shop, hoping to earn a few bob for holding the patrons' horses. They nearly hadn't recognized their stepsister when she emerged from the charity home accompanied by a rangy dowager in a turban. It was only when they heard her speak, when she turned to her companion and pointed out a fat marmalade cat sitting in a shop window, that they knew it was their own Gates.

Ah, but what a changed Gates, in her fancy clothes. They knew someone had coughed up a bit of the ready to pay for such a rig. Demp wanted to rush ahead and greet her, but Sank held him back.

"Look at her," he growled. "She's not going to acknowledge the likes of us. Not in public, at any rate. We'll wait, Demp, and see where she's heading. Maybe she'll lead us to an even bigger fish."

So they stayed in the shadows, always keeping one eye on their quarry. It wasn't difficult—the high, magenta plume in the woman's turban was a hard beacon to miss. They waited across from the teashop where the women stopped, and then picked up their trail again as they walked through Mayfair. When Sank saw which town house they entered, he began to do a dance of rage upon the pavement.

"Bloody blazes, Redemption, do you see that? Do you know who lives there?"

Demp thought he'd have to be a half-wit to forget the home of Griffin Darrowby, where they had barely escaped a beating at the hands of that gentleman's irate servants. "I told you you should have never left her behind with that fellow. I knew he would cozen her."

Sank glanced the flat of his palm across his brother's crown. "You never said any such thing to me. But it looks like he's cozened her all right. Most likely right into his bed. She's not a servant in that house, not with that fancy getup she's wearing."

"Maybe she's working as the woman's companion," Demp suggested, then ducked another slap.

"She's not anybody's companion, except that infernal Darrowby's. I feel it in my bones, Demp. We will just keep watch on this house for a few days . . . see where the grooms go for their pint and chat them up, find out if Gates has any money of her own. This is our God-given destiny, Demp, I know it. This is why we were led to London . . ."

Demp made a face. Only Sanctification could make his plans to extort money from their stepsister sound like a holy crusade. But he went along, because he always went along with Sank. It was easier than fighting back.

* * *

Griffin poured the last of the brandy into his glass and wondered
if it was too late at night to summon Bucket to refill the decanter.
Just because he'd turned into a reclusive sot was no reason to put
an extra burden on his servants. He sipped at the liquor, musing
bitterly at the wretched pass his life had come to. He didn't dare go
out to his clubs—Minerva's most recent letter had gently cautioned him against such idle habits. She had further mentioned a
missive from Lord Pettibone, wherein the vengeful baron had
brought to her attention the advent of Miss Underhill—her former
scullion—into Griff's home. "While I applaud your generosity in
offering this girl employment," she had written, "I cannot but find
fault with her intemperate behavior. One seeks constancy from
one's servants, whereas this girl has shown little loyalty to any
who have given her work."

"Haven't you got anything better to worry about, Minerva?" he
snarled sourly as he tossed her note to the floor, where it joined his
most recent letter from Pendleton, which contained more grim
news of speculations gone awry, and a stack of collection notices
from his creditors.

Griffin set his head on his hands and knuckled his brow. There
wasn't enough liquor in the city to blot out the depression that had
settled upon him like a shroud. He'd been dead wrong to think he
could blithely barter his future for gold. Minerva was not proving
to be the salvation he had hoped; they were not yet even affianced,
and already he was firmly under the cat's paw.

Delphie knocked softly and came into the study. She was the last
person he wanted to see, but his distempered scowl did not deter
her. She came right up to his desk and stood there, with her arms
crossed upon her regal bosom.

He cocked an eye at her. "What has she done now? Ousted
Bucket from his post? Thrown Scotty down a well?"

"*She,*" said the lady in scathing tones, "has done nothing. It is
you who are at fault here. You've been neglecting your responsibilities to her for more than a week now."

He growled deep in his throat. "I brought you here precisely so
that I should be relieved of that obligation. But tell me, how have
I neglected her?"

"Ah, let me count the ways." She held up one forefinger the-
atrically. "One, you have been pointedly avoiding meals, a fact that
has not gone unnoticed by your guest." She raised another finger.
"Two, you have not once complimented her on her appearance.

She told me after her fitting that you are not interested in lady's fashions and wouldn't care if she went about dressed in sackcloth."

Griffin's scowl deepened. "I am hardly in the habit of flattering unfledged young girls."

"Spanish coin is your second tongue, rascal. Don't try to gammon me."

"Any more sins of omission?" he drawled. And then hiccuped.

"Are you drunk?" she said, bending down to peer at him.

He raised his glass in salute. "I'm working on it. It seems the only vice I am allowed these days . . . getting castaway in the privacy of my own home."

Delphinia pursed up her mouth. "Well, that's your own business, I suppose. Now as I was saying about Miss Underhill . . . You have conveniently overlooked several of the girl's attributes."

Griffin nearly laughed. He doubted there were *any* of Gates's attributes he had overlooked.

"Such as," he asked cautiously.

"She can read," the lady stated. "And write I expect, since the one often accompanies the other. And not only English. I overheard Scotty thanking her for the help she'd given him with his Latin."

"You are delirious, Aunt," he said as he turned back to his desk. "The girl is a little savage. Perhaps she has a sort of native intelligence, but she's hardly a scholar."

Delphie snatched up the letter opener from his desk and wrapped him sharply on the knuckles.

"That wasn't called for," he grumbled as he carried his hand to his mouth.

"Now you listen to me, Griffin Darrowby. As I see it, that girl has been mismanaged for most of her life. A truant father, two worthless stepbrothers . . . and you, the one man who has been her ally and friend, blindly refuse to see the potential in her."

"What she has," he said harshly, "is a vivid imagination. Compelling, I will admit, but hardly useful in the real world. Even if she can read, what of it? She has no sense of propriety, and worse, no sense of danger. She is at the mercy of every stranger she encounters, because she is gullible and trusting. Hell, she trusts me, Delphie. Doesn't that tell you something?"

His aunt merely sniffed and then said, "Have you begun your inquiries about a position for her?"

Griffin shifted away from her basilisk gaze. He needed to tread delicately here. Lying to Delphie was not his intention—he only wanted to put her off the scent.

"This needs to be handled carefully," he said in a thoughtful tone. "I must consider all my options . . . take the time to seek out the right employer. She is a blossom that will be crushed in the wrong hands."

"But don't you see, Griffin? She can be anything, do anything within reason, if she's been educated."

"Oh, spare me," he muttered as he pushed back his chair and turned to face her. "You and your causes . . . educating women so that they can seek elevated careers. Even if these things you say about her are true, few would hire a girl with her background. Do you think to make a silk purse out of a—"

"That is a wretched thing to say," she cried fiercely. "Don't you dare call that lovely child a sow's ear."

"She's *not* a child," he bit out. "I wish to God she were."

His aunt circled behind his desk, watching the play of emotions on his lean face. Anger she saw there, and frustration. But it was the glimmer of longing that she noted with satisfaction.

"Oh, my," she said softly as she lowered herself into a chair. "You lied to me, didn't you, when you told me you didn't care for her? I think you care a great deal more than you wish to."

Griffin shifted away from her, but she saw the tension in his shoulders beneath his fine blue coat. "It is hardly your business," he said stiffly. "I didn't ask you here so that you could meddle in my affairs."

"Twaddle!" she snapped. "Your affairs are the talk of the *ton*. I am speaking of your feelings, you wretched boy. I would have bet you had none left, not after all those years with your father. But she's made some change in you. The last time we were in company together, I found you an insufferable peacock. But there's a softness in your eyes now that I've never seen before."

"And a softness in my head," he said dryly, and then added in a faraway voice, "Lord, my life was so simple before I met her. I must have been mad to take her in."

There was sympathy in his aunt's face now, but a measure of caution as well. "Well she's here, Griffin, and you need to deal with her. It's a pity you encouraged her in Cheshire."

"I didn't encourage her," he said. "I rather think she encouraged me. She was someone to talk to late at night, when I couldn't tolerate the forced gaiety of the house party any longer. She is very soothing to be with . . . she is the least judgmental person I've ever met."

"And you've been judged and found wanting your entire life, haven't you? Perhaps you need to avail yourself of her company again. You look as though you could use a good soothing."

"Gates Underhill is more of a problem than a solution," he said. "And I've enough problems to contend with."

She indicated the piles of paper that littered his desk and the floor around him. "I gather you're having a bit of business trouble."

He shrugged. He was tempted to tell his aunt of his financial woes—Delphie would at least offer him some bracing consolation—but he also feared to see the look of pity in her eyes.

"It's nothing that won't eventually come to rights. As for Miss Underhill, if she's been educated, then that's all the better for finding her a decent position. Now, please, Delphie, let me get back to my letters."

His aunt ground her teeth. "She won't require a position if you would do your duty toward her."

Griffin felt the color leave his face. "What do you mean, my duty?"

She leaned forward. "In spite of her bizarre background, she is the daughter of a gentleman. If you would sponsor her in some way, allow her to go about at the fringes of society, she might meet some worthy law clerk or fledgling politician. I'd be happy to oversee it."

He rose slowly from his chair. "You're talking about marriage? You want me to send her off to marry a stranger."

"Surely that's better than working for a stranger. You need only give her a small dowry."

"It is out of the question." His hands were splayed on the edge of his desk, the knuckles showing white. "And that is all I have to say on the matter."

"But—"

"Not another word, Delphie, or I will put her on the coach for Cheshire myself."

When Griffin returned from his early ride the next morning, Gates was lingering in the stall row. He handed his reins to Farrow and called out, "Miss Underhill, will you walk with me?" He indicated the cobbled lane before him.

As Gates moved out of the shadows, he saw there were traces of hay in her hair.

Christ, he muttered to himself, *if she's taken to napping in my stable, I shall go mad with thinking of it.* It was bad enough she slept only two doors away from his bedroom.

He brushed the stray wisps from her hair and shook his head. "You are showing your country roots I fear."

"I was helping Mr. Farrow with Cort's mare," she said. "He was fitting her with a new headstall."

"I trust that you and my aunt are rubbing along tolerably well."

"Oh, yes. She is a bit crusty, as you'd warned me. And I've never met anyone with so many opinions on so many topics. But she says there's nothing wrong with speaking your mind, as long as you've got one." She grinned at him. "And I am pleased to be helping her with her charity work. We're keeping women off the streets, you know."

Griffin tried not to smile. "That is very commendable. There are far too many women on the streets of London."

"You're laughing at me," she said without reproach. "But I don't mind. I did eventually figure out what it meant." She leaned up on tiptoes and whispered against his ear, "She was referring to harlots."

He nodded and tried to disregard the shivery sensation of her warm breath against his skin. "Yes, I am aware that one of Delphie's pet causes is finding legitimate work for fallen women."

Gates sighed as they proceeded down the lane. "I often saw women like that while I was traveling with my father. It was very sad, especially since Papa would not speak to them. I believe they needed his services more than the other townspeople did."

Griffin said nothing, feeling poorly equipped to comment on what harlots required in the way of salvation. His commerce with them had always led in the other direction.

"I think Miss Darrowby has a much better grasp on saving souls than my papa," she continued. "He never knit scarves or took up collections for the poor as she does." She stopped and chewed at her lip. "I'm sorry, I didn't mean to rattle on like that. Was there something you wanted to tell me?"

He didn't hear her. He'd been distracted by the quicksilver flow of emotions on her intent, angular face and by his discovery that she was quite tall—it wasn't surprising that he hadn't noticed before, since he'd never walked beside her. He saw now that they were nearly shoulder to shoulder, and it made him long to discover what it would feel like to kiss a woman whose lips were only inches below his own. Whose breasts would press just below his heart and whose—

"Mr. Darrowby?" They had reached the end of the lane, where it opened onto the side street.

Griffin quickly shook himself back to reality. "Yes, there is something I need to say. It appears I have been . . . distant with you this past week—"

"Have you?" she asked in an airy tone that would have done a seasoned debutante proud.

"And now Delphie has rung a peal over me for neglecting you."

"Poor man," she said with a sly twinkle in her eye. "I am fortunate to have such a dragon on my side. But I expect you have greater demands on your time than entertaining me. Miss Darrowby had no right to criticize you."

Griffin took up one of her hands. "As I told you before, we are friends to each other, Gates. Though I admit I have not been bearing my share of the friendship. But I will."

"You needn't," she said, gently tugging her hand from his hold. The playfulness had faded from her eyes. "I am holding my own now."

He'd never in his life received such a neatly delivered snub. Especially after his uncharacteristic display of humility.

"I've written to Lady Seaton," she continued, "who is one of the sponsors of the charity home, about going to live there as a matron. So you see, you will not need to find me a position after all."

"That's preposterous," he said, striding a little bit away from her in agitation. He spun back. "What sort of life would you have there, Gates? You'd be worse than a drudge. It's one thing to visit the place and do your blasted good works, but quite another to live there, among poverty and disease."

Gates hitched her shoulders. "I knew you would not like it. But I've been here for more than a week, and you have not come up with any other solutions."

"Here's my solution!" He closed the gap between them and thrust her back against the brick wall of his neighbor's garden. His arms closed tight around her and his head lowered until his mouth was inches from her own. "I want you here, Gates," he whispered hoarsely. "With me."

Her eyes were wide as dinner plates as she gazed up at him, reading the unspoken yearning that had narrowed his cheeks and fretted his brow. So it was out in the open at last.

"I c-cannot," she said haltingly. "We both know why I cannot. And there is another thing I sorted out this week when you took such pains to stay out of my way." She met his eyes. "It was because you kissed me."

"What?" He tangled his hands in her long hair and tugged gently.

"In the byre at Bellaire. Oh, I know I was half asleep, but you must admit your kisses are fairly stimulating . . . though I'd never been kissed by anyone, so perhaps I am not a good judge. But the point is, you never expected me to come here. I fear I am something of an embarrassment to you."

"I am rarely embarrassed by anything so pleasurable," he uttered.

"Oh," she said and blushed right up to her hairline.

He lowered his face to her hair, breathing in a subtle whiff of clover and timothy—Gates Underhill's earthy, provocative scent. "And I would like to do it again."

She set her hands against his chest, so warm and solid beneath her trembling fingers. "Oh, Griffin, I think I would like it very much if you did. But Delphie would ring more than just a peal over us."

"We are not children minding a nursemaid, Gates," he said, as he tugged her closer, until her hands were trapped between them. This was happening much faster than he'd intended, but he was never a man to miss an opportunity. And she felt so damned fine. "We can make our own choices."

"You can," she said a bit crossly. "Because you are a man. But I am at the mercy of other people's expectations. Including yours."

"What if I said I *expected* you to kiss me?"

She fought back her grin and said stiffly, "Then I would remind you of Lady Minerva and *her* expectations."

"Hang Lady Minerva," he growled under his breath.

She put her chin up. "And when you are with her, you will say 'Hang Gates Underhill,' in just the same odious manner. You see, Griffin, I am not such a bumpkin as you like to pretend."

"It's Delphie who's put the sauce into you," he said with a

frown. "I recognize her touch. But if you take counsel from a maiden lady, you risk ending up on the same parched, empty shelf."

"Better on the shelf, than in the basket," she said coolly.

Griffin shook his head. "Christ, she's turned you into a parliamentarian, hasn't she? My little wood sprite has quite disappeared."

Gates looked away from him and sighed. "I fear she died the night I ran away from Lord Pettibone—crushed under the wheels of her own foolish hopes."

"Then no more daily miracles? No more consorting with cows?" He sounded almost bereft.

"No, there are so few cows here in London. And even fewer miracles."

Griffin felt something twist inside him. He blinked several times and then slid his hands up to her shoulders. "Then I will find you a miracle, Miss Under-the-hill."

Her mouth drew up on one side and she said a bit sadly. "I would rather you found me a way out of your home. You may not credit this, but it is very difficult to be standing here with you, talking of kissing and such, when I know that it can never happen. And living in the same house with you is . . ."

"A trial," he said softly, completing the sentence for her. "Yes, I know that too well. But since we've finally gotten around to plain speaking, perhaps now it won't be so awkward for us."

She looked doubtful. "Can we go on from here?"

You bloody-well bet we can, he vowed silently. He could barely contain his elation—she wanted this completion as much as he did. There was little he couldn't eventually accomplish with a willing lady. But he needed to temper his desire; Gates was a novice in the school of eros.

"We will go on, Gates," he promised her softly. "And at your own pace. If you come to me, I will see that you are never sorry for it." He brushed his cheek slowly along the side of her face, and felt her drift against him. "And if you do not choose my path . . . I will shrug off my losses and set you free."

"How can you speak of this so calmly?" she implored him. "You are asking me to go against every value I hold precious."

He shook his head. "I have merely laid my cards on the table; it's up to you whether you want to bet against them or fold."

"I do not gamble," she said forthrightly.

He smiled, a sly, half-moon of a smile, and purred, "My dearest girl, you dealt *this* hand yourself."

Gates flung her head back. "Then we will play it out. But I warn you, you will not like my pace."

He stroked one finger along her throat. "I am a very patient fellow, Miss Under-the-Hill."

He was just about to seal their bargain with a chaste kiss, when Farrow called out from the far end of the mews. "Mr. Griffin, you'd best come look at this hay that was just delivered. It's not fit for goats."

Griffin set Gates away from him and drew a deep, shuddering breath. He sketched her a brief bow and went striding back toward the stable.

"Blast!" she murmured with a throb in her voice. It was one of Cort's tamer oaths. She didn't know if there was a word that could do justice to her feelings at that moment. The words they had spoken and the desire that had sparked between them were too frightening for her to deal with at present. She needed time to distance herself from her wayward heart, which longed for the tempting solution he'd offered her. If she followed her heart, she'd likely still end up at the charity home, but as one of its fallen inmates and not as a matron.

She wandered back down the lane and entered the garden, still dazed from the shivery memory of Griffin's hands on her body, and of her own hands pressed against the warm, comforting wall of his chest.

The late afternoon sky was sullen and gray when Gates and Delphie left the home in Whitechapel. A week had passed since Griffin made his offer in the mews lane. Gates had expected him to badger her with his attentions and so was surprised by his subsequent charming and utterly proper behavior. He bantered with her over meals and often sat with her in the evenings, trying not to grimace at her halting attempts to play the piano.

As the women stepped out onto the pavement it began to rain. Delphie motioned Gates to remain behind as she stepped into the street to hail a hackney. Gates hung back inside a recessed doorway, trying to keep the rain off her new pelisse.

She turned abruptly when two men clattered out of the alley beside her. They ran directly toward her through the obscuring screen

of rain and leapt onto the stoop where she sheltered. Her initial cry
of alarm was cut off when one of the men clapped his hand over
her mouth. They quickly pulled her down off the steps and hauled
her back toward the darkness from which they had emerged.

When Gates pried her assailant's hand away and began screaming, a burlap sack was thrust over her head. She felt herself being
dragged backward, away from the street, away from help. She
fought back then, with every ounce of anger she could muster,
flailing about with her fists.

"Damn!" one of the men cried as she made contact with his jaw.
He retaliated by swinging her against the wall of the alley. Her
forehead bounced off the brick surface and she fell heavily to her
knees in the mud. Rough hands grasped her upper arms and she
was again dragged along the uneven ground.

She heard Delphie's roaring cry of anger as if through a fog.
There were several audible thuds and equally audible cries of distress. The men released her then, and went pelting off down the
alley, wailing like banshees.

Delphie was just helping Gates into her room when Griffin
came racing up the stairs. He all but knocked his aunt out of the
way. His hands went to Gates's shoulders, gripping them tightly.

"What's happened?" he asked her breathlessly. When she did
not answer quickly enough, his gaze darted to his aunt. "Bucket
says she was injured. Tell me."

"She was attacked by two ruffians who put a sack over her head.
But I beat them off with my truncheon." Delphie smugly patted her
large knitting bag, where the weapon now lay. "I never walk
through London without it." She pried his fingers from Gates's
arms and led her to the bed. "Steady now, Gates. There's the girl."

"Christ, she's limping."

Delphie turned to him and rolled her eyes. "If that's all the help
you're going to be, you might as well go back to your ledgers."

He backed to the door and shouted out, "Bucket, send Thomas
for the doctor. At once."

"Yes, sir," Bucket called up from the foyer. "I have already
taken the liberty of doing just that."

Delphie peeled the girl out of her wet pelisse and then pronounced, "I'd best fetch her up something to put on her head." She
brushed past him with a look of thin-lipped determination.

When Griffin approached the bed, Gates could have sworn he was trembling.

"I just got roughed up a bit," she said with a tiny smile. "Foot-pads, I expect, trying to steal my purse. I'm really fine," she in-sisted when his somber expression did not go away. "You know me, tough as old boots."

"Old boots, is it?" he said as he seated himself on the edge of the bed. "You look more like a trampled slipper to me." He brushed his fingers above the discolored knot on her forehead. "They hurt you," he whispered as his eyes darkened from blue to deep indigo. "Unless Delphie did this with her truncheon. The woman is a menace."

She grinned. "She saved me, Griff. You should have heard those fellows howling as they ran off."

"Where did it happen."

Gates worried her lip. "In London."

He was not amused by her prevarication. "Gates . . ."

"We were just leaving the charity home in Whitechapel. I'm sure they only wanted to steal my purse."

"Then why the sack? It doesn't make any sense. But I will tell you this, you are not to go there again. With or without Delphie. I never liked the idea of the two of you traipsing around the East End."

"Griffin!" she cried, nearly rising up from the bed. "That is not fair. I am helping those people. No one else seems to care."

"I'm sorry, but I forbid it."

"Forbid?" Her eyes narrowed.

"Find someone else to practice your charity on . . . teach Cort not to bet on ducks, get Scotty to change his linen once in a while. But the fallen women of Whitechapel will have to do without you."

Delphie came in carrying a basin and a cloth compress. Her scowl was not lost on Griffin. "See, I knew you would end up up-setting her. Out now, we want none of you in here."

"I mean it," Griff uttered over his shoulder as Delphie thrust him bodily from the room.

Gates lay quietly as Delphie applied the compress; the pain in her heart was far greater than the throbbing in her head. She had at last discovered a worthwhile occupation, and now Griffin had for-bidden her to follow it. She'd long since stopped thinking of him as an arrogant man, but he had just served her a potent reminder of his tendencies in that direction.

Dr. Oates, an elderly stick of a man, made an even greater fuss over her than Delphie had, clucking over her bumped head and tsking over her wrenched knee. He applied sticking plasters to her worst scrapes and gave her a willow bark potion for the headache he was sure she would develop. Gates's only headache was currently sitting in his study thinking of ways to thwart her.

Unfortunately, she learned later, when the goodly physician made his report to Griffin, he instructed that she stay off her knee for a period of at least two days.

"Two days!" Gates cried when Delphie delivered the doctor's verdict. "I shall go mad."

But Cort and Scotty came to her rescue the next morning and carried her down to the front parlor, where they amused her by cutting out silhouettes of famous people and wild animals, and forcing her to eat far too many sweetmeats. She spent most of her time plotting ways to get around Griffin's edict.

Griff came through the front door and heard laughter spilling out from the parlor. Gates's laughter to be precise. He handed his hat and stick to Bucket and went into the room. His brothers were playing cards with the invalid, who was lying on the sofa swathed in one of Delphie's exotic dressing gowns. "What is she doing downstairs?" he growled.

"I carried her," Cort pronounced.

"Carried her?"

"You know the doctor said she was not to walk for a day or two. And really, Griff, I doubt she weighs more than a bushel of feathers."

"I get to carry her back upstairs," Scotty added with a grin.

"Indeed you will not," Griffin said. "She is in my charge."

"I wish you would stop discussing me as though I were not here," Gates complained to the room in general and then shifted her gaze to Griffin. "I was getting dreadfully bored up there."

"If you are bored, then you must take it up with me."

"As if he'd know the first thing about distracting an invalid," Cort muttered.

"I heard that," Griff said between his teeth. "I believe she has had enough distractions for one day."

He went to the sofa and swooped Gates up in his arms before she could protest. His brothers fell back as he carried her across to the door. She thought of squirming and kicking, but then reckoned it felt nice to be cradled against his chest. She laid one hand against his shirtfront and that also felt very nice.

"Griffin," she said as he reached the foot of the stairs, "will you stay and visit with me?"

She felt the muscles beneath her hand tense. "I am very busy this morning."

"But you said if I was bored . . ."

"I'll have Scotty find you something to read."

She closed her eyes. "My head hurts too much to read."

He tipped his face down to hers. "It didn't hurt too much to play cards."

"Well, you've jostled me. That can't be very good for a throbbing head or a wrenched knee."

"And I suppose Cort was the soul of delicacy when he carried you?"

"No," she said, restraining a chuckle. "He nearly dropped me midway down the stairs. You are a deal stronger than he is, I think."

When Griffin reached her bedroom, he nudged the door open with his knee and crossed over to the bed. He watched as she shifted under the covers and drew them to her chin. She looked up at him so beseechingly that his breath caught in his chest.

"Oh, very well," he said. "I'll carry your lunch up, and then read to you for a while. Will that make you happy?" She nodded once.

At half past twelve he came in bearing a tray. Soup and rolls and a dish of pudding, she saw, as he placed it on her lap. He pulled a chair up beside the bed and opened the book he'd carried in.

"*The Lady of the Lake,*" he read aloud, "by Walter Scott."

She tipped the book down with her forefinger. "Any illustrations?"

"No," he said. "You'll have to use your splendid imagination, Miss Underhill."

"*The Lady of the Lake,*" he began again. "By Walter—"

"Is it about King Arthur?" she interrupted, a spoonful of soup halfway to her mouth.

"Gates," he said warningly, "I suggest you let me get past the title; then you will see what it's about."

She grinned at him. "Go on."

He read to her for nearly an hour, his tone rising and falling with the cadence of the poem. He had a lovely voice, she thought. Deep and rich and sometimes a bit husky. And as he read, the careworn expression in his eyes, which had begun to increase lately, gave way to a soft mellow glow. He even laughed at one point, when his tongue got tangled around a line.

"There," he said, shutting the book upon his knee. "I think that's a sign that I've read enough. I'll leave the book here for you, in case your headache clears."

She sensed with dismay that he was done with her and cast about in her head for some way to make him stay. "Do you like poetry, Griffin?"

He shrugged. "I used to read Donne and Blake in the library at Darrowby. When I wasn't locked in my room for some misdeed or other."

Gates realized it was the first time he had ever spoken of his boyhood home.

"Farrow told me he left Darrowby when you did." Griffin nodded and Gates continued with a trembling heart. "Farrow also said something else . . . he said I should ask you what happened to Gaspar. About those scars on his side."

Griff shifted on his chair. "Do you make everything your charge, Miss Under-the-hill?"

"What do you mean?"

"My horse, your two ungrateful stepbrothers, the women and children of Whitechapel."

She leaned forward, nearly upsetting the tray that lay beside her. He was seated so close she could smell the mingled scents of sandalwood and tobacco on his clothing. "I am only curious over how he came to be marked like that. I recall you told me once that you'd raised him from a foal and I couldn't imagine that you'd let someone hurt him."

He blew out a long breath. "You can stop glowering at me, Gates. It was my father who did it."

"But why?"

"Because Gaspar was young and headstrong, and because he would not respond as swiftly as my father demanded. One day I came into the stableyard and found my father beating the horse with a riding crop. He had spurred the poor beast so cruelly that the blood was running down his sides in streams. I knocked my father down in the dirt and then struck him, just once, with the crop.

So that he would know what it felt like to be helpless against someone's rage. They say he bore the mark on his face until the day he died."

"You never saw him again?" He shook his head. "How long ago did this happen?"

"It was just after I'd left Oxford. I fled from Darrowby with Gaspar and came to London. My mother lived here then, but she refused to take me in. Fortunately, my grandmother had left me a small inheritance, so I was able to make my way in the city."

"Your parents did not live together? Isn't that unusual?"

"Not so strange, in the *ton*. I know a dozen couples who only infrequently share the same roof. But it was more than them living apart—they were completely estranged. My father would have divorced her but for the fact that it would have cost too much. It was cheaper to keep her here, and pay her bills. It was only after his death that she returned to Darrowby—where she queens it over the gentry in Bath."

Gates rubbed at her palm, trying to keep the distress from her face. He could not know how his words sounded to her, the pain that crept into his voice as he'd spoken of his father's rage and his mother's rejection.

Griffin gave a dry chuckle. "If you were a member of the *ton*, instead of a country-bred wood sprite, you'd have been hearing sordid tales of my family's escapades from your cradle. I wager the Darrowbys have furnished more grist for the gossip mills than any family except the Hanovers."

"You almost sound proud of that fact." She was unaware of the rebuke that had crept into her voice.

He lowered his head and fidgeted with the book.

He's told me too much, she thought bleakly. *And now he's embarrassed that I know of these ugly, hurtful things.*

He rose then and set the book on her bed, "I have business to attend to in my study."

"Griffin," she called out as he turned away. "You looked after Gaspar when he needed you . . . won't you let me look after the women and children in Whitechapel. I promise not to—"

"No! It is not open for discussion. Now stop arguing with me or I shall grow angry."

He looks fairly incensed already, she murmured to herself as he went through the door.

* * *

As Griffin came riding up the mews lane, he saw a crowd of urchins gathered near his garden gate.

"Make way," he called out in a stern voice. The children gazed up at him, and then recognizing a gentleman, which in their experience meant a less-than-gentle man, they fell back with cries of alarm.

One of the bolder boys ran forward and caught Gaspar's bridle. "S'awright, sir," he lisped up at Griff. "We bayn't meanin' any 'arm. She said we should come. She said it was proper."

Since Gaspar was singularly unappreciative of the urchin hanging on his bridle, Griff thought it prudent to dismount.

"Farrow!" he called out as he thrust his way past the grimy throng. He led Gaspar into his stall, and then made his way back through the gaggle of urchins. As he entered the garden, he spied Gates and Farrow coming along the path toward him, each carrying a large wicker hamper.

"What is going on here?" he called out. "Half the population of Seven Dials is lurking in my mews."

"I told them to come," Gates said, huffing a little as she clutched the heavy hamper to her chest. Griff immediately reached out and relieved her of it. He lifted the lid and peered inside. Well, at least she wasn't distributing the heirloom silver, he thought with relief, just bread and cheese and apples.

"The loaves and the fishes?" he asked with a quirk of his brow.

"There is too much going to waste in this house. In all these houses," she added, waving one hand toward the adjoining homes. "I've sent around a petition to your neighbors' cooks, asking them to put food baskets in their alleys. Farrow has agreed to collect them, and we shall feed the children here."

"No," Griffin said, and then again, "No," louder this time and with a good deal of temper showing. He took her by the collar and turned her toward the house. "See that? That is where I live. Are any inside that place hungry or in need?"

"But—"

"No, they are not. Because Darrowbys take care of their own. I believe that's all I am required to do."

"We are required," she stated firmly, "to help those less fortunate than ourselves. Those children have no one. Some of them are completely alone in the world."

"More of your papa's Book?" he said dismissively.

"It's in the other Book too," she snapped. "You told me to find another outlet for my charity. This is it. Delphie says it was an inspiration."

He made no response, merely started toward the house, still carrying the hamper. Gates took hold of one of the handles and began pulling it in the opposite direction. Farrow merely stood and gaped.

"Stop that!" Griffin growled. He turned to her, releasing the basket so quickly she nearly tumbled backward. He snatched it from her again and handed it to Farrow, who tucked it under one arm.

"I can't see why the devil you should care," he said. "Who was there for you, who looked after you when you were alone?"

She met his eyes, unafraid of the anger that simmered there. "You did," she said simply. Then she put her head back, squared her shoulders, and walked toward the house.

Griffin watched until she disappeared behind the gazebo, and then swung to Farrow.

"It's no use, sir," the groom said. "She is like a trickle of water that wears down a great stone, drip by drip." He stood there, a hamper under each arm, awaiting his orders.

Griffin muttered, "Oh, go feed the blasted multitude," and stalked off in the wake of his conscience. He didn't see the fond smile his groom bestowed on him or he'd have been even more incensed.

Griffin found her in the library, slamming Scotty's discarded books onto the shelves, her cheeks awash with bright color. He caught her by the wrist, twisted the book from her hand, and tossed it onto the table. The next instant he swung her by both wrists away from the stacks.

"Let go!" she said crossly.

"You give so much to everyone else," he cried. His eyes were blazing now, bluer than an arctic sea. "But what would you give to me? What, Gates?"

"Whatever I am able," she replied softly.

"And what would you ask in return?"

She closed her eyes for an instant. "I told you what I require from you."

"Oh, yes, I remember," he growled, leaning in close. "My blasted good opinion."

"Stop this!" she cried, pulling back from his hold. "You

promised not to taunt me. And I don't know why you are so riled, merely because I saved some scraps of food from being tossed onto the refuse heap in order to feed a few hungry children."

How could he tell her? How could he explain that before long he and his dependents might need those charity baskets as much as the urchins did?

"Hang your good works," he proclaimed. "You're a little hypocrite—so quick to offer charity, and yet refusing to accept even the smallest token from anyone."

He caught up her hand and tugged her through the pocket door, into his study. He placed her before his desk and then drew open the wide drawer. She immediately saw the ten buttons lying there atop a scattering of receipts.

He scooped up a handful of the buttons and shook them under her nose. "You made a mockery of my good intentions. And I so rarely have any . . ."

Gates saw that she had injured him when she returned his gifts. It had never occurred to her that she had such power over him. Not *that* sort of power—to wound or inflict pain.

She wrapped her hands around his fist, stilling it. "I am so sorry," she said in a quiet voice, forcing him to look into her eyes. "I didn't mean to seem ungrateful."

"I don't want your gratitude, Gates." He stepped closer and snaked his arm around her waist.

Her eyes darkened. "Then were you trying to buy something else from me?"

He shook his head slowly. "It won't fadge, my girl. You're not going to make me angry again by implying these were anything more than a freely given gift. If I wanted to cozen you with presents, I fancy I could do better than a handful of buttons."

She put her head back, and tried to ignore the persistent thumping of her heart. Lord, his arm at her waist felt like a fiery brand. "Like that pheasant, for instance? I never did thank you for it."

He offered her a brief, sweet smile. "But you took it, and ate it, and never came chasing after me to return it. Why did these"—he rattled his fist so that the buttons clicked like dice—"so offend your sensibilities?"

She lowered her head. "I thought they were offered out of guilt." He shook her slightly in protest, but she continued. "Because you frightened me in the barn, and because you kissed me in the cow byre. All I could think was that you were soothing your conscience by leaving me expensive baubles."

He tipped her head up with his fisted hand. "I have no conscience, my dear. Not a shred. So it's a good thing you have one large enough for both of us."

He drew back from her, letting his hand linger for an instant on her hip, and then retrieved the rest of the buttons from the drawer. He dropped them onto her open palms, and then forcefully closed her fingers around them.

"Now," he said, "you can redeem them, or gamble them, or pitch them at pigeons, for all I care. But I will not have them back again. Do you understand?"

Gates nodded silently. And tried very hard to keep her happiness from showing on her face. Because it had all just come marvelously clear. It was there in his voice, and most tellingly in his bright eyes. *He did care for her.* She'd known for quite some time now that he desired her, and she had been beguiled enough by that fact to allow him some liberties with her person. But if the yearning expression in his face was any indication of his present feelings, he had gone a long way past mere lust.

She raised her cupped hands to her breast. "I will keep them," she said softly, looking up into his fathomless blue eyes, "in the spirit in which they were given."

"He's gone off to Bristol," Delphie said as she coaxed a male canary onto her finger. "I'm surprised he never mentioned it to you—especially since the two of you have been thick as thieves lately. I am still agog that he came with us to the charity home yesterday and actually *played* with the children."

"Don't say it like that, Delphie," Gates protested. "You make it sound like he'd have rather eaten them for dinner. He only went with us because Cort and Scotty were off at a picnic in Richmond."

Gates had persuaded Griffin to relax his edict; he'd allowed her to return to the charity home, but only if Thomas or one of his brothers escorted her back to Mayfair.

"How long did he say he would be gone?" she asked, trying not to sound forlorn.

"Not above three or four days, I imagine. He has some business with a Bristol shipbuilder."

"Will he look in on his mother at Darrowby, do you think?"

The old woman chortled loudly. "I believe hell will have to freeze over before that event occurs."

"Well, I hope he has a pleasant journey," she said, wondering if she sounded properly insipid.

Cort had been coaching her on the fine art of lady's conversation—insisting that she must speak in a bored voice and never, ever express an opinion that hadn't been voiced previously by a man. It sounded a great deal like the way she conversed with her father and stepbrothers.

She'd also been assisting Delphie with the writing of her latest pamphlet, *The alternatives to marriage: A dissertation on the merits of the single state for women of intellect.* She recalled the way Griffin grinned when she read him an excerpt. He'd pronounced his aunt a female Moses, ready to lead her bluestocking flock into the promised land—where there were no irksome husbands and endless lending libraries.

His mellow humor enchanted her and made her forget that behind his easy smile lay a trap called desire. No, perhaps not a trap so much as a shadowed cavern, wherein sublime riches and dazzling wonders awaited her. Gates dared not step into that fearsome, enticing place, but she couldn't prevent herself from hovering at the threshold.

But in spite of his mellowed behavior with her, Griffin still seemed preoccupied with something, and spent endless hours in his study, poring over ledgers. Gates did not want to imperil their newfound harmony by pressing him for an explanation, but she worried over him just the same.

Now he'd gone away, once again without a word. He'd not even left her a solitary button. She stood beside the cage of her favorite canary pair, a yellow-gold male and his toffee-colored hen, and whistled a mournful tune. The male immediately caroled out a song—a far happier one than hers.

"I think we both need a walk," Delphie said briskly, noting the forlorn expression in Gates's eyes. "Fetch your pelisse now."

Gates ran to her room, always eager to be outside, even if it meant a sedate stroll through Green Park. A bonnet sat at the foot of her bed, an elegant creation of cream-colored straw embellished with knots of amber velvet ribbon and cream-colored feathers.

"Oh, Delphie," Gates cried out, turning as she came into the room. "Where did this come from?"

"Madame LaSalle's, if the name on the hatbox was correct."

Gates was grinning. "No, you know what I mean."

"He left it for you . . . he wanted it to be a surprise."

Gates was already sitting at her vanity table, trying to push her mass of hair up onto her head to accommodate the bonnet. "I gather you were his accomplice in this."

Delphie bit her lip. "The boy does have a cozening way about him."

Gates at last managed to tame her hair and set the bonnet upon her curls. She swung around to Delphie wearing an expression of concern. "You must wonder why he does such things for me."

Delphie raised one hand. "Lord, child, I have eyes in my head. He can barely breathe when you are in the same room."

"I want you to know that I have never . . . we have never—"

Delphie laid a hand on her arm. "You will follow your nature, Gates, and nothing I do or say will change that. I cannot say the same about my nephew, since his nature has altered so much in these past weeks that I hardly know him. Still, the man's a fool."

Gates lowered her head, afraid of her next words, afraid to hear the harsh voice of reason.

Delphie leaned down to tweak the velvet bow beneath her chin and whispered, "Only a fool gives a bonnet to a pretty girl and doesn't wait around to see how she looks in it."

Sank and Demp resumed their patrol of Griffin's home once they'd recovered from their shellacking at Delphie's hands. Her battering had not deterred them from their goal, only made them more cautious. They found they could mingle with the urchins who waited in the mews at noontime and receive a free handout from the grizzled groom. If the man questioned their presence—two grown men among so many children—he never said a word, but dutifully handed them a piece of bread or a wedge of cheese.

Shortly after they'd followed Gates at Darrowby's home, Demp had had the good fortune to meet the Darrowby footman at a pub called the Harp and Garter. He'd been informed that the young lady who lived in the house was most definitely not the master's fancy piece, not with that Tartar of an aunt standing guard over her.

"He's going to marry our Gates!" Sank had cried jubilantly after Demp shared this tidbit with his brother. "'Else why would his aunt be there to chaperone her, all right and proper?"

Demp looked dubious, but did not want to risk a slap for voicing his doubts. It seemed the more wretched their finances became, the more likely Sank was to box his ears. He prayed that it was true, that Gates was about to make an advantageous marriage. He'd known some man would snatch her up once she went out into the world—she was a very pretty girl, after all—only he hadn't thought it would be a handsome nob with a fine, big house.

Sank was still dancing gleefully around their tiny room. Demp feared his capering would rouse the landlord of the boardinghouse. They had been lodging there since they'd first arrived in London with Darrowby's purse. That money was long spent, though, and their rent was weeks overdue.

"Shush!" Demp cautioned him.

"If he's to marry her," Sank crowed, "then he'll pay handsomely to get her back."

Demp jumped up from his rickety chair by the window. "By all that's holy, Sanctification, you're not planning to abduct your own sister. I will not allow that. No, I will not."

Sank bore down on him and soon had him pinned on the floor. "Underhills stick together," he snarled.

"But she's an Underhill too," Demp cried. "She's the only *real* Underhill. We are Marsdens, Sank. Her papa gave us his name because our father disgraced his."

"It makes no difference. Do you think once she's married to that rogue, that we'll see a penny of his money? We must do something now, before they are wed and disappear from town."

"Why would they disappear? He lives here."

Sank rolled his eyes. "He has an estate near Bath. When men marry they always take their wives back to their family homes . . . so they can start them breeding, you see."

"Why can't they breed in London?"

Demp received one more clout for his foolish question, before his brother climbed off him. He staggered to his feet. "And if I help you with this, you will leave her in peace afterward?"

Sank took a drink from a dented tankard and then drew a hand across his mouth. "Afterward, yes. While she is here, I can't promise to leave her alone. She always was a winning little thing, and you can't blame a fellow for his appetites, now can you, brother?"

Demp said nothing. He thought he was going to be sick to his stomach.

* * *

Cort and Scotty were doing their best to keep their fears at bay. They knew Griff would be traveling perilously close to Darrowby on his way to Bristol. Though it was a remote possibility, he might just take a look in on their mother. "He'll find out about the Gorgon's money troubles if he goes there," Cort lamented. "*And* he'll know we kept the news from him."

"How will he know we interfered?" Scotty asked and then remembered the off-putting letters he'd forged in Griff's handwriting to his mother. That was fairly damning evidence. "What shall we do, Cort? He's liable to throttle us both . . . you've seen how angry he can get when he's been thwarted."

"I'll take his anger any day, over that icy, cutting disdain. He's the only man I know who can put a crease in a fellow's skull with just a glance."

They went striding back and forth, crossing and recrossing the library. "Nothing," Cort at last exclaimed. "I don't see any way out."

"Wait," Scotty said, holding up one hand. "We need to prove to him that we had his best interests at heart. So he'll be grateful to us when he comes home. Here's what we should do . . . while he's away, we liquidate everything we can get our hands on . . ."

"Liquidate? Are you mad?"

"No, just listen. We each have three hacks, we sell two. You have a carriage and pair, which, if I may point out, you rarely use. We will sell that—"

"Now just a minute . . ."

"And I've plenty of fripperies that the Gorgon's sent me for birthday's and whatnot . . . tie pins, watch fobs, which should fetch a bob or two."

"You are completely insane . . ."

"Look, Cortland, this was your idea . . . you're the one who read Griff's mail and then burned it. You're the one who coerced me to forge those letters to the Gorgon. We need to show Griffin that we are sorry for what we did, and the only way I can see to do that is to perform some sort of penance. And in addition to that, we can show him that we can practice economy here in the house . . . Gates tells me things are handled very wastefully. And I can imagine how much that Frog in the kitchen earns . . ."

"Marchand? I heard him tell Bucket that the Dutchess of Stratfield offered him a bonus to come and cook in her kitchens."

"Then we will tell him he is welcome to go."

"But who will cook for us then?"

"I *will*." The slim figure came through the partially opened pocket door that lead to Griff's study. Gates shook her head. "You two are the worst conspirators . . . I could hear you hissing at each other from down the hall." She bit her lip and her voice lowered. "So why are you going to sell your horses and practice economy?"

"Griffin's rolled up," Scotty blurted out before Cort could stop him. "Cort read some letters in his desk—he's been skirting disaster since the spring."

Gates eyes went wide. "Jehosephat! Are you sure?"

"That's why he went to Bristol," Cort said. "To ask a shipbuilder he once backed to loan him some money. If you care to look in his desk, you'll see the draft of his letter to the man."

"I do not care to," Gates said severely. "And I will see that there is a lock installed on it before he comes home."

Cort turned from her with a sullen, guilty frown. Scotty stepped closer. "If the *ton* learns he is ruined, he might be ashamed to ask for Lady Minerva's hand."

Gates mulled this over and said with a tiny dollop of hope, "Is it possible she won't marry him now?"

Scotty shrugged. "It's anyone's guess. Even without money, he's still a splendid-looking fellow."

Gates could not argue with that. She drew her reserves around her—this was not the time to feel jealousy. Griffin needed her. "If Marchand leaves, I will help in the kitchen. I can do wonders with turnips." She grinned when she saw the look of horror on their faces. Apparently an aversion to turnips was a shared Darrowby trait. "No, I was attempting to be humorous. I can cook, especially if there are recipe books. And," she continued, "we can use tallow candles—they're pence cheaper than beeswax—and only light fires in certain rooms, which will economize on fuel."

"He will be impressed by our thrift," Cort said with feigned assurance. "And then maybe he will not have our heads for prying into his affairs."

Or mine, Gates thought, *for joining with his brothers in their scheming.*

Chapter Twelve

"Another letter from Darrowby?" Sir Thomas asked as he strolled into Minerva's sitting room.

"Yes," she said, smiling up at him before tucking the note into a blue-ribboned bundle and placing it in the top drawer of her desk. "He is nothing if not a faithful correspondent."

"And what is the news from London? Are wasp-waisted coats again in style for men? Has Prinny taken yet another aging mistress?"

She shot him a look of irritation. "You needn't make Griffin sound like such a fribble, Thomas. Anyway, he is currently in Bristol, looking into some investments. So you see, he is being quite tame in his pursuits . . . Possibly even tedious," she added with a sigh.

"Ah," Sir Thomas said as his brows rose. "You've bridled the rake and now you find him a trifle boring. What is the saying, my dear . . . be careful what you wish for?"

She picked up a pen and began to tap it nervously against the silver inkwell. "I don't know what I expect from him. I have heard no rumors to his discredit—well, barring the highly unlikely one about a naked woman hammering at his door in the middle of the night—and now he has become a pattern card of respectability. My aunt in Hyde Park writes that he rarely goes to his clubs, and that he is at home with his two brothers most nights. His maiden aunt has also come to stay with him; he hired that Underhill girl, who went off with Lord Pettibone, to be her companion."

Sir Thomas merely nodded. Gates had been sending him regular updates from London in her brash, scrawling hand. Very reassuring updates.

"It sounds as though Griffin has put his past behind him, does it not, Thomas?"

"Indeed it does," he said dryly. "You should feel reassured, Minerva. But tell me, has he also been able to articulate his feelings for you? I recall that was your chief concern. That he should love you."

"No," she said with a sigh. "He never writes of his feelings. It's all banking and investments . . . shipping and mining. I swear he doesn't want a wife, Thomas, but a business partner."

"It's flattering, I believe. Most men wouldn't think a lady capable of interest in such things."

"Oh, I am capable," she grumbled. "But I have my own holdings to deal with. And mine interest me only slightly more than his do. This was never to be a marriage of wealth, Thomas. I have all that I need. And if Griffin loved me, if any man could love me as Lucas did, I would wed him, even if he were a pauper. But a woman needs a bit of romancing, to hear sweet reminiscences . . . not corn prices."

"Oh, he *has* piqued you, my dear. What do you say we put off our cataloging chores in the library and go for a drive to Paultons? It might put the roses back in your cheeks."

Her hands flew to her face. "Lord, I must look positively hagged, for you to say that. You never notice my appearance . . ."

"Minerva—" He kept himself from speaking. She couldn't know how utterly untrue her words were.

"You needn't apologize," she said with an attempt at lightness. "There are enough men in the world who live only to flatter me. It's a relief sometimes that you are not one of them."

He took up his walking stick and moved away from her. "If a man does not flatter you, Min, it doesn't mean he's blind to your charms."

"Gallantry, Thomas?" she baited him. "I am quite overcome with shock."

"Fetch your wrap," he said gruffly. "And stop making a May game of my poor attempts to cheer you."

"Lucas was right," she said as she joined him in the doorway. "You are an old sobersides."

He bowed his head so that his mouth was beside her ear, "And you are a hopeless tease. Is that how you made Lucas laugh? By bedeviling him with his own shortcomings?"

She nodded, "Mmm. And that's also how I made him love me. No one had ever dared to tease the starchy master of Bellaire before he met me."

"Then it's an odd path to love."

"Oh, not at all . . . teasing is a token of fondness. Of great fondness."

"Is it?" he mused softly. "Then I gather you are practicing on me until your Mr. Darrowby returns."

Minerva was rendered speechless by this statement. Could Sir Thomas have no idea how much he meant to her, of how much she had come to rely on his company and his steady presence in her home?

Already they had made great headway in the library. Thomas had discovered several rare volumes of illumination, and she had ordered a showcase built to display them. Together they'd poured over the pages, tracing their fingers over the gilded letters and fanciful animals that adorned each chapter opening.

He was quiet on their drive, his focus on his horses, a pair of lively grays. She'd always considered Thomas to be a sedate, cautious fellow, but he drove to an inch, and rode as well as any man in the county. She now wondered if his slow, deliberate manner with her was natural to him, or if he'd acquired it during his frequent visits to Bellaire, which had begun while she and Lucas were still newlyweds. What if she had met him before her marriage? Would he have maintained that same courtly distance from her, or would she have seen an animated, engaging man? Did Sir Thomas de Burgh even know how to flirt?

She was rocked out of her musings when the curricle hit an uneven patch of road and she was forced to take his arm to steady herself. By way of an experiment, she left her hand there on his upper arm. She could feel the flex of his muscles as he brought his horses under control.

Damn that walking stick! she fumed. *It's fooled me into thinking him less than robust.* And damn his insistence on emulating the way Lucas had treated her, as though she were made of porcelain. Lucas had been a man in his fifties when he'd wed her. She doubted Thomas was much more than forty, closer to her in age than he'd been to Lucas. And yet she'd always thought of the two men as contemporaries . . . sharing their interests in books and music. Thomas had been her husband's protégée, she now saw. Not his peer.

When they reached the inn at Paultons, Sir Thomas climbed from his seat and went around the curricle to assist her down. He held out one hand, but she leaned forward and put both her hands on his shoulders. He threw his head back and gazed up at her, his eyes now clouded with uncertainty.

Gray, she thought. *A fine, clear shade of gray, like an autumn twilight.* How silly that she'd never noticed. Or the way his thick brown hair waved slightly over his ears and at his collar.

Are you a handsome man? she wanted to ask, as he at last put his hands around her waist and swung her down from the carriage. *For I cannot tell . . . You have been a fixture in my life for so long, that I see only Thomas, my friend, Thomas, my confidante, Thomas, my starchy conscience.*

"What is it, Minerva?" His hands were still at her waist. "You look as though you'd seen a ghost."

And she had, she realized. The ghost of her husband, who had been her friend, and her confidante, and her equally starchy conscience. Lucas had also been her lover . . . a man who, after a lifetime of dry, dusty pursuits, had found and shared unutterable bliss in his wife's loving arms. She wondered what sort of lover Sir Thomas would be, and then felt herself blush. But she knew from her own dear husband that a man who was sedate and cautious in his daily life, was not necessarily either of those things in bed.

Find another man like Lucas, Thomas had repeatedly told her.

And she, blindest of creatures, had had that very man right under her nose.

When Griffin's coach reached London, it was late afternoon. His mission in Bristol had been a waste of time. Even old and trusted business partners feared to ally themselves with him, as if he bore a taint that would sully their own endeavors. It was another grating reminder that his prospects for recovery hinged on the wealthy widow. The woman who demanded his love in return for sharing her fortune.

Fool that he was, he'd thought he could have it all—a secure future with Minerva and a delightful clandestine relationship with Gates Underhill. But he hadn't seen the trap he'd set for himself: by keeping Gates close by him, he'd made her a virtual part of his family. She frolicked with his brothers and accompanied Delphie on her missions of mercy. She spent hours in the stable talking to Farrow and conferred with Bucket on the merits of one racehorse over another. She had even charmed his frosty valet by exhibiting her talents with a needle and thread on a brocaded waistcoat that Griffin had torn.

Gates had integrated herself into his household with her unaffected manners and, with the exception of Marchand, she had won favor with everyone. He had purposely surrounded her with people who would guard her virtue until he was wed to Minerva, but

they had somehow become watchdogs in perpetuity. Unless he intended to replace all his servants and disassociate himself from his
brothers and his aunt, Griff could no longer blithely take the girl as
his mistress. If he dared they would, to use Delphie's favorite expression, boil him in oil.

Which thought left him in a sour, frustrated frame of mind. He
would never possess Gates Underhill on his own terms. If he took
her now, it would confirm Minerva's worst suspicions. If he took
her later, he would be a pariah in his own home. And it would furthermore betray Minerva. Surely a man owed some loyalty to the
woman who was going to bail him out of impending bankruptcy.

"Ah, but I am bankrupt," he muttered to himself as the coach
rounded Hyde Park corner. "As morally bankrupt and as con-
scienceless as any Darrowby born."

It was a startling revelation. And a distasteful one. Griffin had
spent so much of his life battling against his legacy of anger and
brutality that he'd never stopped to examine the other unsavory
traits that had been bequeathed to him by his sire. He was auto-
cratic, selfish, prideful, and remorseless.

He thought again of the ten buttons Gates had initially returned
to him—a testimony of conscience from a woman who refused to
be in his debt. Gates Underhill was gentle, generous, humble, and
possessed more scruples than a pontiff. She was the light to his
darkness, the gold to his jet. At that moment he would have traded
all the wealth in the kingdom for the sure knowledge that he would
one day awaken beside her . . . would know the comfort of her
arms and of her soft, soothing words.

With sudden and startling clarity he realized why he'd been
working so hard to rebuild his finances. It was not so that he
wouldn't have to go to Lady Min empty-handed. It was so he
wouldn't have to go to her at all! Now that his plans had crumbled,
he saw that he'd been making them with Gates in mind.

It was true she made him angry. But she also made him laugh,
and she sometimes came very close to making him cry. She
touched him in a place that had been so barren and so cold for most
of his adult life. Her father had missed the mark when he'd rechristened her Gates of Heaven. There was a more fitting Biblical name
Griff would have chosen—Balm in Gilead.

He wasn't yet sure what course he would follow with her; he
was still facing his own ruin. But he knew above everything, that

he needed her with him. And he could not have that if he married elsewhere.

The front hallway was dimly lit and smelled of pork fat. Bucket was not in the front hall, so Griffin drew off his greatcoat and hat, and went immediately into his study. The hearth beneath the marble mantel was cold and had been swept clean of any kindling. He lit a candle and the room filled with the same acrid scent that had permeated the hall. "Tallow," he muttered, as he leaned over to observe the brownish candles in the brass stand. They'd often used tallow candles in Spain. He hated tallow candles.

"Bucket!" he called from the doorway. He waited for several moments and when his butler did not appear, he went down the hall and called his name again. Scotty peeked his head out of the library. He was wearing a woolen muffler around his throat. "Hullo, Griff."

"What the devil is going on here?" he said. "Have we fallen on such hard times that we cannot any longer afford to heat this place? And why in blazes are there tallow candles in every room?"

"Er," Scotty stammered. "You'd best talk to Cort. He was in charge while you were gone." He disappeared back into the library.

"Bucket!" Griff called again in his most carrying, captain-of-light-cavalry voice. "Cortland!"

He stood in the shadowy hall and wondered where his household had disappeared to. He ran down the steps to the basement level and knocked loudly on the door to Bucket's room, waiting impatiently for a response. Marchand's door next received his assault and again there was no answer. He was muttering sourly as he strode into the kitchen, his booted feet echoing crisply on the slate floor. There were pots simmering on the cooking racks above the blazing hearth, but of Marchand, his temperamental chef, there was no sign. The door to the larder opened and Gates emerged carrying a jar of preserves.

"Oh," she said, stopping short at the sight of him. "You're here." She set down the jar and went to the stove, where she began to stir a pan of sauce with a wooden spoon. She was wearing a long white apron over her gown and had pulled her hair up into a knot at the back of her head. If he hadn't been so distracted, he would have thought she looked utterly delicious.

"Yes, I'm here. And I'm wondering what is going on in my house. Tallow candles, no fires lit upstairs . . . and I shudder to think what else."

"Economy," she said without turning away from her task. "We are practicing economy."

A look of growing suspicion crossed his face when he realized there were several recipe books opened on the kitchen table. To his knowledge, his chef had never once referred to a book to create his miraculous concoctions.

"Oh, no," he uttered. "Tell me that Marchand is still here. Tell me that he is merely sulking in his room over some slight from Bucket or Wilby."

"He is gone to the Duchess of Stratfield," she said. "Because he was frightfully expensive, and besides, you don't need to be French to prepare a decent meal—"

"A decent meal!" Griffin exclaimed. "The man was a genius with seafood, an artist with lamb, and . . . and his way with a cream sauce has been celebrated by at least three poets. And you have the nerve to call his sublime efforts a decent meal?"

Gates had been blowing on a spoonful of the white sauce, and after Griffin finished his diatribe she held it up to his mouth. He made as if to swipe it away, and she stamped one foot.

"At least taste it, you insufferable snob."

"Snob!" he railed, and as his lips shaped themselves to do justice to the word, she slipped the spoon into his mouth.

"Mmmm!" he muttered, tugging it out by the handle. "How dare you . . ." But he was distracted now. The essence of brandy and cream and something subtle he couldn't quite put his tongue around were mingling inside his mouth. *"Mmmm,"* he said again, slower this time, as he licked the back of the spoon.

"Well?" she asked, putting her hands on her hips and cocking her head.

"Oh, Gates." He sighed blissfully. "This is heaven."

"Not bad for a farm girl from Cheshire," she said triumphantly. "Now if you will leave me to my cooking, Cortland will be home at any time. It is he who must tell you about our plans to economize."

She shooed him from the room, but not before he had refilled the wooden spoon from the simmering pan. "And mind you don't burn your tongue," she called after him.

When she turned back to the stove she was grinning. Some sage had once pronounced that the way to a man's heart was through his stomach, and if the look on Griffin Darrowby's face when he'd tasted her sauce was any indication, he would be her slave for life inside a fortnight.

Cort arrived home just before dinner, and Griffin must have pounced on him immediately. Gates could hear their raised voices even in the recesses of the kitchen. When Bucket came into the room to fetch up the first course, he made a slashing motion across his throat with one hand.

"That bad," she said with a sigh. "I had a feeling he wouldn't take the news with any good grace."

When she entered the dining room to take her place at the table, the tension was palpable. Even Delphie was sitting in silence, all her peppery energy diffused by the strained expressions of the men sitting around her. Gates escaped to prepare the dessert course—a frothy concoction of meringue and strawberry preserves—and when she returned to the dining room, Griffin refused to even look at her.

She waited until later that evening to brook him. She knew he usually retired to his study with a decanter of brandy after the meal was finished. It was prudent to give the mellowing liquor some time to work before she entered the room.

"Griffin?" she said as she cracked the door. "Might I have a word?"

"Come to gloat, have you?" he said wearily without turning from his desk.

"No," she said as she crossed over to him. "I merely wanted to see how you were faring."

He looked up at her then, and she saw a flicker of bleak despair in his eyes. "I am faring just fine, thank you." He poured a measure of brandy into his glass and saluted her before he swallowed it. "What man wouldn't be faring fine to discover himself at the mercy of two striplings and a farm girl?"

"They, er, we were only trying to help. Your brothers sold their horses, did you know that? And Cortland sent his curricle off to Tattersall's."

Griff slammed his glass down on the desk and leapt to his feet. "I will not be an object of pity!" he cried. "Not in the *ton*, not among my friends, and certainly not among my own family. My finances are nobody's bloody business but my own." He leaned toward her, his eyes black with rage. "Do you understand that, Miss Underhill?"

"We will not speak of these things outside this house," she said staunchly, refusing to back down in spite of the fierce glare he was leveling at her.

"And do you think my servants will be so discreet? They are no doubt sniggering behind their hands at my comedown. Tallow candles, indeed! And what servants know, soon the whole of the *ton* knows. And then every tradesman I have ever done business with will be hammering at my front door looking for payment."

Gates took him by the shoulders and forced him back into his chair. She knew he hadn't expected her to be so forward, which was why he allowed her to manhandle him in such a way. She then perched on the edge of his desk and said bitingly, "It's a pity you have so little faith in them. In truth, *they* have a deal more faith in you. Wilby and Bucket, and Farrow, of course, have all agreed to work for their board only until you come to rights. Robert has a mother to look after, but he said he would work at half pay. Now, how do you feel about that?"

Griffin's response was to pour himself another brandy. Gates plucked it out of his hands and sipped at it gingerly. "Thank you," she said primly. "Cooking gives one a rare thirst."

"Devil take you," Griff muttered as he set his elbows on the blotter and looked away from her.

"I gather," she said more gently, "that your mission in Bristol did not go well."

He looked over his shoulder at her and smiled grimly. "Why am I not surprised that you knew about that? It's bad enough that Cort's been filching letters from my desk, but did he have to share them with half the world? And to answer your impertinent and extremely prying question, no, it did not go well. Even old friends want nothing to do with me these days."

"Here," she said, wrapping his fingers around the stem of the glass.

"I don't need anything more to drink," he growled.

"I know. I thought maybe you'd like to pitch it across the room."

"I fear I need something more substantial than a glass to do justice to my frustration. Maybe I should pitch you across the room, Miss Under-the-Hill."

She nearly grinned. "Speaking as someone who is a professional glass breaker, I doubt I would make a very satisfactory crash."

"Oh, Gates," he cried, halfway to a chuckle, as he spun back to her. "Why do things seem less bleak when you are with me?" He reached for her hands, capturing them in his own. His eyes lifted to meet her even gaze. "My little turnip."

"Don't call me that," she chided him softly. "You hate turnips."

"I may have to revise my opinion," he whispered as he raised her hands to his mouth. "I've never before met a turnip who smelled of vanilla and strawberries."

"Cozening man," she said under her breath. She leaned forward and laid her cheek against his golden hair—which shimmered no less brightly in the light of tallow candles. They remained so for several minutes, until the mantel clock chimed midnight. Griffin released her hands and sat up. His eyes were no longer clouded. Instead they shone with a bright wonder.

"You'd best get some sleep," he said in a low voice. "I expect you will be up at the crack of dawn to make me a six-course breakfast."

She grinned down at him. "I was thinking of poached eggs en croute, with truffles and caviar."

He groaned. "Then I will be the best-fed pauper in this city."

She slid from the desk and was halfway across the room, when she stopped, "Griff? I heard you yelling at Cortland before dinner—" She was sure half the square had heard him. "And I am glad of it."

"Because he deserved it, you mean?"

She retraced her steps to his desk. "No, because I think it's about time you started behaving like a brother, and not like a stiff-necked schoolmaster. It's not natural, the way you act with them. Anger is a good thing, when it serves to bring people closer together."

"What the devil are you talking about? Anger never served anyone—"

"Farrow says you forgot how to be angry when you were a boy. He says that—"

"I don't give a damn what Farrow says."

"But it's true. And what's more, I believe it's why you tolerate me, because I make you angry so often. You need to let out some of your rage now and again. Otherwise the top of your head would fly off, like the lid on a kettle that's been left on the hob too long."

Griffin was regarding her with something akin to astonishment.

"Even God gets angry," she added. "It's in the Bible and in Papa's Book, as well. But I'm sorry about repeating what Farrow said—it was in confidence and I never should have told you."

"See what I mean about servants and gossip," he said. "Nothing stays a secret once *they* learn of it."

"Yes," she said, putting up her chin. "I see your point. You wouldn't want Lady Minerva to think you were after her money."

Griffin shrugged. "I told her how things stood with my finances before I left Bellaire. It hardly fazed her. But I can't go to *any* woman with my creditors at my heels."

"No," Gates said stiffly. "That would never do for a Darrowby."

Gates kept busy the next morning, cooking, helping Delphie with her birds, and then seeking refuge in the garden with her shears. She had only cried a little the night before, for being such a gullible and foolish girl. Just because Griffin had kissed her hands and sat with her cheek resting upon his head for what seemed like an eon, did not mean he had any intention of altering his plans with Lady Minerva.

It had been a blow to discover the widow was unperturbed by his wretched finances. Gates had harbored some vague hope that when the lady discovered the true state of Griffin's affairs, she would discourage his suit. But that was clearly not going to happen.

She still puzzled over why Griffin was trying to rebuild his fortune. It seemed a pointless goal, in light of the lady's enormous wealth. But there was masculine pride to consider and no man wanted to be labeled a fortune-hunter. She could imagine how that would rankle a man like Griffin Darrowby. And here she was, helping him reduce his expenditures, so that he could go to his lady with his pride intact.

She threw down her shears and kicked them across the garden path.

Gates went into the study the next morning to ask Griffin why he'd missed his breakfast. He looked as though he hadn't been to bed at all. His face was unshaven, his cravat at half-mast, dangling down over his opened waistcoat. The brandy decanter at his elbow was suspiciously empty.

"I received this last night from Pendleton," he said hoarsely, holding up a wrinkled paper. "Lord Pettibone has purchased the mortgage on this house, and is beginning foreclosure proceedings." She gave a loud gasp. "We've been checkmated, Gates. Do you know what that means . . . ? It's a chess term—"

She was nodding when he said crossly, "But of course you play chess. How silly of me to think otherwise. I forget there's not a blasted thing you can't do. Read Latin, doctor horses, balance a ledger, rescue urchins . . . Christ, you probably compose Elizabethan madrigals in your spare time, when you're not advising the prime minister."

Gates kept a solemn face so as not to provoke him further, and perched on the arm of a chair. "This is very bad news, isn't it? Can he actually take your house from you?"

Griffin nodded. "Can and will."

"Oh, Griffin," she said with a tiny throb in her voice. "This is my fault. If you hadn't gone to him that night at Rippon's, if you hadn't—"

He cut her off abruptly. "I did what needed to be done. To protect you. I . . . I forgot that I'd become vulnerable. That money equals power and that the lack of it puts you at the mercy of men like Pettibone."

She looked thoughtful for a few seconds. "I suppose this is not a good time to make a confession," she said nervously.

"Nothing you say can shock me," he uttered. "I have lost the ability to be surprised."

"Since I feel responsible for this new disaster, I would like to approach my mother's father on your behalf. You asked me once if her family had any money, and I did not answer you quite truthfully. I believe my grandfather is a wealthy man." She hesitated and then said in a low voice. "A very wealthy man."

"You also told me her family wanted nothing to do with her or you. Why would that have changed?"

Gates looked pensive. "I read in the *Times* last week that my grandfather is very ill. I thought perhaps he might want to patch things up with me."

"Ah, a deathbed reunion, is that what you fancy, my girl?" Then a look of uncertainty clouded his face. He turned to her and asked cautiously, "Gates, why would the *Times* print something about your grandfather in Cornwall?"

"He's not in Cornwall at present," she said softly. "He has been staying at his house in London." Her voice rose a notch. "Oh, please don't be angry when I tell you. I didn't think it mattered, after all. But now I might be able to aid you, if I can make him see reason."

"Who is he, Gates?" It was too late she saw, the anger was already flashing in his eyes.

"Arthur Bembroke," she said weakly. "Viscount Conklin."

Griffin's mouth fell open. He was clearly not as beyond surprise as he'd thought.

He rose from his chair and loomed over her. "You are Lord Conklin's granddaughter?"

She swallowed audibly and then nodded.

He threw his head back and gave a harsh shout of laughter. "Sweet Jesus! This is a new low, even for the Darrowbys. I have set a viscount's granddaughter to laboring in my kitchen. I can't wait to hear what the *ton* shall make of it. It's almost too delicious."

Gates leaped to her feet and grasped his arm. "You didn't 'set me' to anything. I work for you because I want to. Because I . . ." Somehow she couldn't quite bring herself to say the words. He would scoff at them in his present mood. Declarations of love needed the proper forum.

"You work for me," he drawled wearily, "because you are a meddlesome, managing chit, who can never leave anything alone." Though his words were cutting, the expression in his eyes was brimming with fondness. "And I have never thanked you," he added softly, "for staying here and helping me battle through this wretched situation."

Her eyes brightened. "I never wanted your thanks, Griffin. It is I who owe you. So please say you will let me do this one thing for you . . . let me at least speak to my grandfather."

"I cannot keep you from him, Gates. But do not go there expecting a reward."

She looked down at her hands, twisted together against her skirt. "You think he will refuse to acknowledge me? Am I so unworthy of his consideration?"

Griffin reached out and cupped the side of her face with his hand. "He is the luckiest man on the planet to have you for a granddaughter. And a blind old fool to have left you to fend for yourself. But I wasn't speaking of his ethics, just now. Conklin was ruined, as I was, by his investments in the Indian mine. I heard it from Pendleton himself."

There was a rare expression of defeat in her eyes. "Perhaps he had other investments."

Griffin shook his head. "According to Pendleton, it was hearing of the mine disaster that made your grandfather ill. He collapsed in Pendleton's office and had to be carried out on a litter."

She raised her eyes to him after a moment. "I . . . I can't seem to muster up any sympathy for him, as sick as he may be. My mother died without a single member of her family beside her, and all because of that stubborn old man."

"You and your father were beside her, Gates. I'm sure she was easy in her heart."

Gates sniffed back her tears. She had other business to tend to besides weeping over what was past.

"Well, what's to be done now? You can't let Pettibone take your home."

"I'm damned if I know," he said. "I can sell the furnishings and the paintings. I've a collection of Restoration plays that might fetch a good price at auction. But it won't be enough to pay off the mortgage." He looked away from her. "The Earl of Carnes told me I could name my price for Gaspar—"

"No!" she cried. "No one else can handle him, you know that. They will beat him."

He set his elbows on the desk, his chin on his fists. "There is another way," he said musingly. "One I swore years ago never to pursue." He tipped his head toward her and grinned. "But if you were willing to petition your fearsome grandfather, why then, how can I balk at petitioning the Gorgon?"

She set a hand on his shoulder. "She *is* your mother. She must have some maternal feelings for you."

"Well, there's only one way to find out." He drew a sheet of paper from a cubbyhole and dipped his pen in the dragon inkwell. "What do you think? A tone of earnest supplication?"

"That'll be the day," she muttered. "Just try not to insult her too grievously. Why not say that you've a financial proposition to discuss with her. From what your brothers tell me, she always welcomes a chance to come to London."

"Ah, but not to get her pockets picked."

Gates leaned over his shoulder. "If you do it properly," she whispered into his ear, "she'll never know what hit her. I have some experience of your methods of getting your way with unsuspecting females."

He pivoted around. "As if you've ever let me cozen you," he complained.

She backed away, all the while grinning at him. "Write your letter, Griffin. I have potatoes to boil."

He merely rolled his eyes skyward for an instant, and then turned back to his desk. "Before you return to the kitchen, would you tell Bucket to take down all the paintings in the main hall. No, on second thought, we'll wait with that. It wouldn't do for the Gorgon to get wind of my plight the instant she walks through the door. If she even comes," he added with a scowl.

She'll come, Gates murmured to herself. And it was more of a prayer than a reassurance.

Chapter Thirteen

It was late in the afternoon, four days later, when an elegant post chaise drew to a halt before the house. Gates was in the front parlor with Cort and Scotty, writing out a list of items to be sold, when they heard the commotion on the front walk and ran to the window. Gates watched as a slim, stylishly dressed, blond woman was handed out of the carriage by a liveried groom.

"Great bleeding Christ!" Cort moaned. "We're done for now."

"She's come here to help Griffin," Gates explained trying to tamp down her jubilation. Griff had cautioned her not to tell his brothers of his plan, in case it came to naught, and she had complied. But as she took in the shocked dismay in both their faces, she thought perhaps she should have warned them of their mama's impending visit.

"Oh, that's washed it!" Scotty exclaimed as he snapped the drapery closed. He glared at his brother. "There's nothing for it now, Cort. I'm going to tell her it was your idea."

"The hell you will! I'm not the one who wrote the blasted letters."

Scotty's face turned a deep crimson and looked as though it were going to explode. *"Aooww!* How could I have let you bamboozle me? But I can see it won't matter which of us takes the blame. The Gorgon will have our heads, and if she don't, Griffin will skin us both alive."

Gates was staring at them in complete bewilderment. "What in heaven's name are you talking about?"

"We never told you," Scotty said penitently. "Cort was also intercepting our mother's letters to Griff. It turns out she's—"

"She's going down the hall," Cort interrupted from his position beside the door. "Griff was in his study all morning, so she's probably been taken there. C'mon." He hooked Scotty by the arm and dragged him out of the parlor.

"Have you lost your wits?" Scotty cried, pulling back.

"We've got to hear what she says. Maybe there's a way to get around this mess."

Still awash with curiosity, Gates trailed them down the hall and into the library. The brothers went immediately to the pocket door that led to the study and placed their ears against the oak panel.

She stood in the center of the room. "I don't think—"

Cort crossed to her and covered her mouth with his hand. "You've got to keep silent," he hissed.

She nodded. He drew her back to the door. Gates also put her ear against the panel and listened with all her might.

Griffin watched his mother arrange her skirts as she settled into one of the armchairs.

"You're looking well, madam," he observed. "Though I don't believe you were quite so blazingly blond the last time we met."

She set a hand to her coiling coiffure. "I think this color becomes me enormously. It's all the crack in Bath, if you must know."

"The gentlemen must be going about with shaded spectacles then."

She pouted. "It's easy for you now, Griffin, in the glory of your youth. But wait until *your* looks begin to fade, and the ladies no longer cast lingering glances at you. You'll take to the bottle fast enough then."

He nearly laughed. Here he sat, on tenterhooks over this interview, and his inimitable parent was lecturing him on hair dye. It was almost a relief that some things changed so little over time. He recalled Gates's instructions—that he was not to insult her.

"But then I have far less cause for vanity than you, Mama. I only hope I bear up as well."

This transparent flattery was met with visible preening on her part. "Thank you," she murmured. "I believe that is the first kind thing you have said to me in many years. A mother likes to know she has the approval of her son, even if she has . . . been imprudent at times."

Griff thought it a poor word for how she had treated him, but kept it to himself.

"In truth I was a little afraid to come here," she continued. "Your other letters were so harsh; I suspected someone else had written them. Imagine my horror when you so callously instructed me to sell my coach and four, and to auction off the Darrowby silver. But then your most recent letter was much more welcoming. It convinced me that I was best off coming to settle things with you in person."

"Other letters?" Griffin murmured. "The fact is, madam, the one I sent on Monday was the first I'd written to you since I returned from Spain. That was in May."

She gave a nervous laugh. "Oh, no, Griffin. You are mistaken. I have your letters here in my reticule." She patted the richly beaded bag in her lap.

"May I see them?" he asked. She fished them out and handed them to him. He scanned each one rapidly, and as he did so, his eyes hardened and his jaw clenched.

"This is not my hand," he pronounced thickly, holding up the first two. But the ruse that had been perpetrated on her worried him far less than the content of the letters. They had clearly been written in response to her pleas for money.

"Of course it's your hand," she protested. "As if a mother wouldn't know her own son's handwriting. Even if you have always been a poor correspondent."

He stood up and growled, "I did not write these letters. But I have a pretty fair notion who did."

There was a noise from behind the closed pocket doors. Griffin went striding over to them, but by the time he'd slid them open, Gates alone was standing there. He could hear his brothers footsteps racing along the hall toward the front door.

"Abandoned by your conspirators, eh?"

She winced. "I was, er, cleaning." She plucked a feather duster off a nearby tabletop. "See?"

"Well, you'd best come in here and meet my mother."

Gates tucked the duster under one arm, like a field marshal's baton, and preceded him into his study.

"Mother, may I present Miss Underhill of Cheshire. Miss Underhill, my mother, Lady Constance Darrowby."

Gates sank into a respectable curtsy. She then moved forward and boldly took up the lady's hand. It lay limp and cold against her palm, like a dead halibut. "I am pleased to meet you, Lady Constance. I see now why your sons liken you to a fabulous Greek myth."

She dipped again, shot Griffin a sly glance, and took herself back to the library. He followed and slid the doors shut after leveling her with a grim frown.

His mother was trembling with affront when he turned back to her. "You . . . you introduced me to a *servant*? Have you gone wit-less?"

"Witless?" he echoed, and then smiled. "Yes, I expect I have. But Gates is no servant."

"She was carrying a cleaning implement of some sort," his mother pointed out archly.

"We are practicing economy in this household," he said. "And we all do our part."

"Then who is she?"

My darling, Griffin was tempted to reply. *The warm heart of this once-cold house.*

He coughed slightly. "She is Delphinia's companion."

"I have heard nothing of this."

"You don't hear all there is to know in Bath, madam. She has been with Delphie for some time now."

"She needs to be taught nicer manners," she said, rubbing at the hand where Gates had touched her.

Griffin said under his breath, "I'm afraid that will require a bet-ter man than me."

Lady Constance resumed her seat. "Well, Griffin, will you please tell me what has been going on here. I have been writing to you since early September about the state of my finances."

"What," he said, "gambled away all your pin money?"

"I explained in my letters," she cried fitfully. "Oh, please, Griff, don't make me go through it all again." She plucked a delicate square of lace from her bag and began to dab her eyes. "You think I am heartless, but I can't tell you how my heart has been wrenched by this betrayal. I have never felt so much pain."

He suspected that if she were truly having financial woes, then her hard little heart must be breaking over it. "For God's sake," he snarled. "Stop your theatrics and tell me straight out what has hap-pened."

She put up her chin and said in a breathy, wilting voice, "I've lost everything, Griff."

His face paled. There might have been theatrics in her voice, but the truth of her words lay like dull cinders in her once-bright eyes.

"Tell me," he said more gently.

"Old Higgins, the lawyer who administered my jointure, died in the winter. His son took over the handling of my affairs—Young Higgins," she said. "Only he wasn't so very young. Close to forty, I'd say. And with the most lovely smile and the most wonderful—"

"Ah, no, madam," he moaned. "Please, don't regale me with details of this paragon's person. Just tell me what Not-So-Young Higgins did with your jointure."

She sighed. "He convinced me to invest in one of those new steam engines. I know nothing of such things, but he told me I wouldn't find a better opportunity in this lifetime."

Griffin cocked his head. "I don't believe he was wrong. What happened?"

"I cannot be sure," she said with a little sob. "I merely signed a power of attorney—so that he wouldn't have to pester me over every little thing. But then the magistrates came to me—"

"Magistrates?"

"Yes, they asked me if I knew where he had gone. His other clients were nearly rioting in Bath. He had taken all their funds and ridden off. But I knew he wouldn't have done such a thing to me. We were . . . that is, I was . . ."

"Please," he said, holding up one hand. "Imagination suffices. So he absconded with all your money?"

"Everything, including your brother's trust funds. He even took my diamond and emerald necklace . . . the one your grandmother gave me. He offered to have the clasp repaired. It had snapped, you see, one night while we were—"

"Madam! I understand that this knave was your lover. You needn't keep reminding me."

"He was very charming," she said sullenly. "And you know I have so little amusement in my life."

"You shall have even less now," he said without rancor.

Her eyes filled with tears. "You're not going to help me. I can see it in your face. It puts me in mind of *his* face, of all those times when he was harsh with me. Your father was so intolerant of my nature, but I thought you were better than him, Griffin. Not a hard man, only a distant one."

Griffin got up and paced to the window. "I am at present neither hard nor distant, Mother. I am, if plain truth be spoken, bankrupt."

"No!" She came to her feet in a rush of satin. "You are wealthy. Even in Bath they speak of the fortune you made on 'Change."

He turned to her and smiled grimly. "As I said before, they don't know everything in Bath. I am punting up the river tick with a vengeance. Every investment I had went sour this spring. Boats sank, crops wilted, and landslides inundated mines. This house is mortgaged and about to be foreclosed on. I find myself a veritable

Job, for all the trials I have had to withstand. I cannot help you. But, for what it is worth, I believe I would have helped you, were it in my power."

Something in his lost expression must have stirred the last shred of maternal concern that remained in her breast. She went to him and touched his sleeve. "I was very proud of you for making your own way, Griffin. I know it was mostly to spite your father, and I am ashamed to say, I hope he was duly incensed by your success. But what is to become of us now? We cannot sell Darrowby or any of the land."

"I have been gnawing on that very problem these past months." He rubbed at his brow with his knuckles. "Lord, I even contemplated marriage to an heiress—"

Lady Constance grasped his arm through the sleeve of his coat. "Minerva Stargrove! Of course! Viscountess Upworth told me she was sure you were courting the widow. You see, Griffin, we do know a few things in Bath." Her voice lifted gaily. "Oh, my blessed boy. This is all that is wonderful." She tapped at his wrist with her fingertips. "But naughty, naughty Griffin. For scaring me so. Of course that is the solution. Scotty needn't give up Oxford, and Cort can live in a better part of London. Why, from what I hear, Minerva Stargrove is up to her eyeteeth in gilt. I can have the drawing room at Darrowby redone in the Egyptian style and order new hangings for my bedchamber."

She was flitting about the room, her head cast back as she cataloged the things she could buy. "And I shall order a new wardrobe—it wouldn't do for the mother of the groom to look dowdy. And I can—"

"No!" He'd caught her up by the shoulders. "It's not going to happen, so you can stop redecorating and refurbishing. I'm not going to marry Minerva Stargrove."

She shook him off and smiled deliriously. "Of course you are."

He had an inkling then of why his father had been driven to violence around this woman. She was surely the most self-indulgent, care-for-none in the history of females.

"I have not offered for her," he said in a strained voice. "Though I led her to believe that was my intention. Which is why I have not written to tell her of my change of heart—such a message should be delivered in person."

"Oh, pooh!" she said crossly. "What idiocy is this? You hold the

Stargrove fortune in the palm of your hand and tell me you can blithely whistle it down the wind?"

"There are other commodities I have come to value more than money."

Lady Constance shot him a long, speculative look. "There is someone else?"

He nodded. "Very much so."

"Has she any prospects?"

"Not a one, save that she is resourceful and amusing and confoundedly pretty."

The lady sniffed. "I hope those attributes will still console you when you are living like a parson."

Griff nearly smiled. "She at least will not mind living like a parson. Her father happens to be one."

She threw up her hands. "This is my penance for going off and leaving you. To see you married to some nonentity with nothing to recommend her but a pretty face." Her eyes narrowed. "You've filled her belly," she muttered. "That's it, isn't it? She's schemed her way into your bed and now expects you to make an honest woman of her. The harpy!"

"She has done nothing of the kind," he said as the last of his patience evaporated. "And if you ever again speak of her in such a way, I will cut you, madam. As though you were invisible to me."

Again her eyes grew wet with tears. "Are there no gentle feelings inside you for your own mother, Griffin? I have come here, on my knees, to ask for your help. You must know how difficult that is for me. And I'm met with simpering vows of affection for some young woman . . . I hesitate to name her a lady."

"She is much more than a lady," he said softly.

"Yet you," she continued, "would place this . . . this stranger before your own family? No, don't stop me, Griffin—hear me out. When I left Darrowby all those years ago, it was so difficult to part with you. You were my favorite child, beautiful and clever. But you were also the only one of us who was strong enough to stand up to your father. Don't you remember how badly Cort stuttered and how Scotty rarely slept through the night? And I won't even go into my own travails in that house. But he never seemed to reach you, Griffin. You were a little soldier . . . braving the worst of his tempers to distract him from the rest of us. It was because of you that I was able to leave, to take my other babies to a safe place." She stopped to draw a breath. "So I cannot and will not believe you would now leave us at the mercy of the harsh world, not when it is within your power to protect us."

With a graceful motion, she drew up the hem of her gown and turned for the door. He was reminded of her departure from Darrowby, when she had raised the train of her carriage dress in just such a manner. He felt anew the shredding pain of abandonment and rejection.

"You blighted my youth," he said in a voice he hardly recognized as his own. "With your selfish affairs, which enraged him and made him lash out at me. And ultimately with your leave-taking, which deprived me of my brothers." A thread of pain stitched its way into his words. "And now you ask me to blight my adult life, as well, by pressing me to marry where I do not love." He took a halting step toward her. "You expect me to give up a girl who is more than air and sunlight and life itself to me, so that you can buy new hangings?"

She put her chin up. "I expect you to do what is right for your family," she said. "Precisely because that is *not* the Darrowby way. Your father would have married this churchmouse and sated himself with her, were that his pleasure. He always put his own pleasure first. But *you* are not your father, Griffin."

With that potent salvo she sailed from the room.

Griffin stood unmoving for fully five minutes after her departure, his thoughts tumbling inside his head like dice in a paperboard box. Several coherent thoughts at last managed to fight their way out of the chaos. She was not going to save him from disaster . . . she had engineered a disaster of her own.

She had also brought several truths home to him. Cort and Scotty would have nothing, no prospects, no future. All the Darrowby servants, his own and his mother's, who had served the family for decades, would be turned out. The elderly retainers would have no pensions, no sureties for their old age. His mother's fate he was less concerned with. She would find a well-heeled man to look after her—if he knew the Gorgon, she had probably driven off to the park in her chaise to look for suitable candidates.

And then there was Gates. Child of a careless, rambling father and granddaughter of a broken, bankrupted peer. They made a pretty pair, he and his wood sprite, with not a penny between them. Only an as-yet-unspoken love. But could love endure in poverty?

He was not sure it could. He had never been without money—even when he left Darrowby he'd had his grandmother's bequest. He wondered how his love for Gates would stand up against deprivation and hunger. Against the sharp arrows of ridicule from his peers and stares of pity from his friends. He'd been the object of such things during his boyhood—a sorry joke of the *ton,* Lady Constance's bartered son—and had sworn he would never be again.

He walked like one in a trance to his desk and poured himself a brandy. But he couldn't raise it to his mouth, his hands were shaking so badly.

You are not your father. He'd put his pleasure first.

Was that what he was doing with Gates? God, his mother had twisted the truth with her viper's tongue until he had no idea where the rightness of things lay. Was he shirking his responsibilities so that he could pleasure himself with a woman? And if that was all he wanted, why not ally himself with a rich one?

"Griffin?" Gates peeked her head into the room. "I heard her go out."

He nodded as he settled on the edge of the desk. "Mmm. She's gone."

She came toward him. And then stopped when she saw the look of numb disbelief in his eyes.

"I'm sorry you caught me eavesdropping." She bit at her lip, an expression he usually took the time to admire. But it did not move him. "I heard enough of what she said. She hasn't any money left, has she?"

"Not a groat," he said as he raised the glass and drank deeply. His eyes challenged her over the rim. "So tell me, Miss Under-the-Hill, where is your daily miracle today? Where in bloody blazes is anything even remotely resembling a miracle?"

She laid her hands upon his chest. "The miracle is never about money, Griffin," she said. "It is not about material things. It's about beauty and wonder. Trust is a miracle . . . and caring." Her voice lowered to a husky whisper. "Love is a miracle."

"Love?" he echoed harshly. "What has that to do with me? You just met my mother . . . can you believe there is room in that vain creature's heart for such a thing? Fortunately you never met my father, but I assure you, love was as foreign to him as charity to a miser. Those two people made me, Gates. They shaped me and molded me in their image. So what can I know of love?"

He twisted away from her and crossed the room. She caught up with him and forced him onto one of the chairs, holding him down, her hands at his shoulders.

"This is so hard for you," she said with a wavering sigh as she slid onto the chair's arm. "For a time I did have parents who loved me. And I truly don't know which is worse, Griffin. Never knowing love, or knowing it and then losing it."

She heard his voice break as he answered in a bleak, lost tone. "The worst is . . . wanting love . . . and knowing you will never have it."

He thrust his face hard against her shoulder, trying to muffle the sound of his dry sobs. She held on to him for dear life, her arms tight and her voice soothing as she murmured endearments against his bright hair. When at last he drew back from her, his face was pale, his hair a disordered tangle above his brow. It was the face of a child, she realized, because his pain was that of a child.

"There," she said whispering a golden lock back from his forehead, "that's been a long time coming."

He looked away. "I'm sorry you had to witness it. She rather knocked the slats out from under me. I'm all right now. But . . . I . . . I think I need to be alone."

He couldn't be alone; Gates understood that. Already his detachment was returning, the icy manner that kept her at arm's length. She was not going to let him go, not after he'd shared his grief with her.

She slid down to kneel on the carpet. "Look at me, Griffin. I'm not going to try to cajole you out of this distemper. I think you need to experience it. But don't you dare imagine yourself unloved." He quirked one brow at her. "Your brothers worship you, if you only had the sense to see it. And Delphie harbors a very deep affection for you. Farrow and Wilby and Bucket would do anything to aid you. That sort of loyalty must be akin to love, don't you think?"

When he made no comment, she went relentlessly on, now clutching his lapels between her fingers. "You are so blind to love now, I wonder if you were equally blind to it as a child. Like a covered garden where no sunlight could penetrate."

"A covered garden also keeps out the darkness," he said as his eyes hooded over.

She gave a ragged cry and pounded his chest with her fist in frustration.

He caught her hand in an iron grip. "Don't," he said between his teeth. "Don't ever hit me. *He* hit me. Too many times to count. I wasn't only blind to love, Gates. I made myself blind to pain and rage and despair. I was alone in the wilderness—you cannot know what that is like—and I schooled myself to feeling nothing."

Her eyes darkened. "How dare you assume that I don't know what it's like in the wilderness. I traveled the countryside with a madman, sleeping in the open, shivering in the rain. But I never closed myself off from my feelings, the only feeling I turned my back on was fear. Because fear cripples you more than all those other things combined."

He tapped the back of his hand against her jutting chin. "I always wondered how you managed to stay serene in the face of all your trials . . . I admired you for it, more than you can know. Now I see where your serenity comes from—unlike me, you believe that no one can take anything from you. Nothing that counts, at any rate."

She mulled over his words, and then nodded slowly. "I never expected more than I got, Griffin." Her hand reached for his and gripped it tight. "But somehow I got so much more than I expected."

He raised their joined hands to his lips and kissed her knuckles. "So did I," he said hoarsely. "I feel things when I am with you, Gates. Things I haven't dared to feel in so long."

Her eyes danced. "You mean anger and irritation and frustration?"

"Oh, yes." He was watching her face as he bit tenderly into the soft skin he held to his mouth and the look in his eyes made her tremble. "But there are other feelings, some of them so fine I cannot put a name to them, they are so foreign to me. And all because a managing, meddlesome farm girl took her ax and crashed in the roof of my covered garden."

"I didn't have an ax," she said mischievously. "Sank sold it to a peddler, if you will recall."

He slid his hands to her shoulders and pulled her forward until their brows touched. "I recall everything, Miss Under-the-Hill. From the minute you spooked my horse and sent me into the water, to the look on my mother's face when you curtseyed to her with a feather duster under your arm. You banished the Gorgon, my heart. I doubt there's a woman in this hemisphere who could have done that."

Gates grinned and rubbed her cheek against his. "Well, she was very intimidating. And very beautiful." She hesitated an instant. "Is that her real hair color?"

He laughed outright. "Lord, Gates, you have seen the idol's feet of clay. Or head of clay. She hasn't been a true blonde for a decade. And she'll despise you for having noticed."

Gates snapped her fingers under his nose. "I don't give a fig for your mother's opinion. You forget I have been educated by the formidable Delphinia Darrowby, who could have your mother for breakfast."

"Mmm. It appears I have surrounded myself with Amazons to fight my battles for me."

"Favors returned," she said. "You certainly did battle for me enough times."

"And will continue to, my heart. Will you let me protect you . . . ? I promise always to keep you out of the wilderness."

When she nodded, he reached down and drew her into his lap. She squirmed to settle herself and heard him groan deep in his throat. "Sit still," he growled, "Or I might need to kiss you."

"Indeed?" she said in her best bored-debutante voice. Then she laughed softly and put her arms around his neck. "What if I need to kiss you? Would you mind?"

Griffin was about to reply that it was not a matter of joking, when she took his head firmly between her hands and set her half open mouth against his. His body reacted instantly, like a spring that has been too tightly wound. Her kiss was not tentative, but it spoke of unschooled passion. His blood surged with the need to instruct her, to display his vast, accumulated knowledge of sensation and sensuality. But there would be plenty of time for tutorials—his present and only desire was to taste her.

He uncoiled from the chair, carrying her with him to the patterned carpet. His knees straddled her as he arched her up into his arms and took her mouth in a searing, draining kiss. His tongue danced against her teeth, her soft nether lip, and then it found its mate in the welcoming dark. They tangled and tasted, tongues and lips shaping into supple curves of shared delight.

Gates cried out against the onslaught to her senses, fear and shivering awe mingling in her wordless moan. In the next instant her fingers raked through his hair, finding a purchase in those gilded strands. She tipped his head, angling it slightly, purposely deepening the kiss until he too moaned and shivered.

"Gates . . ." he crooned. "Oh, God . . ."

He was out of control, so far out of control. Her touch burned through him like an intoxicating fire, a blazing nimbus that easily immolated the last vestiges of the stone sarcophagus he had erected around his heart. He was free now, he realized in a moment of startling lucidity. Then the moment was gone, and he was lost again in the glory of her mouth, and the sweet, yielding length of her body.

His hands caressed her—if such sweeping, pressured strokes could be called caresses. But she rose up under his desperate touch, eager for the heat of his palms and the harsh tracing of his splayed fingers. When he laid her back on the carpet and slid down beside her, she tugged his face close and smiled—an expression as ancient as Eve. Her Levantine eyes were half-closed and glazed with passion. She whispered close against his ear, "There is . . . no paradise . . . but this."

He lowered his head to the well of her throat, beading moisture on her glowing skin with tiny, rapid kisses, feeling the pulse of life against his lips as he suckled softly just below her ear. He heard her stifled laugh at the tickling sensation, and then her gasping sigh as he increased the pressure of his mouth.

"You liked that," he taunted in a husky, barely audible voice.

In answer she shifted her head and, like a sweet, barely tamed vixen, took his earlobe between her teeth and bit down slowly till he was writhing in delight. Then she pulled aside the crumpled remains of his neckcloth and set her mouth against the hollow at the base of his corded throat. Griffin cried out as her tongue darted against him, hotter even than his fevered skin.

When he pulled back from her and sat upright, her eyes were dancing up at him. "It's much nicer when I'm awake," she said, hitching her shoulders so sensuously that he felt his arousal increase tenfold.

He set his fist on her chin and massaged it gently. "If you'd kissed me like this in the cow byre, my little savage, we'd have set every hay bale ablaze."

She shifted to her side and curled her hands against her throat. "This is a very comfortable carpet." she murmured. "Much nicer than a stone floor." Her eyes teased him. "I could sleep here . . ."

Christ. He blew out his breath. "No. No one sleeps on the floors in my house."

He rose shakily to his feet and then raised her up by one hand. She needed to support herself against the back of his chair, but she smiled in spite of it.

"Wait here a minute," he said, wrapping one arm around her and giving her a swift hug.

He returned in less time than it took for her to pour and drink a glass of brandy.

As he came into the room, she spun to face him, a charmingly guilty expression on her face. He thought she looked more beautiful than an autumn twilight, all wood sprite now, with her tangle of curls and her lambent amber eyes. A drop of brandy had pearled on her ruddy, swollen mouth.

"That's the first time I've ever seen you look contrite," he said as he crossed to her and finished off the liquor in the glass without removing the stem from her hand. "And probably the last." He let his fingers drift up her arm to the cap of her shoulder. "Set the glass down, Gates," he ordered in a trembling voice.

She opened her fingers and dropped it straight onto the carpet. By some miracle it did not break. Her eyes laughed, her mouth curled into a grin, and in the next instant he had caught her up against his chest.

"The house is ours," he murmured into her hair. "I've given the servants the night off, and Delphie has been sent off to harass my mother at her hotel—a fitting revenge, don't you think?"

"What of your brothers?" she asked, and then remembered their panicked flight. "Oh, I suppose they are halfway to Darrowby by now."

"The moon will not be far enough away, once I am on their trail . . ." His voice drifted off. "But I've other pursuits at the moment."

Gates tightened her hold on his shoulders. "Pursuit implies that one person is trying to flee."

Griffin laughed. "Semantics, my heart. Now come with me . . ."

When Gates awoke, it was early morning. The first fingers of dawn were exploring the carpet in Griffin's bedroom, creeping through the draperies, which had been purposely left open. Griffin had wanted to see her by moonlight. She shivered again at what he had seen—and what she had seen.

They had stripped off each other's clothing with careless, grinning abandon, until he was clad only in his breeches and she in her chemise. But they might as well have been naked—Griffin's breeches had clung like a supple, second skin, and her muslin shift was only a gossamer barrier, and then not even that when he slipped it off her shoulders and took her breast in his mouth. That sensation eclipsed every wondrous feeling she'd ever known. He had tasted her with slow hunger, until her keening cries echoed up to the high, molded ceiling.

Her conversations with the fallen women of Whitechapel had not prepared her for such a languid, silken conquest. Again and again Griffin had brought her, aching and trembling, to the brink of some dark chasm. His hands had touched her with both reverence and hunger, and she didn't know which moved her more. And he had begged for her touch, setting her splayed hands upon his bared chest. She'd instantly complied, tracing her fingers over the sleek muscles, feeling the soft, springing curls that laced its center and led her fingers down to the taut muscles of his belly. He'd cried out when she stroked over the waistband of his breeches, and then rolled onto her so swiftly her breath had whooshed out of her. His kiss had left her equally breathless.

She could now hear the distant cries of street hawkers, out beyond the square. It would be daylight soon, and she had no idea of what the past night would mean to her future. Though Griffin had not taken her virtue—he had been so compelling in his restraint— he had surely taken her soul. The physical hunger he'd aroused in her still simmered, but it paled beside her yearning need for his love. And though he had spent half the night whispering endearments against her ear and throat and breast, he had never once said the word she longed for.

He shifted on the bed beside her and canted one long leg over her thighs. His arms drew her back against his chest, until they were fitted together like a pair of parentheses. One hand drifted to her breast, while the other lost itself in the tangles of her hair.

"I think you know what I need to do now," he murmured groggily against her nape. "I . . . I must go to Bellaire tomorrow."

Her heart stopped.

Even in his half sleep, he must have felt her tense. "You've got to understand, sweetheart . . . it's the only way." He placed a lingering kiss on her shoulder, and then yawned audibly. "And I will need to get a special license."

"If it were done, 'tis best it were done quickly," she quoted in a remote, lost voice.

"Mmm." She felt his smile as he drew her even tighter against him. "I knew you would understand."

*   *   *

Gates waited until Griffin was asleep before she shifted out
from under him. Holding her pain deep inside, as one cradles a
wounded limb to the body, she fled to her room. She plucked a
dress from her wardrobe and then tossed the rest of her dresses into
the bandbox from Madame LaSalle's shop. She'd earned them, she
reckoned—she had cooked and stitched and gardened, and never
received a penny of pay. Not to mention her recent interlude with
the master of the house. She had neglected to ask the ladies of
Whitechapel what the going rate was for an evening of sport.

A tiny, ragged sob tore from her throat, and she stifled it with
one hand.

Griffin rolled over and his arm fell onto the pillow beside him.
It was empty and cool to the touch. His eyes opened then, and he
raised himself up on one elbow. In the bright light of morning, he
saw that Gates was not in the room. Her gown, which he had care-
lessly tossed onto the floor the night before, still lay in a delicate
heap. She was probably off in the garden or preparing breakfast in
the kitchen. It occurred to him that she might be a bit shy of him
this morning, in spite of her usual fearlessness. He grinned.

As for himself, he felt as though a ponderous weight had been
lifted from his shoulders. What was it she had said . . . *fear cripples us more than all those other feelings put together.* He'd lost
his fear last night in the sanctuary of her sweet arms. His mother's
waspish accusations had totally evaporated.

"Gates of Heaven," he murmured as he turned his face into her
pillow and inhaled the arousing scent of clover and sunlight and
passion. She had become his salvation, the one person who exalted
him and humbled him at the same time. "My sweetest, dearest
girl," he murmured against the soft linen. What he felt for her went
so far beyond desire, he doubted a word had been coined that could
express it. Love would have to suffice.

He slipped from the bed and began to dress for travel, tugging
on his boots and wishing that Wilby would magically reappear.
But then it had been worth it, giving his servants the night off. Not
that they wouldn't guess what had transpired in this room last
night. Which meant he'd best make haste to Bellaire.

He scouted the house for Gates, peeking into the main floor rooms before he went down to the kitchen. The hearth was cold and the table was

empty save for one of Bucket's racing forms. A whisper of disquiet stirred against his neck. He ducked out the back door and scanned the garden, where a cool October breeze bent the heads of the last hardy flowers of summer. Gates was not there.

He went back to the kitchen, stole a bun from a basket in the larder, and then went upstairs to his study. He needed to leave instructions for Bucket.

The half-eaten bun fell unnoticed from Griff's hand when he saw the ten buttons sitting on his desktop. He snatched up the note beneath them, not caring that several of the gold and jet baubles went tumbling to the floor.

"Griffin," she had written in a hand that shook so badly his heart clenched in pain, "I am going back to Cheshire. I understand why you need to go to Bellaire—marrying Lady Minerva is the only way to keep your home—but I cannot stand by while you do it. If you have any kindness for me in your heart, you will not ever seek me out. Please do not. I have returned your buttons because they were not offered in any spirit I can accept. That was my misunderstanding, you see."

"You didn't misunderstand, Gates," he murmured. He had to rub his eyes before he could continue.

"I would be lying if I said I did not care for you, but I must distance myself from you while I still have a shred of self-respect left. Anyway, I couldn't bear it if you left me again without saying good-bye. This time I am the one who has that dubious honor."

She hadn't even signed it, he saw, only left behind the wrinkled imprint of her scattered teardrops.

Sweet Jesus! This meant she was alone on the road somewhere. Alone and penniless. Well not quite penniless—last night he'd teased her over the pocket of cloth she had pinned to her chemise, which contained the buttons and several gold coins. She confessed that Sir Thomas had given them to her, and he'd growled out his jealousy. She'd had to kiss him for quite five minutes before he'd been reassured.

He quickly scribbled a note to Bucket, and then went upstairs to pack his valise. If he traveled on horseback, he might just overtake the stage before it reached Cheshire. It would be rough going, but he'd cut his eyeteeth riding overland in Spain. And when he caught up with his runaway, there would be a reckoning that would rival Salamanca for pyrotechnics. He could hardly wait.

Chapter Fourteen

Gates walked out of Lord Conklin's town house in a daze. It had been a fleeting impulse, visiting her ailing grandfather before she returned to Cheshire. Her uncle, the soon-to-be fifth viscount, had just seen her to the door, his pale face narrowed by worry as he bowed over her hand. She had assured him she would be quite safe on the mail coach and thanked him for the small purse he had given her.

Her grandfather had been barely lucid at first and had thought she was her own mother.

"Maria," he had called when she stepped into his large, over-heated bedchamber. Her uncle had hovered nervously in the background; clearly fearing the sight of her would send his father into a fatal collapse. But the old man had roused noticeably and spoken soft, halting words of regret and shame. More than once Gates had to wipe away a tear. Her grandfather lamented that there was nothing he could do for her and Gates had seen the truth of his words. The elegant exterior of the house was belied by the empty rooms and denuded walls of the interior. The same fate that awaited Griffin's home, unless he married Lady Minerva.

Gates was making her way along the pavement, when a portly, balding man stopped her.

"Miss Underhill?" he crowed. "It's Mr. Pendleton, Mr. Darrowby's business manager."

Gates had seen the man several times at the house, his face always set in grim lines. Now he was grinning at her with barely contained elation.

"It is the most wonderful news, my dear. Quite the most wonderful, unexpected news. Ah, but I see I confuse you . . . let me say it outright. It's the mine in India, which Mr. Darrowby invested in so heavily . . . the company was attempting to clear away the rubble at the mine's entrance, to appease the local maharajah, and they discovered gold in the rock. Oh, such a great deal of gold, tumbled down from the side of the mountain." He grasped her hands and shook them wildly. "He has come about, Miss Underhill! All the investors are now very wealthy men, because, you see, the land they leased included the mountain. What great forethought that was. I am just now on my way to visit Lord Conklin, who also suffered a great loss in the landslide."

"You must tell him immediately," she said intently. "And I will go home and tell Mr. Darrowby."

Mr. Pendleton bowed quickly and went off toward her grandfather's house. Gates raced along the pavement, back toward Rutledge Square, praying that Griffin had not yet left for Cheshire.

She knew he did not want to barter himself for gold. If he had his own gold, which virtually seemed to be the case now, he could decide his own future. If even half the things he'd said to her last night were true, then she might be the person he chose to share it with.

She was rounding the corner into the square, her mind singing with the joyful news she had to deliver, when two men stepped out from between the brick church and the adjoining house.

This time they did not have a burlap sack, only a very sorry-looking pistol.

"Come along, Miss High-and-Mighty," Sank said. "You won't get away this time."

Gates nearly tumbled back off the curb. "You?" she cried. "It was you who attacked me?"

"Sorry," Demp muttered. "We didn't mean to be so rough with you. It was all the damn rain . . . made you slippery as an eel."

"Oh, and is this a kindness?" she stormed, pointing to the pistol.

"I'll use it if you won't come along," Sank growled. "Don't think I won't." He cocked it and raised it under her nose. "We've been waiting weeks to get you alone, without that old harridan or those two young coves close beside you."

Gates raised her eyes above the pistol—she could see the upper windows of Griff's town house beyond the ornate railing of the square's fence. She was so close to his home, so close to delivering the message that would keep him from traveling to Cheshire.

"No!" she said with a sob. "I must go home. Here—" She thrust the purse her uncle had given her at Sank. "Take this. It's all I have."

"This is only a tidbit," Sank said as he tucked it into his greasy waistcoat. "We've got our eyes on a bigger prize. Your fancy man will pay handsomely to get you back from us."

"He's going away!" she cried as they manhandled her out of the square. "He doesn't want me!"

Both brothers rolled their eyes scornfully. "You never could tell a proper lie," Sank declared.

They took her by hackney to a rundown boardinghouse in Whitechapel and dragged her up to their tiny room. She screamed in protest when they bundled her into a narrow wardrobe and shut her inside. Through the door she heard them arguing over the composition of their ransom note.

"He won't pay you!" she wailed, thumping her fists against the door in impotent fury. She railed at them for nearly an hour before she slumped down on the dusty floor and began to weep bitterly. Griffin would be on his way to Bellaire by now to ask Lady Minerva for her hand. Gates knew a gentleman did not cry off once he was betrothed. Griffin was as good as married.

It was airless in the tight confines of the wardrobe and she soon fell into a feverish sleep.

Sometime later, the door was abruptly flung open and daylight poured into the darkness. She awoke at once and lay there against the side wall, gasping and disoriented.

"I've sent Demp to Rutledge Square with our ransom note," Sank announced. He took a long pull from the gin bottle he held, and then set it on the rickety table behind him. "But we're glad to be rid of him, aren't we, my sweet little Gates." He loomed over her and grinned, his eyes bright with lust.

The bile rose in her throat as she felt the first stirrings of fear. She thrust herself upright, pushing away from the wall with both hands, and cannoned into him with her shoulder. He stumbled backward, tangling his long legs in the chair behind him.

Gates snatched up the gin bottle and swung it hard against the side of his head. The bottle shattered, scattering shards of glass over his shoulders and her arms.

A fine weapon, she fumed, *that disintegrates when you use it.*

Sank was weaving, but still on his feet. A trickle of blood snaked down his left temple; it matched the red rage in his eyes. "You shouldn't have done that," he said thickly.

Her gaze darted frantically around the room, looking for a more durable weapon as Sank closed the gap between them. She tried to slip around him, but he caught her about the waist and wrestled her into his arms. Her hands and legs flailed as he twisted her face up toward his wet mouth.

"Papa will cut out your liver!" she raged, angling her head back and away from him.

He merely laughed. He was nuzzling her neck, his hands groping along her back and sides, when she heard a muffled cry from the doorway. Sank hissed as he was abruptly wrenched away from her.

"You damned cur!" Demp cried, thrusting his brother back against the wardrobe. "I knew I shouldn't have left you alone with her. You promised me . . . you promised you wouldn't bother her."

Sank said a very nasty word, then added sanguinely, "But I'm not bothering her, she was begging for it." He fisted one hand and took a step forward. "Now go deliver our note, or I'll make you watch while I take her."

Demp glanced at Gates and saw the fear trembling in her eyes. His jaw set.

"I don't think so, brother," he said under his breath. His fist plowed into Sank's chin with an audible crack. A brief gleam of shocked comprehension lit Sank's eyes before he crumpled lifelessly onto the planked floor.

"Now go!" Demp said, turning to Gates. "You don't want to be here when he wakes up."

"Come with me?" she cried. "You are not like him, Redemption. You always protected me."

"No," he said a bit sadly. "I mostly went along with him. But not any longer. I'll take his purse and buy a passage to America." He grinned at her. "I've always had the yen to see a red Indian." He winked. "And there's a bully boy of a sailor at the grog shop who's lookin' for likely lads who want to, er, ship out to India." He prodded Sank's shoulder with his boot toe. "I believe we might have a candidate here."

"That will take some of the starch out of him," Gates said with a grin. She ran to Demp and hugged him. "God speed, Redemption . . . Or will you be Raymond now?"

He shook his head. "Think I'll keep the name. I feel like I redeemed myself today."

Gates had no coins to pay for a hackney back to Griffin's house, so she ran until she thought her sides would burst. She staggered into the empty front hall, and heard a jumble of voices coming from the parlor. There seemed to be a dozen people in the room—unfortunately not one of them was Griffin. Lady Constance was seated on the sofa; beside her stood a genial-looking, gray-haired man. Delphie was striding about the room, muttering at Cort and Scotty. Wilby, Bucket, and Farrow had ranged themselves along the walls, out of harm's way.

When they saw Gates in the doorway, they all gaped.

"What the devil are you doing here?" Cort said.

"You're supposed to be haring off to Cheshire," Scotty added.

"I was . . ." Gates began. "Oh, but it's such a long story. And I must find Griffin? Is he still here?"

Bucket shook his head as he stepped forward. "No . . . he, er, left me this note."

Delphie snatched it from his hands, raised it up and read aloud. "'Gates has gone haring off to Cheshire. I am bound there as well.'" Her gaze lowered to Gates. "What happened here last night?"

Gates blushed ten shades of scarlet and hung her head. "It doesn't matter. Nothing matters now. He's gone off to propose to Minerva Stargrove."

"He can't do that," Scotty protested. "Everyone knows he is in love with you."

Gates's head shot up at his words.

"He's chasing after you, my girl," Delphie added calmly. "It's quite clear."

Farrow stepped forward and coughed uneasily. "That's what I thought this morning, Miss Underhill, when he told me you'd gone back to Cheshire." He lowered his eyes. "But then he told me he was bound for Bellaire, and when I asked him why, he said, 'Unfinished business.'"

"I'll boil him in oil," Cort grumbled. "Of all the wretched things to do. If he'd only waited an hour."

You can say that again. Gates sighed to herself. And then looked up at Cort. "What do you mean?"

Lady Constance rose from the sofa and took up the hand of the man standing beside her. "After talking to Griffin yesterday, I realized it was my duty to help him. Mr. Ashley Bentwood of Virginia"—she smiled at the man beside her—"has been kind enough to ask for my hand in marriage."

Gates tried not to goggle. Griff's mother hadn't wasted a minute finding a mate.

"Er, we met in Bath last month," she said, and then tittered, "but he was so enamored of me, he followed me here to London."

"Disgustingly rich," Cort whispered audibly to Gates. "Bank-

ing, don't you know. Griffin don't need the wealthy widow now.
Mr. Bentwood's going to buy back Griff's mortgage from Pettibone."

Mr. Bentwood came forward. "Miss Underhill, am I to understand that you would like to stop Mr. Darrowby from reaching
Cheshire? Because we arrived here in my new coach, which I
would be happy to place at your disposal."

Gates spun from one earnest face to another, feeling as if she
might swoon.

"If we travel past sundown each night," Delphie observed in
her best commanding-officer voice, "we might just beat him to
Bellaire."

"That would be presumptuous, Delphie," Gates said. "We can't
know that he wants me, after all."

"Oh, please!" Delphie cried, throwing her hands up. "Will
someone talk some sense into this girl?"

To everyone's surprise, Farrow was the one who stepped forward. He set his hand on Gates's arm and said softly, "He never
looked so heartsick as when he rode off this morning, miss. Trust
me, I've known him his whole life. It's you he wants, and no mistake."

"Besides," Cort added stoutly. "I doubt he's going to walk right
into Lady Min's parlor the instant he gets there and pop the question. He might not do it until the next day or the next. In which
case you will reach Bellaire in plenty of time to stop him."

"But what of Lady Minerva?" Gates responded bleakly. "She
will have all her expectations dashed if he arrives at her house and
does not ask her for her hand."

"Hang Lady Minerva," Cort grumbled. "We'd much rather have
you in the family." His blue eyes danced at her. "Besides, I doubt
she can cook worth a tuppence."

"Or make Griffin smile as you do," Scotty added as he took her
hand and squeezed it encouragingly.

Gates drew a deep breath. She'd been following Griffin Darrowby from place to place for some time now, and with little hope
of reward. And now the best reward of all might be within her
grasp, if she had the fortitude to follow him one last time.

"Yes," she said after a moment, her voice now full of joy. "Oh,
yes. We must follow him. Thank you, Mr. Bentwood." She ran to
the banker and took his hand.

"The least I can do," he said, leaning forward to whisper in her ear. "If we are to be the two new members of this family."

Less than half an hour later, Gates found herself ensconced in the banker's extravagant coach, sitting beside Delphie. Cort and Scotty lounged back on the seat across from them. Gates tried to stifle her nervousness as they set off; she knew only an act of God would keep Griffin from reaching Bellaire before they did—he had a three-hour lead and he was on horseback. She prayed Cort was right—that Griff would not propose to Minerva as soon as he arrived.

With all the hubbub in the parlor, Gates had forgotten to tell Griff's family about his startling economic recovery, so she now regaled Delphie and the brothers with the tale. She was glad she hadn't said anything in front of Griff's mother—she quite liked the idea of Lady Constance playing the martyr for her son's sake, even if it was a small penance the woman was paying by marrying the wealthy Mr. Bentwood.

Griffin expected to reach Bellaire by early afternoon of his third day of travel. He knew he'd been making good time, not stopping at posting houses to sleep till after dark, and setting off each morning with the dawn. He'd been puzzled at first that no one at any of the stagecoach stops had seen Gates, but then he remembered she was traveling with only a few coins in her pocket; he doubted she would be leaving the coach to dine at the various stopovers. He prayed that she'd acquired enough mistrust of strangers while in London not to be taken in by anyone. He prayed it hourly.

Somewhere outside Paultons, Gaspar threw a shoe. He more than threw it, he half stumbled over it and went down in a tangle of thrashing legs. Griffin cursed as he dusted himself off and got the horse back on his feet. There was something about this vicinity that played havoc with his riding skills.

It took Griff nearly an hour to reach the village, gingerly leading the horse. The smithy was off at the Benchleys' farm seeing to a draft mare, so Griff was forced to cool his heels and his thirst at the Badger Barrow, where he passed the time discovering whether Gates had traveled through the village that day. Opinions varied. Several villagers claimed she had driven past in a donkey cart, while others said she'd been missing since mid-September. One old codger swore he'd seen her ride by on a broomstick.

When the smithy at last appeared, Griffin breathed a sigh of relief. But the man was inclined to chat, and so prolonged Griffin's agony for another forty-five minutes. Once Gaspar was pronounced fit, Griff remounted and continued along the road for another three miles, past the stile that had gotten him into such trouble in September. That was when he remembered he hadn't asked in the village for directions to the Underhill farm. He cursed roundly and soundly for ten minutes, until he arrived at the long drive to Bellaire. Surely someone on the estate would know the way through these cursed woods.

He left Gaspar in the care of a stable lad and went briskly around to the front of the house. No mind that he was travel-stained and had not spared the time to shave that morning. The lady would take him as she found him.

He muttered, "Don't bother yourself, I'll find her," to Stubbin as he strode past the astonished butler. He was at present in no mood for niceties.

Lady Min looked up from doing her accounts in her lilac-papered sitting room just as he came through the half-open door.

"Griffin?" she gasped. "I was not expecting you. This will not do, you know. I cannot—"

He swept her out of the chair and caught her by both arms.

"You wanted me delirious with love, as I recall," he said through his teeth. "Well, you can congratulate yourself, my dear. I am as besotted as a schoolboy with his first crush. The only prob—"

Before he could finish, she gave a sharp cry of dismay and broke free of him. He watched in startled surprise as she bolted from the room, her skirts lashing about her heels.

"Well, that's a damned fine welcome," he said to the painting of a black horse over the mantel.

Lady Min fled directly to the library, where Sir Thomas de Burgh was arranging the illuminated manuscripts in their new showcases.

"Oh, Thomas," she cried. "Griffin has come here. He . . . he loves me . . ." The rest of her message was lost in incoherent sobbing. The magistrate's face grew pale and his fine gray eyes lost more than a bit of their brightness.

"You must be very happy, my dear," he said in a stilted, whispery voice. "Let me be the first to con—"

"I don't want him to love me!" she wailed miserably. "He has come two weeks early . . . before I could . . . before I had a chance to . . ."

Sir Thomas moved instantly to her side. He couldn't prevent himself from wrapping his arms around her and coaxing her head onto his shoulder. She was trembling all over; he felt his breathing tighten.

"What is it, my heart? You must calm yourself. I cannot bear to see you like this."

Her head snapped up. "What did you call me?"

He looked away from her. "I'm sorry, Min. It was just a slip." And then he steeled himself to tell her the truth. It wouldn't matter, after all; she'd be off to Darrowby within a few months and he'd probably never see her again. The bleak thought that she would never know of his feelings lent him courage. Better to be heard and dismissed than never to be heard at all.

"No," he said, setting her back from him, so that he could look into her eyes. "I am not sorry I called you 'my heart' . . . for that is what you are. And have been for such a very long time . . ."

Minerva dashed her tears away with an impatient hand. "Thomas?" Her voice rose a notch when she saw the emotion simmering in his eyes. "Oh, my dearest Thomas! My dearest, dearest love . . ."

He kissed her then, bent her back, and kissed her with such fire and such open hunger that he put to flight every misconception she'd ever had about him being a cautious, careful man.

They nearly didn't hear Griffin's polite cough from the doorway of the library. Minerva looked up and gave what would have been called a squeak in a less elegant lady.

"Well," Griffin drawled, leaning back against the doorpost and crossing his arms, "this is a very happy circumstance."

Sir Thomas tightened his hold on Minerva. "Darrowby, I think you and I need to have a talk."

Griffin sketched a bow. "I am at your disposal, Sir Thomas."

Once the chaise drew up in the stableyard of Bellaire, and its occupants determined that Griffin was in residence there, Gates insisted that she enter the house alone. She could think of nothing less subtle than parading through the front door with Delphinia,

Cort, and Scotty in tow. What she needed to say to Griffin required privacy and tact.

She chose to go in through the kitchen entrance, sailing past the mighty Stubbin with a practiced sneer. He wondered who the pretty, stylishly dressed young lady might be, and further wondered why she was in his kitchen. Harris knew her instantly, though, and rose up from his chair with a deep bow.

"He's in the library, I believe," he said, at once grasping the situation.

"Will you ask him if he will see me?" she said in a small voice.

Noting her bleak expression, he shook his head and smiled. "Go on up now. You won't be sorry."

Gates went up the steep narrow stairs, glad to put the kitchen behind her. Her sojourn there seemed to have been eons ago. She heard soft voices coming from the library and turned to flee; she dared not approach Griffin unless he was alone. But then the sound of his voice drew her forward, against her will.

From the shadows she looked through the open door of the library and saw Griffin and Lady Minerva standing beside Sir Thomas. Griff held a glass of champagne raised in a toast, his other hand rested on Minerva's arm. "To true love," he said gaily. He tossed back the drink and then leaned over to kiss Minerva's cheek.

Gates made a tiny, strangling noise, and three pairs of eyes shifted at once to the doorway. She fled then, down the hall and out through the front door. She was lost in the darkness of the woods before the three celebrants had even reached the front steps.

"Damnation!" Griffin snarled. He turned to Sir Thomas. "Now would someone please tell me how to find that wretched farm."

Gates knew she was a fool to have come here, back to the farm. But she couldn't bear to face Delphie and the boys so soon after her humiliation. Imagine, walking in on Griffin while he was toasting his bride-to-be. It was much worse than falling out of the cherry tree. She couldn't bear seeing anyone just then. And no place on earth was more solitary than this farm.

She wandered onto the porch and found a letter from her father tucked into the door frame; some kind soul had doubtless carried it from the village. It had yellowed slightly over the passing weeks.

She broke open the seal and scanned the words, and then, trembling slightly, she reread it more slowly.

Her father, it seemed, had been preaching in Glasgow and had been struck and knocked unconscious by a wind-tossed brewery sign. The owner of said brewery, a widow of middle years, had taken him into her home and nursed him. And miracle of miracles, when he came to, his visions and voices had totally disappeared. The widow lady had been so taken by his gentlemanly air, that she had promptly suggested marriage, whereby her papa found himself thrice married, and to a woman, he assured Gates, of great wealth.

The envelope contained a bank draft for a large sum of money.

It was so horribly unfair, she thought, as she lowered herself down to the top step. Now that Griffin was affianced to Lady Minerva, and no longer needed money, it seemed to be rolling in from every direction. Gates wanted to lay her head down and cry, but could not even muster up one tear. Her pain was that great. She needed something to do, to keep her mind away from the cutting edge of anguish and loss.

Marching resolutely into the barn, she began to drag the broken flotsam that littered the floor out into the yard. She piled everything beside the woodshed, using the pitchfork to heap the debris around its walls. Then she brought the tinderbox out from the parlor and set one of the sacks on fire. The resulting blaze was most satisfactory—the other burlap sacks caught, and then the dried, stiffened harness traces. When the shed itself began to burn, she had to step back from the heat. Fire crackled and blazed, as glowing embers rose about the conflagration and drifted harmlessly into the air.

She was so intent on the fire that she didn't hear the horseman approaching.

"Going to throw yourself onto the pyre?" Griff asked as he slid from Gaspar's back.

She spun to him in alarm. He was disheveled and travel stained, and she thought he had never looked more glorious in his life. Or more unattainable.

She held the pitchfork toward him menacingly. "I don't want to see you. Ever again. Now go away. There is nothing for you here. Nothing."

"I believe we played this out once before." With very little effort he deflected the tined end of the tool and grasped the wooden handle. He twisted it from her grasp and tossed it onto the ground. "I know you went to Bellaire, Gates, we all saw you there."

"Yes, I saw you with Lady Minerva," she said bitterly. "I heard you toasting her. I . . . I came too late, you see. Too late to tell you that you are rich. Disgustingly rich, to use your brother's expression."

"I know," he said. "Delphie told me about the Indian mine that's swimming in gold . . . and about my mother's American banker, as well. She and my brothers are at present making themselves at home at Bellaire." He was moving forward toward her. With intent. She backed away, and then turned and fled into the barn. She skittered up the ladder to the loft, forgetting how fast he was, and now agile. This time she didn't even have a chance to reach for the ladder, he was that close behind her.

"Damn it, Gates!" he cried. "You needn't run from me." He held out his hands. "Never again."

"Oh, yes I do. I know what you want. You've got your wealthy bride now, so you think you can come here and cozen me into being your mistress. But I won't."

"When have I ever sweet-talked you into anything, my girl? No, it's been sparring and brangling every step of the way. I think that's why I care for you so much, because you're the only soul who's ever really roused me to anger."

Gates saw the look of tender affection in his eyes and hardened herself against it. "There is only heartache for us, Griffin," she said softly. "Money won't lessen that. I'd give back everything I now possess to change things, but it's too late."

"And what do you possess, Miss Under-the-hill? That you make so free with."

She named the sum mentioned in her father's letter and Griff's eyes widened. "You see, Papa has married a rich widow in Glasgow. But none of that matters now. You must leave."

"Indeed I must not."

Gates threw herself facedown in the straw and gave a muffled groan of frustration. "Please go. I can't bear this any longer."

"I suppose there's nothing for it but to marry you now," he mused, as he reached out to stroke her tangle of hair.

"Oh!" she stormed, coming upright again abruptly and slapping his hand away. "This is infamous! You would throw over Lady Min, now that you know my father has money."

"And your grandfather, as well," he added slyly. "I can jus
imagine the dowry he will give you."

"Why does such wicked behavior not surprise me? You are un
scrupulous, avaricious—"

"Don't forget lecherous," he drawled as he carried her back
down to the floor of the loft. "That seems to be foremost in my
thoughts right about now." And then he kissed her hard.

"No!" she cried as his fingers bit into her shoulders.

She recalled the first time they'd enacted this scenario in the
loft. She'd swooned. Now she wanted nothing so much as to shoot
him between the eyes. Except that she also wanted to kiss him
back, to respond to the urgent pressure of his mouth, that was mak
ing her ache with ten times the longing she'd ever felt before.

His hands were on her body, as they'd been that heavenly night
in his bed. Skillful and ardent, he coaxed her into this dance, where
he alone knew the steps.

"I can't believe," she gasped, once she had broken away from
his insistent mouth, "that you would promise yourself to one
woman, and then come directly here to dally with another."

"But you dally so awfully well, my little savage." He traced the
plump line of her bottom lip with his thumb and smiled at her will
ful frown. "And I hate to argue with you, knowing how little like
lihood there is of getting you to attend me, but I am promised to
no one." She started to protest, but he silenced her with a judi
ciously placed kiss.

"There," he said after he'd regained his breath. "It's taken me
while to figure out how to keep you quiet. But it's pleasant work
after all. Now listen to me, Gates. Are you listening?"

She nodded sullenly.

"Lady Min is going to marry Sir Thomas. Not me. Him. It was
their betrothal I was toasting in the library. Honestly, Gates
you've got to stop eavesdropping on people, you only ever get half
the picture."

"Thomas? And Minerva?" Her eyes lit up with understanding
"Oh, Lord. It makes sense now. I knew there was someone he
cared for who did not return his regard. He is such a wonderful
man . . . I am so happy for him." Then the repercussions of this
revelation dawned on her. "And that means—"

"Yes, my turnip. I am still a free man."

"But I thought . . . that night in London, after we'd . . . when you said you had to go to Bellaire. I thought you meant you had to propose to Minerva . . . to save your house."

He tipped her chin up with his thumb. "I went there to tell her in person that I could not offer for her . . . because I was in love with someone else."

Gates felt her breath hitch.

"Still," he went on," it does seem a shame. I've wasted all this time courting a woman whose heart was given elsewhere. Very lowering to a man's self-esteem. I shall need to look about for another lady, because I find myself unaccountably set on marriage. You don't happen to know of a likely candidate? No, probably not. I am the worst sort of fellow . . ."

Gates narrowed her eyes, obscuring the rush of joy she was feeling. "It would take a saint," she pronounced with feeling.

"Or," he drawled, just before he kissed her, "merely a parson's brat."

Epilogue

Griffin tugged off his riding gloves as he came out of the barn and headed across the yard toward the house. The tumble-down farmhouse with the sagging porch had been razed and re-placed by a tidy stone manor with a roof of crisp red tiles. He always marveled that he found himself living on the same property where he had once been held captive in a woodshed. But then he had been made a captive in more ways than one during that fateful misadventure.

Goats and chickens still ranged over the yard—his wife never ceased to be amused by their antics. In the fields beyond the farm-yard, a dozen mares with foals at their sides browsed on the rich green grass. The foals were blood bays for the most part, which was not surprising, since Gaspar was their sire. The temperamen-tal horse had turned into a lamb once he'd been set out to stud. It was usually the other way round, Griff knew. But then Griff was the first person to acknowledge that domestic bliss had a way of mellowing a fellow.

As he approached the house, the front door swung open and a tiny savage came hurtling toward him. Her dense, curly hair was tangled into knots and her pinafore was half off one shoulder and smeared with jam. "Papa!" she cried, lifting her plump arms to him. There were many things he was proof against, but this was not one of them. He plucked her off the top step and burrowed his head in her neck. That smell, that divine baby smell that she re-tained, even though she had been walking and talking for a year now. It always brought him to his knees.

"Oh, you've found her." The tall woman came through the open door. "I was scribbling away in the study and she just disappeared. She always knows when you've come home."

"Unlike her mother, who loses herself in her good works." The pleasure in his eyes as he regarded her, belied his complaint. "Who has Delphie got you sponsoring now? Fallen actresses? Abused cart horses?"

"Soldiers," Gates said, wiping at an ink smudge on her forefin-ger. She also had one on her chin, and Griff hoped she wouldn't discover it. He had plans for that smudge, once his daughter was set down to her supper. "We are starting a farm for veterans who were disabled in the war. A place where they can support themselves and their families."

"I have to applaud your Utopian ideals," he said as he came up the steps toward her. "Even if they never do make a profit."

"The profit is in the people we aid," she said as she leaned over to kiss her daughter's sticky cheek. "And we have so much, Griff, you and I."

"Yes," he said, as he leaned his head to one side and brushed her chin with his own. "Yes, we do." He set his daughter down and watched her as she skirted her mother's flower beds and made a beeline for the nearest goat.

Griff slid an arm around her waist. "She is so much like you," he said softly. "It takes my breath away."

Gates grinned. "She is like me until she wants something. And then it's imperious frowns and peremptory orders, just like a true Darrowby."

He tipped her head up to him with his free hand. "You broke the Darrowby curse, my heart. You gave us a bonny brown-haired girl."

Gates patted her slightly swollen stomach and made a face. "I fancy this next one will be a boy, though. He frets something fierce."

He held up one hand in protest. "Don't look at me. You were the one who wanted another child so soon."

"Yes, and you grit your teeth and forced yourself to do your manly duty."

"Well, it wasn't that much of a hardship." He traced his mouth along her chin. "Pity all my duties aren't that pleasant."

She turned into his whispering kiss, so that their lips met. It was still a shock to her, how potent it always felt, this intimate contact that was the precursor to passion. She watched his bright eyes go hazy as he deepened the kiss. Felt his work-hardened hands slide to her hips as he tugged her against him.

"Do you think your ailing soldiers could spare you for an hour or so?" he asked raggedly.

"What about your daughter, sir? We can't leave her unattended or she'll end up down the well."

Griffin didn't miss a beat. He turned and shouted, "Farrow!" from over the porch rail.

The gray-haired groom appeared at the door of the barn.

"Will you look after the hoyden for us? Gates needs me to help with her . . . correspondence." He ignored his wife's chuckle. "Set her on her pony if you like. But don't let her ride alone, no matter how she cries for it."

The groom moved forward and swept the little girl up in his arms. "I recall it was the same with you, sir. Headstrong to a fault, like all Darrowbys." He smiled and carried his squirming bundle into the barn.

Griffin turned to Gates. "I suppose you'll want the naming of the next baby?"

"Well, it's only fair," she protested. "You named our daughter, if you will recall . . . while I was still too dazed to think clearly."

"I had no choice," he said simply, as he took up her left hand and carried it to his lips. The gold ring she wore glinted in the sun, a flawless topaz set about with small diamonds and stones of faceted jet. "She *is* a Daily Miracle. As you are, my dearest love."

Farrow kept his arm around his charge as they slowly circled the small paddock. Daily Darrowby thumped her heels against the pony's black-and-white sides and laughed in delight.

When she suddenly began to cry, Farrow pulled her down from the small saddle and cradled her in his arms. "What is it, my poppet?"

"Hurt-th my eye," she said with a sniffle, knuckling her brow.

Farrow took out his large white handkerchief and gently dabbed away the piece of chaff that had lodged beneath her lid. He grinned at her. "Better now? A shame to cry when you've got such pretty eyes."

"Mama call-th them pixie eyes," she lisped, touching a finger to the corner of one slanted, grassy green eye.

Farrow's fond gaze beamed down at her, a gaze of exactly the same grass green shade as the child's.

"You have your grandfather's eyes, my poppet," he said in a low, soothing voice. "But remember, that is our little secret."

Daily grinned. *"Thecret,"* she said and crossed her heart. She quite liked secrets.